# *Deep is the Heart*

$$\langle \phi_n | \phi_m \rangle = \langle \phi_n | \int_{-\pi}^{\pi} dx\, |x\rangle \langle x | \phi_m \rangle$$

$$\phi_n(x) = \langle x | \phi_n \rangle \quad \phi_n^*(x) = \langle \phi_n | x \rangle$$

$$\langle \phi_n | \phi_n \rangle = \int_{-\frac{L}{2}}^{+\frac{L}{2}} dx\, |\phi_n(x)|^2 = \int_{-\frac{L}{2}}^{+\frac{L}{2}} dx\, \tfrac{1}{L} = L \cdot \tfrac{1}{L} = 1$$

$$\langle \phi_n | \phi_{n'} \rangle = \langle \phi_n | \int_{-\frac{L}{2}}^{+\frac{L}{2}} dx\, |x\rangle \langle x | \phi_{n'} \rangle$$

$$\langle \phi_n | \phi_{n'} \rangle = \int_{-\frac{L}{2}}^{+\frac{L}{2}} dx\, \phi_n^*(x)\cdot \phi_{n'}(x)$$

$$\langle \phi_n | \phi_{n'} \rangle = \tfrac{1}{L}\int_{-\frac{L}{2}}^{+\frac{L}{2}} dx\, e^{-ikx} e^{ik'x} = 0 \;;\; h \neq h'$$

$$\psi_a - \psi_b = 0,\, 2\pi \ldots \Rightarrow e^{i\psi_a} = e^{i\psi_b} \quad \{|Q\rangle, |L\rangle\} \quad |\psi\rangle = \sqrt{\langle\psi|\psi\rangle}$$

$$\psi_n(x) = \tfrac{1}{\sqrt{2L}} e^{i\psi_o}\left(e^{i(\frac{2\pi}{L}n+\psi_o)x} + e^{-i(\frac{2\pi}{L}n+\psi_o)x}\right) \quad \rho = \hbar\tfrac{2\pi}{\lambda}$$

$$= \tfrac{2}{\sqrt{2L}} e^{i\psi_o} \cos\left[\left(\tfrac{2\pi}{L}n + \psi_o\right)x\right] \;;\; \psi_n\left(x = \pm\tfrac{L}{2}\right) = 0 \quad \hbar = \tfrac{h}{2\pi}$$

$$\Rightarrow \left(\tfrac{2\pi}{L}n + \psi_o\right)\tfrac{L}{2} = \tfrac{\pi}{2}(2\ell - 1),\; \ell = 1, 2, \ldots \Rightarrow k_o = \tfrac{\pi}{L} \quad \begin{pmatrix}1 & 0 \\ 0 & 1\end{pmatrix}$$

$$\psi_n(x) = \sqrt{\tfrac{2}{L}}\cos\left[\tfrac{\pi}{L}(2n-1)x\right] \;;\; \psi_a - \psi_b = \pi \;;\; \psi_n(x) = \sqrt{\tfrac{2}{L}}\sin\left[\tfrac{\pi}{L}nx\right]$$

$$\hat{H}\psi_{ns}(x) = -\tfrac{\hbar^2}{2m}\partial_x^2\psi_{ns}(x) = \tfrac{\hbar^2}{2m}\left(\tfrac{\pi}{L}[2n-1]\right)^2\psi_{ns}(x)$$

$$E_{ns} = \tfrac{\hbar^2}{2m}\tfrac{\pi^2}{L^2}(2n-1)^2,\; n = 1, 2, \ldots \;;\; \hat{H}\psi_{na}(x) = \tfrac{\hbar^2}{2m}\left(\tfrac{2\pi}{L}\right)$$

$$\hat{H}\psi_a = -\tfrac{\hbar^2}{2m}\partial_x^2\psi_a(x) = \tfrac{\hbar^2}{2a}\psi_a(x) - \tfrac{\hbar^2}{2m}\tfrac{A}{a}(x-x_o)^2\psi_a(x)$$

$$a \approx 10^{-14}\,m$$

$$= -\tfrac{\hbar^2}{2m}\left(-\tfrac{A}{2a} + \left(\tfrac{A}{2a}(x-x_o)e^{-\frac{k-x_o}{4a}}\right)\psi \;;\; V(x) = \tfrac{\hbar^2}{2m}\tfrac{A}{a}(x-x_o)^2$$

$$|\psi(x)|^2 = |\psi_o|^2 e^{-\frac{(x-x_o)^2}{2a^2}} \quad \hat{H} \to \hat{H} = -\tfrac{\hbar^2}{2m}\partial_x^2 + V(x)\;;\; \hat{H}\psi_a = \tfrac{\hbar^2}{2a}\tfrac{A}{a}\psi_a = E_a\psi_a$$

$$\int_{-\infty}^{+\infty} dx\, e^{-Ax^2} = \sqrt{\tfrac{\pi}{A}} \quad V(x) = \tfrac{1}{2}m\omega^2(x-x_o)^2 \to m\omega^2 = \tfrac{\hbar^2}{m}\tfrac{A}{a}\psi \Rightarrow \boxed{\omega = \tfrac{\hbar}{2ma}}$$

$$A = \tfrac{1}{2a},\;\Rightarrow\; |\psi_o| = \tfrac{1}{(2\pi a^2)^{\frac{1}{4}}} \quad E_a = \tfrac{\hbar^2}{2m}\tfrac{1}{2a}$$

$$[\hat{p},\hat{x}] = \tfrac{\hbar}{i}\;;\; \hat{p} = \tfrac{\hbar}{i}\partial/\partial_x \;/\; \hat{H} = \tfrac{\hat{p}^2}{2m} + \tfrac{1}{2}m\omega^2\hat{x}^2 \qquad V(x) \qquad \langle(x-x_o)^2\rangle$$

$$a^2 + b^2 = (a + ib)(a - ib)\;;\; a, b \in \mathbb{R}\;;\; 2.\;(a\hat{p} + ib\hat{x})(a\hat{p} - ib\hat{x}),\, a, b \in \mathbb{R} = \langle\psi_a|(x-x_o)^2|\psi_a\rangle$$

$$= a^2\hat{p}^2 + iba\hat{x}\hat{p} - iab\hat{p}\hat{x} + b^2\hat{x}^2 = a^2\hat{p}^2 + b^2\hat{x}^2 - ba\hbar \int dx\, |x\rangle\langle x| = \mathbb{1}$$

$$\hat{H} = (a\hat{p} + ib\hat{x})(a\hat{p} - ib\hat{x}) - ba\hbar\;;\; a^2 = \tfrac{1}{2m}\;;\; b^2 = \tfrac{1}{2}m\omega^2 = \int dx\,\psi_a^*(x)\langle k|$$

$$D_{\psi}:\; C^+ \tfrac{1}{\hbar\omega}(a\hat{p} + ib\hat{x})\;;\; C^- = \tfrac{1}{\hbar\omega}(a\hat{p} - ib\hat{x}) \Rightarrow \hat{H} = \hbar\omega c^+ c^- + \tfrac{1}{2}\hbar\omega = \int dx\,\psi_a^*(x)(x-x_o)^2\psi_a(x)$$

$$\left(\begin{smallmatrix}\omega & \frac{t}{\hbar}\\ -\frac{t}{\hbar} & \omega\end{smallmatrix}\right)|\omega, t \in \mathbb{C}\} \;\{\pm 1\}\; iSU(2) \cong S^3 \quad A \to \omega \bar{A}\omega^{-1} = \int dx\,\psi_a^*(x)(x-x_o)^2\psi_a(x) = \int dx\,(x-x_o)^2$$

$$\omega = \left(\begin{smallmatrix}0 & 1\\ 1 & 0\end{smallmatrix}\right),\; \sigma_2 = \left(\begin{smallmatrix}0 & -i\\ i & 0\end{smallmatrix}\right),\; \sigma_3 = \left(\begin{smallmatrix}1 & 0\\ 0 & -1\end{smallmatrix}\right)\;;\; S_i = \tfrac{\hbar}{2}\;;\; i\epsilon_{ijk}$$

## A.V. Zeppa

outskirtspress

DENVER, COLORADO

This is a work of fiction. The events and characters described herein are imaginary and are not intended to refer to specific places or living persons. The opinions expressed in this manuscript are solely the opinions of the author and do not represent the opinions or thoughts of the publisher. The author has represented and warranted full ownership and/or legal right to publish all the materials in this book.

Author's Disclaimer: This book is a work of fiction. It is a story written entirely from the author's imagination. Any reference to historical events, real people, or real locations is used fictitiously. The characters and events in the story are products of the author's imagination. Any resemblance to real people, living or dead is entirely coincidental.

Deep Is The Heart
All Rights Reserved.
Copyright © 2015 A.V. Zeppa
v4.0 r1.0

Cover Photo © 2015 istockphoto.com. All rights reserved - used with permission.

This book may not be reproduced, transmitted, or stored in whole or in part by any means, including graphic, electronic, or mechanical without the express written consent of the publisher except in the case of brief quotations embodied in critical articles and reviews.

Outskirts Press, Inc.
http://www.outskirtspress.com

ISBN: 978-1-4787-5231-8

Outskirts Press and the "OP" logo are trademarks belonging to Outskirts Press, Inc.

PRINTED IN THE UNITED STATES OF AMERICA

In the garden of dreams

there is an awakening of spirit without compromise

it is hidden between the heart and mind

and the reality of the journey forward.

Those perfect footsteps and youthful innocence

are imperfections that make it human.

Deep is the Heart

# CHAPTER 1

## David

On a clear autumn evening near the shores of Lake Michigan the night sky welcomed billions of stars once again. David walked up the hill behind his house knowing it was going to be another perfect night for viewing. He had his backpack on and his telescope carefully cradled in both arms, holding it against his chest. He was carrying it to his favorite place in the whole world. This nightly ritual was David's way of traveling to the stars, a place that truly felt like home.

He put the telescope methodically in place when he got to the top, and then took his headphones out of the backpack and adjusted them over his beanie. His iPod contained every album made by Rush, a rock group he really liked. *2112* was his favorite. Listening to Rush while stargazing took him to places no one knew about. It was his own secret world. He cranked up the volume and then synced the telescope with earth's orbit.

David could always feel the harmony between music and the universe. The combination of those two entities reverberated through his thin pale body, making his neural wiring fly at the speed of light. He looked deep into the crystal darkness as the music summoned the universe to respond in its own solitary way. In an instant the Northern Lights made their first appearance of the year dancing hypnotically just for him. His smile grew wide because he knew it couldn't get any better than that. He wished his friends could see the significance of it all, but they rarely hung out with him when he did his geeky science stuff.

David spent his nights studying math, physics, and the universe while other people at school partied, got drunk, and smoked weed. His ultimate goal was to become a physicist like his heroes Albert Einstein, Carl Sagan, and Benjamin Eldridge.

That goal was closer than he realized because of a letter he had received earlier in the day. David was usually the first one home so he always got the mail before heading inside. He opened the mailbox and a letter from Columbia University was staring back at him. He froze for a couple of seconds, afraid to touch it. But he quickly let go of the negative thoughts and reached in, hoping for the best. He stood in the driveway reading the simple measured words he had longed to hear.

*Dear Mr. Emerson,*

*It is our pleasure to inform you that you have been selected for a personal interview with Columbia Universities' Office of Admissions. You have been selected to the next level in the Early Decision process because of your SAT score, your personal essay, and your academic background. It is apparent that you are a hardworking, very responsible and dedicated young man. We are proud to extend this invitation to the next step of your academic career with a personal interview on Saturday, October 10th at 11:00 am. The interview will take place at Pupin Hall, room 514, located on Columbia's Morningside Heights Campus. Once again, congratulations on being selected for a formal interview.*

*Sincerely,*
*Stacy M. Bergen*
*Admissions Officer*

David must have read the letter at least ten times hoping the reality of it would finally sink into his brain. As his telescope moved with earth's orbit, so did his thoughts. He sat there with headphones blaring, and that vast expanse above him applauding, while he tried to grasp how close he was to his perfect dream. He didn't know whether to smile or cry.

He secretly wished he had that special someone to share the moment with, but knew he'd never find that person in a remote place like Harbor Springs. That was the harsh reality of being gay in the middle of nowhere. He also understood how hard it was going to be to leave home. But he knew he had to in order to achieve his dream, and maybe find that special guy who had to be out there somewhere.

David often wondered what it felt like to have a boyfriend, but it was impossible to find out since he was the only openly gay guy at school. Most of the guys avoided him like the plague. And if they did acknowledge him, it was only to call him a faggot or queer. It had been that way ever since coming out in middle school.

David came out to his parents at the age of twelve. It was one of the hardest things he had ever done because he was afraid they would hate him. He thought about staying in the closet until he got older, but knew he would end up hating himself. So he confidently let his mother and father know, hoping for the best. His mom took it pretty well, but his dad...he just got up and walked out of the room. He looked at his mom and the tears came. She kissed him on the cheek and left. He sat there waiting, hoping they would come back. It happened minutes later, but his dad wouldn't look at him. He stared at the air and the walls and his hands while his mom asked questions.

The two of them tried to logically work through what it was all going to mean. She told him the truth. That being gay in a small conservative town would make his life extremely difficult. David understood her concerns, but he also understood that he couldn't hide that part of his DNA for one second longer.

There was the obvious adjustment period for his family, especially his dad. He was ashamed and embarrassed about having a gay son. But when David was severely beaten by four homophobic boys in middle school a few months later, he broke down and begged for his forgiveness. Now their relationship has never been stronger.

David noticed a silhouette out of the corner of his eye slowly coming up the hill, jarring his mind out of the past. He hoped it was his father. They always had nice talks whenever they stargazed together. It was a way to see another side of the person who had brought him into the world. His father wasn't some big fancy executive or a person of prominence in the community. He never even finished college because love got in the way. David knew how different they were in many respects, but they did share a philosophical bond that made both of them view the world with optimistic eyes.

But as the silhouette got closer, he could tell it was Tyler, his best friend and secret crush. He took his headphones and beanie off and shook his shaggy blond hair to make himself look presentable. He watched Tyler stop a couple of times and look up. He smiled because it looked like the Northern Lights were coming right down on top of him.

"Well, I see you have a front row seat again," Tyler said, plopping down next to David.

"This is fucking awesome. I have to come out here more often."

"Yeah, it's unbelievable tonight." David leaned back on his elbows to get a better view. Tyler leaned back too so they could be shoulder to shoulder. Neither one said a word for a minute or so. David eventually broke the silence. "What are you thinking about?"

Tyler was thinking about one thing in particular but was petrified to talk about it. He asked something else instead. "Do you think there are other worlds out there with people like us? I mean, we can't be the only people in the whole fucking universe, right?"

"With all of the exoplanets astronomers are now finding, I would think there are millions of planets that could support life as we know it. So yeah, I think there are intelligent beings out there like us."

"What the fuck is an exoplanet?"

"They are planets orbiting around distant suns. Astronomers are finding them by the hundreds. It's very cool."

"Do we have telescopes that can see them?"

"No, not yet, unfortunately."

"So how do they know the planets are really there?"

"Astronomers use something called radial velocity. They also use microlensing to detect them as well. Extremely small velocity variations can be seen through the displacement in the star's spectral lines…."

"Hey Einstein, STOP! STOP! I don't know what the fuck you're talking about anymore..lol

It just seems crazy to think about other worlds and stuff."

"I guess it does seem a little weird. But even though most of the exoplanets they've found are gas giants like Jupiter and Saturn, they have found a few terrestrial planets similar to earth orbiting around the sweet spot of their suns."

"What do you mean by terrestrial, and sweet spot?"

"Earth is a rocky planet with an active core and it's in the perfect position relative to our sun to support life."

"Oh. Cool. That's kind of amazing when you think about it."

David started pointing out some of the constellations and then they took turns looking through the eyepiece. At one point David re-calibrated the telescope to show Tyler something unique.

"Take a look at this." Tyler looked and saw a fuzzy ball of light about the size of the moon.

"What is it?"

"It's the Messier 4 Globular Cluster in the constellation Scorpius. It's about 7,200 light years from our solar system and has some of the oldest stars in the universe. Cool, isn't it?"

"Yeah, I've never seen anything like it. Is it in our galaxy?"

"Yes. Basically everything we're looking at right now is in the Milky Way. Less than a hundred years ago scientists thought the Milky Way *was* the entire universe. That is until Dr. Hubble discovered other galaxies."

"I didn't know that."

David gazed ardently at Tyler's handsome profile while he looked through the eyepiece. He sighed. His crush was getting the best of him. He wanted to tell Tyler how he felt, and almost did, but chickened out once again. They ended up talking about music, the Northern Lights, and the Tigers until he decided to tell Tyler about the letter. "I received some good news in the mail today." Tyler turned towards him. "Oh yeah?"

"Yeah. I got a letter from Columbia University. They want to interview me. I've made it to the next level of their admissions process."

"Are you kidding me? That's fucking awesome." Tyler gave him a congratulatory hug, making David's body instantly come alive. "I can't believe that I might actually get in.

The thing is, they only admit approximately eleven

percent who apply, so the odds aren't in my favor. But at least they want to interview me."

Tyler knew how important this was to David because it was all he had talked about since ninth grade. "They'd be fucking idiots not to accept you. You're everything they're looking for. I mean you got a perfect 2400 on your SAT. You're a goddam genius in math and physics. What more could they want?"

"Please quit saying the genius thing, ok?"

"Sorry. I guess I'll just keep the truth to myself then." Tyler smiled. David smiled.

"Well it's probably not enough, but I guess I'll find out in a week. My dad and I are flying to New York next Friday. I'm really excited and really scared."

"Man, I can't believe my little David might become an Ivy Leaguer."

"I'm happy that I at least have a chance. I don't care about the whole Ivy League thing. I want to go there because they have one of the best math and physics programs in the world." Tyler gave him a knowing grin. "And let's not forget about that Eldridge guy being a professor there." David smiled at his keen perception. "That's a big reason too. I want to take every class he teaches if I get in. He is one of the leading physicists in the field of String Theory."

David felt good about how everything was coming together, and that he got to share the news with his best friend. That meant the most.

A few minutes later Tyler finally got to the reason why he

stopped by. "Melissa's having movie night tonight and she sent me here to make sure you come this time."

"I'm up for a movie. Sounds like fun. What are we going to see?"

"*The Signal*. We have to be there by ten."

"I don't like scary movies, you know that."

"Come on, they're fun. And anyway, I heard this one isn't gory. Please come."

"Honestly, those movies give me the creeps."

"I'll protect you. I promise. I'll put my arm around you and hold you and I won't even try to cop a feel." Tyler bumped his shoulder against David's and grinned.

"Yeah, and if you do that everyone will think you're gay."

"I don't care. You're my best friend and if I wanna hold you then I'm gunna hold you. Ok?"

"Ok. Thanks."

"Anytime."

Then David's smile faded. "Is Brad going to be there?"

"Probably. Is he bothering you again?"

"Yeah. He's been picking on me more than usual lately. He hates me and lets me know every chance he gets."

"I'm going to kick his fucking ass tonight."

"Please don't. I don't think Melissa would appreciate it. Thanks for offering though. He just spews his little gay jokes at me and I ignore him. I don't think he would physically hurt me, although it looks like he wants to at times."

"He picks on you because he's insecure, and you scare him. He can't compete with you, so giving you shit is the only way he can feel good about himself. I can't figure out why Melissa even likes him. I mean his personality sucks and I've seen him in the showers. Believe me, it's nothing to write home about," Tyler said, trying to make David laugh.

"Come on, be nice." That visual made David giggle. "He's jealous because Melissa and I are close and he doesn't want anyone butting in on his boyfriend time. He's even told her that he doesn't want her hanging out with me anymore."

"What a pin dick. Fuck him. I'll talk to Melissa and get this shit straightened out."

"Don't worry. We've already talked and she isn't going to let him control her life."

"Well, little old Brad and I are going to have some words very soon."

David looked up at Tyler's shadowed face and smiled. "Let's pack everything up so we can get scared out of our minds." They stood next to each other, their fingertips just inches apart as they looked skyward one last time before making their descent back to earth.

# CHAPTER 2
## Marco

The Upper East Side of New York City has always been an oasis of wealth, style, and creature comforts most teenagers only dream about. It is a Garden of Eden for the chosen few who are lucky enough to have been born into that alternate universe. Marco Valerio was one such teenager.

Marco lived in a two-story Park Avenue penthouse and attended Pembrooke Academy, one of the finest private college preparatory high schools on the Upper East Side. It was located in a seven story 1920s Art Deco building on Madison Avenue. He had everything a senior in high school could ever imagine: wealth, good looks, intelligence, and an exceptional gift for writing.

Marco wasn't some stuck up rich kid like a lot of people at his school, but he was self-assured and driven by his passions. His priorities were really quite simple. He loved to write, he loved to hang out with friends, and he loved to have sex with the endless supply of hot guys who were constantly hitting on him. That was his one true weakness. But those attributes, and his sexual appetite, made him one of the most popular guys at school.

11

Σ

Marco stood in front of the mirror making sure his hair looked just right while *Crystalized*, by The xx played in the background. He always looked flawless in his school uniform. He hated to wear it, so he bent the school's strict dress code to his liking with his own fashionable flair. His burgundy blazers were hand tailored and always fit perfectly, and so did his array of black Armani skinnys. And of course over three dozen pairs of Gucci shoes were needed, because how dare one wear the same shoes more than once a month. Marco knew how hot he looked, and so did everyone else. He finished his ensemble with a white Armani dress shirt and a skinny black tie. He looked in the full length mirrors turning in different positions to make sure he looked perfect at all angles. This was his morning ritual Monday through Friday.

Macro had it all going for him and he knew it. The combination of his Spanish and Asian lineage gave him an exotic look no other student at Pembrooke even came close to having. He turned heads wherever he went with his tall slender body, pitch dark hair, olive skin tone, and eyes that could melt the sun. He was the envy of every guy at school. And now he had one more piece of Rhodium that could be added to his already impressive collection. Laying on his desk was a letter from Columbia University.

*Dear Mr. Valerio,*

*It is our pleasure to inform you that you have been selected for a personal interview with Columbia Universities' Office of Admissions. You have been selected to the next level in the Early Decision process because of your SAT score, your personal essay, and your academic background. It is apparent that you are a hardworking, very responsible and dedicated young man. We are proud to extend this invitation to the next step in your academic career with a personal interview on Saturday, October 10th at 11:00 am.The interview will take place at Pupin Hall, room 514, located on Columbia's Morningside Heights campus. Once again, congratulations on being selected for a formal interview.*

*Sincerely,*
*Stacy M. Bergen*
*Admissions Officer*

Marco had applied as an Early Decision candidate to Columbia University, and now they wanted to interview him in one week. He couldn't believe that he was being considered for their world renowned writing program. It was a dream come true. Marco hoped the 2140 he received on his SAT would be high enough to get him in.

He never told any of his friends how much he wanted to go there. He kept that particular dream to himself. He looked at that confident demeanor reflecting back in the mirror, knowing his writing prowess and physical attributes would help him grab that elusive gold ring.

His phone rang as he walked from his dressing room back to his bedroom. It was Zander, his best friend. "Hey, what's up?"

"You won't believe it. I got the IDs last night," he said, excited as hell.

"Cool. How did you get them so fast?"

"I promised to neck the guy five times..lol."

"Are you serious?"

"You know I'm only kidding, although he was pretty hot. I wouldn't mind necking him. But seriously, when you wave two crisp one-hundred dollar bills in someone's face, things get done. So are we still on to hit Retro's tonight?"

"Of course. It's college night and I need to see some hot college boy ass shaking it on the dance floor. I'm getting hard just thinking about it."

"Keep it in your pants, unless you want me to come over and take care of it for you. I'd love to get at that piece of yours."

"Cut it out. We'll find some hotties tonight and both get what we want. They have to be ten times better than what we've been fucking. I'm so bored with immature guys that don't know what they're doing. I need to experience someone older who really knows how to fuck."

"Yeah, I know what you mean. You'll have them eating out of your hands like you always do. Maybe some of your charm will attract a few my way. Just don't take them all, ok?"

"Ok, I'll leave a few for you..lol Come on, you're hot as hell and you know it. We'll show those college boys how Upper East Side gay boys party. I'll see you in a few."

He was excited to finally be going to one of the hottest gay bars in Chelsea. He heard how great college night was from Thomas, a cute guy from another prep school he occasionally had sex with. Thomas had gone to Retro's a few weeks earlier. He told Marco all about it when they skipped school one afternoon to fuck. Now he was only hours away from his own sexual ecstasy.

Marco loved sex pure and simple. He didn't like to complicate things by staying tied to one guy. He did have his share of boyfriends over the years, but always ended up cheating on them. He simply didn't want to connect emotionally. He finally had enough of the boring boyfriend routine and decided that one night stands were the only way to go. He loved to use guys because it was uncomplicated, unemotional. It was the perfect way to satisfy his raging hormones without all of the bullshit. The guys he fucked knew where they stood, so everyone got what they wanted. But even though this plan had been working flawlessly, every now and then he wondered what it would be like to have a real boyfriend, someone he actually liked, or maybe even loved. He didn't have a clue why he would think about love, because sex was his perfection.

Even though he was excited about going to Retro's, he was more excited about the possibility of matriculating at Columbia. It had been his goal since the age of twelve. Both of his parents had gone to Princeton and wanted him to follow in their footsteps, but they reluctantly understood their son's desire to follow his own path. They supported Marco by not interfering or trying to manipulate him, although this was especially difficult for his overbearing mother.

While taking the elevator down to the lobby he decided that he needed a bit of extra inspiration. He knew he would be late for school, but told Max, his father's chauffeur, to drive by Columbia's main campus before dropping him off. He hoped it would help him get through the coming week in one piece. The next eight days were going to change his life in the most profound ways.

Marco's mind drifted to the past as the Escalade made its way across Central Park North. He started thinking about Dylan, his one true boyfriend from seventh grade. He smiled while remembering the great times they had together. Dylan was the first boy Marco had ever kissed. He had the biggest crush on him and finally let him know when they went to a Halloween party together. Marco knew he was gay by the age of ten, but had never acted on his desires until he met Dylan a couple of years later. He was instantly attracted to him, so they became friends. The Halloween party was where Marco got the courage to tell him.

The party was at his best friend Claire's penthouse, so he knew where they could sneak off and be alone. He had it all planned out. During the peak of the party he told Dylan that he wanted to ask him something but needed to ask in private. They went to the den at the other end of the main floor. Marco closed the sliding doors, and without saying a word, leaned in and kissed him. He waited to be pushed away, or punched, but Dylan did neither. Instead, he put his arms around Marco and started kissing him with more intensity. That was the moment he had fallen in love. From that point on they were inseparable for the rest of seventh grade.

They had countless sleepovers where they could be themselves with no one making judgments. The emotional connection they shared went way beyond any poetic words he could ever write.

Marco also experienced the pain of losing love. During the summer between seventh and eighth grade Dylan's father was transferred to Japan. It almost killed him when Dylan moved away. They tried the long distance relationship thing, promising to stay together, but reality got in the way. During the fall of that year Dylan sent a breakup letter to Marco saying that he was going out with a girl from school. He ended the letter by saying that he would keep the love he had for Marco locked in his heart forever. Those words tore him to shreds. He vowed never to get close to anyone again.

Marco wiped his eyes and forced his mind back to the present before completely losing it. He didn't know if what he had with Dylan was love, a teenage crush, or just the elation of coming out to someone. He had written about it many times through the tragically flawed characters in his stories. He took quiet comfort in those characters because love was no longer part of his DNA.

Marco looked with fervent eyes as Max slowly drove past the front gates of Columbia. He watched as students made their way inside, wishing he could do the same. He wanted to extract whatever bits of experiential awareness and poetic alchemy lay in wait just for him, knowing it would help him write sentences that would slice through skin, making one bleed with each word read. This singular goal was far more erotic than the loveless sex he constantly craved.

# CHAPTER 3

## Tyler

OCTOBER

True friendship runs deep in the hearts of those it magically embraces. Like a crescent sun eclipse, it is one of those rare gifts that very few people receive and genuinely appreciate. No one really knows why it happens, how two people randomly meet and then easily share their passions and dreams within emotional perfection. This humanistic connection always strikes when least expected, and if a person is lucky enough, it lasts a lifetime. Sometimes it even enters into that other realm where two become one.

Tyler helped David carry his telescope down the steep well-worn path. They talked about a book they were both reading as they made their way back to the house. Halfway down the hill Tyler almost dropped the telescope twice because he was looking up instead of watching where he was going. Once the telescope was safely back in the bedroom, Tyler flung himself onto David's bed, leaned against a couple of pillows and began his usual ritual. His eyes went from poster to poster while David was busy taking things out of his backpack.

Tyler had seen these posters a million times, but always enjoyed looking at them because they were so different from his own. They made him feel happy and content for some reason. He knew those images were some sort of complex puzzle, an intimate journey, that if constructed correctly, would allow him to enter deeper into David's unique world.

His eyes went from image to image as he thought back to that pivotal day when they had become friends. It happened during a little league baseball game. Tyler was one of those natural athletes that every parent and teammate admired. He was a pitcher, catcher, third baseman, and shortstop. He also had the highest batting average and the most home runs on the team.

David, on the other hand, was not athletic at all, so he was constantly getting picked on. Even the coach and his own father criticized him in their clever little ways. Tyler felt sorry for him because he could see that his heart wasn't in it. During one of the first practices he overheard his father talking to David's father about their glory days in high school when they played. That's when he knew David was being forced to play.

Things got pretty intense when two assholes on the team started taunting David relentlessly, calling him a bitch and dick muncher whenever the coach was out of earshot. Just before the start of their sixth game, Tyler finally had enough of their shit and told them to shut the fuck up. They turned on him, calling him David's faggot boyfriend. He lost it and proceeded to kick both of their asses in front of everyone. The coach ran into the dugout and grabbed Tyler, but he pulled away and let the coach have it too. "I'm fucking tired of everyone picking on David. You know what's been going on but you don't do a fucking thing about it?" The coach started to yell at Tyler, but suddenly stopped, like he had just remembered his own days as a bully.

He composed himself and gave the entire team a lecture about supporting one another. When he finished his speech, he took the two bullies off to the side to let them know they were benched for the next two games. Tyler moved over and sat next to David and tried to calm down. He caught his breath and then asked David if he wanted to hang out after the game. They became best friends from that day on.

Tyler smiled at that memory while continuing to go from poster to poster. There were images of the universe in different stages of evolution, clusters of mystical looking galaxies, supernovas, black holes, and futuristic looking spacecraft. Scattered in between those were pictures of Rush, Geddy Lee, David Gilmour, Thom York, and Chester Bennington. They were musicians David admired and listened to. There weren't any posters of pretty girls or sports cars like Tyler had hanging on his walls.

He ended the poster game by staring at the wall next to the bed. He studied the fierce eyes of Einstein and Eldridge. He knew David was made from the same mold because his eyes had that same intensity.

Just below those pictures were some new ones he had never seen before. He looked closely at one in particular because the guy looked a lot like him. "Who are these guys?"

David walked over to see who he was talking about. "Oh, them. Let me introduce you to Ezra Miller, Freddie Highmore, and Keir Gilchrist. I think they're really fine actors, and I think they're cute too." Tyler felt a jealous ping hit his stomach with those words.

"You know something, I kind of look like this Keir guy, don't you think?"

"Weird coincidence, isn't it?" David said, with a sly grin.

Tyler looked at the picture again and then turned back and caught David checking out his body. David quickly looked away, wanting to run out of the room. Tyler sensed his embarrassment and tried to let him know that he didn't mind. "Well, I think you have excellent taste in guys. It's kind of cool that I look like him." David didn't say anything, so Tyler bumped his leg against his and smiled. "Hey, it's all cool, ok?"

"Thanks." Still feeling embarrassed, David turned and walked back to his closet to gather himself, and to find something else to wear.

Tyler's mind was going a mile a minute at the thought of David checking him out. It made him feel good, but it also added to the mixed emotions he had been wrestling with. He needed to calm down, so he turned onto his side and noticed a whiteboard filled with weird looking math equations leaning against David's guitar. "What's all this?" Tyler asked.

David turned to see what he was talking about. "Oh that. I'm learning some new math for
M-theory. It's interesting stuff."

"I love how your mind works. You are unbelievable, you know that?"

"Awe, that's so sweet of you to say."

Tyler tried his hardest not to, but he was checking David out as he stripped down to his boxers while looking through his closet. He admired David's slender frame, smooth chest, and slight six pack abs. This scared him because it excited him. He thought David was hot, but felt guilty about it, like he was doing something very very wrong. It didn't matter to Tyler that David was gay, but being gay himself was something he wasn't ready to deal with. He knew how difficult it was for David, and didn't know if he could ever be that strong.

After David had come out in middle school Tyler began looking a little closer, trying to see what made him tick. It wasn't because he was afraid of him, or afraid to be seen with him. It was because of what he was feeling. He wanted to figure it out but denied himself to seriously go there. It was easier to hide within the straight persona instead of facing the truth. But the feelings he had for David were now getting too intense to ignore, so he finally decided to go for it.

He looked away for a second and tried to gather up all of the courage he possessed. Then he turned back towards David, who was zipping up his jeans.

"Which one should I wear?" he asked, holding up two t-shirts.

"The Red one." While David slipped the red t-shirt over his head, Tyler scanned his sexy v-lines and cute little abs into his brain, making his heart almost pound right out of his chest.

David shook his shaggy hair back in place and asked, "Do I look all right?"

"You look prefect as always."

"Thanks. I think I need a haircut though." David giggled because he couldn't see anything through his long bangs.

"Please don't cut it. I really like the way it looks."

David parted his bangs with his fingers. "Thanks. I kind of like it too."

Tyler tried to move but was paralyzed with fear. He wanted to hold David in his arms and never let go. He wanted to feel David's heartbeat in rhythm with his own. He wanted to know what being gay felt like without having to hide. He sat up on the edge of the bed, took a deep breath, then stood up and looked into those determined blue eyes hoping the right words would come out. "David?"

"Yeah?"

"We've known each other for a long time, and I've always been honest with you, right?"

"Yeah. We've always been honest with each other. That's what best friends do."

"I feel the same way, so…" Tyler's voice trailed off.

David gave him a worried look. "What's wrong?"

Tyler was shaking slightly. "Y-you know, if I were gay, I'd ask you out in a heartbeat. I just wanted you to know that. I hope you don't think that's a weird thing to say, but it's the truth. It's how I really feel and I just wanted you to know."

Tyler saw the shock on his face and hoped he hadn't gone too far. David couldn't believe what he had just heard, but he did hear it, and for the first time in his life was able to look at Tyler's gorgeous face and gorgeous lips without the fear of getting caught. "That is one of the nicest things anyone has ever said to me." Tyler smiled and then slowly put his hands on David's waist and pulled him close. "I really mean it."

"I know you do." David had wished for this moment on a million falling stars and now his wish had come true. Being held by Tyler felt perfect. He whispered, "Tyler?"

"Yeah?"

"Would you kiss me?" At that point David's whole body began to tremble. Tyler held him against his chest and rubbed his back. Once David relaxed, Tyler pulled away and looked into his loving eyes, and then leaned in and kissed those soft beautiful lips. Sparks flew in every direction as soon as they connected. They were encapsulated with emotions that had been patiently waiting for years to meet. That first kiss, and their soft caresses, made them realize how connected they had always been. A few minutes later Tyler reluctantly pulled his lips from David's. He whispered, "That was nice."

"It was magic," David whispered back, barely able to get the words out. He smiled as the tears fell one by one. "You're the first guy I've ever kissed. I've wanted this to happen since seventh grade."

Tyler suddenly felt dizzy. The years of fear, like ghosts under the bed, had entered his thoughts once again. He tried to push that fear away because he was in love with David.

"You're the first guy I've ever kissed too, so we're even." He tried keeping his feelings in neutral, but his heart wouldn't let him. Tyler asked, "Will you be my date tonight?"

David kissed him on the cheek. "I would be honored."

All of a sudden Tyler's phone chimed. It was a text from Melissa asking him to do her a favor. His hand was shaking slightly as he read it. "Melissa wants us to get the pizzas. I g-guess we better get going."

"Yeah, I guess. We don't want the pizzas to get cold."

# CHAPTER 4
## David

David was trying to process what had just happened as they drove to the pizzeria. He couldn't believe that he had finally kissed Tyler. It was a dream come true. He loved how normal it made him feel. How their bodies fit together perfectly. How those sexy arms held him so close he cried. How kissing Tyler's brooding lips sent shockwaves through his entire body. He wanted to tell him so many things, but kept silent because he could see fear written all over Tyler's face.

Then the guilt came. Kissing Tyler was the happiest moment in his life, but he felt like he had played a giant trick on his best friend, plotting and scheming for years just to get to those lips.

Little did he know, but Tyler was thinking the exact same thing. He couldn't bear to look at David because he felt like he wasn't being honest. He looked straight ahead as he drove, silent, lost, feeling ashamed. Tyler hated feeling that way because deep down he knew there was nothing to be ashamed of. There was nothing wrong with being in love with David. He knew that. But he also knew his parents and the rest of his family would never understand that in a million years. They would never accept that he was gay, and in love with another guy.

David sensed that Tyler was having second thoughts, so he decided to let him off the hook.

"Tyler, we should talk about what happened, but I'll understand if you don't want to right now. I just don't want you to feel obligated in any way, ok?" Tyler didn't answer. After a long thirty seconds, David tried again. "Look, I like you a lot, and I know what happened is a scary thing. So you get to choose. We can see where this thing between us might go, or we can pretend that it never happened and just stay friends. I'll accept whatever you decide."

David watched Tyler let out a sigh. It sounded desperate and sad. "Thank you for understanding. I am confused, but I don't want to pretend it didn't happen. I liked that it happened. Please believe me. I don't ever wanna hurt you, so I hope you'll be patient while I'm trying to figure this out."

"I understand. Take all the time you need. Just know that I'm here for you, ok?"

"Thanks."

David was finally able to relax and even crack a smile. All in all it had been the most perfect day he had ever had. He received a letter from Columbia University. He had his very first kiss from the guy he was in love with. He glanced at Tyler and noticed how the light from the dashboard gave his face an angelic glow.

$$\oint$$

Melissa lived on Little Traverse Bay in a sleek sprawling

ranch that emulated the early twentieth-century designs of Frank Lloyd Wright. Her father was a wealthy corporate lawyer who commuted between Chicago and Harbor Springs. He was a huge fan of Wright and felt his philosophy of blending architecture and nature was the perfect way to live. That's why he chose Harbor Springs to build his one of a kind home.

Melissa started living in Harbor Springs year round the summer she started eighth grade. She was tired of the pretentious preppy scene in Chicago and wanted out. She became friends with David the very first day of school. They met in English class. She sat next to him and introduced herself because she thought he was cute. She knew he was definitely boyfriend material even though he looked a lot younger than her. David introduced her to Tyler later that day. The idea of David becoming her boyfriend evaporated when he came out at school a couple of weeks later. With the exception of Tyler and Melissa, every single one of his friends shunned him.

Δ

David and Tyler walked in the side entrance that led to the kitchen. Melissa's mother greeted them as she fussed about getting everything prepared. "Hi boys. Thank you for getting the dinner." She went to get her purse. "Tyler, let me give you some gas money."

"No thank you Mrs. Nolan. Just eating all this good stuff is payment enough."

David stood next to Tyler with an infectious grin. "Hi

Mrs. Nolan. Thank you for buying dinner. It's so nice of you to feed us all the time."

"David, how have you been? I haven't seen you in quite some time."

"I know. I've been really busy with school and college applications."

"You need to come around more often. We miss seeing that beautiful smile of yours."

David blushed. "I will, I promise."

Melissa came into the kitchen a minute later and gave them hugs. "I thought for sure you weren't going to come tonight," she told David. "You can't keep your eyes in the stars all the time. It isn't healthy." He giggled. "Watching spooky movies is healthy?" They went to the great room to talk in private before everyone else showed up. "I just miss hanging around with you. I barely see you in school anymore." She kissed David on the cheek and gave him a miss you hug.

"I'm sorry. Thanks for sending Tyler to get me." David looked his way to see his reaction. Tyler's somber stare gave his facial features contorted linear depth, making them look broodingly animated.

"Hey, are you ok?" Melissa asked Tyler, playfully slapping his arm.

"Yeah, I'm good." Then he looked at David and said it again. "I'm definitely good."

He smiled. "David got a letter from Columbia University today."

A panicked look fell across Melissa's face even though

she was trying to hide it. "You got in? That's fantastic."

"No. I didn't get in yet." Then he looked at Tyler. "I didn't want anyone to know yet."

"I'm sorry, but I'm excited for you, that's all. Melissa is family."

David grinned. "You're right. I'm sorry."

Tyler gazed into those deep blue eyes. "I'm really proud of you."

All of the excitement had returned to David's voice as he explained. "I did get a letter, but it's only for an interview. It's the next level of the Early Decision process, so I'm keeping my fingers crossed."

"I can't believe it. That is so cool." Melissa meant it this time and gave him another hug. And that's when Brad walked in and started spouting off like an idiot. "Back off star man, she's mine. Oh yeah, I forgot, her kind of equipment don't register in your gay brain. Sorry dude, she's all yours." Melissa turned and gave Brad a look that could kill. "You're a fucking asshole, you know that. Maybe you should just leave now."

David didn't want to dignify his comment with a response, but Tyler did. "David is my date tonight and you've insulted both of us." Brad looked like a deer caught in headlights. So did Melissa. "All right, all right. I'm sorry for being an asshole. I didn't mean anything by it." David watched with satisfaction when Brad tried to kiss Melissa and she dubbed him. Then she asked,

"Are you guys really on a date?" Tyler took David's hand in his. "Yeah. It's a bromance date." Her smile grew wide. "Very

31

cool. You guys make a very cute couple." Brad looked like he was going to throw up.

Within a few minutes everyone started showing up and the night got under way. It turned out to be a couples night even though it wasn't planned. Brad couldn't help himself and started gay bashing again. "Hey guys, David is Tyler's date tonight. They're having a bromance," he said, thinking everyone would laugh. It was just the opposite. The girls thought it was cool.

Tyler put his arm around David's waist to let everyone know that he was serious. He hoped the panic lying just under his skin wouldn't begin to leak out and make him run away. David couldn't believe that Tyler was being affectionate in front of everyone. An odd silence fell while everyone processed what was happening. Lucas finally spoke up. "I think everyone here knows your friendship is really special. I think bromances are cool. Why don't you sit next to me and Kathy during the movie."

"We'd like that. Thanks," Tyler said. David gave him a sympathetic look and then apologized in front of everyone. "I'm sorry I got you into this mess. We don't have to do this. I'll understand." He wanted to give Tyler an out, but Tyler wasn't having any of it.

"I asked you to be my date tonight and you accepted. This isn't a pity date if that's what you think." Then he did what he thought he'd never do. He kissed David in front of everyone. And it wasn't just a friendly little peck. It was as real and emotional as it gets. Everyone stood there in shock because no one had ever seen two guys kiss in real life. Tyler slowly pulled away after a minute or so and looked at David without saying a word.

Brad couldn't take it any longer and asked Tyler in a condescending voice, "So, you're gay too? I can't fucking believe it. I thought you were kidding. Fuck me, everyone is turning fucking gay."

David started to go after Brad, but Tyler grabbed him just in time. "David, don't lower yourself to his level. He doesn't understand anything." He looked at Brad. "What I am is none of your fucking business, so get over it."

Melissa was seething and told Brad to leave. David didn't want to ruin the night so he tried to calm everyone down and reason with Brad. "You need to let this gay bashing thing go. You're not hurting Tyler or me in the least. Let's just enjoy hanging out together."

That wasn't close to being good enough for Melissa. She took Brad outside to talk. He looked totally defeated when they came back in a few minutes later.

Things finally got back to normal when everyone gathered in the kitchen. The conversation started off with the usual school and work gossip, and then eventually made its way to the colleges everyone applied to. Melissa lamented how this was the last year everyone would be together. That observation made David feel sad because it was the beginning of the end of everything he had ever known. It felt tragic. It felt final.

David decided to put those feelings in his pocket so he could enjoy the excitement of everyone talking about their dream colleges. He decided not to say anything about the Columbia letter because he didn't want to upstage anyone. He even gave Tyler and Melissa a pleading look at one point. They understood.

Kevin, Lucas, and Kathy were applying to Michigan State. Mike, Brad, Emma, and Aubree were applying to Central Michigan. And Tyler and Melissa were applying to the University of Michigan. David was being heavily recruited by U of M, MIT - Massachusetts Institute of Technology, and a dozen other world renown universities. He kept that to himself. His parents were the only ones who knew. He knew moments like this one were coming to a close, so he decided to etch the night into his memory banks forever.

Twenty minutes later everyone headed to the great room. Pillows and blankets were set up in everyone's favorite spots on the floor. After everyone got cozy, Melissa turned the lights off and the movie started.

David was a nervous wreck sitting next to Tyler. He wanted to hold his hand but was afraid to, so he decided to just enjoy being next to him. A couple of minutes into the movie Tyler leaned close and whispered, "Remember, I'll protect you." He took David's hand in his and gave it a gentle squeeze, and then their fingers intertwined.

# Chapter 5

## Marco

It was twelve-thirty in the morning when Marco and Zander cabbed down to 17th Street and 5th Avenue. They got out at the corner, took some Molly, and walked a half block to Retro's. Marco was excited to finally be going to his first gay club. He lied to his parents, but it was worth it. He told them he was sleeping at Zander's, and Zander told his parents he was sleeping at Marco's. This scheme always worked because their parents were preoccupied with their own social lives.

The plan for this particular night was to dance with and entice as many college guys as possible before choosing one to have sex with. They would each go their separate ways after the club closed and head to their guy's dorm or apartment. This fantasy had been floating around in Marco's head for weeks and now it was finally happening.

They saw all these extremely hot guys standing in a line when they walked up. Having so many gay boys in one place made Marco's skin tingle. He couldn't wait to have sex with someone older. A burly guy with a half dozen piercings and twice as many tattoos was checking IDs at the entrance. Marco was nervous because he wanted to get in there so bad.

35

Being seventeen sucked as far as he was concerned.

Every guy standing in line checked Marco out. He knew it and played it. He posed and teased as he chatted with Zander. He let a couple of guys know he was interested with a wanting look. He had played this game a million times and loved how easily it worked.

Five minutes later they were through the door. They had entered an alternate universe where the real games were played. A sexy papi in a black speedo pointed to a stairway leading to the lower level. "The coat check is that way guys." Marco started following Zander downstairs when someone grabbed his ass. He turned around and was face to face with black speedo papi. He told Marco, "You're fucking hot. I'd love to tap what you got." The idea of an older guy fucking him made his body come alive. "I just might let you before the night is over." Marco's hand brushed his package as he turned around and headed down the stairs. He caught up with Zander at the coat check. Another hot papi in a red speedo took their jackets. The guy gave Marco his ticket and also slipped him his number. "Give me a call when you get a chance."

"I definitely need to give you a call," Marco said, his eyes on the bulging prize that awaited.

On their way upstairs Zander became fatherly. "He's way too old for you. He must be a least thirty."

"Yeah, I know, but did you see that package? I wanted him to take me in the back and fuck my brains out."

"Come on, let me save you from yourself."

⚔

The dance floor was packed with at least two hundred of the hottest college guys Marco had ever seen. He loved the atmosphere and the intensity of the music. Everywhere he looked there were go-go boys in speedos dancing. They made sure their junk was eye level so guys could stuff dollar bills in. Zander yelled to Marco, "You should do this. You'd make thousands a night with that body of yours."

"Yeah, I wouldn't mind doing it for the adrenaline rush."

Someone caught his eye. He walked over to a blond go-go dancer, his perfect shiny body slithering, seductively simulating perfect sex. Marco's eyes were riveted, hypnotized by his beauty, hypnotized by the Molly. The guy moved his hips back and forth, making his abs and v-lines come alive. He moved within inches of Marco's face and proceeded to give him a private show. Marco stuffed a fifty into his speedo, making sure it was in good and deep. The guy leaned down, "I'd fuck you in a second if I were gay." Marco smiled at the thought of doing a straight guy. He put it on his mental list.

Marco moved through the crowd checking guys out and eventually found Zander. They were at the bar ready to buy some drinks when four guys came up and pulled them onto the dance floor. The uninhibited fun had now begun. He closed his eyes and felt the music course through his excited body. He breathed in the sweat and hormones and unemotional lust, his body screaming for it all. He was surrounded by sexy intellectual college boys who wanted the same thing he wanted. He had finally made it to heaven.

Guy after guy hit on him as the early morning unfolded.

They rubbed against him. They kissed him sexy wild. Even violently at times. They caressed his cute little ass and enticing package, begging to fuck him. It was a game he loved to play before choosing the lucky one.

It was two thirty when Marco found Zander making out with a blond haired cutie named Darren. He was a student at New York University. Marco thought about stealing him away, until a gorgeous guy tapped him on the shoulder and asked him to dance. Marco smiled his smile and followed him to the dance floor, then moved in close and started making out with him. Marco knew he was the one. They Danced for the next twenty minutes, refusing to let anyone join in. The way they danced expressed what they both wanted, so Marco made his move and took that guy by the hand and walked off the dance floor in search of Zander. He spotted him and his guy standing by the DJ booth. Marco needed to fill Zander in on his plan. "Go for it if he asks you to go home with him. Text me at some point and let me know where you're at, ok?"

"Yeah, ok. You do the same."

They had their guys, so all they had to do was get invited to their place to fuck the night away. Marco and his guy went to the lower level so they could talk.

"What's your name?"

"Jordan."

"I'm Marco."

"You're really cute," Jordan said.

"So are you." They started kissing like it was their last day on earth. The bartender interrupted them when their drinks were ready. They found an empty table.

"Is this your first time here?" Marco asked.

"No, I've been here a few times."

"Did anyone ever tell you that you look just like Usher when he was a teenager?"

"Yeah, I've heard that before. I can assure you it wasn't me who was on *Moesha* back in the 90s," Jordan laughed. "Marco, you are just about the cutest guy I have ever seen. I mean it. What nationality are you?"

"Spanish and Asian mix."

"Very nice. Very sexy." He leaned in and nibbled on Marco's lips. Marco loved how aggressive Jordan seemed to be. It was measured. It was dominant. It was sexy. He loved the way Jordan's full luscious lips felt against his. The way Jordan used his tongue to slip inside his body.

"What college do you go to?" Marco asked, after they came up for air.

"Columbia."

"Really? I love Columbia."

"Yeah, me too. I'm a junior."

"So tell me, what's it like?"

"I love it. It's everything I thought it would be. The professors are fucking brilliant and accessible. And the campus is amazing. You work your ass off, but there's a lot of fun to be had as well."

"Very cool. What's your major?"

"I'm majoring in Mathematics and minoring in Philosophy."

"Nice. I've applied as an Early Decision candidate. I'm actually going for an interview next Saturday."

"I hate to ask, but how old are you?"

"Eighteen."

"Cool. We could hang out if you get in." Jordan started rubbing Marco's leg and asked, "Would you like to go to my apartment and well, you know."

"Yeah, I wanna get all over you." Marco slid his hand to Jordan's crotch and rubbed it. Jordan closed his eyes and sighed. He had him exactly where he wanted.

"Where do you live?"

"112th and Amsterdam. It's near The Cathedral of St. John. Do you know where that is?"

"Yeah, I've been in that area a few times. Let's grab a cab and do it."

Marco sent Zander a text letting him know where he was going. His fantasy was about to become reality. He was going to break night by having the best sex of his life with an Ivy League college hottie.

≈

It was 9:30 in the morning when Marco finally left Jordan's apartment. They exchanged phone numbers even though he knew he'd never call him. Diplomacy was part of chase.

Marco walked down 112th toward Broadway thinking about his night of uninhibited sex. He spotted a restaurant on the corner and went in. He texted Zander to let him know where he was. Zander responded a couple of minutes later saying he was still at Darren's near Washington Square Park.

"How good was it? That guy was fucking hot," Zander said.

"It was perfect. I can't even tell you how many positions we did it in."

"Same here. Let's talk when we meet up."

"I'm at Tom's Restaurant at 112th and Broadway. Cab up here."

"Cool. See you in about forty-five."

Marco sat there drinking coffee thinking about Jordan. The night had gone just as he planned. Even though it was the best sex he ever had, he didn't feel as satisfied as he thought he would. Instead, he felt kind of lonely and depressed and didn't know why. He went through the whole night in his mind hoping to find a clue. It didn't make sense, so the only cure was to either have more sex or go on a writing frenzy. He sipped his coffee and let his mind wander. He started formulating an idea for a new story as a way to analyze his night of conquest. He called it *Empty Victories*.

# CHAPTER 6

## David

OCTOBER

FRIDAY

The view over Lake Michigan was breathtaking. David had only been on a plane a few times, but each time he flew he always enjoyed looking down at Grand Traverse Bay, Lake Michigan, and the numerous sand dunes that dotted the shoreline. As a kid he liked to pretend that he was a god looking down at the earth from Mount Olympus. But this time his mind was elsewhere. The New York City skyline, Columbia's campus, Tyler, and the life he was potentially leaving behind preoccupied his synapses. David's mind reeled backward as the plane flew forward. He started thinking about the aftermath of his date with Tyler. How everything began to unravel the very next day.

The following morning he texted Tyler to let him know what a great time he had at Melissa's. He also asked if he wanted to hang out later in the day. Tyler didn't text back until eleven-thirty that night. It was short and cold. He told David that he was scared and confused. David knew he was in all out panic mode. He told him once again that there was no pressure on his part, and to take all the time he needed to figure things out.

Tyler didn't text or come over on Sunday like he usually did, and the drive to school Monday morning was quiet and strained. David tried to get a conversation going but Tyler wasn't interested. Melissa tried to help, but it was no use. David stared blankly at the road hoping Tyler didn't hate him.

Then things went from bad to worse as soon as they got to school. A lot of people stared at them as they walked to their lockers. One of Tyler's jock friends walked up and asked, "How was your date with your boyfriend? Did you give him tongue?" Tyler told him to fuck off. He walked away from David and Melissa totally pissed. The news of their date spread all over school like wildfire. Tyler was teased mercilessly the entire day. David felt terrible because he didn't deserve the grief he was getting.

He was even getting picked more than usual. Two guys from Tyler's baseball team grabbed him as soon as he walked out of his Calculus class. They shoved him against the lockers and accused him of turning Tyler gay. They both threatened him, but Derrick, the bigger and more ignorant of the two, made it personal. "I hate faggots you fuckin cocksucker. You're a fuckin disease that's gotta be wiped off the earth." It was the first time since middle school that David felt real fear. He knew Derrick meant it.

He went into protection mode and decided to eat lunch in the physics lab. Christian, his friend and lab partner came in near the end of lunch and told David what was going on.

"I was standing in line getting lunch and overheard Tyler and his friends talking. He told them that he didn't really ask you out on a date. He said it was just something he wanted to do to piss Brad off. He said the kiss was meant to do the same thing." David put his book down. "Did he say anything else?"

"No, but his friends did. They blamed you for everything and told Tyler not to hang around with you anymore because his rep is getting ruined by all the faggot rumors."

David felt nervous and alone. He looked down at the table and ran his fingers through his hair.

"Thanks for letting me know."

"Just to let you know, I didn't believe a word Tyler said. He likes you. I see the way he looks at you whenever you guys are together."

"Please don't let anyone else know that. Please?"

"No problem."

David felt like he was choking to death. He couldn't breathe. He put his head on the table and tried not to cry.

Tyler had successfully avoided David the entire day until it was time to go home. He walked into David's physics class and asked if he was ready to leave. David could see how nervous Tyler was about being seen with him, so he decided to help him out. "I'm going to be staying late today, and for the rest of this week and next week because of this experiment I'm working on. I also need to get here an hour early. My dad is picking me up later, and said he would drive me to and from school for the next couple of weeks. That way you don't have to wait around or pick me up in the morning. I appreciate you asking though."

"Cool. See you around." Tyler headed for the door and

disappeared. David cried himself to sleep for the next three nights.

It was 2 am Thursday morning when David suddenly woke up in a confused state. He thought it was a dream, but he heard it again. Someone was tapping on his window and calling his name. He crawled out of bed and crouched down as he moved toward the window. As he got closer he saw Tyler standing in the yard looking down at the snow. He opened the window as quietly as he could and whispered "Do you want to come in and talk?"

"Thanks." As soon as Tyler slid through the window he started crying.

"I'm so sorry for everything. I lied about us. I panicked."

"It's ok, I understand. I'm sorry your friends found out." He hugged Tyler and rubbed his back. "Let it all out." He finally calmed down a few minutes later. "I'm such a fucking coward. I don't know how you've taken it all these years. I really don't"

"First of all, you're not a coward. The haters are. Sadly, the world is filled with them. They hate what they can't comprehend. It's that simple." They spent the rest of the night talking and decided to just be friends for the time being. David knew it was for the best, even though his heart was shattered.

The next thing on David's mind was his father's indifference about the interview. He couldn't figure it out. His mother was excited about it. They talked about college life and New York all week. But his father didn't show any emotion one way or the other. He never brought it up once. His silence reminded David of his reaction when he told him he was gay.

All of a sudden it hit David like a bolt of lightning. What if he did get accepted and didn't get a full ride scholarship? Could his parents afford to send him? Did they even want him going to college in another state? That had to be it.

In truth, his father hadn't said anything because he was afraid he would jinx it, and he would never want to do that. David's father was a gifted baseball player in high school and had elaborate rituals he always followed. Superstitions are an integral part of the game, and he had them big time. Most athletes have rituals to keep the good karma from going askew. Nobody, but nobody ever talks about a no hitter when a pitcher is pitching one, or when a batter is on a hitting streak. So there was no way he was going to jinx his son's dream of getting into Columbia University by talking about it.

David was the first person in his family to be going to a major university. His parents were very proud of this fact. Even if he didn't get into Columbia, they knew he would be going to some other prestigious university because of the scholarship offers he was getting on a weekly basis. His SAT score had opened the flood gates with full ride scholarships and promises of an unequaled math and science education. David took all of it in stride while his parents were in awe of what was happening.

David needed to know if his father was ok with his college choice. "Dad, thank you for taking me to New York. I really appreciate it. I can't believe this is actually happening. I was just wondering if you are ok with this. You've been pretty quiet since I got the letter." His father gave him a reassuring smile. "Believe me son, I am. This is your dream. Your mom and I are proud of everything you've accomplished. We both want this to happen because you've worked so hard to get where you are. No father could be prouder than I am right now. I've been waiting for the perfect time to give you something." He reached into his laptop case and pulled out a small worn box and handed it to David. "I hope this brings you good luck." David thanked him and opened it up. It was his dad's Titans baseball lapel pin from his days as a short stop at Traverse City West High School. "That pin was given to me by the Booster Club when we came in first place in the regionals my junior year. We wore them the following year when we won the state championship. I want you to have it because it helped me achieve one of my dreams."

"Thank you. This is awesome." David carefully took it out of the box to get a good look. He had never seen it before. "Would you put it on for me?" His father pinned it on his shirt and made sure it was straight. "There you go." David kissed his dad on the cheek, then said, "I love you."

∂

The view of the Manhattan skyline while crossing the Queensboro Bridge sent shivers down David's spine. He could see three iconic structures making their presence known: The United Nations Building, the Chrysler Building, and the Empire State Building. He took pictures and sent them to Tyler and Melissa. His smile grew wide as the cab made its way into the heart of Manhattan.

His Father made reservations at the Hotel Newton ten blocks from Columbia's campus, so they were headed in that direction. The cab drove west on 59th street, which allowed David to see many other iconic images of New York: The Plaza, Central Park, horse drawn carriages, and doormen standing outside ultra-modern apartment buildings. He kept thinking to himself, *I'm actually here and it feels perfect.*

"Well, what do you think?" his father asked.

"It's overwhelming. To tell you the truth, I'm scared." His father could see the panicked look on David's face and tried to reassure him. "I'm afraid too. I'm not used to things being so busy. We definitely aren't in Harbor Springs anymore. But don't worry, it is just all new to us. Try to relax and enjoy it."

"I'll try. It just feels a little crazy." David tried to find the confidence that had always gotten him through the rough times. He kept himself occupied by taking pictures and sending them to his mom and his friends.

After checking into the hotel, they got a map of the city at the front desk and started walking north on Broadway towards Columbia. David felt like he was in the land of OZ as they walked from block to block. He liked the tall buildings that lined the street and the wide crowded sidewalks. It was all a little unsettling until he realized how close he was to the campus.

Walking those last four blocks felt just like the first time David had gone on The Gatekeeper roller coaster at Cedar Point. It was scary and exhilarating. He saw the Columbia

Bookstore sign and started walking faster. When he got there he peeked through the window to see what it looked like inside. "Do you want to go inside on our way back to the hotel?" his father asked.

"Definitely. I want to buy a Columbia t-shirt." David walked the last two blocks without saying a word. He went up to the gates and touched them so he would know they weren't a mirage. Then he looked up at the statues of Science and Knowledge and smiled.

"Are you ready to go in?" his dad asked.

"I'm more than ready." They walked through the gates and followed a red brick walkway that lead to the center of campus. In a nanosecond the goosebumps came, making the hair on his arms stand straight up. David was now standing right in the middle of his dream.

As soon as they walked past the journalism building the entire campus greeted him. David was surrounded by an enclave of stately academic buildings, manicured lawns, and intimate gardens. He kept walking until he was in the absolute center of campus.

Once there he turned to his right. There stood Butler library, windows ensconced in a warm glow with an orange purplish dusk as its majestic backdrop. He then did a one eighty and was greeted by Low Library. It reminded David of the Parthenon because of its elevated and centered position.

David's father purposely lagged behind. He understood that David needed to experience the moment by himself. To see for himself, and to understand how his hard work and academic abilities brought him to that very spot. He took a few pictures of David, hoping he wouldn't mind. He wanted to capture the moment for him. As his father looked through the lens snapping away, he noticed a slight glow all around David's body. It gave him a warm feeling because he knew that glow was destiny surrounding his beautiful, loving son.

David finally turned to his father with an infectious grin. "What do you think?"

"Impressive and intimidating."

"I know what you mean." David walked over and gave him a hug. "Dad, thank you for everything."

"You're welcome son. You belong here."

"I hope so."

"There is no doubt in my mind."

A couple of minutes later they decided to find Pupin Hall. They walked up the steps in front of Low Library so David could take some pictures. From there they walked through a maze of hedgerow which lead to another red brick walkway. The Mathematics Building was on the left, Pupin Hall was straight ahead. "Dad, this is where they split the uranium atom for the first time back in 1939."

"I didn't know that."

"That breakthrough was the beginning of the Manhattan Project."

David felt like he was entering a holy shrine as they walked into Pupin. He could smell the decades of history and knowledge as they made their way down the main hall. A minute later he found the room where his interview was going to take place. He checked out a couple of the student bulletin boards before they left. From there they spent the next half hour walking around the campus taking pictures. David kept touching the Titan baseball pin hoping it still had some of its special powers.

# CHAPTER 7

## Marco

Marco sat at the dining room table with his parents while dinner was being served. It had been a long week on several fronts. He thought about everything that happened as he ate. He found out on Tuesday that several of his peripheral friends had gotten fake IDs. They found out about Zander and him going to Retro's from Zander, and wanted to tag along on their next excursion. They bugged Marco all week about it. He was angry with Zander because the last thing he wanted was college night turning into the typical high school bullshit scene. That was the very thing he was escaping from. He hadn't talked to Zander since Tuesday after telling him to stay the fuck away from him until further notice.

Then one of his ex's wanted to get back together with him. Marco didn't want to go anywhere near that fucking nightmare. He tried to let Jason know that it was really over, but Jason turned it into the typical yelling and drama scene. Half of the school watched it go down outside of the biology lab. Jason was totally out of control, yelling at Marco one minute, and then pleading with him to take him back the next. Marco

52

tried to calm him down and explain that he wasn't interested in settling down with just one guy. Then a couple of Jason's girlfriends got into it, calling Marco a player and a slut. He finally walked away vowing never to hook up with anyone from school ever again.

The other thing that had been on his mind all week was the Columbia interview in the morning. He emailed a portfolio of his best writing on Monday as requested by the admissions office. That made him extremely nervous. What if they didn't like anything he had written? He didn't like the feeling of that uncertainty one bit, and it had slowly enveloped him to the point where he had a hard time sleeping all week.

"Marco, how has school been?" his father asked, trying to start a conversation.

"Interesting to say the least, but it's finally over."

His father started to ask what happened, but his mother abruptly interrupted their conversation.

"So what are your plans for the weekend dear? You know your father and I are leaving for the lake house in the morning. We need to get away from the city for a few days. I'm exhausted."

"I have that interview at Columbia tomorrow," Marco said, but really wanting to tell her to go fuck herself.

"Oh. I forgot all about that," his father said in a semi-indifferent tone. "Good luck with that son. I'm sure you will impress them on all fronts."

Then his mother started in on him. "Are you sure you won't consider Princeton? I could make a phone call to my dear friend Harold anytime you like. He is the Dean of Undergraduate Studies." She took a sip of wine and waited for his response.

"Thanks, but I think I'll see how this interview goes first. Columbia is my first choice, so I'm concentrating most of my time and energy on that right now. But just to let you know, I am in the middle of my application for Princeton just in case Columbia doesn't work out. But please don't make any phone calls on my behalf. It is important to me that I get in on my own. I do appreciate your concern though." Marco said, trying with every ounce of energy not to get angry. He couldn't believe how unconcerned his father was, and how manipulative his mother was being, even after she promised she wouldn't interfere.

"Well, let us know how everything turns out," his father said.

"Will do, sir."

"Do you want Max to drive you there tomorrow?"

"No, that's ok. I'll take a cab."

"I transferred an additional ten thousand to your debit card today. That should hold you over until we get back on Tuesday."

"Thank you. I'm planning a little shopping spree in SoHo right after my interview."

Marco actually felt like buying some weed instead so he could get stoned and forget how hurt he was.

After he finished eating, he excused himself and went to his bedroom to unwind and write. He checked his phone and saw at least thirty messages. He read a few of them. Claire and Cynthia were wondering where he was at. The others were invitations to parties and to hang out. Four messages were from Zander. Marco turned the phone off and threw it on the bed. He hit the dimmer switch, put some music on, and sat at his desk and started re-reading what he had written the night before. The story was about absolute power over others. How easy it was to control human beings. Human nature. It made him smile as he continued on.

The mundane world disappeared as Marco journeyed into the mind of a young prince who was worshipped by the masses. His manipulation was poetic, sterol, charming, vile, empathetic, cold. His blade cut without a sound, and he loved to watch. It was his only entertainment. It was his heart's desire.

The prince enhanced his own life by sucking the life out of foolish useless souls. He was clever by pretending to love them as they gave him everything, regardless of the damage it caused. He was masterful, and they applauded and bowed to his God-like power. "We just want to worship your handsome face, your perfect physique, your hypnotic words. We aren't deep, we promise. We aren't deep...we aren't deep... we aren't deep," they chanted over and over until they could chant no more.

Three hours had gone by when he finally stopped to read the new pages. He knew this character would become one of his favorites because the prince knew what he wanted and understood how get it.

It was 1:00 am when Marco finally decided to get some sleep. He couldn't remember the last time he had gone to bed that early on a Friday night, but he wanted to be well rested for the interview. He hated to admit it, but he was still nervous. Almost afraid. It seemed like his life's work was riding on that one interview. He turned the phone on to check his messages out of curiosity. There were at least another twenty wondering where the hell he was. He smiled knowing he could fuck every one of those guys if he wanted. He turned the phone off, undressed, took care of business, and fell fast asleep.

# CHAPTER 8

## David

10 AM

The morning was crisp and inviting as the sun peaked through the timeworn buildings of main campus. Those solemn buildings stood silent and proud, inviting young minds to learn the secrets of life. They offered the chance to build layers of knowledge and wisdom and courage. Requirements to expand one's mind.

David and his father were having breakfast across the street from campus. They sat at a table near the front window so David could look at the entrance while he ate. He wanted this more than anything. So did his family and friends. His mom and sister had called earlier and wished him good luck. And he got texts from Tyler and Melissa wishing him the same.

It was 10:35 when his father suggested they head to Pupin Hall. David felt paralyzed for a moment, and then felt like running in the opposite direction. "Dad, I don't know if I can do this."

"Yes you can. You are going to impress these people, believe me. Just be yourself and good things will happen. Are you ready?"

"Ready as I'll ever be, I guess"

They crossed the street and walked toward the front gates, and that's when some guy ran right into David, almost knocking him to the ground. The guy grabbed him just in time and apologized.

"I'm really sorry. Are you ok?" David looked into those dark brown eyes and gave him a shy smile. He was staring at one of the cutest guys he had ever seen. "Yeah, I'm fine. No harm done."

"Please forgive me, I wasn't looking where I was going,"

"I wasn't looking where I was going either," David said, trying to stop himself from staring.

There was a nanosecond of silence that seemed like it lasted a year. "I'm Marco Valerio," the guy said, quickly fixing the awkwardness.

"My name is David Emerson."

"Cool. Are you a student here?"

"No, but I hope to be next year. I'm here for an interview."

"So am I. There must be a bunch of us around here today. Let me wish you good luck. I hope you get in."

"I hope you do too." David didn't want him to leave, so he introduced his father. They shook hands and exchanged the usual niceties, then Marco turned back to David, "Well, I need to get a coffee before this thing starts. It was nice meeting you. Hope to see you around campus in the fall." He turned and walked away.

David sighed as he walked through the gates. He looked over his shoulder hoping to get one last glimpse of Marco. He had been in New York less than twenty-four hours and already had his first crush.

When they got to the plaza in front of Pupin Hall, David's father gave him hug and wished him good luck, and then went to sit on one of the benches with the other parents. David walked toward the doors, turned and gave his father one last wave before heading inside. He walked to room 514 and entered a nice reception area where four other potential students were sitting. They looked as nervous as he was. He signed in and took a seat. He needed to relax, so he checked out the latest science news on his phone. A message popped up from Tyler just as he started reading. "I just want you to know that I'm thinking about you and hope everything goes well. You deserve it." He smiled and texted back, "Thanks," then continued reading. He was so engrossed in an article about the Higgs Boson that he didn't notice someone else had come in. That person sat down and tapped him on the arm. "So we meet again." David looked up and saw those dark eyes and that smile. "H-hi," was the only word he could find.

"I didn't think I'd see you again." Marco took his phone out. "Let's exchange numbers just in case we both get in. It would be nice to have at least one friend on campus."

"I agree." David tried to hide his nervousness as they traded phones and entered their numbers. Marco was about to say something else, but the receptionist called his name. They both stood up and shook hands. "Good luck in there," David told him.

"Same to you."

A nicely dressed older woman opened the door and welcomed Marco. He gave David one last smile and then disappeared through the door. David sat back down hoping they would run into each other again sometime.

He started concentrating on his own interview at that point. A few minutes later a young guy, maybe thirty or so, opened the door and called David's name. He knew his moment had finally arrived. He was calm and resolute, vowing to show them he was worthy of being a student at Columbia. They shook hands and introduced each other. The admissions officer's name was Timothy Logan. David followed him to an office that had a mahogany table and two burgundy leather chairs. David sat quietly as Timothy opened his folder and took out his application, essays, and SAT score. He laid everything out in front of them and smiled. "I'm sure you are a little nervous, but you have nothing to be nervous about. I am extremely impressed with your academic credentials."

David breathed a sigh of relief after hearing those words. As the interview progressed, he found out that Timothy wasn't an admissions officer at all. He was doing his postdoctoral work in physics. He explained that he had received a PhD from Cal Tech, and that the Physics Department liked to interview the Early Decision candidates themselves and give their own recommendation. "All departments work close together at Columbia to ensure that we matriculate intelligent well-rounded students."

The interview lasted a little over a half an hour and covered a wide range of topics, beginning with David's goals, the math and physics programs, and student life at Columbia.

David noticed how insightful and open Timothy was while they discussed various topics. He was happy to know that he wasn't some condescending professor locked into a traditional mindset.

They talked about important breakthroughs in mathematics, String Theory, Supersymmetry, and Dark Matter. Timothy also explained how the research opportunities worked, telling David that he wouldn't have any problem getting on a research team if he matriculated. When the interview was over, they stood up and shook hands. "David, it was a real pleasure getting to know you."

"Thank you for giving me the opportunity to be interviewed."

David walked back into the reception area in a euphoric daze.

"By the look on your face I'd say the interview was a success."

David smiled. He couldn't believe Marco was still there. "I think it went pretty well. At least I didn't faint. How did yours go?"

"I thought it went well too. There was an admissions officer and a professor from the English Department interviewing me. We had an interesting conversation about my writing."

"You're a writer? That is so cool."

"Yeah, I love writing short stories. But I'm working on a novel right now, which is something totally new for me." They walked out to the hall so they could have some privacy.

"What's your major?" Marco asked.

"Math and Physics. If I get in I'll be double majoring."

"Wow. So you're one of those math and science gods? I would never have thought that."

"Why?"

"You don't look like...excuse the derogatory term, a geek. You look more like a musician to me. Like you could be in One Direction or The Wanted." David blushed. "You guessed right. I am a musician too. I play the guitar and sing a little, but I'm definitely a geek when it comes to math and physics. They have a great program here."

"I'm definitely a writing geek."

"I'd love to read some of your stories sometime."

"Cool. I'll send a couple to you." They exchanged email addresses.

"Where are you from?" David asked.

"The Upper East Side. I've lived in Manhattan my whole life. Where are you from?"

"Michigan."

"Cool. What's it like there?"

"Different from here, that's for sure. I live in a little town called Harbor Springs. It's in Northern Michigan right on Lake Michigan. I've lived there my whole life too."

"You're a long way from home. Welcome to the Emerald City..lol"

"Thanks. I've wanted to go to Columbia since seventh grade. I've only been in New York for a day, but I know I belong here. Does that sound crazy?"

"No, not at all. I know where you're coming from. I hope we both get in because we deserve it."

"I hope so too." Something was definitely happening between them. David could feel it.

"I don't mean to be forward, but I think you're a very cool guy and I'm glad I almost knocked you down this morning. It is kind of like fate," Marco said, with a strange grin.

"Yeah, I've been getting that same feeling." David wondered if Marco was gay. He hoped so, but his luck in that department was non-existent.

They finally walked out to the plaza. Even though neither one wanted the conversation to end, Marco knew it was time to go. "David, it was very nice meeting you. Enjoy the rest of your time here and have a safe trip home." They shook hands again. "Thanks. It was nice meeting you too."

David stood by the entrance watching Marco walk toward lower campus. Then he spotted his father looking at Marco too. He hoped that he wouldn't ask any embarrassing questions.

David walked over and sat next to him. "So, how did the interview go?"

"I think it went really well."

"That's good to hear. I'm proud of you. This whole thing is amazing to me," his father said, as he gave David a hug. After filling his father in on the particulars of the interview, they walked around the entire campus one last time. Then his father surprised him with tickets for a touristy tour of Manhattan. They walked to The Cathedral of St. John's on

Amsterdam Avenue and waited for one of those red double decker tour buses. A few minutes later their journey around Manhattan began. They would catch a flight back to Traverse City late Sunday afternoon.

# CHAPTER 9

## Marco

SATURDAY MORNING

10 AM

Sometimes the longest journey only requires a few steps, but taking those steps can be one of the hardest things a person will ever do. Sometimes they are taken by sheer determination and a need to excel. And sometimes fate dictates them. They might even make a person bump into the very thing that could change their life forever.

It was ten in the morning. Marco sat at the breakfast table in the sun terrace checking his messages. He finally decided to send Zander one. "We will talk later today," was all he wrote.

He knew he couldn't stay mad at his best friend, but he still wanted him to sweat it out for a few more hours. Then he read a message from Lisa that said she went to college night at Retro's with some guys from school. They all had fake IDs. She said they couldn't get in because the line stretched all the way down the street. They tried to get into another gay bar a couple of blocks away, but were turned away because the guy knew the IDs were fake.

Marco felt vindicated. He made up his mind to hit Retro's by himself. He needed to score another college hottie.

He read a few more messages and then turned his thoughts to the interview. A few minutes later Rosa served him a nice hot breakfast while she conveyed a message. "Your mother and father left for the lake a couple of hours ago. They said good luck with your interview. They are proud of you."

"Thanks for letting me know."

Marco sipped his coffee and ate his breakfast while looking towards Central Park thinking about what he was going to say at the interview. He had several strategies in mind depending on how the whole thing proceeded. He was never at a loss for words, and knew his personality and looks would impress the admissions officer. He smiled to himself because this special day had finally arrived.

"You look very nice," Rosa said, as she poured him more coffee.

"Thanks. I want to look like a college student but still have some class."

Marco always looked hot in Armani Suits. He was hotter than most of the models in Manhattan.

≜

It was 10:40 when Marco's cab pulled up in front of Columbia University. He got out and started walking toward the entrance. In his excitement he bumped into one of the cutest guys he had ever seen, almost knocking him to the ground. He quickly grabbed him to break his fall.

"I'm really sorry. Are you ok?" he asked.

He was mesmerized by the intense blue eyes staring back at him. Marco felt like he had just bumped into an angel. "Please forgive me, I wasn't looking where I was going."

"That's all right. Don't worry, I'm ok. I wasn't looking where I was going either."

"I'm Marco Valerio."

"My name is David Emerson."

"Cool. Are you a student here?"

"No. But I hope to be next year. I'm here for an interview."

"I'm being interviewed too. This is so cool. There must be a bunch of us here today. Good luck. I hope you get in." David wished Marco the same. He didn't want to leave but knew it was time to go before it became awkward. He told David that he was going to get a coffee before his interview started. He reluctantly said goodby and walked away. As soon as he walked across Broadway he turned around to see if David was still there. Sadly he wasn't. He reminded Marco of Dylan for some reason, and that made him smile.

$$\Sigma$$

Marco walked through the gates sipping his coffee wondering why his interview was in the physics building rather than Philosophy Hall. It didn't make sense. When he got there, he stood outside gathering his thoughts while he finished his coffee. When he walked into room 514 he couldn't believe who was sitting there. He smiled and then quietly sat next David. "So we meet again." David looked up from his phone, smiled and said hi.

Seeing those blue eyes and that cute smile again made Marco's heart melt. He knew it was fate playing its hand, so he asked, "Would you like to exchange phone numbers? We could get to know each other better just in case we both get in. It would be nice having at least one friend here in the fall." Marco's heart raced frantically as he waited for David's answer.

"Yeah, definitely."

They exchanged phones and put their numbers in. His hands were shaking slightly as he pressed each number. He had never felt this nervous around any guy except Dylan. A minute later an admissions officer called his name. David wished him good luck. Marco did the same. He stood up and said, "This should be interesting."

The admissions officer and a professor from the English department interviewed Marco. They started out by discussing twentieth century fiction because that was Marco's area of interest. Hemingway, Steinbeck, Salinger, McCullers, and Forrester, were influential in his development as a writer. He admired the skillful ways in which each author looked at human nature and its inner workings. Those particular authors were catalysts for his own writing style.

Marco needed to show them that he was more than just a pretty face. He opened up completely so they would understand how serious he was. The professor was impressed with his portfolio, asking questions about several pieces of prose he found insightful. Marco explained his motivation for each story and what he was trying to achieve with certain word choices and imagery. At that point the conversation became a bit more animated because they were now on the same page philosophically. He thanked them for their time and consideration when the interview concluded. He returned to the reception room where one student was still sitting there waiting to be called in. He hoped that David was still being interviewed so he could see him again. He decided to wait for a while just in case.

As he sat there waiting, Marco realized he was crushing on David. He thought that feeling had disappeared years ago. He crossed his fingers hoping he was still inside. Five minutes later he heard David thanking the admissions officer for the interview. His heart began to race. When David walked through the door, Marco stood up and asked, "So, how did it go?" David looked at him and smiled. "I think pretty well actually. It was a lot different from what I had envisioned. How was your interview?"

"I thought mine went well too. It was a little intimidating at first because I had two people interviewing me. But we ended up having a great conversation about the writing process."

Marco couldn't take his eyes off of David. He wanted to grab him and kiss those perfect lips right then and there, but fought that urge with all his might. Marco's gaydar worked every time, but for some reason he couldn't tell if David was gay or not.

"You're a writer?"

"Yeah, I love to write. It takes me to places no one else

knows about. You know, I go to my own little world to live and breathe with my characters. I know it sounds crazy."

"No, not at all. I can definitely relate."

"What's your major?" Marco asked.

"Math and Physics. I'm going to double major."

"Wow, that is so cool. So you're one of those math and science gods. I would never have thought that because you don't look the part."

"What do you mean?"

Marco felt embarrassed as he tried to say something intelligent. He was just too enamored with David to find the right words. "I don't know, but you don't look like, please excuse the term, a geek. You look more like a musician to me. You look like you could be in One Direction or The Wanted."

"You're right. I am a musician too. I play guitar and sing a little, but I'm definitely a math and science geek," David said, with a slight laugh.

"I'm a geek too. I think we have a lot in common." Marco was flirting and could see that David didn't have a clue, so he changed tactics.

"So, where are you from?"

"Michigan."

"Cool. What's it like there?"

"I love it. I'm from a small town in Northern Michigan, right on Lake Michigan. I've lived there all my life."

"Well David, You're a long way from home. Welcome to the Emerald City..lol"

"Thanks. Where are you from?"

"The Upper East Side. I've lived in Manhattan my entire life."

"Wow, that is amazing."

"I like it. I wouldn't want to live anywhere else."

"I hope I get in so I can live here too. I love this place already."

Marco couldn't help himself and started flirting again. "I don't mean to be forward, but I think you're a very cool guy. I'm glad I almost knocked you over. It's kind of like fate or something."

"Yeah. I'm glad we met." They talked for a few more minutes and then walked outside to the plaza. Marco knew it was time to go. "It was really nice meeting you. Let's stay in touch." He shook David's hand. "I hope you have fun while you're here." Then he reluctantly walked away. He made his way to Broadway, got in a cab, and headed to SoHo to do some shopping. He leaned his head back against the seat and reflected on everything that had just happened. He was in seventh heaven. A few minutes later he sent David a text. "Enjoy the city and have a safe flight back home. Please keep in touch."

# CHAPTER 10

## David

David and his father got home a lot later than anticipated Sunday evening. Their plane was delayed twice. First there was an hour and a half delay because the terminals were overbooked. Then their plane didn't have a full crew, so they were delayed for another hour waiting for one more steward to show up. David didn't mind because it gave him time to do some homework. He was the only student at his school taking Multivariate Calculus, a college level course he was flying through with ease. David enjoyed this level of Calculus because it gave him a greater understanding of curves, surfaces, scalar and vector fields.

Even though David was tired, he couldn't wait to tell his mom and sister all about the trip. They sat around the kitchen table talking and eating the reheated dinner she had saved for them.

"Mom, New York City is unbelievable. It was kind of overwhelming at first, but dad and I got used to it pretty quick. It's actually easy to get around. We went on one of those double decker tour buses to see everything. Even if I'm not accepted at Columbia, we have to go there for vacation. You would love it. Dad and I can show you around Manhattan. There is so much to see and do."

David's father agreed. "I was impressed. Honestly, I didn't think I was going to like it, but once I decided to just go with the flow, I started to enjoy the energy."

"I'm happy you boys had a nice time. What was the campus like?"

David's eyes lit up. "The campus is perfect. I stood in the center of it taking the whole thing in. It felt surreal. I really want to go there. I want you and dad to be proud of me."

"Honey, your father and I are proud of you. Getting or not getting into Columbia is never going change that."

"Yeah, I know. It's just…Thank you for saying that."

She leaned over and kissed David on the forehead. "So tell me about the interview."

"I was so nervous at first, but dad calmed me down. I went into the interview and just tried to be myself. A professor from the Physics Department interviewed me instead of an admissions officer. His name was Professor Logan. Mom, he was really young and really smart. He explained everything I needed to know about the math and physics programs. We talked for over a half hour. I thought the interview was a success. I know I did my best, so I'm satisfied regardless of the outcome."

While they continued eating dinner and talking, David's thoughts kept drifting to Marco.

"What are you smiling about?" his mom asked.

"I guess I'm just smiling because it was so awesome." David didn't want to tell her that he met a cute guy and was crushing. He decided to keep that to himself.

⊔

Tyler and Melissa picked David up Monday morning and headed to school. They wanted to hear all about the trip as soon as he got in the truck. David pulled up pictures on his phone and explained where everything was in relation to Columbia's campus. Tyler thought the campus was in midtown Manhattan because David said it was on Broadway.

"No, it's not in midtown. Broadway runs diagonally all through Manhattan. Columbia is on the Upper West Side in a place called Morningside Heights. It's near the Hudson River, Riverside Park, and Harlem."

Tyler asked, "You mean you'd be going to college in the hood?"

"Yeah, I guess I would be. Harlem looked pretty cool. My dad and I stopped there on the bus tour and walked around on 125th street. It was interesting. There were street vendors selling all sorts of stuff, the Apollo Theater, and an eclectic mix of people walking around. I could feel a real sense of history."

"Whenever someone mentions Harlem I think about Law and Order or the Harlem Renaissance," Tyler said.

"Funny you say that. While we were walking around, I was thinking about Langston Hughes, Cab Calloway and other artists we learned about in American History."

All of a sudden David's phone buzzed. He smiled when he saw who the text was from. Melissa glanced over to see who it was. "Who's Marco?" she asked, with a curious tone in her voice.

"He's a guy I met on campus."

"Someone's got a crush on a boy named Marco," Melissa sang. She grabbed the phone out of his hand and read the message aloud.

"Hey David, I just wanted to make sure you got home safely. I hope you enjoyed your stay in New York. It was very nice meeting you. I was wondering if you would like to skype tonight. I'll be home all evening. Let me know. Have fun at school, I know I won't..lol"

David blushed as Melissa read it. "Awe, that is so sweet," she said, giving the phone back hoping he wasn't mad. Tyler hadn't said a word because he was jealous. He knew he shouldn't have been, but he was. He tried to shake it off and convince himself that he was happy David had met someone. But the twinge in his stomach hurt like crazy. Tyler asked, "Is he gay?"

"I don't know. I don't think so, but I hope he is."

"What does he look like?" Melissa asked.

David smiled. "He is one of the cutest guys I've ever seen. He's almost as cute as you, Tyler."

Tyler smiled and grabbed the steering wheel tight, trying to keep his emotions in check. It made him feel good that David still thought he was cute. Melissa looked at Tyler. "Think of the possibilities if you were gay."

"Leave him alone Melissa," David said, hoping she would drop it.

"I just thought, you know…." her voice trailed off.

It went dead silent except for the sound of the truck cruising down the road. David's mind went back to the night when he and Tyler kissed each other. All three were thinking the same thing; David and Tyler being boyfriends. Even though David had wanted that to happen since eighth grade, he knew Tyler wasn't ready.

He finally broke the silence. "You should have seen what Marco was wearing. He had on this perfect looking suit and expensive looking shoes. He looked like one of those models you see in magazines. His facial features were unique too. I've never seen anyone who looks like him. He kind of looked Asian and Spanish to me. He's tall and thin and has gorgeous jet black hair. He's very charming and sophisticated too. Needless to say, I was intimidated. I looked like such a geek compared to him. All I needed was a pocket protector to complete my wardrobe."

"David, you're cute and sophisticated too. You just don't know it," Melissa said, telling him the truth. Then came words of warning. "Well, he sounds like a typical New York preppy guy. Those types can be dangerous in more ways than one."

"Come on Melissa. That's nothing more than stereotyping," David said, looking somewhat annoyed.

"Have you ever seen that reality show NYC Prep? The students on that show are so fucking rich. They have no idea how the rest of society lives. You have to be extremely careful hanging around with the privileged few," she countered, knowing this from experience.

David looked at her strange for a second, taking in what she said with some seriousness.

"You're right, Marco is wealthy, and he confirmed it when

he told me that he lived on the Upper East Side. But he wasn't at all like you're describing from that stupid show. Melissa, you're not that way. Reality TV is fake. You know people say and do all sorts of weird things to get their few minutes of fame. Why do you watch that stuff anyway?"

"look, I'm not trying to be negative, but you need to take it slow with this guy if he turns out to be gay, and you end up going to college together."

"Yeah, yeah, ok mom," David said. He turned his head and looked blankly down the road.

He started feeling insecure. "You know, I loved being at Columbia, but at the same time I felt inadequate. I've been thinking that maybe I won't fit in there. The rich and the average probably don't mix very well. Honestly, sometimes I don't even know what I'm thinking. I should just go to college here and forget all about New York."

Talking about Marco was supposed to make him happy, but instead it made him apprehensive about the whole situation.

"That's bullshit David. You belong at Columbia not because you're rich, but because you're so fucking smart, and because you have the passion and strength to succeed. Columbia should be happy that you applied there. I don't think they're seeking perfect looking rich people. I think they're looking for people like you who will learn and contribute something meaningful. Don't be afraid. You've never been afraid, so don't start that shit now," Tyler said, hoping to shake David out of whatever insecurity he was feeling. A minute later they pulled into the school parking lot.

"Thanks for saying that. It means a lot coming from you. I guess I'm just scared about the future." Tyler looked at David wanting to say something else, but couldn't find his own courage.

David got out of the truck and sent his reply saying he'd love to Skype. Marco responded a few seconds later with a thumbs up.

While they were walking towards the doors, David decided to friend Marco on Facebook. He knew it would let him know that he was gay, because it said so in his profile. He was proud to be out and wanted Marco to know the truth. He figured that if he didn't accept, then their friendship was never meant to be. He pressed the request button just before he walked through door.

∞ ∫

It was 11:45 am when David's Chem class let out. He met up with Tyler at his truck and headed into town to get some lunch. He noticed that Tyler looked like he was in a bad mood. "Is anything wrong? You seem like you're lost in your thoughts."

"No, I'm fine. I just have some stuff on my mind that I'm trying to work out. I'm sorry I'm not very good company today."

"You know I'm right here if you need to talk, ok?"

"Thanks, I know you are." Tyler looked at David for a quick second giving him a little half smile, then kept his eyes fixed to the road so he wouldn't reveal the truth.

They sat down in their favorite booth at Mary's Diner and ordered sliders and fries. While they waited for their food, David decided to check his Facebook page again to see if Marco had accepted yet. There was nothing. No response. This had him worried. He knew the whole gay thing probably blew any chance of being friends.

Melissa, Brad, and Kathy came into the restaurant a few minutes later and sat at the booth across from them. Brad was giving David and Tyler dirty looks as usual. Melissa put the leash on him quickly. A few other people came in from school, so things got noisy and fun. Then Emma came in and strategically sat next to Tyler. David smiled because he could tell she was trying to put the moves on him. He thought about what a cute couple they'd make if it ever happened.

He sat there eating and looking out at the harbor and lake. He had a sinking feeling in his stomach, like destiny was playing a dirty trick on him. But then it happened. He got a message from Marco. He discreetly took his phone out and kept it under the table so no one could see. David's smile grew wide as he read the words that made his wish come true.

"Hey David, I'm sorry that I couldn't friend you sooner. My school confiscates our phones as soon as we walk into the building. They give them to us at lunch so we can communicate with the outside world..lol I'm at lunch with friends right now. I noticed your profile says that you're gay. I just want to let you know that I'm gay too. I can't wait to skype tonight so we can get to know each other better. Enjoy the rest of your day."

David sent a text back telling Marco that he looked forward to skyping, and that he was happy to know he was gay too. David spent the rest of lunch looking at Marco's Facebook page trying to get to know him better. It turned out to be one of the best afternoons David ever had.

# CHAPTER 11
## Marco

Marco stood in his dressing room getting ready for school. He normally hated Mondays because his weekends of writing and sex were interrupted. But something was radically different about the weekend he had just experienced. The interview at Columbia, and meeting that cute blond guy from Michigan made him happy for once.

David had been on Marco's mind all weekend. He was different from the guys he went out with. He could tell that David was somewhat shy, yet very determined. He found that endearing. He also knew David was probably off the charts academically because of what he was majoring in. This scared and fascinated him. But the thing he liked most about David was that he was real.

It was a perfect autumn morning so Marco decided to walk the ten blocks to school. He sent Zander a text saying that he was on his way. He made his regular stop at the Nector Cafe and ordered his usual Caramel Macchiato. He decided to send David a text while he waited.

"Hey David, I just wanted to make sure you got home safely. I hope you enjoyed your stay in New York. It was nice meeting you. I was wondering if you would like to skype tonight. I'll be home all evening. Let me know. Have fun at school, I know I won't..lol"

Marco had just finished up when Zander tapped him on the shoulder. "Who are you texting? The hot piece of ass you fucked yesterday?" Marco gave him an exasperated look.

"Come on. I don't fuck everyone I meet. I'm not that shallow. If you really want to know, I was texting a guy I met at Columbia University on Saturday."

"What were you doing there? Did you hook up with that guy from Retro's again? I thought your mantra was one night stands only."

"Fuck you." Marco got his Macchiato and walked outside. Zander followed. "I'm just playing with you. I'm sorry." Marco calmed down and let him in on his big secret.

"I was at Columbia because I'm being considered as an Early Decision candidate. And while I was there I met a guy from Michigan who is being considered too. We got to know each other a little, so I wanted to know if he got home ok. There's more to my life than just having sex. Give me a little credit."

"I didn't know you applied to Columbia. You could have told me."

"I didn't want to say anything in case nothing came of it."

"Well, I think it's cool. I hope you get in."

"Do me a favor, don't say anything to anyone, ok?"

"Yeah, no problem. So, tell me about this guy."

Marco took a sip of coffee wondering if he should say anything. He decided that he needed to tell someone how he felt. "This is between me and you, ok?"

"Yeah, of course. What's his name?"

"David. David Emerson. And I really like him. I might even be in love with him. It was so fucking weird, I felt like I got hit by lightning when we met."

"Wow. You've never used the 'L' word as long as I've known you. Is he gay?"

"I don't know. I hope so. But even if he isn't, I still want to get to know him. I just hope we both get in so I can find out." Zander was about to say something witty, but Marco's phone buzzed. It was David. "Hey Marco, it's really nice hearing from you. I'm home safe and I did have a great time in New York. I'd love to skype tonight. How does nine sound?"

He responded with a thumbs up, and then in his excitement, let Zander read it. He looked at Marco and shook his head. "You've really been bitten. I can't believe it. You need to slow down my friend. Shit, you don't even know if he's gay or not. What does he even look like? Is he hot? Remember, you have a rep to protect."

"He's one of the cutest guys I've ever seen. He has blond hair, kind of long and emo styled. He has Gorgeous blue eyes, long eye lashes, and a smile that made me want to get all over him. Shit, I almost did."

"He sounds hot, but you need to take your time before using the 'L' word. You're scaring me."

"I trust my instincts, and they tell me he's the real thing, and what I'm feeling is the real thing." Marco took another sip and smiled. "Well, I guess I'm happy for you. But what are you going to do with him living so far away? Where in the hell is

Michigan anyway? Is it even part of the United States?" Marco gave him another fuck you look. "He only lives six hundred miles away." Zander was trying to help him see reality. "You need to keep your options open. There are lots of pretty boys right here, and you've only just begun to tap them."

Marco didn't respond. They walked the rest of the way to school in silence.

▽

It was 12 noon when Marco, Zander, and Claire got their phones from the office and headed to a Sushi restaurant for lunch. As they walked, Marco checked his messages. The first one he saw was David's. It was a friend request from Facebook. Marco immediately accepted and started scanning his page. When he got to David's profile, it revealed what he had hoped.

"He's gay. David is gay."

"Who's David?" Claire asked.

"You don't even want to know," Zander said, shaking his head.

Marco texted David explaining why he hadn't friended him sooner. Then he told him that he was gay too. He received a reply back a minute later. "Hey Marco, It's good to hear from you. I'm happy to know you're gay too. I can't wait to skype tonight. I'm glad we met the way we did."

Marco must have read that text a half dozen times. He looked up at the clear blue sky and thanked whoever, or whatever was looking down on him. He sent his reply. "Same here, see you tonight."

They ended up skyping until three in the morning. Marco had a hard time falling asleep because his emotions were all over the place. His body was on fire fantasizing about having sex with David. As that was happening, his mind tapped into that one emotion he avoided like the plaque. He knew having a boyfriend meant caring for someone other than himself. He honestly didn't know if he could do it.

¾

They skyped whenever they could over the next month and a half. Marco couldn't write coherently until he saw David's face on his screen. And David sacrificed many nights of stargazing so he could gaze into Marco's dark brown eyes. They wanted to tell each other how they really felt, but decided not to cross that line until they got to know each other better. This required a certain level of honesty, something that was difficult for Marco. Within the first week of skyping they became comfortable sharing personal details.

"When did you figure out you were gay?" Marco asked.

"I knew for sure when I was ten. At least that's when I knew what it meant. I came out to my parents the summer between 7th and 8th grade. Then I told my friends when school started."

"How did everyone take the news?"

"My parents and sister were shocked at first, but eventually adjusted. After I came out at school, some of my friends became former friends."

"That's too bad, but I'm sure you expected some negative reaction, right?"

"Yeah. It got pretty bad for a while. So, when did you come out?"

"When I was fourteen. The whole thing was anti-climactic though. My parents and Rosa, our housekeeper, had known for a while and were just waiting for me to figure it out."

"Wow! Were you shocked by that?"

"No. It made me laugh. I was really trying to hide it, but they could see right through me. They even knew my friend Zander was gay too."

"That is very interesting. I wonder if my parents knew too and just didn't say anything."

"I wouldn't be surprised. Mothers seem to know these things."

"Yeah, I think you're right. My mom took it a lot better than my dad."

"So tell me all about your boyfriends," Marco said, knowing he was being nosy. David looked away from the camera embarrassed. "I've never had a boyfriend."

"No way. I don't believe that for a second."

"It's the truth. Remember, I live in a small town in the middle of the woods. I'm the only person who has ever come out at my high school."

"I'm sorry. I shouldn't have asked."

"No, it's ok." David didn't say anything for a few seconds wondering if he should tell him about Tyler. He knew he needed to be honest. "I've only been kissed twice, and that was by a friend a couple of months ago." Marco felt every jealous bone in his body wake up with that revelation.

"Was it a he or a she?"

"A he. His name is Tyler."

"Is he gay? Does he like you? Do you like him?" Marco was almost hyperventilating as he asked.

"I have to be honest. I've had a crush on him since 8th grade. As far as him being gay, I think he is at least bi."

"So have you and Tyler, like, you know, experimented or anything?" Marco was now totally jealous and totally turned on. He hated what he was thinking but couldn't help himself. David's face turned ten shades of red. "No, no, nothing like that. But we did go on a date."

"How did it go?"

"The date was perfect, but Tyler kind of panicked over the next few days, so we decided to stay friends."

"Have you guys talk about it since? I mean, does he know if he's gay or straight yet?"

"No and no. I don't want to put any pressure on him. I'm waiting for him to figure it out, and then hopefully he'll talk to me. He was there for me when I came out, and I want to be there for him."

"I'm impressed. You guys must be really close."

"He's my best friend." David gave Marco a look that said he didn't want to talk about it anymore. "So, how many boy-friends have you had?" David asked, turning the tables on him.

"I've had a few over the years," Marco said, trying to stay as vague as possible.

"How many is a few?" he asked, getting jealous himself.

"I've had six boyfriends." Marco said, deciding not to count the twenty-plus guys he had sex with, because he didn't consider them boyfriends. This was his way of telling the truth.

"Wow! That's a lot of boyfriends," David said, even though he wasn't surprised.

"I guess, but only one of them really meant anything to me."

"What was his name?"

"Dylan. We were boyfriends in 7th grade. We kept it a secret because we weren't out. I really liked him, but we broke up a couple of months after he moved to Japan. The long distant thing never works out."

"It must have been hard."

"Yeah, it was." As soon as Marco said that they gave each other panic stricken looks.

They were both wondering if they were doomed by the distance thing too.

As the weeks went on, Marco and David shared their feelings about friends, family, school, and what they wanted to do in life. They were both strategically dancing around the idea of becoming more than friends, but neither one had the courage to make the first move.

# CHAPTER 12
## David

Time changes destiny into incalculable emotions that play out on both the literal and metaphorical landscape. It is like two suns that are being pulled into each other's gravitational fields and then collide to form an entirely new realm of possibility. It is where two hearts can easily feel each other's vibrations and emotions with just a single touch. It is a physicist's dream to experience this phenomenon. It is a writer's dream to extract the meaning of what those suns are going through. In the end, there isn't a thing that can be done except to hold on for dear life.

David's life had always been a process of diverse layers set within his love of math, science, family, and friends. They were the most important things in his life. Nothing could ever change that. But his personal aspirations were making it hard to come to terms with the impending separation from those he loved. He didn't know what solar system he would eventually end up in, but he knew it would be life altering. He just wished he could figure out a way to have both.

David's trip to New York had changed everything. The first thing that changed was his relationship with Tyler. They had become a lot closer. Tyler started hanging out with David and his science friends after school, and David spent more afternoons at Tyler's house playing video games and talking. Sometimes when everything was quiet and they were alone, Tyler would put his arm around David and hold him close. Sadly, all of this was happening at the same time he and Marco were becoming closer. David was being pulled in two directions, something he hadn't planned on. He loved Tyler and would do anything to become his boyfriend. They had talked about it several times, but Tyler was still struggling with his sexual identity. The last thing David wanted to do was ruin their friendship, so he backed off.

One night while they were stargazing, David told Tyler about skyping with Marco. He said that they had a lot in common even though they came from different worlds. Tyler was jealous but tried not to show it. "So what do you guys talk about?"

"Just about anything really. That's the cool thing about it. Marco is easy to talk to. I hope you can meet him someday, then you'll know what I'm talking about."

"Yeah, that'd be nice. So, you like him then?"

"Yeah. We've become skyping friends."

"Do you like him more than just as a friend?" Tyler's voice quivered when he asked. David didn't know how to answer at first, but decided to tell him the truth. "I very easily could, but I'm not ready to go there right now."

"Why? I mean, if you like him, then you should go for it." David adjusted the lens trying his hardest not to cry. He was thankful it was dark because he knew Tyler was looking at him. David wanted to shake him and yell, "*Please figure it out soon! I love you,*" but said nothing.

Tyler was obviously jealous, but still too scared to face the truth. He looked up at those stars and wondered why everything had become so fucking complicated.

An hour later they started packing things up. "I hope this didn't bore you," David said, while placing the telescope in its case. "It was great tonight. I couldn't believe all the meteors we saw."

"Yeah, that was pretty cool. I made tons of wishes."

"Me too," Tyler said, hoping the most important one might come true one day.

Just before they were ready to leave, David turned to Tyler and asked, "Can I hug you?"

"Yeah, I'd like that." They stood on top of David's hill in each other's arms as the stars fell from the sky.

⤳ ∃

It was a little after four when David, Tyler, and Melissa headed home from school. It had been a long stressful day. David had taken two major exams, Tyler gave an in depth presentation about the benefits of capitalism, and Melissa had a test in AP French.

It was cold and windy as they ran through the parking lot and jumped into Tyler's truck.

So, what do you guys wanna do? I don't feel like going home yet," Tyler said.

David smiled and made a suggestion. "Do you guys want to hang out at my house? I could give you a lecture on black holes and singularity, then you could take a quiz."

"I could give you a black eye with a single punch," Melissa said, and then started tickling him. "Cut it out, I was only kidding."

"Yeah, let's hang at your place," Tyler said, reaching over Melissa to get in on the fun.

As soon as they got out of the parking lot, David connected his iPod to the stereo and played *My Body*, by Young the Giant. Melissa cranked it up and started singing at the top of her lungs. David and Tyler quickly joined in.

Ten minutes later they were singing along to *Cough Syrup* when Tyler finally turned into the driveway. As they got closer to the house, David stopped singing. He saw his dad's car parked at a haphazard rushed angle. He knew something was wrong because his dad never got home before six. Tyler and Melisa were still singing as they got out of the truck, but David was dead silent as he quickly walked towards the house. His mom opened the door as he was making his way up the porch steps. His dad and sister were standing next to her.

"Dad, why are you home so early? Is something wrong?" he asked, bracing himself for the worst.

"Everything is fine. My boss gave me the afternoon off because I worked late on Sunday."

"Oh. That was nice of him." David calmed down.

Tyler and Melissa said hi and followed David into the house.

"Why don't you guys go fix yourselves a snack," his mom suggested.

"Thanks Mrs. Emerson, I'm starving," Tyler said. He did a quick maneuver around David and Melissa and disappeared into the kitchen. David asked his mom what was for dinner, but she cut him off. "Eat a snack first and then I'll tell you." He gave her weird look and said, "Ok."

When he walked into the kitchen he saw Tyler looking at something on the counter. "What are you looking at?"

"See for yourself." Tyler moved to the side. David stopped in his tracks when he saw an overstuffed 9 x 12 envelope laying there. A million thoughts flooded his mind as he read the words, Columbia University Office of Admissions. His mom, dad, and sister walked in to see his reaction.

David walked to the counter, picked it up and held it to his chest. "Wow," was all he could say. "Well dufus, are you going to open it up or hug it to death?" Tyler said, bumping David with his arm. He knew what that packet meant, and so did everyone else watching.

David could barely breathe as he opened it. He took the admissions letter out and started reading in silence for a few seconds, then read it aloud.

*Dear Mr. Emerson,*

*I am delighted to inform you that the Early Decision*

*Committee on Admissions has voted to offer you admittance to Columbia University. As is tradition, a Certificate of Admission is enclosed. The committee is convinced that you will make important contributions during your undergraduate and graduate years with us. Please accept my personal congratulations for your outstanding achievements.*

*We are also happy to inform you that you have been chosen to receive the Gates Millennium Scholarship, which will pay your tuition, room and board, and book Fees through graduate school.*

*In anticipation of the questions you may have, we have assembled the information in the packet for your careful review. Once again, congratulations on your acceptance to Columbia University.*

*Sincerely,*
*Stacy M. Bergen*
*Admissions Officer*
*Columbia University*

Tears were falling by the time he finished reading. David looked up and tried to smile. His mom and dad went over and hugged him. Tyler and Melissa stood to the side waiting for their turn. Conflicted emotions filled the room as everyone began putting his achievement into their own rationale. It hit David hard when Tyler hugged him and said, "I'm going to miss you."

As they continued celebrating, David's thoughts turned to Marco. He wondered if the same envelope had found its way to his house. He wanted to text him, but decided not to just in case it hadn't come yet. What if Marco didn't get in? Would he be ok? Would he still want to be friends? He knew it was a stupid thing to think, but it did cross his mind. He decided not to say anything unless Marco brought it up the next time they skyped.

# CHAPTER 13

## Marco

December

Marco, Zander, and Claire decided to cut their afternoon classes and do some shopping. Claire had received a call during lunch from Prada saying something interesting had come into the boutique that she might like. Shopping was a way of life for the three of them. It was as important as oxygen. And having a limitless supply of funds made it that much more enjoyable. It was close to Christmas break and things were beginning to wind down at school, so taking the afternoon off was no big deal.

"I want to stop at Gucci and Armani to see if anything new has come in. I crave new high tops, skinny's, and t-shirts," Marco said, while cabbing down Park Avenue.

"You look hot in faded tees," Zander said.

"Yeah, I know."

"That ego of yours is making it crowded in here," Claire said, with a mischievous smirk.

"Hey, I'm just being honest."

"I hate to admit it, but it's true. All I know is that we're going to Prada first," Claire insisted.

"I wonder what I should buy today. I've been looking like a

raggedy Upper West Sider lately." Zander made that comment while watching a homeless guy rummage through a garbage can.

"Are you making fun of the other side of the tracks?" Marco asked, already knowing the answer. "Of course. I hate looking typical."

"Arrogance suits you well."

"Why thank you."

Claire decided to change the subject. "Marco, are you still skyping with that guy you met? What's his name?"

"David. Yeah. We've been having a great time chatting and getting to know each other," he told her, trying to sound nonchalant.

"I can't figure out why you're waisting so much time on this guy. Shit. He lives like thousands of miles away in Montana or Siberia or some fucking place. Nothing is ever going to come of it, you know that. I don't get it." Zander was totally exasperated. "I mean, it's gotten to the point where we hardly hang out anymore."

"Look, who I talk to shouldn't concern either one of you. David is a great guy. I like him a lot. And it doesn't concern me at all that he lives far away. There is just something about him. You guys would never understand. Let's just drop it and have some fun." A minute later they got out of the cab at 58th and 5th Avenue and hit the stores with a frenzy.

✄ ✎

It was around 4:30 when Marco finally got home. He had

spent a perfect afternoon hanging out and shopping. He put his bags off to the side in the entrance hall and hung his leather jacket in the closet. Rosa came from the kitchen and greeted him. "Well, it looks like you did a little shopping today," she said, shaking her head and smiling.

"You know it is my one weakness," he said, trying not to look guilty.

Rosa couldn't hold back any longer. "Something came for you about an hour ago," she said, pointing towards the living room. Marco turned and saw a big overstuffed packet lying on the coffee table. He gave her a serious smile and then walked into the living room and sat down on the couch. He looked at it with wonder, like it was some sort of alien being. He touched the Columbia insignia with his fingers knowing it had happened. He carefully open the packet up and read the congratulatory letter. "I got in. I actually got in." He tried his hardest not to cry.

"I'm so proud of you papi. I know your mother and father will be too." Rosa gave him a kiss on the forehead. Marco wiped his eyes. "Thank you for everything. You've always supported me." He stood up and gave her a heartfelt hug.

Then his thoughts went to David. His hands were shaking in his excitement as he texted, "I can't believe it, I got in. Did you find out yet?" He started going through the packet while he waited for David to text back. He didn't have long to wait. He crossed his fingers when his phone buzzed. "Congratulations!! I got in too :)" Marco jumped off the sofa and yelled, Yes! Yes! David got in. Another text came a few seconds later. "I can't believe we both got in :) I'm celebrating with my family and Tyler and Melissa right now. I'll text you when things calm down. Let's skype tonight :)" Marco responded, "This is the best day of my life. Just think, we get to go to college together. I'll show you all around the city. Can't wait to talk."

Marco sat by himself going through the rest of his packet while David celebrated with his family and friends.

He waited patiently for his parents to get home so he could tell them the good news. They were supposed to be home by six, and it was after six-thirty. He sent his father a text to see where they were. Ten minutes went by before his father replied. "We're running a little late. Your mother bought a new piece of art and wants me to meet her at the gallery. See you soon." That scenario was the typical shit he had to deal with. He went to his bedroom, cranked the music up and started writing.

It was almost eight o'clock when his parents finally made it home. Rosa knocked on Marco's door and told him dinner would be ready in five minutes. He was sitting on his bed with the Columbia packet all spread out while he talked to Zander. "I wish I were going there too. It would have been perfect rooming together," Zander told him. "Yeah, we could have really made our mark on the place." Marco said, and then got an idea. "Why don't you apply? There's still time you know."

"I'd love to, but my parents won't let me. They want me to go to Brown. I'm a legacy, so it's all about fucking family tradition. It sucks because I have no say in where I want to go."

"I completely understand. My parents tried to get me to attend Princeton on the same premise."

"Life sucks."

"Hey, I gotta go. My parents are home and I need to let them know the good news. Later."

Marco's parents were in the middle of a heated discussion when he walked into the dining room. They stopped arguing and both put on plastic smiles. "How was school today?" His father asked.

"Good. I got an A+ on one of my short stories. My English teacher told me that she submitted it to the Scholastic Art & Writing Competition."

"How nice dear," his mother said.

His father looked very pleased. "If I'm not mistaken, that competition is very prestigious. I know that some of the winners have gone on to remarkable careers in the arts."

"You're right. Ms. Birchmier said that past winners include Truman Capote, Andy Warhol, and Robert Redford," Marco said, trying to stay calm.

"Well, I'm sure you will win. You always do. I would love to read the story," his mother said.

He was happy that they were in better moods. "I have something else to tell you. My acceptance letter came today from Columbia."

His father smiled, got out of his chair, shook Marco's hand, and then gave him a hug.

"I'm proud of you son. This is great news."

His mother, on the other hand, gave him a forced smile. "That is so nice dear. Congratulations." She put her fork down and took sip of wine. He could tell by her body language that she was angry. "Mother, why can't you be happy for me just once? I worked my ass off to get into my dream school." He looked at his father like, what the fuck.

"Of course she is happy for you," his father said. She tried to fix the situation, but only made it worse. "Marco, I am happy for you, but…well…, it's just that I had already called my friend Harold at Princeton. He said that you would easily matriculate once your application was received. We…I mean, I was hoping that you would want to go to Princeton to keep the family tradition alive."

"I told you that I didn't want you calling your friend. You promised you wouldn't."

His father knew nothing about it, and gave her a look that could kill. "Don't worry about Princeton, son. Your mother was just trying to help. Both of us are very proud of you. I'm proud that you did it on your own."

"Thanks. It means a lot coming from you." Then his father got down to business. "Have you thought about accommodations yet? Are you going to commute or get an apartment?"

"Actually I've decided to stay in a residence hall for the first year," Marco told him.

His mother gave him an exasperated look. "Dear, why would you want to do that? Let us buy you a nice apartment close to campus. You have no idea what it is like living with people from god knows where."

"Mother, I want to live in a residence hall to have a different experience. That's what going away to college is all about."

"Well, I hardly think that you have thought this through in a logical manner."

"Son, I think it is a splendid idea to experience dorm life. Your mother and I did, and we enjoyed it. We'll put off buying an apartment until your sophomore year, unless the perfect apartment becomes available. We can buy it as an investment, or as a gift to you. Who knows, you may end up liking dorm life and live there for your entire undergraduate years."

"Thanks, I appreciate it."

After Marco finished dinner, he excused himself and went to the kitchen. Rosa was cleaning up. She was concerned. "Are you ok papi?"

"Yeah, it's no big deal."

"Your mother is proud of you whether you know it or not. Just give her some time."

"I can't ever please her no matter how hard I try." Rosa gave him a hug. "She will come around. You'll see." He thanked her and grabbed a vitamin water out of the frig and then headed to his bedroom. He took the back hall to the stairway so he wouldn't have to see his mother's scowling face again. He plopped down on his leather chair and gave Claire a quick call to let her know he got into Columbia. She was happy for him, but also a little put off because he had kept it a secret. They talked for twenty minutes or so as he explained why he didn't want to say anything about it. She forgave him, but dragged her displeasure out for effect. Marco hated to do it, but he cut their conversation short so he could skype with David.

# Chapter 14

## Skyping

"Hey, how are you holding up?" Marco asked, as he admired David's handsome face. He wanted to pull him through the computer screen and fuck him all night long. Even though he was falling in love with David, the idea of using him as a sexual object sent him over the edge. Marco had been fantasizing about it for weeks.

"I'm doing great." David couldn't stop smiling. "What a day this has turned out to be. It feels like I've been floating in the sky since I found out."

"Yeah, me too. I can't believe we both got our letters on the same day. I just wish we could have shared this big moment together."

"Me too." David brushed his bangs out of his eyes with his fingers, but they fell right back. Marco thought it was adorable. "I really like the emo look you have going."

"Thanks. I've never had my hair this long before, but I kind of like it this way."

"It suits you perfectly. You can start a new trend by becoming the first emo physicist."

David Laughed. "I never thought of that." He shook his head so his bangs completely covered his eyes. "Do you think anyone will take me seriously looking like this?"

"Of course they will. They'll just think you're a modern day Einstein with emo hair. That guy's hair was outrageous."

"Yeah, it was."

Marco realized his flirting was becoming a little too obvious, so he decided to tone it down. The last thing he wanted to do was scare David off. "Do you know which residence hall you'll be living in?"

"Yeah, it's called Hartley. It's right across from Butler Library."

"Cool. They put me in John Jay, so we're practically next door neighbors. Wouldn't it have been cool if they had put us in the same residence hall?"

"Definitely. They put me in Hartley with the other scholarship students. But we're close enough anyway."

"You received a scholarship? That is so cool."

"Yeah, without it there is no way my parents could ever afford to send me to Columbia, even though they would have tried to make it happen. I was lucky enough to get the Gates Millennium Scholarship. It pays for everything, even my books and food, right through graduate School. I never thought in a million years that I would actually get it. I guess I was just lucky."

"They saw what a genius you are."

"Thanks for saying that, but that's so far from the truth."

"Don't be modest now, you know it's true." Then Marco decided to take it a step further. "Plus they probably thought you were really cute too. Only cute geniuses get that scholarship."

He crossed his fingers as he waited for a response.

"Y-you too," David said, tongue tied.

"You too what?" Marco asked, putting him on the spot.

David's face turned bright red with embarrassment. "I-I mean, you're cute too."

"Why thank you for the compliment."

"I've wanted to tell you that for a while."

"Same here. I'm glad we finally got that out in the open."

"Yeah." David's hands were shaking slightly as he tried to process what was happening.

Marco knew exactly what he was doing, but David's heart was pounding wildly knowing he had just entered uncharted territory. He needed to calm down, so he changed the subject.

"So, your parents must be happy about the good news."

"My father is very happy for me, but my mother is another story. I thought she was going to choke on her dinner when I told them. She didn't waste any time before telling me that Princeton was the better choice." He looked away embarrassed.

"Give her some time," David said, realizing he had put his foot in his mouth by asking.

"She makes me so angry sometimes. It's all about the legacy bullshit for her, and wanting to impress her friends. She thinks Princeton is superior to Columbia, which is totally not true." "You're right," David said. "They're both Ivy League and constantly battling it out with Harvard, Yale, and MIT as the top university in the nation."

"She knows that, believe me. The thing she can't stand the

most is that I did it without her help. I know I sound vindictive and spoiled, but you have to know my mother to fully understand her devious nature. She has a motive for everything." David could see the hurt in his eyes and wanted to give him a hug to make him feel better.

They sat there in silence for a minute or. Marco cooled down and apologized for his outburst. "I'm sorry I went off. You didn't need to hear all that."

"It's ok. I'm glad you felt comfortable enough to share your feelings. That means a lot to me." David hoped that Marco could see how much he liked him.

"I feel like I can tell you anything, and you understand. Thanks."

"Anytime."

It was Marco's turn to change the subject. "So, does it snow a lot where you live?"

"Yeah, it snows tons around here. Right now we have over four feet on the ground."

"That is a lot of snow. We get some snow in New York, but it turns brown and ugly and then disappears. I love watching it from my windows whenever it does snow. I always get a warm feeling for some reason."

"Me too. I love a good snowstorm. It makes the world quiet and reflective."

All of a sudden a brilliant idea popped into David's head. "Let me show you what it looks like outside right now, ok?"

"Sure."

David put his coat and boots on and took his iPad with

him. He turned the lights on outside so Marco could see the huge snow drifts.

"That is unbelievable. I can't believe how much snow there is. I love it. And just think, it's only December," Marco said.

"It can get pretty overwhelming at times, but you get used to it."

"What do you do for fun with so much snow?"

"There is lots to do here in the winter. I have a pretty nice telescope, so I stargaze every chance I get. I love to cross country ski and walk through the woods with my snowshoes. I also have a snow machine and hit the trails with my friends on the weekends. There's never a dull moment."

"All of that sounds incredible. I've been skiing a few times, but that's about it," Marco said, leaving it at that. He decided not to say anything about his ski trips to Colorado, Utah, and Switzerland for obvious reasons. "What's a snow machine?"

"We call snowmobiles snow machines in Michigan." David pointed his iPad at four of them parked side by side in the driveway.

"Wow, they look awesome. Are they fun to drive?"

David had another brilliant idea. "Marco, would you like to come for a visit over the Christmas break?"

"Yeah, I'd love to. Will you take me riding on your snow machine?"

"Of course. Actually, I'm sure my dad will let you drive his after I show you how to drive mine," David was excited about the possibility of seeing Marco again. "Come with me." He walked back inside so he could ask his parents. "Mom, dad, where are you?" he called, while taking his boots off.

"We're in the kitchen." David walked in and propped up his iPad on the island so everyone could see each other. He felt a little awkward skyping with his parents, but this was really important.

"Dad, you remember Marco, right?"

"Of course I do. Hi. It's good to see you again."

"It's nice to see you again, Mr. Emerson."

"Mom, this is Marco Valerio."

"Hi Marco. It's nice to finally meet you."

"It is very nice to meet you, Mrs. Emerson."

"Marco was also accepted at Columbia today." David's mother and father congratulated him.

"Thank you. I'm sure it has been an exciting day for everyone. Both of you must be very proud of David."

"Yes, we are."

"The reason why I got all of us together is to ask if Marco could come for a visit during Christmas break." His parents looked at each other for a second, then his mom said, "It's ok with us. Marco, will it be ok with your parents?"

"I'm sure it will be fine with them. I'll have my father give you and Mr. Emerson a call.

While we're all together, I would like to invite David to New York over the break as well. I could fly in for a few days, and then David could fly back with me," Marco suggested, hoping David wouldn't be angry for suggesting it.

A huge smile erupted on David's face. "Mom, dad, can I go?" he asked, crossing his fingers.

"Well, I don't know. What do you think, dear?" His dad gave David a serious look, and then grinned. "That sounds like a good plan to me."

Marco watched with envy as David hugged and kissed his parents. It was easy to see how much he was loved. "I'll make sure my father calls tomorrow to confirm everything, and to give you the flight information so David and I can fly back together."

"Thanks, we appreciate that," David's mother said.

David thanked his parents again and then headed to his bedroom so they could talk in private.

"I can't wait until you get here. It will be nice to hang out together. You can meet Tyler and Melissa. And, oh yeah, I'll take you snowmobiling on all of the awesome trails around here."

I'm looking forward to it. I'm up for anything you want to do. I just wish we could make time go faster."

"Me too." They continued talking well into the night making plans and anticipating the moment when they would be standing face to face.

# CHAPTER 15

## David

David was still in seventh heaven when Tyler and Melissa picked him up for school the next morning. He didn't get very much sleep, but it didn't matter because he was running on pure adrenalin. He couldn't wait to tell them the good news.

"Hey guys, Marco is coming to spend a few days here during Christmas break. And then I'm going to fly back to New York with him to spend a few days with his family."

There was an awkward silence. Tyler and Melissa were trying to process the fact that Marco actually existed. They both panicked for different reasons.

"Um...that sounds interesting. I'm looking forward to meeting this guy you're so crazy about," Tyler said with zero enthusiasm.

David could tell he wasn't happy about it by the inflection in his voice. "I think you'll like Marco if you give him a chance. He's really nice."

"Don't you think he'll get bored with the whole Michigan wilderness thing?" Melissa asked, trying to think of an excuse for David to un-invite him.

"I don't think so. He told me he's looking forward to getting out of the city for a few days. We are going to stargaze, and I'm going to take him riding on the trails, and he can hang out with us. Maybe we can have a movie night and get everyone together," he suggested.

"Well, all I know is that you better keep this rich boy entertained, I know from experience. You remember Matthew and Julie from Chicago don't you?"

"Yeah, they were really nice."

"Well, every time they came to visit they were bored," Melissa groaned. "I don't invite them anymore because I got tired of their bitching and trying to get me to move back to Chicago."

"Marco's not like that at all."

"He might not be, but just know this. Cute rich boys are extremely spoiled and need constant attention. And another thing, he might even look down on you because you're not rich. Status is everything with certain people," she warned.

"Melissa, you're rich and you don't look down on me."

"I'm different. You know I've never been into the status thing. I decided to live here so I could get away from pretentious assholes and the private school bullshit."

"I think Marco is a lot like you in that regard. He isn't spoiled or pretentious at all. You'll see when you meet him," David told her, trying to sound optimistic.

He sat there quietly looking out of the window wondering why they were both being so negative. "Look, it's ok if you guys don't want to meet him. I understand. It's just that I like him a lot, and I think he likes me, and meeting you guys would give him a better understanding of who I am. You can tell a lot about someone by the friends they hang out with."

Melissa knew she had gone too far. Tyler felt the same way. They shamefully looked at each other while David stared out the window. Melissa finally nudged him with her shoulder.

"You better bring Marco over so we can hang out or Tyler and I will drag you two out of your house." David turned and gave them a faint smile.

"We're sorry for being assholes," Tyler said, knowing he had hurt David's feelings.

"You deserve to find a great guy. I really mean that," he added.

"Thanks."

Tyler wanted to tell David how he really felt, but still couldn't go there. The idea of coming out to everyone was terrifying. He was losing David and couldn't do anything about it.

As they walked towards the school entrance, David asked another favor of them. "Hey guys, please don't say anything about me getting into Columbia, ok? And please don't say anything about the scholarship either."

"Why?" Melissa asked.

"Because no one else knows which colleges they're going to attend yet. Plus it will seem like I'm bragging. I'd just rather keep it between us for now if you don't mind."

Melissa looked straight ahead for a few seconds knowing she was in trouble again.

"David, I kind of already told Brad, Kathy, and Lucas. I'm sorry, but I was just so excited for you."

"And I told Jim, Andrew, and Emma," Tyler sheepishly added.

David sighed as he gathered his thoughts. "It's ok, don't worry about it." He knew it going to be a long day. He just hoped that no one would care, or at least not say anything nasty to him.

℧

News of David's Columbia acceptance and scholarship spread around school quickly. When he walked into his math class second period, everyone stood up and applauded. The same thing happened in physics. The principal even came in to congratulate him. He informed David that he was the first student at his high school to be accepted at an Ivy League College.

Students and teachers came up and congratulated him the entire day, which made him feel proud of what he had accomplished. He wasn't used to the spotlight, so he tried to keep a low profile by just going about his day like always.

David was getting some books out of his locker after 7th period when Brad walked up and actually said something nice to him. "Hey David, I think it's really cool that you got into Columbia. If anyone deserves it around here it's you. I mean that. And Melissa said your scholarship pays for everything right through grad school. That's awesome."

David couldn't believe what he was hearing. "Thanks Brad. I appreciate it."

"Look, I know I've been a fucking jerk picking on you for,

you know, being gay, and being a nerd. I'm sorry. I really am." He hesitated for a few seconds, trying to find the right words. "Look, the truth is, I've been jealous of you for years. I mean, you have it all, and you've never bragged about it. That's the cool thing about you. I wish I could be more like that."

David stood there dumbfounded not knowing how to respond to his confession. It felt like he was in a surreal dream. It was so out of place, but Brad seemed truly remorseful.

"Apology accepted. Maybe we could start fresh from here on out."

"Cool, I'd like that. Will you do me one favor though?"

"Sure. What do you want me to do?"

"Punch me in the face as hard as you can. I've been such an asshole and I don't want to live with this guilt for the rest of my life." David smiled and said, "Ok, here goes." Brad closed his eyes, waiting for the punch. David made a fist and lightly tapped him on the chin. He opened his eyes with a look of disbelief. "Can I just give you a hug instead?" David asked.

"Sure." David hugged him and said, "Your friendship is all I ever wanted."

⇄

As soon as David got home from school he made a snack and watched an astronomy lecture on-line. It had been a long emotional day and he needed to relax. After dinner he went stargazing. He stood on top of his hill looking at his world, his universe, while *Earthshine* by Rush played through his headphones. He was fully connected to his existence as he thought about how much his life had changed in the last twenty-four hours. Even though he didn't know what the future held, one thing was certain, he was ready to take the ride.

Eventually David's mind drifted to Marco's impending visit. He couldn't wait to bring him to his little mountain, the place that defined every atom in his body. Sharing that spec of earth with him was important because David felt like he could be the one. With a slight breeze and the quietude of the forest, David closed his eyes as the music played, feeling completely connected to the energy of the universe. And he could feel it. The universe was rotating. He always knew it did.

That night David decided he would ask Marco to be his boyfriend.

# CHAPTER 16

## Marco

All Marco thought about while he got ready for school was the moment when he would finally be on a plane to Northern Michigan. He needed to see David in the flesh so he could ask him to be his boyfriend. He didn't want to understand how that blond haired angel had managed to resuscitate emotions he thought were long dead. He just wanted to hold him in his arms to keep them from fading away.

*The reality of innate characteristics can cause binary stars to be placed in a state of unstable equilibrium, often resulting in eventual destruction.*

As usual, Marco met Zander at the Nector Cafe on their way to school. He definitely needed a heavy dose of caffeine. He pulled an all-nighter skyping with David, and then writing until it was time to go to school. Marco sipped his Macchiato and yawned repeatedly while they discussed their agenda for the weekend.

Zander tried to entice him back to life. "Let's go to Retro's tonight. We haven't been there in like forever."

"I'm not in the mood for that scene right now. Maybe some other time."

"Come on. I need some more of that hot college ass. I'm horny as fuck, and you have to be too, unless you've been getting some and not saying anything."

"I haven't had time to fuck around. I've been in a writing frenzy for the last month and a half. I pulled another all-nighter last night because I can't stop. It's like I'm on fucking Aderall," Marco said, hoping Zander believed this half-truth.

"That's cool. But I'm sure you need sex as much as I do. I know you. You've never gone this long without getting laid." It was the brutal truth, and Marco knew it. And even though he stroked it a couple of times a day trying to relieve the urge, his body still craved random sex.

Zander went into pleading mode. "Come on Marco, you need to fuck as bad as I do. Go with me tonight. I'm begging you."

Marco had been turning guys down for the last six weeks because of David, but Zander's pleading had momentarily broken David's spell. "Ok. I'll go," he said, with a guilty smile. He did his best to rationalize what he was about to do. David wasn't his boyfriend yet, so he was free to do as he pleased.

❦

The dance floor at Retro's was packed once again with the hottest guys in the city. Marco felt those familiar jolts of electricity run through his veins as guy after guy hit on him. He realized how much he missed this part of his life, and didn't care about anything except getting laid. He was in his element and loved it.

The Molly he had taken gave him the perfect buzz. He had been craving it for weeks. He wanted to fuck every guy there. At one point he even went after Zander. "I wanna give you what you've always wanted," Marco yelled in his ear. He grabbed Zander's hand and put it on his crotch. He moved it up and down for him as his lips found Zander's. Ten minutes went by before they came up for air. They smiled their Molly smiles and went their separate ways for more action.

It was 3am when Marco finally decided to hook up with a guy named Trevor, one of a dozen or so hot blond twinks Marco had his eye on. They danced and kissed and groped until the club closed, then headed to Trevor's apartment.

They started going at it as soon as they entered Trevor's bedroom. They took turns stripping each other naked, and then got into some wild kissing, touching, and licking. Both had bodies every guy and girl envied. They were slender, defined, and well hung. They proceeded to devour each other with perfect loveless sex. Marco spent the next two hours having the sluttiest sex he had ever had. Six weeks of jacking off had been driving him crazy, so he told Trevor that he could do anything he desired. And he did.

And when Marco thought it couldn't get any better, it did. His ultimate fantasy was about to become reality. He was exploring Trevor's body when he heard the apartment door open. "Who's that?" he playfully moaned.

"Cameron. My roommate."

"Oh."

A few seconds later the bedroom door opened and he

walked in. "Very nice. I see you've been having fun without me." He focused on Marco and smiled. "What's your name?"

"Marco."

"Hi Marco. You are fucking hot."

"Thanks, so are you." Marco spread his legs to give him a better view.

"Mmm." Cameron's eyes were riveted on his raging hard-on.

Trevor kissed Marco on the cheek. "Do you mind if he joins us?"

"That sounds hot." And with that, Marco took his sexual fantasies to the next level by having his first three-way. Trevor and Cameron fucked him every way imaginable, ravaging every inch of his quivering naked body. The lingering effects of the Molly, and the poppers he repeatedly inhaled, made him moan and scream and beg for more. And they gave him what he desired. It was by far the best sex he had ever had.

≈ ≭

It was 11 am when Marco finally woke up. His body felt like it had been beaten up. It was the perfect kind of pain he always enjoyed. He lay there, his fingers rubbing his chest and stomach, thinking about going another round with them. Sadly though, he didn't have time. They were out of it anyway. He quietly slipped out of bed, grabbed his clothes and went to the bathroom to pee and freshen up. He couldn't believe how hot sex with two guys could be.

He looked in the mirror ready to enjoy the satisfied smirk he always had after gratifying sex. But this time it wasn't there. He looked again. Nothing. He shrugged it off because every erotically touched muscle in his body reminded him of how good it was. He slipped out of the apartment and texted Zander so they could meet up and share their stories.

David never entered Marco's mind until later that evening when he suddenly pulled his conscience from the clutches of a guilt-ridden nightmare. He sat up in bed, sweaty and panic stricken, a layer of grief covering his perfect olive skin. He was surrounded by darkness except for the slivers of dull sad light coming through his bedroom windows from some other wounded reality. He wiped his tear-stained face and tried to focus his eyes to see, to see what he had done.

# CHAPTER 17

David and his father were at the airport in Pellston waiting for Marco's plane to arrive. It was delayed a couple of hours because a snowstorm had dumped eight inches of snow the prior night, and that morning. It was early-afternoon when planes finally began to land. David stood in the waiting area nervously looking out at the runway. He watched the snowplows methodically go back and forth trying to keep the runways clear. "I just wish it would stop snowing."

"Marco will get here safe and sound. Don't worry." His father squeezed David's shoulder for reassurance. "I'm sorry. I guess I'm just nervous."

"Nervous in what way? Because flying through a snowstorm is dangerous? Or is it because Marco is coming to see you?" David gave him a look that said the obvious. His father tried to ease his anxiety. "Making new friends can be nerve racking, but it's always interesting when you connect on a certain level. Marco seems like a sincere friendly guy, so it should be fairly easy."

"You're right, he is a nice guy. I've enjoyed skyping with

him. He's perceptive, intelligent, and has this dry sense of humor that makes me genuinely laugh."

"He sounds complicated, but in a good way. I was kind of wondering, is he gay?"

"Yes." David knew what was coming next.

"Do you like him more than just as a friend?"

"Yes, I think so." David felt slightly embarrassed sharing that secret.

"Well, I'm happy for you."

"Thanks dad. That means a lot."

"I know it's been hard living here and not having opportunities to date. But that will definitely change once you move to New York. The only advice I can give you is to take your time with the whole dating thing. Stay level headed. Relationships can get a little crazy if you're not careful. I don't want to see you get hurt, and I don't want someone taking advantage of you either."

"I'm trying to take things slow. Liking someone is a lot more complicated than I ever thought."

"You're right about that. Most relationships are complicated, but real relationships are worth the effort. I'm glad you're thinking this through rationally."

David smiled a tiny bit. "Sometimes I think being rational and liking someone is an equation that can't be solved." His father shook his head agreeing before giving him a little more advice.

"When you start college in the fall, please be careful. New York is a big city, and it is filled with people who love to take advantage of unsuspecting people. I'm sure it will be an interesting place to attend college, but it can also be very dangerous if you aren't on your guard."

"Dad, I'm not going to put myself in a situation I'm not comfortable with. I've thought about that too, believe me."

"I'm glad." His father breathed a sigh of relief, then reiterated his current unease. "I'm not trying to tell you what to do, but I hope you will take your time with Marco and really get to know him before, you know.... I hope that makes some sort of sense."

"It does make sense. I like Marco a lot, but you're right, I don't really know him the way I need to yet. I will take it slow, I promise. Anyway, I don't even know if he likes me that way. He hasn't dropped any hints or whatever you're supposed to do. And I don't know how to let him know that I like him, let alone ask him on a date. I have zero experience in the dating world."

A mischievous grin began to appear on David's face, and his father noticed. "What are you smiling about?"

David could feel his face getting hot. "Well, actually, I kind of lied. I did go on a date a couple of months ago."

"You did? Who with?" his father asked, with a surprised look.

"Tyler. He asked me if I would be his date for one of Melissa's movie nights, and I said yes. Honestly, I don't think it qualifies as a real date, but we hung out together the entire night."

"Wow. I would have never guessed. Is Tyler gay?"

"Will you promise to keep what I'm about to say just be-tween you and I?"

"Of course."

"That means you can't say anything to mom, ok?"

"I promise."

"Well, I definitely think he's questioning. I've suspected it for a couple of years. If he is gay I want to be there for him when he comes out, like he was for me."

"I'm glad. I don't know how your mom and I would have handled things if Tyler hadn't been there for you, and for us." David's face went ashen at the thought. "I wouldn't be here right now if it wasn't for him. Gay or straight, I want to be there for him. I want him to be happy."

At that point David decided to tell his father everything because his emotions were getting the best of him just think-ing about it. "Tyler kissed me twice that night."

"Oh," his dad said, slightly shocked. "Were you expecting that to happen?"

"No, but he shared something personal with me, so I asked him to kiss me, and he did, and it felt perfect. It was like I knew we were made for each other."

"So, I take it you like Tyler too?"

"Yeah. I've had a crush on him since 8th grade. I never seriously thought for even a second that he might feel the same way about me. So, as you can see, this whole situation has be-come rather complicated."

"I can see that. Just know that you have plenty of time to work this out. Be patient."

Twenty minutes later they watched Marco's plane land. David breathed a sigh of relief as it taxied safely down the runway, its lights blinking triumphantly as remnants of the snowstorm continued to gently fall.

David was standing next to his father just beyond the waiting area when Marco finally walked out of the jetway in a sea of people. His heart went into hyperdrive as soon as their eyes met. Marco was trying to politely maneuver his way through as quickly as possible while David walked towards him. As soon as they were face to face, Marco put his backpack on the floor and gave David a lingering hug. "It's good to see you again."

"Same here. I'm really happy that you're here. I'm sorry about all the snow, but this is typical Michigan weather. How was your flight?"

"The flight was good. I apologize for the delay. I hope you and your father weren't too bored waiting around."

"No, not at all. I'm just glad you're here safe and sound."

David's father hung back just long enough to give them a few moments alone. "Marco, you remember my dad."

"Of course." They shook hands. "It's nice to see you again Mr. Emerson. Thank you for extending the invitation to visit David."

"I'm happy that you could make it. And congratulations on your acceptance to Columbia. Your parents must be very proud of you."

"Thanks. They are. I'm sure you and Mrs. Emerson feel the same way about David."

"We definitely do. I'm sure it is an exciting time for everyone."

While Marco skillfully exchanged pleasantries, his thoughts remained focused on David. He couldn't believe that he was finally standing next to him. Underneath his skin, Marco's veins were pulsing wildly knowing his heart was feeling something real for the first time in years. And his eyes reaffirmed that David was an angel sent just for him. Marco loved how his shy smile and confident words revealed that timeless paradox of innocence and knowledge. It shook Marco to his very core knowing David possessed both attributes.

"I hope you're hungry," David said, skillfully interrupting the parental twenty question game.

"I am a bit hungry as a matter of fact."

"Good. My mom is making roast beef for dinner."

Marco's face lit up. "Actually, I'm starving. I love roast beef."

"I remember you telling me, so my mom is making it just for you."

"That is so nice of her."

"Let's head to the baggage claim and get your luggage and get out of here."

Marco made a request while they waited for his luggage. "Will you take me for a ride on your snowmobile after dinner?"

"I was planning on it. The trails are unbelievable right now."

"Cool, I can't wait see what it is all about."

卅

The ride back to Harbor Springs gave Marco a chance to see some of the vast Michigan wilderness. Marco's favorite writer came to mind while absorbing his new surroundings.

With each mile further into the forest, he began to feel the quietude, the isolation, the loneliness one must come to know and embrace, that solitary rite of passage through fear, through loss, through self-destructive doubt, through near-death, in order to find some sliver of truth. Hemingway almost succeeded. Marco was determined to.

A half hour later the road began snaking through the forest in roller coaster-esque fashion as they got closer to Harbor springs. It twisted around hill after hill, rising and falling like an age old fairy tale before making the final ascent to the crest, revealing a deep blue expanse pristinely wedged between the forest and sky. "Is that Lake Michigan?" asked Marco, eyes wide.

"Yeah. What do you think?"

"It's so blue. So alive. I thought it would be frozen solid. It is the second time today that I have seen what perfection looks like."

"Yeah, I never get tired of the view."

A couple of minutes later they turned onto Tamarac Trail and then finally into David's driveway. It had been freshly plowed, adding at least two more feet of snow, making the snow banks close to seven feet high. No one said a word as the house came into view. The Christmas lights were twinkling soft and warm all across the front porch, and on seven pine trees adjacent to the house, giving it an enchanted look. "Your home is beautiful," Marco said. "It looks just like a Christmas card."

"Thanks. My dad and uncles built it." David was proud of that fact.

"I am truly amazed. You have an artistic eye Mr. Emerson."

"Thanks. It was definitely a labor of love."

David's mother opened the door and greeted them as they walked up the front steps.

"How were the roads? I was starting to get a little worried about you guys."

"They were fine." David's father said, giving her a 'look what I brought home' smile.

He gave her a kiss and then moved to the side. David was all smiles as he gave his mom a hug. "Mom, this is Marco." She shook his hand. "Marco, I am happy that you could come for a visit."

"It is very nice to meet you in person Mrs. Emerson. Your home is breathtaking."

"Thank you. Come in out of the cold you two." David gave his mom a shy smile as he followed Marco inside. She gave him the mom look of approval.

"Well Marco, as you can see, we are a little off the beaten path," she said, with a slight laugh.

"I love it. I feel like I've stepped into another world." While Marco was taking off his leather jacket he noticed David's sister staring at him from the kitchen entryway. He gave her his tried and true smile and said hello. David took his jacket and introduced her. "Marco, this is my sister Audrey."

"It is nice to meet you Audrey. You have a beautiful name."
She blushed ten shades of red. "H-hi," she stuttered with an
enamored gaze. "I like your name too."

"Why don't you guys go to the great room and relax.
Dinner is almost ready. I'm sure you boys are starving," said
David's mom.

"That's for sure. Dinner smells delicious Mrs. Emerson."

"I made Roast Beef. David told me it was a favorite of
yours."

"It definitely is. Thank you for making it."

"I'll call you guys when it's ready."

Marco couldn't believe what he saw when he followed
David through the entryway into the great room. He looked
around in quiet awe at the twenty-five foot vaulted ceiling,
the post and beam construction, the hand hued logs, the field-
stone fireplace blazing away, and a Christmas tree at least
twenty feet tall, decorated with hand-made ornaments, tin-
sel, and vintage multi-colored Christmas lights. Everything
about the room reflected warmth, family, and love. It wasn't
pretentious, or staged, like most aspects of his world.

"David, this room makes me feel like I belong here."

"I know what you mean. I love to sneak in here after everyone has gone to sleep. I like to cuddle up by the fire and
read, or play guitar, or think about crazy theories."

During dinner David and his family enjoyed Marco's stories about growing up in New York City, and all of the places
he had traveled. The conversation gave David a chance to know
more about him without having to ask a million questions

himself. The tension that was evident when they first sat down had all but disappeared when the conversation became more animated. Everyone started sharing funny stories about their past. Marco couldn't remember the last time he had laughed so hard and felt so normal. For David, his worries about their different upbringings were slowly being laid to rest.

When dinner and the stories finally ended, David and Marco helped clear the dishes from the table, rinsed them, and put them in the dishwasher. This was a first for Marco. Everyone pitched in, which made him feel like one of the family.

"David, why don't you help Marco take his suitcases to the den and get settled," his dad suggested, knowing they probably wanted some privacy. David's smile confirmed that observation. "Come on Marco, I'll show you where you'll be sleeping and then I'll take you on a quick tour of my bedroom and give you your Christmas present and then I'll take you snowmobiling through the woods," he said, all in one excited breath.

"Cool. I need to give you your gift too." Marco put the dish towel on the counter and thanked David's parents for the excellent dinner, and for making him feel so welcome. They got the suitcases from the foyer and made a quick beeline to the den. "I love the rustic ambiance," Marco said, when they walked in.

"I hope this will be comfortable enough for you. The pullout couch has a pretty firm mattress, and there are sheets, pillows, and blankets in the closet. I'll help you set everything up."

"Thanks. This den has a cozy feel. I'm sure I'll sleep well." Marco began to scan the bookshelves, which were methodically arranged into areas of fiction, non-fiction, history by centuries, and of course math and science. "This is an awesome library."

"As you can see, my family likes to read."

Marco took the suitcase he was holding and laid it on the floor. He opened it and took out David's present. "Merry Christmas."

"Thank you so much. Let's go to my room so I can give you your present. We can open them together." Marco's enjoyed looking at David's cute little tush as he followed him down the hall. He wanted to kiss David. He wanted to feel David's slender body against his, and... Marco realized that he needed to slow his mind down before he completely lost it.

David, on the other hand, was nervous about revealing his entire life to someone he liked, but barely knew. He held his breath when they walked in to his bedroom, hoping for the best.

Marco didn't say anything for a few seconds as he took it all in. The small intimate space revealed what David was all about. "Your bedroom is awesome. It is you without a doubt."

"Thanks. I didn't have any grand plan or anything as you can probably tell. Everything in here is what I'm passionate about," David said, beaming with pride. He walked over to his desk and got Marco's present. "Merry Christmas. I'm happy that you came to visit me."

Marco looked at the vintage Santa wrapping paper and smiled. "Thank you for inviting me. And thank you for the gift." He wanted to hug David but resisted the urge. "I want you to open your gift first if you don't mind."

"Ok." David could tell it was a book. He carefully unwrapped it and smiled when he saw the title. It was Benjamin Eldridge's latest book, *Beyond our own Universe: New Theories in Dimensional Planes.* "Thank you so much. This is one of my favorite books."

"You're welcome. I assumed that you already had a copy, but I don't think you have a copy like this one. Open it to the title page." David couldn't believe his eyes. It was signed by Professor Eldridge, along with a personal message.

*To David,*

*Congratulations on your matriculation to Columbia University. I look forward to having you as a student in the near future.*

*Benjamin Eldridge*

David was stunned. "Oh my god. I don't know what to say." Marco was grinning ear to ear. "Do you like it?"

"I love it. How did you get this?"

"Oh, I have my ways. You told me how he has inspired you, and he is the head of the math and physics departments, so I paid him a little visit."

"I don't know what to say."

"You don't have to say anything."

"C-can I, uh, can I give you a hug?" David asked, hoping he wasn't being too forward.

"I'd love a hug." Shyly, awkwardly, David put his arms around Marco and gave him a quick squeeze and started to let go, but Marco wouldn't let him. Without saying a word Marco pulled David close and began to rub the small of his back hoping it would relax him. Within seconds Marco could feel the tension disappear. "This feels nice," he whispered.

"Yeah, it feels...." David whispered back, his words disappearing.

Marco moved his head closer to David's until they were cheek to cheek. Then his hands made their way to those sexy slender hips, which made David's body tense up again. "Are you ok with this?" Marco asked. David didn't answer. Marco pulled away a little hoping he hadn't blown it. He could see conflict and a quiet sadness in David's eyes, like he was trying to figure something out. A moment later, a slight smile appeared on David's face as he moved his body closer. "This feels perfect. Thank you for the gift."

"You're welcome. I'm glad you like it." At that point Marco decided to go for it. He looked into David's blue eyes, feeling vulnerable, feeling alive for the first time in years. Then he slowly leaned in until their lips met. The kiss was soft, almost hesitant at first, until Marco's tongue began to move slow and sexy all over David's slightly open lips. David reciprocated a moment later, sending shivers down both of their spines.

David gently pulled away after a minute or so because he was trying to stay in control of his emotions. Marco acquiesced even though he wanted to take it to the next level.

David gave Marco a shy glance and said, "That was really nice." Then he leaned close and kissed Marco on the cheek. "You have to open your present now." Marco picked it up and read the attached note. "I know you are going to change the world with your words. Merry Christmas."

"That is so nice of you to say." When he unwrapped it, two books by Earnest Hemingway were staring back at him. *In Our Time* and *The Nick Adams Stories*. "I love these books. Thank you so much."

"I figured you probably had copies already, so I talked to a friend of mine who owns the bookstore in town to see if I could get special additions, and she came through for me. In Our Time is a third addition, and The Nick Adams Stories is a first addition."

Marco looked concerned. "David, you shouldn't have spent your money on me like that."

"I wanted to get you something special, and besides, I got a nice discount."

"Well, ok then. This is the best gift I've ever received."

"Awe, I'm glad you like them."

Marco kissed David on the cheek and whispered, "I've never met anyone like you."

David didn't respond right away because he was trying to see the real person behind that perfect face. He was trying to see into those dark haunting eyes that were magnifying his conflicted emotions and making his heart fall in love. "Marco, I don't have any experience with any of this, but I want to let you know that I really like you. I wanted to tell you that a month ago, but I was petrified."

"I really like you too. You're all I've thought about, and I couldn't get here fast enough to be with you." David's eyes started to sting as his guilty feelings began to overwhelm him.

"I'm sorry. Please don't cry. I'll do anything you want me to." Marco gave David a hug hoping it would calm him down.

"You didn't do anything to make me cry. It's me. I need a little time to figure some things out." Marco understood. "David, we have lots of time."

They put their arms around each other and held on for dear life.

$$\forall \therefore$$

Marco followed David to the utility room where they stored the snowmobile gear. He laughed while slipping into one of David's snowmobile suits. "I feel like I'm wearing one of those NASA space suits."

"Yeah, they feel bulky and weird at first, but you'll get used to it."

Big Christmassy snowflakes were falling as they walked across the driveway to where the snow machines were parked. David gave Marco some safety tips about riding and then checked to make sure the survival kit was under the seat. He also checked to make sure they had a full tank of gas. "We don't want to get stuck twenty miles in the woods without the essentials," David said.

They spent the next couple of hours riding the trails all

around Harbor Springs. David took Marco to some of his favorite places that had great views of the harbor and Lake Michigan. At one point David decided to let Marco drive, so he gave him a quick lesson. He loved wrapping his arms around Marco's waist while he cautiously drove down the trails. They were both having the time of their lives.

It was snowing pretty hard by the time they made it back home. They shook the snow off once they were on the porch, and then stood there for a couple of minutes watching the snow fall. Marco couldn't believe how peaceful it looked, and how beautiful the Christmas lights looked twinkling away in the snowy silence. "You are so lucky to live here," Marco said, almost in a whisper. "I know I am. It looks magical when it snows like this." They both turned and looked at each other, each thinking how perfect the moment was. Marco slowly leaned in and Kissed David. A few minutes later they headed inside to get warm.

After hanging up their suits and helmets, the smell of hot chocolate lured them into the kitchen. When they walked in the mood lighting was set perfectly, and two full mugs and a dish of homemade cookies were waiting patiently on the counter to be devoured. There was no one in sight, which was unusual for early evening. But David understood what was going on. He would thank his mom and dad later. They ended up in the great room sitting on the floor by the fireplace listening to music and talking deep into the night.

≜ ≼

The next day turned out to be crystal clear and slightly warmer, about twenty degrees, but the weather channel said it was going to snow later in the afternoon.

"Hopefully we'll have a clear night tonight so I can take you stargazing. But if not, we can try again tomorrow night. It's always hit or miss this time of year," David explained while they ate breakfast. "Cool. I've never gone stargazing." They sat at the kitchen table eating scrambled eggs, bacon, and toast with homemade raspberry jam. At one point Marco started grinning like a little kid. David smiled. "What are you thinking about?"

"I was wondering if you would be interested in building a snowman with me. I've never made one before."

"Sure. The snow should be perfect for building one."

Just as they were finishing with breakfast, David got a text from Melissa wondering what they were up to. "Do you guys want to come over for a movie night? Everyone is dying to meet him."

He looked at Marco. "My friend Melissa is having movie night tonight. Do you want to go?"

"Yeah, that sounds like fun."

"Great." David texted back saying they would be there at 7pm. He attached two smily faces and two thumbs up to let her know things were going well. "You have to see Melissa's house. It is amazing. It's right on the harbor and has an incredible view of lake Michigan."

"I can't wait to see it."

"I hope you don't mind hanging out with my friends. They really want to meet you."

"I'm looking forward to meeting Melissa and Tyler." Marco got quiet for a moment as he tried to find the right words. "David?"

"Yeah. Is everything ok?"

"Everything is perfect. I just want you to know that I've never had a Christmas break like this. It's one of the best I've ever had. I mean it." David blushed at those kind words. "I feel the same way. I'm glad you're having fun. I can't wait to hang out with your friends in New York."

They cleaned up the kitchen, and took turns in the bathroom trying to look as hot as they could for each other. This was the normal routine for Marco, but a brand new world for David.

They spent part of the morning building a snowman and having a snowball fight. They both felt like they were ten years old again. At one point while they were goofing around, David's dad started chopping wood in back of the pole barn. The barn was situated a couple hundred feet from the house, tucked away in a wooded area. Marco was curious about the echoed chopping sounds. "What's that?" he asked.

"Oh, that's my dad chopping wood. We heat the whole house with two energy efficient wood burning stoves. My dad and I usually cut eight to ten cords of wood in the fall and winter to make it through the year."

"That is so cool. It makes everything smell so good out here."

"Yeah it does. And it's great exercise too."

"Can I try to chop some wood?" Marco curiously asked.

"Sure, but you need to be very careful." They finished the snowman off by dressing him up with one of David's beanies and an old scarf. They took a couple of selfies together with there creation, making funny faces and giggling like little kids. "My friends are going to get a kick out of this," Marco said. He sent them to Zander and Claire along with a text, "I'm having the time of my life!!"

David's father was pleasantly surprised when they walked up and asked if he needed any help. "Dad, Marco wants to learn how to chop wood. Will you teach him how?"

"Sure. Just remember, the main thing is safety first." He gave Marco a pair of goggles, work gloves, and an axe. He demonstrated how to attach a log to the axe and then come down on a larger stationary log just right.

"Mr. Emerson, do you split all of your wood like this?"

"No. In the fall David and I use chain saws to cut everything into eighteen inch lengths. Then we use a log splitter to do about eighty percent of the chopping. We have a system to get most of our wood split and stacked in a couple of weekends."

"Well, you definitely don't have to go to a gym to keep in shape," Marco said, exhausted after five minutes of chopping.

"Marco, let's take the snow machines out for a ride," David said, rescuing him before he had a heart attack.

"That sounds like a good idea. Go have some fun. Thanks for helping, Marco."

"Anytime Mr. Emerson."

David's father smiled as he watched them walk back to the

house. Even though he wanted David to take it slow, he hoped that they would become boyfriends at some point. He had a good feeling about Marco, and trusted David's judgment.

The snow machines were all gassed up and ready to go. Marco was a little nervous about driving solo, but David assured him that he was going to have a blast once they hit the trails. They did a quick safety check and then headed down the driveway and onto the side of the road. A couple of minutes later they were cruising down a freshly groomed trail zipping past snow-covered pine trees and an eternity of snow crystals reflecting in the rays of the sun.

Marco felt totally free for the first time in years. He finally relaxed and started enjoying the silent wilderness around him. He wanted to absorb it all, become part of it, the same way Hemingway had done a century earlier. With his body gliding effortlessly like cogent words on a graceful page, he could feel strength, individualism, and truth in the purest sense. Qualities he needed to acquire in much greater depth. It made him realize how far he was from becoming a relevant writer.

He also realized something else. David already possessed those attributes with the same conviction as Hemingway and Einstein. It was an epiphany that shook him into self-doubt. He knew he had certain advantages David would never come close to attaining, and yet, behind David's shy exterior, he possessed steely resolve, quiet individualism, and lived a life that was truth personified. How could this have happen? Marco was angry and jealous. His Upper East Side pedigree was supposed to have guaranteed him those qualities. The truth was staring at him from all directions, but he just couldn't see.

Twenty minutes later they came to the end of the trail, about a quarter mile from the Lake Michigan shoreline. They parked their machines on a bluff and took a much needed break. They pulled off their helmets and kissed. "Are you having fun?" David asked.

"This is an unbelievable experience. I can't even put it into words, but thank you for taking me out here."

"You're welcome." David pulled up his seat and took out his thermos. "There's nothing better than hot chocolate and a view of Lake Michigan in the winter."

"As I said last night, you are so lucky to be living in a place like this."

"I know. Sometimes I pinch myself because it all seems like a dream. You know, I haven't traveled much, but I really can't picture any place better than this, although New York City is a close second."

"New York is definitely unique. It's an artist's paradise. It's a microcosm of human civilization, beauty and ugliness in all its glory. But it is where people like us need to live in order to realize our goals. But when I look around at all of this, I feel something completely different. A writer could really get to know himself and create without the distractions and posturing of city life." Marco took a couple of sips of his hot chocolate and continued. "I love New York but hate all of the posers who just want to suck the life out of you and then move on to the next victim. To be honest, I'm a participant at times because that's just the way it is. I guess I'm just weak. I know I sound jaded or spoiled or whatever, but New York will eat you alive if you aren't careful."

"I believe you. But I also believe you are strong enough to walk away from the bad stuff if you really want to. I hate the thought of having to leave all of this behind, but I want to be a physicist and I can't become one here. I'm really scared about moving to New York, but it's what I need to do. So I have to be brave."

"David, you have nothing to worry about. I know you'll be able to handle it. Hey, maybe we could look out for each other..um, you know, help each other stay focused in the fall."

"I think that is a great idea." And then without any fear whatsoever, David kissed Marco to seal the deal.

As they cruised down Lakeview Trail into Harbor Springs, a disquieting sense of guilt began to overwhelm David. His heart was being torn to shreds because he was in love with Tyler and Marco. Why did it have to happen? He felt ashamed. He felt like he was cheating on both of them even though he was boyfriends with neither.

When they entered Harbor Springs, David decided to take Marco past an affluent residential area where three story Victorian mansions lined the dormant landscape like patriarchal relics, cold, empty, hoping that the coming spring would give them new life once again. As Marco rode past he saw his own privileged life staring back at him, the surface beauty, the intimidating status, the self-absorbed emptiness. He sped up until he was side by side with David, ignoring those three story empty shells. He couldn't get out of there fast enough. A couple minutes later they parked their snow machines at Mary's Diner and had lunch.

Marco sipped his coffee, trying to shake the chill from of his body. "This is definitely an affluent little town. It reminds me of several exclusive Long Island resort towns."

"You're right. A lot of wealthy people from Chicago have summer homes here. Without them Harbor Springs would pretty much be a ghost town. Chicago money is the life blood of our economy. It works pretty well because most of those people just want to blend in and enjoy the area. That's how I met Melissa. Her father is a corporate lawyer in Chicago and loves it up here, so he built an awesome vacation home. I know you're going to like her. She's the nicest person I know other than Tyler." Just the sound of Tyler's name made Marco jealous. He needed to figure out a strategy against this potential adversary. "So, tell me more about Tyler."

David's adorable smile appeared in an instant, and that's when Marco knew.

"He's athletic, smart, funny, honest, and the best friend I've ever had. He knows me better than anyone. He stood by me after I came out in middle school. He's always been there for me, and I've tried to be there for him. He never lets on, but I know he protects me from certain people at school who would love to hurt me if they ever got the chance. I think of him as my guardian angel." Marco did his best to sound upbeat. "Tyler sounds like the perfect friend. You two are fortunate to have each other."

"I know. I don't know what would have happened to me if we hadn't met." The guilt resurfaced with a vengeance as soon as David said those words.

All of a sudden Marco's phone buzzed. It was a text from Zander. "The pic you sent of yourself sitting on that snow thing in that god awful outfit makes you look like a fucking hillbilly. I'm going to start calling you Jethro from now on..lol And what's with all the fucking snow. I'm sitting on the beach in the Cayman Islands getting the perfect tan and drinking a margarita smoothie, something you should be doing with me right now." A selfie of Zander holding his drink against the backdrop of a turquoise shoreline was attached to the text. Then another message popped up.

"The guys are so fucking hot down here. I'm getting laid every night. You would be too."

Marco messaged back. "Fuck you. You're an asshole." He put his phone away only to have it buzz again. Curiosity got the best of him, so he read the text. "Sorry. I'm just fucking with you. David is hot ;-) Now I understand. Later

"Who was that?"

"Zander."

"I can't wait to meet him and the rest of your friends."

"They are an interesting group to say the least."

After lunch they walked to the harbor and entered an area on the docks where a long row of rustic shanties sat side by side like time capsules of the past. They looked sad and near death, so Marco was surprised to find out they were specialty stores that sold all sorts of things. Souvenirs, smoked fish, books, ice cream, and artwork by local artists from the area. David took Marco to the The Harbor Bay Book Store, his favorite shanty. It was the last one on the dock and had the best view. His neighbor, Mrs. Tariel owned it with her husband. It was his favorite place to read during the summer.

They walked in and found her standing in front of her easel painting away. She was one of the well-known local artists. She looked up. "David, I'm so happy to see you. Merry Christmas." She put her brushes down and gave him a hug.

"Merry Christmas Mrs. Tariel. I'd like you to meet my friend Marco Valerio. He's visiting from New York."

"Marco, it is so nice to meet you."

"It is nice to meet you. You have a wonderful store. I love the rustic ambience, and the location."

"Thank you. I've tried to make it feel homey and inviting. David, why don't you show Marco around while I make us some coffee."

"Great idea, thanks." They went from section to section until they got to the section that was inspired by David. "Mrs. Tariel surprised me with this a couple of years ago."

Marco smiled. "Very cool." She had assembled an array of LGBTQ fiction, non-fiction, and informational books for teenagers who were gay, transgender, or questioning. They were surrounded by books on mathematics, physics, and astronomy. "It is quiet back here, so anyone who is gay or questioning can check things out without everyone staring at them. We are trying to change attitudes as much as we can."

"I didn't know you were a rebel. Good for you."

David smiled and grabbed Marco's hand. "Come with me." They headed out the back door to the freshly shoveled patio. "This view is heaven."

"Yeah. It's my favorite place to read. During the peak of the summer tourist season I help Mrs. Tariel out. It has been the perfect summer job for me."

"I'm sure it has."

"The funny thing is, I don't even care about the money. I would work for free if she'd let me, because she was the first adult to support me after I came out. Her sister Karen is a lesbian, and her best friends, Todd and Brock are gay. They live in Chicago and have been partners since college."

"Very cool. Have you ever met them?"

"Yes. They vacation here every summer. I was in eighth grade when I first met them. They spoke at a school assembly along with Mrs. Tariel, a psychologist, and the president of the Michigan chapter of GLSEN after some guys beat me up for being gay."

Marco gave David a pained look. "I'm sorry. I didn't know."

"Yeah, it was a bad time, but I think some people learned from it."

Marco hugged David and kissed his forehead. "If you don't mind talking about it, I'd like to know what happened. I'll understand if you don't want to, but I think it would help me to get to know you better."

David leaned against the railing trying to decide. "I don't mind talking about it." He took a deep breath. "So, after I came out, all of my friends, with the exception of Tyler and Melissa, disowned me. It didn't take long before they started to bully me by calling me a queer, a cocksucker, and all the other typical expletives associated with being gay. When that was no longer entertaining enough, four of my ex friends started randomly punching me. They punched my arms, chest, and back really hard, and shoved me against the lockers and walls every chance they got. They attacked me whenever Tyler or the teachers weren't around.

After a month of that things seemed to settle down, so I thought they were finally getting over it. But I was so wrong. One day they jumped me when I was coming out of my math class. They dragged me to an empty classroom and put duct tape over my mouth, duct taped my hands behind my back and duct taped my ankles together, then proceeded to beat the shit out of me. I thought I was going to die because they went at me like animals. This one guy, Jason, who I had known my whole life, held me up while the other three punched and kicked me repeatedly. The last thing I remember before I blacked out was hearing someone yell, 'You die now you fuckin queer.' I was in a coma for nine days. The police told my parents that I was lucky a couple of girls just happened to look into the classroom. They screamed when they saw my body face down on the floor covered in blood. One of the girls ran to get help and the other one called 911. My doctors said that I would have died if she hadn't called because I had gone into cardiac arrest. They used the defibrillator and had to give me three jolts to bring me back. After I regained consciousness I told the police who had beat me, and they were arrested. Of course they denied it, but the DNA tests did the trick. The trial was statewide news and even made its way to the national news as part of a piece on the rise of gay hate crimes."

David stopped at that point and took a deep breath. Marco stood there doing everything he could to keep from crying. "Hey, don't feel sad. I survived and I'm ok now." Marco wiped his face with his sleeve. "I don't know what to say. I can't believe anyone would want to hurt you."

"Yeah. It made me a stronger person. And it made me appreciate how fragile and temporary everything is. It also brought my dad back to me."

"What? I don't understand."

"When I came out to my parents, my dad had a hard time accepting it. Our relationship was really strained, basically nonexistent from that point on, that is until I awoke from the coma. I'll never forget it as long as I live. Tyler was sitting next to my bed when I started regaining consciousness. I tried to let him know that I knew he was there by moving my fingers. When he finally noticed, he put his hand in mine and started crying and telling me how much he loved me. Then he yelled for my parents and that was all I remembered. I blacked out for another two days. When I woke up the second time my dad was sitting next me rubbing my arm and staring at the wall. He looked lost. He didn't realize I was awake so I moved my hand and put it on top of his. He turned and looked at me like he was seeing a ghost, or a second chance. He put his hand in mine and started crying uncontrollably, asking for my forgiveness over and over. He told me he was sorry and loved me more than anything. The pain and the hate my friends inflicted on me was worth it because my dad loved me again."

Marco's body shook slightly, and it wasn't from the cold. He tried to find the right words. "You and your dad are lucky. Second chances are rare in this world."

"We are lucky."

"So, what happened to them? How many years did they get? I hope those mother fuckers got life."

"Because of their age and having no prior offenses, the charges against them were plea-bargained down to a hate crime assault. They spent two years in a juvenile facility downstate. As far as I know they have to see a psychiatrist a few times a week and do community service until they turn eighteen. Two of them have already turned eighteen, and the other two will be eighteen in March and May. Fortunately, all four families moved away from here, so I haven't had to worry about them."

"David, I…." Marco was lost for words.

"Yeah, it was a pretty bad time, but I'm still here, and I'm happy. I just kind of look at everything as a gift now. That includes meeting you." David smiled, and then put his hand in Marco's.

$$\Sigma$$

It was 7pm when they headed over to Melissa's. There was a light snow falling just as the weatherman had predicted, so David wasn't too disappointed about not being able to stargaze. It was supposed to clear up over the next couple of days, so he was hopeful about taking Marco to his special place.

David seemed relaxed on the surface as he drove and chatted with Marco about school and friends. But on the inside he was a nervous wreck trying to figure out his dilemma. He was in love with Tyler, and had fallen in love with Marco. He assumed they weren't in love with him, but if by some small chance they were, he honestly didn't know how he could choose one over the other.

Being logical and keeping his emotions in check were proving to be an impossible task because Marco was sitting next to him being charming as ever, and Tyler was a few miles away waiting for them to arrive. David felt like he was betraying his best friend, and leading Marco on. He started having second thoughts about the whole evening, especially when he visualized the three of them in the same room together. He wanted to turn around and go home, but it was too late to be a coward.

David had talked to Melissa about his feelings a few days prior to Marco's arrival. He explained what she already knew. She gave her typical straightforward advice.

"The first thing you need to do is be honest with yourself. What are you looking for in a guy? Make a list of qualities you would want a boyfriend to have. Once you've figured that out, do Tyler and Marco possess any of those qualities? If they do, don't wait around for them. You need to talk to the one who is the one and make your feelings known. Ask him to be your boyfriend. If he says yes, then you need to let the other one know in case they have feelings for you. It isn't an easy thing to do. Personally, I think both of them like you, but they're afraid to say it, just like you are."

"Why is this so complicated? I never thought..." David looked at Melissa totally lost.

"Welcome to the wonderful world of dating."

"Thanks a lot. Multivariate Calc is ten times easier compared to this."

Melissa smiled, and then went for the jugular. "I know it's Tyler. You're in love with him. You need to tell him." Those words were shots to his heart, hitting him with blunt force. In a barely audible voice David said, "I don't want to pressure him. I don't want him to panic like he did the last time."

"David, you need to tell him that you're in love with him and that you want him to be your boyfriend. You can't wait around any longer, especially with Marco in the picture."

"That's what I hate about this whole situation. I pressure Tyler, and if he isn't ready, then I settle for Marco. Is that fair to Marco?"

"Yes it is. It's ok to like more than one guy. I know you like Marco a lot, but you and Tyler have something unique, and you have to know how he feels about you. If he doesn't feel the same way, then you can move on without having a guilty conscience."

"You're right as usual."

"It's not about me being right, it's about your happiness. I think you are lucky to have two guys in your life that you like. I think Marco would love to be your boyfriend, and I know

Tyler is scared and confused, and you're protecting him, but you need to talk about it."

David and Marco pulled into the last space in the driveway and were welcomed by a spectacular array of Christmas lights highlighting the sleek facade of the house. David was surprised to see so many cars already there. Marco's eyes were transfixed as they walked up the driveway. "This home is outrageous. It screams individualism. I love it."

"Yeah. And look at that view of the harbor. It's incredible."

They got halfway up the walkway leading to the front entry when Marco stopped and started taking pictures. "Let's take a selfie with the house as a backdrop." David turned and stood next to him and posed. After they took a few cute ones they started making funny faces and fake gang signs while Marco clicked away. Unaware they were being observed, Melissa stood at the entry doors watching David have the time of his life. It made her smile to see him so happy. She opened the storm door and asked in her best motherly voice, "Are you children ready to come in out of the cold yet?" They both turned around quickly, like they had been caught doing something terrible. David grinned, "Yes mommy. Will you make Marco and me some hot coco?" Marco gave Melissa a nervous grin as they walked towards her. David's heart started beating faster and faster with each step. "Melissa, I'd like you to meet Marco."

"Hi Marco, it's nice to finally meet you," she said, in a somewhat guarded tone. She could see how much David liked this guy, so she decided to be as fair as possible in her assessment.

"Melissa, it is so nice to meet you," Marco said, not knowing if he should shake her hand or give her a hug. He did neither because she abruptly turned and gave David a hug and kiss instead. He knew he had been dissed, but pretended not to notice. "Melissa, your home is amazing. I love the Frank Lloyd Wright influences."

"Thank you. This house is my father's pride and joy." Marco walked from the foyer into the living room to take it all in. David followed, and then Melissa. She discreetly checked Marco out, calculating his Neiman Marcus Bomber Jacket was in the four to five thousand dollar range, and his Gucci high tops were at least eight hundred dollars. Everything else he was wearing screamed New York fashion runway. Marco knew he was being scrutinized. It was what he had expected.

David didn't have a clue about the chess game Melissa and Marco were playing through body language and conversation. Stalemate was on the horizon, so Melissa changed tactics. "Why don't we head to the great room, everyone has been waiting for you guys to show up."

When they walked in, everyone stopped what they were doing and stared at Marco. Like it was preordained, his presence mesmerized every person in the room. He would have them eating from his hand in mere seconds. He smiled his confident smile while he quickly scanned the guys, trying to figure out which one was Tyler. In an instant he had locked eyes with his competition.

David gave everyone a nervous smile, "I'd like you to meet my friend Marco Valerio."

Everyone took turns introducing themselves and making small talk. David watched the looks on Emma, Kathy, and Aubree's faces as they checked Marco out from head to toe. Brad, Mike, Kevin, and Lucas introduced themselves next.

Tyler stood a few feet away watching Marco charm everyone, David included. Just the thought of having to shake that guy's hand made him want to puke. He wasn't ready for this at all, this nightmare he had created, but decided to put on his best game face when he was finally introduced. "Tyler, I-I'd like you t-to meet Marco," David said, stuttering like crazy. Tyler and Marco stared each other down with feigned smiles as they shook hands. David wanted to cry.

Tyler spoke first. "Welcome to the wilderness Marco, I hope you've been having fun."

Their eyes stayed locked on each other like two demigods ready to battle it out for the golden haired treasure. "I definitely have been. David has been the perfect host," Marco said, in a measured neutral tone. He continued, "David has told me a lot about you, how close you guys are and everything. It's an honor to hang out with you." He hoped to disarm Tyler with those words.

Tyler had a strategy of his own. "I hope we can get to know each other better. Any friend of David's is a friend of mine." He turned to David and gave him a hug. "I'm glad you guys could make it tonight."

"Me too." David said, feeling like his whole body was coming apart at the seams. He took a deep breath so he could calm down. "Thanks again for the awesome Christmas present. You shouldn't have spent so much money."

"I know how much you love Rush, and I wanted to make sure that you had all of their remastered CDs before heading to New York."

"That is so sweet of you." And then those other words slipped out. "I love you so much."

"I love you too." Tyler said, without hesitating. He gave David another hug.

Marco look away to give them some privacy, and because he didn't want that image floating around in his head for even a second.

All of a sudden a pillow came flying out of nowhere and hit Tyler in the back of the head.

"Get your ass over here and help us set the room up," Brad said, standing next to Lucas like a typical smart ass kid who was trying to pick a fight. "Excuse me while I go help those two morons," Tyler said. He threw the pillow back and helped them set everything up.

Melissa's parents made a brief appearance. "Merry Christmas David."

"Merry Christmas Mr. and Mrs. Nolan. I would like you to meet my friend Marco Valerio."

"Merry Christmas Marco. It is nice to meet you."

Marco shook their hands. "It is nice to meet the both of you. I think your home is amazing. It is a living breathing piece of art."

"That is so kind of you to say. Not many teenagers

appreciate this kind of architecture," Mr. Nolan said, beaming with pride. Melissa gently but strategically changed the conversation to the night's movie options. Her parents took the hint and excused themselves.

Strategies were flying all over that great room between Marco, Tyler, and Melissa. Everyone else partied away, oblivious to the Shakespearian tragedy that was slowly unfolding.

Melissa put on some music. The conversations became more animated and filled with laughter.

Tyler discreetly watched how affectionate Marco was being with David. How their bodies touched every now and then. The shy smiles they exchanged. How happy they seemed to be. That's when he knew he had made the biggest mistake of his life. He had squandered so many opportunities to tell David that he was in love with him, and now it was too late. It was a secret he would keep forever so his best friend could be happy. He just hoped Marco understood how special David was and would treat him with the love and respect he deserved. He had to let Marco know this before the night was over.

Marco, on the other hand, knew Tyler was in love with David. His gaydar was working perfectly. He could see the tender way Tyler looked at David when he thought no one was watching. And the nervous stutters and shy gazes from David whenever Tyler was near him, said it all. Tyler was his competition. Marco needed to make some strategic moves in order to win David's heart.

Melissa decided to commandeer Marco into the kitchen

so they could talk. She wanted to see what he was all about. A few seconds later Brad came over and picked David up and slung him over his shoulder so they could have one of their epic pillow fights. Brad dumped him on the couch and started hitting him with a pillow. Mike and Lucas joined in but Tyler came to the rescue, grabbing a pillow and knocking both of them away. David got up, grabbed a pillow and it became two against three as they all laughed hysterically.

They finally stopped their nonsense and continued to set up viewing spots. They were short a couple of blankets and pillows, so Tyler and David went to get more from the lower level linen closet. It was one of the quietest walks they had ever taken. It was all being said without saying a word, but David didn't want it to rest there. He needed to let Tyler know that he was in love with him. Tyler started to open the closet door but David put his hand on it and held it closed. He looked Tyler in eyes. "I need to tell you something."

Tyler looked away, his heart breaking but trying to summon whatever strength he had left. He put on the performance of his life. "David, please...please don't say anything. Not now. Please"

"I have to," David said, as his eyes started to sting. "I'm in love with you. I always have been."

Tyler wanted to tell him the truth, but the other truth was still in the way. "I don't know what I am or what I feel or what I'm supposed to feel." David broke down. Tyler put his arms around him and rubbed his back. "Please don't cry. Please. I want you to be happy. You don't have to wait any longer."

A couple of seconds later Brad yelled, "Where in the hell did you guys go?"

"We'll be there in a second," Tyler yelled back. They both wiped their eyes and headed back upstairs without saying a word. Brad and the guys could see something had happened, but wisely left it alone. David did a quick beeline to the bathroom. Tyler handed the blankets and pillows to Brad and stared blankly into the fireplace.

After everyone had eaten and cleaned the kitchen, they headed back to the great room. Melissa pushed three buttons on the wall and made the theater system come to life. The movies chosen were *Elf* and *The Perks of Being a Wallflower*. It was a couples night once again so everyone cozied up on their blankets. David and Marco went the platonic route and sat next to each other, leaning against the couch. Marco wanted to hold David's hand but wisely decided not to go there. He could tell David's emotions were in a volatile state. The last thing he wanted to do was miscalculate.

Tyler was the odd one out and sat by himself near the fireplace. He did his best to pretend he was into *Elf*, but David and Marco sitting next to each other was driving him crazy. He wanted to get the hell out of there and go home.

As the movie played, Melissa discreetly watched David who was discreetly looking at Tyler every few seconds while Marco pretended not to notice. Ten minutes into the movie David couldn't take it any longer and finally crawled over to Tyler. "Will you come sit with me?"

"I'm fine right here. Please don't worry about me." David's

feelings were hurt, but he understood. Marco could see how hurt David was when he crawled back, so he did the honorable thing and crawled over to Tyler. "David needs you. Please." Without saying a word, Tyler followed Marco back and apologized to David.

Everyone enjoyed watching *Elf* for the umpteenth time. It was a Christmas tradition. The New York scenes became topics of interest for the girls. They asked Marco all sorts of questions about the city. He tried to explain what it was like living in Manhattan without letting on how privileged his life actually was.

Things settled down into reflective quiet when Melissa put on *Perks*. The scene where Patrick asks Charlie to keep Brad's sexuality a secret made Tyler realize how his own fears had made him lose David. He got up without saying a word and went to the bathroom to calm down. His hands were shaking as he put cold water on his face and looked in the mirror. Staring back at him was an image partially intact and fading fast.

Once composed, Tyler veered off to the kitchen on his way back to get something to drink. He poured himself a glass of orange juice and drank it while looking out the window at the falling snow. His eyes started to sting a little, making the outside Christmas lights blur. He was wiping his eyes when he heard a voice. "The snow looks beautiful." He turned around and saw Marco standing next to the island. "Sorry, I didn't hear you come in."

"I was wondering if I could get something to drink."

"Yeah, of course. Let me get it for you." He got a glass out of the cupboard and pressed it against the ice maker. Marco tried to find the right words while Tyler filled his glass with orange juice. "I hope my being here isn't too awkward." Tyler handed him the glass and then took a sip from his, trying to stay calm. "No, it's not awkward. I'm glad you guys are getting to know each other."

"I'll back off if you want me to. I sincerely mean that. I can see you and David have something special together and I don't want to harm that in any way." Tyler looked down at the counter desperately trying keep the truth from spilling out. "I appreciate your concern, but..." His voice became soft. "David is my best friend. All I ask is that you never hurt him. Can you promise me that?" Hearing those words and seeing the look on Tyler's face hit Marco hard. "I promise. I would never do anything to hurt David. Please believe me." Tyler hoped he was telling the truth. "We should probably get back." It turned out to be a long night for all three of them.

✂

With only one more day left before heading back to New York, David's parents decided to take them to Boyne Mountain for a day of skiing and snowboarding. David and Marco had the time of their lives. Both were excellent skiers, but only so so on snowboards. They had a blast trying to get down the hill in one piece. They also snuck as many kisses as they could whenever they were alone.

Everyone met back at the lodge later that afternoon so they could have dinner and relax before heading home. With a crystal clear night being promised from somewhere on high, David couldn't wait to take Marco to his special place.

Ω

Marco followed David up the steep incline on the freshly shoveled path that led to the top of his hill. David was surprised to see that the viewing area had been cleared off as well. He would thank his father later. After putting the telescope in place, he turned around to see the reaction on Marco's face. Marco didn't say a word as he took it all in. The deafening silence, the crescent moon casting shadows, the black silhouettes reaching toward the sky, and the white crunching cold, were poetically juxtaposed against the vastness of the multicolored Milky Way. It sent chills down Marco's spine. "David, this is…." His words disappeared. David smiled. "Welcome to my secret world."

"I feel like I just entered heaven."

"This is heaven. It's a place where you can think and dream and be yourself without the interference from the world below."

"I've never seen so many stars in my life."

"Yeah. Seeing the galaxy this way is magical." As soon as those words were spoken, a flurry of meteors began falling through earth's atmosphere over Lake Michigan.

"Look at that," Marco said, pointing at the sky.

"Let's pretend they're shooting stars and make a wish."

Marco gazed at David affectionately. "I've already received my wish."

"W-what did you wish for?" David asked, stuttering once again.

"To meet someone like you."

They looked at each other, their eyes saying everything that needed to be said. David put his hand in Marco's. "Thank you for saying that."

"It's the truth. I hope you believe me." David squeezed his hand. He knew it was now or never. "Marco, I really like you and…I…I was wondering….would you be my boyfriend?"

"I would be honored to be your boyfriend."

"Really?"

"Yes, really."

David let out a huge sigh of relief, smiled, and tried on the new words. "We're boyfriends. You and I are boyfriends. I like the sound of that."

Marco's heart soared. He looked up at the Milky Way and yelled, "I want the whole universe to know that David Emerson is my boyfriend." He put his arms around David not ever wanting to let go. Neither one said a word as the warmth of their bodies glowed while billions of stars shined down on them.

Marco pulled away just a little and put his hands on David's angelic face. Then he slowly leaned in until their lips met. It was their first kiss as boyfriends. A distant rumble echoed mysteriously across the entire sky. Neither one heard it at first, but as their kiss intensified, so did the thunderous rumble. David suddenly pulled away and looked toward the western horizon. "Did you hear that?"

"Hear what?" Marco asked. He put his arms around David and started kissing him again. The sound of thunder intensified tenfold as flashes of light exposed the distant horizon.

A shiver went down Marco's spine, making his whole body shake. He stopped kissing David and asked, "What's going on?"

"This is so cool. It's Thundersnow."

"What?"

"Thundersnow. A winter thunder storm." They stood there listening to the low menacing roar and watched the flashes of light approach from the west. David smiled. "This is so rare. I've only seen this once before. It happened the year I came out."

"It seems so surreal," Marco said, in an uncomfortable tone.

David held his hand. "Don't be afraid. I'll protect you." He kissed Marco as the wind kicked up and the thunder roared through the sky.

# CHAPTER 18

David gave his parents one last hug before boarding the plane for New York. Marco thanked them for their hospitality. "Mr. and Mrs. Emerson, I had a wonderful time. It was so generous of you to let me spend some time with David and your family. I promise to take good care of him."

"We are counting on it," David's father said as they shook hands.

After all of the goodbyes and hugs were done, they walked down the ramp of the jetway. David turned and gave his parents one last wave before disappearing from view. He tried to put that first separation from his family into context so he could calm his anxious feelings. He should have been excited about the trip, but something was gnawing at him. Something deep down bothered him. This trip was the prelude to everything he had ever wanted, and now that it was happening he couldn't understand his trepidation. He began to wonder if his dream should just stay a dream because he was scared stiff to leave his family and his friends.

"Hey, are you ok?" Marco asked as they entered the plane.

David came out of his thoughts. "Yeah, I'm fine."

"I hope you won't get angry with me, but I upgraded our seats to first class."

"Really? Are you kidding? You shouldn't spend your money like that." It made David feel inadequate that Marco was spending money on him when he couldn't return the favor.

"I didn't upgrade our seats to show off, I just want us to be comfortable, and to have a bit more privacy. It's my way of showing you some New York hospitality."

"Thank you. This is the first time I've ever flown first class."

A hot looking steward welcomed them aboard and personally escorted them to their seats, a whole six feet away. Marco smiled at the obvious flirting. The steward couldn't keep his eyes off David.

"So, are you excited to see New York again?"

"Yeah. It's all I've thought about since the interview. It's exciting even though I'm nervous about it." Marco put his hand in David's. "Why are you nervous? We are going to have a great time, I promise."

"I know. It's just…I'm nervous about leaving home and being on my own and meeting your parents and all of your friends."

"I know how you feel. The first time away from home is always the hardest because you're on your own and have to rely on your survival skills. The first time I traveled by myself was scary. I felt like I had been abandoned."

"How old were you?"

"Thirteen. My parents sent me to summer boarding school

in Windsor, England. I was homesick to the max. It felt like I was being punished. Then two guys from Switzerland started picking on me as soon as I got there. They made fun of my skin color and for being mixed race. They called me an Asian nigger and a slant-eyed poof. Then other guys started picking on me. And I got homesick on top of that. I finally got so fucking frustrated that I challenged those two guys to a fight in front of everyone. I was in my fourth year of martial arts training, so as soon as I got into my fighting stance they backed off and walked away. No one bullied me after that and I eventually became friends with some pretty cool people."

"You were really brave. I don't know what I would have done in that situation."

"I learned two valuable lessons that summer. You have to stand up for yourself. And being on your own is part of growing up. Whether you know it or not, your parents are slowly letting you go. They trust you and know you're going to be ok."

"You're right. It just feels strange."

"And please don't worry about my parents or my friends. They are going to love you."

Marco kissed him hoping it would have a calming effect.

Something else had been bothering David and he needed to let Marco know. "Don't take this wrong, but as you know, we come from very different situations and I'm afraid that I might not fit into your world. Do you know what I mean?"

"Yeah, I think so. Look, there is no difference between us at all. My parents are wealthy, not me. I do have a lot of privileges, but if you really think about it, you and I are on exactly the same page. We are both broke. And whether you know it or not, you're one of the richest people I know. Look where you live and how smart you are. You have a loving family and great friends. I'll take all of that over a large bank account any day."

David knew Marco was right, but he also knew their worlds were light years apart. He hoped they could find a way to make it work. "I hope your friends like me. I'm kind of shy around people I don't know."

"Please don't worry about anything. I love your shyness. It makes me want to hug you and never let go. And underneath that shy exterior is someone who knows exactly what he wants and isn't going to let anyone or anything get in the way. My friends will see that soon enough. Actually they already kind of know you."

"What do you mean?"

"They've checked you out on Facebook and I've been bragging about you. I know some of them will probably try to hit on you, so be prepared."

David started blushing. "You'll protect me, right?"

"Of course I will."

Fifteen minutes later David was hanging on for dear life as their jet raced down the runway, pushing them back in their seats as it rose majestically into the blue Michigan sky. David was heading to a world of wealth and privilege that only a few teenagers had ever experienced. Little did he know that he was in for one hell of a ride.

3

David was so excited to see the Statue of Liberty and the Freedom Tower as they flew around the lower tip of Manhattan. He had forgotten all about being homesick as he looked at that emerald skyline.

"It gives me goosbumps every time I see Manhattan," Marco said.

David kissed his cheek. "I've never seen anything like it. Just think, we get to go to college together down there." Marco moved closer so that his face brushed gently against David's.

"It's ours for the taking."

Φ Χ

They walked to the baggage claim and were met by Marco's chauffeur.

"I hope you had a pleasant trip."

"We did. Max, I would like you to meet David Emerson."

"I'm very happy to meet you Mr. Emerson."

"It is nice to meet you too. Please call me David," he said, feeling embarrassed.

They walked outside to where a black Cadillac Escalade limousine was parked.

"What about our luggage?" David asked.

"The porters are getting it," Marco said in a casual tone. David shook his head knowing he had now entered Marco's world.

Max opened the limo door. David thanked him and slid into the back where plush leather seats faced each other within the glow of mood lighting. Marco slid next to David and immediately kissed him. After they composed themselves Marco asked, "What do you think of all this?" David looked at his surroundings. "I'm completely overwhelmed."

Marco smiled. "So am I because you're here with me."

"Awe, I feel the same way about you." David leaned in and kissed Marco on the cheek.

"Would you like something to drink?"

"Sure." Marco got a couple of sodas out of the mini fridge. David took a few sips and tried to calm down. He discreetly adjusted himself because kissing Marco had gotten him all worked up. Marco tried to get him to relax. "I just want you to know that I'm not showing off with all of this. My father never lets me take a cab to the airport for safety reasons. You know how protective your parents are, right? Well, so are mine, and this is one way they protect me. Hopefully the limo thing doesn't bother you."

"I'd be lying if I didn't say that I'm intimidated, but I'm also amazed that real people live like this."

"Cool, I'm glad this isn't freaking you out. I want you to experience my world just like I did yours. We're both lucky to live where we live."

A few minutes later the porters brought their luggage and then they were off to the Upper East Side.

Cruising onto the island of Manhattan in a limousine was beyond David's wildest dreams.

He couldn't wait to tell Melissa all about it. He decided not to say anything to Tyler, fearing it might upset him. The guilt he felt about being in love with him and Marco made his insides ache even more after he made his choice. He gave Marco a kiss and asked, "Do you always ride around in this limo whenever you go out?"

"No. I only use it if I'm going somewhere special with friends or with my parents. Remember, this is my parents ride. I love walking and taking cabs. I never use the subway if I can help it because it's so dirty and overcrowded. We'll go on it so you can see for yourself."

"I love walking too. I think it's a great way to see the city."

"I can't wait to show you my hang out spots and take you shopping. Shopping during the Christmas holiday in New York is so much fun. The Christmas lights look fantastic, and 5th Avenue looks like heaven when it's all lit up," Marco said, grinning like a little kid.

"That sounds like fun."

David looked out of the side window at all of the beautiful apartment buildings along Park Avenue as they made their way to Marco's place. He had to keep pinching himself to make sure it wasn't all some sort of crazy dream that he was about to wake up from. A couple of minutes later they pulled up in front of a beautiful Art Deco building. The doorman walked up and opened the limo door for them. "Marco, it's good to see you. I hope you enjoyed your trip to Michigan," Maurice said.

"I had a wonderful time. I would like you to meet David Emerson."

"It is very nice to meet you sir," he said, shaking David's hand.

"It's nice to meet you."

"Marco, your parents arrived home about an hour ago."

"Great." He held David's hand and walked into the lobby.

"Well, this is where I live. What do you think?"

"It's unbelievable," David said, looking at all of the Christmas decorations and a beautifully decorated Christmas tree. Two ornate chandeliers lit up the lobby in a warm glow, and he loved the marble floor with its classic Art Deco inlay.

"I love the Art Deco period. It reminds me of old 1930s films. And just think, you get to live here." David loved everything about it.

"Yeah, I know I'm lucky. I love this place."

They took the elevator up to the 28th floor. "Please don't be nervous when you meet my parents. My mother is a little off the wall, but my father is a great guy."

"I'm looking forward to meeting them."

Marco took his keys out when they got to his apartment door. It was a masculine looking mahogany door with beautiful carvings. It was twice the size of a standard door.

"Wow, this door is awesome," David said, as his fingertips caressed the carvings engraved in the wood.

"I think it's pretty cool. My father brought it back from India a few years ago. He is really into Hinduism. A priest gave it to my father as a gift because he donated $100,000 dollars to their temple. A hundred grand is a lot of money here, but it's a fortune in India. It equates to a little over six million rupees."

"That's an amazing story."

"There's more. This door is thought to have special

religious significance. It has ties to one of Hindu religion's three major lords. It was supposedly touched by Vishnu. He is a very important lord who reincarnates himself into different forms to help the people on earth during times of crisis." David immediately took his hand away from the door. "I'm sorry I touched it."

"Don't worry, everyone touches it. My father thinks it keeps all of the bad vibes out. I don't believe in that stuff. I just think it looks cool."

David looked down the hall and noticed there was only one other door. He thought that was a little strange. "How many apartments are on this floor?" David asked.

"Just two. Ours and Mr. Jensen's. He's this eccentric art dealer."

Marco gave David one more kiss before opening the door. "Are you ready?"

"As ready as I'll ever be."

He opened the door to a world David never could have imagined.

"Well, this is where I live." David realized that he was now at the epicenter of wealth and privilege as he stood in the sleek spacious entrance hall.

"This is unbelievable."

Marco grinned. "Yeah, I like it." He led David to a large gathering room decorated in an elegant modern motif. It had a winding staircase off to the side leading to the upper level. David never realized that penthouses could have more than one floor. "I don't mean to be nosy, but how big is your house?"

"It's has eighteen rooms on two floors. My parents bought half of the 29th floor ten years ago and doubled the size. We also have an enclosed rooftop terrace. I'll show it to you later." Marco felt proud. He looked at David's face and knew he was spellbound. "I love the modern furnishings. It reminds me a little of Melissa's house. Your parents have excellent taste."

"Yeah, my mother does have a flair for visualizing how a room should look."

David walked over to a wall of floor to ceiling windows and couldn't believe the view. Park Avenue was just below, followed by Madison, 5th Avenue and Central Park. He could see a good section of the park and the Upper West Side.

"You are so lucky. What is it like to live here?"

"Well, you know how you feel about living in Harbor Springs, right? I have that same feeling living here. We both live in a little part of heaven."

"That's for sure."

"Marco, is that you?" he heard his father call from the library.

"Yeah, we're in the living room." A few seconds later Marco's parents walked in and gave him a hug. Then Marco introduced the cute blond guy standing next to him.

"Mother, father, I would like you to meet David Emerson."

"David, it is so nice to finally meet you," Marco's father said, shaking his hand and welcoming him to New York City.

"It is nice to meet you too sir," David shyly responded.

"You are an extremely good looking young man. Is your

blond hair natural?" Marco's mother asked, while shaking his hand and looking him over with a fine tooth comb.

David felt his face turn a few shades of red. "Yes, this is my natural color."

"Mother, I completely agree with you that David is very good looking," Marco said, smiling as he took David's hand in his. He gave his mother a look that said to tone it down.

"Why don't we sit down and get comfortable. Rosa will bring us some refreshments in a couple of minutes. Dinner will be ready in about an hour," his mother said.

"Marco, I'm excited to hear all about your trip," his father said.

"It was fantastic. David was the perfect host."

"I'm glad you had a nice time." Marco's father had a wistful look on his face as he looked at the two of them. "David, you live in a beautiful area of Michigan. I've been to Traverse City several times on business. All of the lakes and peninsulas are breathtaking. On one of my trips I drove up to Old Mission Harbor on the peninsula between the east and west bay. The views were spectacular." David relaxed a bit when he said that.

"It is beautiful on the peninsula. I'm lucky to live where I live."

"You won't believe what we did. David took me snowmobiling. We went on these awesome trails deep in the woods. It's one of the most beautiful places I've ever seen. At one point we came out of the woods at the top of this hill and Lake Michigan appeared right in front of us. The endless blue of the lake surrounded by snow covered forests made me feel like I was part of it."

"So you went snowmobiling. I've never been, but it sounds like it could be entertaining."

"We have to get a couple of snowmobiles and go riding," Marco suggested.

"Maybe we can plan that out for next year."

"Mr. and Mrs. Valerio? Maybe you could make a trip to Michigan next year with Marco and we could all go riding. We have some of the best trails and plenty of snow," David suggested, hoping he wasn't being too forward.

"That sounds splendid. We just might have to take you up on that offer," Marco's father said, truly excited by the idea. Marco's mother got this look like she was getting indigestion. "I think that might be something you boys could do without me."

"Mother, you need to lighten up and try something new for a change," Marco said, giving her the look.

David sensed her apprehension. "Mrs. Valerio, even though I live in the country, there are plenty of other things to do besides snowmobiling. Harbor Springs and Charlevoix are very nice tourist towns with great shopping and excellent restaurants. Many people from Chicago have lake homes where I live. Marco even told me that it reminds him of Long Island."

"That sounds more like my style dear," she said, trying to be polite.

Rosa finally came in with the appetizers, which alleviated a little of the tension Marco's mother had caused. She set the tray on a serving table next to the bar and then gave Marco a slight hug on his shoulder. "It's good to have you home. Did you have fun?"

"I had a great time. Rosa, I would like you to meet David Emerson."

"Hi David." She gave Marco a discreet look to let him know that she approved of the cute boy sitting next to him.

Marco's father was curious about David. "Marco tells me that you want to be a Theoretical Physicist."

"That's right sir. I love math and science and I'm excited about attending Columbia in the fall."

Marco's mother chimed in at that point, continuing with her rude observations. "It must be a burden for your parents to send you to such an expensive university."

That observation and her unflattering tone pissed Marco off. He couldn't believe she would say something so snobby. "Mother, David received the Gates Millennium Scholarship. Let me educate you on just what that is. It is one of the most prestigious scholarships in the United States. Only one thousand students receive it in a given year. David is one of the recipients. It pays for every aspect of his college through graduate school. And oh, one other thing. David scored a perfect 2400 on his SAT."

David felt self-conscious as he looked down at the floor.

"Your parents must be very proud of you," Marco's father said.

David looked up. "Yes they are. I'm fortunate to have gotten the scholarship. My parents could never have afforded to send me to Columbia without it. The university also offered me a paid internship to work in the physics department doing research. That will give me some additional spending money, and it will also help pay for trips back home during the holidays. It is important to me that I do this all on my own," David said, letting Marco's mother know that he was not ashamed of his middle class upbringing.

At that point Marco decided to get some distance from her, so he told them that he was going to take David on a tour and then hang out in his bedroom until dinner was ready.

"I'm sorry my mother was being such an asshole," Marco whispered, as they went from room to room.

"Don't worry about it, I understand," David said, even though he didn't. He was used to people hating him because he was gay, but he had never met anyone who hated him because he was middle-class. He started thinking that Melissa was right about being in over his head.

"I just want you to know that shit she pulled was not about you at all, it was about me. She can't stand the thought of me making my own decisions. She refuses to let go, so she constantly tries to shred my life to pieces. She knows I like you so she has to rip you apart to let me know that I'm fucked up."

"That is sad," David said, trying to comprehend why a mother would do that to her own son.

They took a private stairway to the second floor and finally made it to Marco's bedroom. David couldn't believe what he saw. It was everything a guy could ever want.

"This is unreal?" David said, totally in awe as he looked around.

"This is my little sanctuary," Marco said, beaming with pride.

"I don't want to sound nosy, but how big is your bedroom?"

"Counting the dressing room and on-suite, I think it's around fourteen-hundred square feet."

"I've never seen a bedroom like this. I mean, you have a living room and an office in here."

"Cool, isn't it? It's like having my own apartment. All I need is a separate entrance and I'd totally have it made."

They walked over to Marco's office area so he could show David where he did most of his writing. David loved the modern furnishings and atmosphere. It fit Marco's personality to a tee. "This must be an inspiring place to write. I can't believe the view you have from here."

"Yeah, I love to look down on Park Avenue and watch the city in motion. I get a lot of ideas for stories when I look out there and let my mind wander. Come on, let me show you the rest of the place." They made their way to Marco's dressing room. It was at least three times as big as David's bedroom. It had special lighting, custom made cabinets, racks and racks of clothes, and a whole separate section for Marco's numerous pairs of shoes. One wall even had floor to ceiling mirrors. David looked at the thousands of dollars in clothes and shoes and didn't know what to say. His closet was only five feet wide by three feet deep. He owned four pairs of jeans, two pairs of dress slacks, fifteen shirts and sweaters, and five pairs of converse sneakers. Marco recognized the look. "I know it looks like I'm a spoiled brat, and in reality, I probably am. Shopping is one of my weaknesses. Whenever I'm feeling down, shopping picks me up. I know all of this is over the top. I'm sorry."

"You have nothing to be sorry for. This is your life and I would never judge it or judge you for a minute. I think we just have to get used to each other's lifestyles. This relationship is a new thing for both of us."

"Thanks for understanding." Marco put his arms around David and kissed him. They spent the next hour listening to music and talking. Marco even got some of his writing out so David could read it. He was impressed by the style and depth. "Marco, this is amazing."

"Thanks. I'm slowly developing a style that feels right."

David sat quietly reading a few more pages while Marco nervously watched. Marco's phone started buzzing, startling both of them. It was Rosa texting to let them know that dinner was ready. Then, as he was putting his phone in his pocket, Zander sent a text. "Why don't you and your li'll ole country boy drop by. I'm having people over tonight and they all want to meet the guy who has stolen you away."

Marco texted back, "Fuck off. We'll be over around eight, and you better be nice or you'll have to deal with me."

♯ ∽

To Marco's surprise his mother was very gracious during dinner. She even complimented David several times and truly seemed to enjoy hearing about his growing up in Northern Michigan.

Then things turned slightly awkward again when she asked a personal question. "David, I do not wish to pry, but maybe you can answer a question for me. What is it like growing up as a gay teenager in a conservative part of the country?"

"Well, it's not like it is in New York. Marco is fortunate to live in a place that pretty much accepts the gay community. To tell you the truth, I had a rough time when I first came out. My mom was ok with it, but my dad had a hard time, which was understandable. Most of the people who I thought were my friends started bullying me after I came out. I only had two friends who stood by me. Six months after I came out four guys jumped me at school and hurt me pretty bad. I was in a coma for a few days and the doctors didn't think I was going to make it. But I did, and as I lay in that hospital bed, I vowed that I would never be ashamed of being gay."

Marco's parents looked semi-shocked by what David had just told them. "I am sorry that you had to experience that kind of hatred," Marco's mother said, now feeling ashamed of her prior comments.

"You are a brave young man," Marco's father added, sympathetically.

"I would never want to go through that again, but I have to show everyone that I'm proud of who I am. Every once in a while someone will say nasty things, that I'm a perverted queer, or that I'm going to hell, but for the most part they leave me alone. Please don't feel sorry for me." David changed the subject at that point. "Thank you for inviting me to stay with you and Marco. This is a dream come true for me."

"We are happy that you could spend a few days with us," Marco's father said.

After dinner they went back to Marco's bedroom to get ready for a night with his friends. A half hour later they said their goodbyes and cabbed over to Zander's penthouse. Marco was excited to have everyone meet his new boyfriend. "I just want to warn you that Zander is a real piece of work. Don't let anything he says bother you, ok?" David gave him a weary smile. "Thanks for the warning."

"He can be a real asshole at times, but he is one of my best friends. My best friend is Claire. I can't wait to introduce you. She reminds me a lot of Melissa."

"She must be a great person then."

"Yeah, she is. Claire's been there for me since we were little kids. I think all of us gay boys need to have that one special female in our lives."

You're right. I love Melissa more than anything." David started feeling homesick all of a sudden.

Their cab finally pulled up to Zander's apartment building on Madison Avenue. David felt anxious as the doorman opened their cab door and escorted them into another beautifully decorated lobby. David felt like a celebrity holding Marco's hand and having the staff fawn all over them. It amazed him how no one thought twice about the gay thing. When the elevator doors opened this older woman walked out and commented on what a handsome couple they made. They thanked her, wished her a happy holiday and then stepped into the elevator. David smiled at how normal he felt being accepted as just a person instead of someone always having to wear the gay label and feeling bad about it.

As they rode the elevator to the twenty-third floor Marco asked, "Well, are you ready to meet my crazy friends?"

"I'm a little nervous, but yeah, I am. Please stay close to me though, ok?"

"Believe me, I will. I don't want anyone hitting on you."

Zander's housekeeper wished both of them Merry Christmas and pointed towards the noise. It went dead silent when they walked into the entertainment room hand in hand. David stayed calm even though a zillion pairs of eyes were on him. Marco broke the silence by wishing everyone a happy holiday. He gave David's hand a gentle squeeze, then turned and kissed him.

His friends seemed stunned by that kiss. Zander panicked at the thought of an emo bastard twink having his best friend under a spell. Marco's sudden affectionate side confirmed that David was a real threat in more ways than one.

"I'd like you to meet my boyfriend, David Emerson."

David smiled and said hi. The tension eased as everyone started talking again. One by one people began introducing themselves. The girls seemed nice for the most part, but the guys were on edge and aloof. David felt the best strategy was to get in good with the girls first. Claire was the last charming female to introduce herself. "David, I'm happy that we finally get to meet." She gave him a friendly hug and then kissed

Marco on the cheek. A few seconds later Zander walked over and gave Marco a hug, forcing David let go of Marco's hand. After they got through hugging, Zander turned and finally acknowledged David. "I'm Zander. It's nice to meet you."

"Hi. It's nice to meet you too." He gave David a forced smile and then focused on Marco. "I missed you. You should have partied with me in the islands. It was fucking hot." Marco gave him a vicious look, but that just made Zander faux smile even more.

"I'm sure you didn't miss me then. I had a great time in Michigan. It was the best vacation I've ever taken," Marco said, giving him a fuck you look of satisfaction.

There was an awkward silence at that point. Fortunately the rest of Marco's friends came over and introduced themselves. From that point on Zander started getting in his little digs.

He leaned against Marco as he checked David out. "Marco, your country boy is smokin hot. Now I know why you flew all the way to Canada to be with him." David was surprised by his comment, and the fact that Marco's other friends laughed. Marco immediately went to David's defense. "Yeah, I had to go to the other side of the earth to find a guy who is real, compassionate, and smart. He's nothing like New York guys, thank god."

"Hey, I'm only joking. David, please don't take anything I say seriously, ok?" Zander tried to smooth the situation. Claire sensed the tension building, so she took David by the hand and lead him to the couch so they could talk. Marco leaned in close to Zander and said, "Come with me." The rest of the guys followed. Marco was fuming by the time he closed the library doors. "You need to fucking cool it or we're leaving. Who in the fuck do you think you are?" he yelled, trying to hold back from decking him. "Hey, I'm sorry, ok? I promise I'll be good." Adam, Camilo, and Sean stood there grinning like they were in on some big secret.

"Are you really serious about this relationship?" Zander asked.

"Yeah I am. We officially became boyfriends a couple of days ago."

"Cool. Have you fucked him yet?" They all gave Marco the look, knowing how much he liked to talk about his sexual encounters.

"That is none of your business. Get your smut minds out of the gutter for once."

"I'll bet he's a great fuck. He has a cute little ass, and I bet he moans nice and soft for you."

"I'm going kick your ass if you don't stop."

"Come on, I'm just fucking with you. I do have to admit he is one of the cutest twinks I've ever seen."

"Look, you don't have to believe this, but I've changed. I like David a lot. He's one of the nicest guys I've ever met. Give him a chance and you'll see."

Marco walked back to the great room to see how David was doing. Claire was sitting next to him trying to keep Tracy, Debra, Eve, and Becca from stripping him naked. Marco could see they were crushing on him big time. Eve moved over and made room for Marco. "Claire has been telling me all sorts of things about you," David told him.

"I hope she hasn't incriminated me in any way."

"I would never do that." Claire said, with a sly grin.

"She was telling me how long you guys have known each other, and that you're best friends."

"Yeah, Claire and I have a special bond."

Zander and the guys finally came back and joined in on the conversation. "So David, tell us all about Michigan."

"Sure. I live in Harbor Springs. It's in the northern part of the state near Lake Michigan. It's pretty remote but I've enjoyed growing up there."

"Are you a farmer? You know, do you live on a farm?" Zander asked, in a serious tone.

Marco shot daggers at him and the rest of the guys. David knew what was going on.

"No, but there are quite a few farms in the area. I live a few miles from Harbor Springs on fifteen acres. My dad and my uncles built our house."

Claire strategically took over the conversation at that point. "I think you and Marco make a great couple. Some people refuse to let go of the past." Then she said something that shocked everyone. "Marco told me that you had a perfect score on your SAT."

"So, you're the quiet genius type," Zander said, unable to hide the jealous glare.

David didn't know what to say. He wanted that conversation to end. "I'm not a genius. I just do well on things like that."

Marco was getting the last laugh because his friends couldn't comprehend what his boyfriend was all about. David changed the topic. "Zander, your home is amazing."

"Thanks."

"Do you like living in New York?"

Zander gave David a dirty grin. "I love it to death. I wouldn't want to live anywhere else. It's the epicenter of everything worthwhile. There is always something going on, and so many cute guys for the taking."

Adam chimed in at that point. "David, you need to know that Zander is a total slut." Everyone laughed. Zander gave Adam the finger. "You would be a slut too if you could ever get any women." In unison, Marco and Claire told them to shut the fuck up.

Everyone settled down and they spent the rest of the evening listening to music and talking about nothing in particular.

It was just after two in the morning when the party started breaking up. They were putting on their jackets in the entrance hall when Zander made his next move. "Do you guys want to go to a rave tomorrow night?" Everyone said yes except Marco. "I think we'll pass. David and I have other plans."

"Come on, you have to show him how we have fun." Zander turned to David and pleaded.

"Please try and talk your guy into going?"

"What's a rave?" David asked.

Zander started to explain but Claire interrupted him. "Raves happen at certain dance clubs around the city. There are famous DJs who spin their style of music as people dance and party. It's a lot of fun, but you have to be careful because things can get strange."

It didn't sound like fun to David, but he didn't want to spoil everyone else's fun. "Do you want to go? It sounds interesting."

"I'd love to go if you want to," Marco said.

David hesitated for a moment. "Well, you said you were going to show me the real New York, so I think it would be an interesting experience."

Zander got all excited because the trap was set. "Cool, we'll pick you guys up at midnight and head to the Pyramid Club. David, you are going to have the best time of your life."

And with that, everyone said their goodbyes.

David put his head on Marco's shoulder as soon as they got in the cab. "Your friends are nice."

"I'm glad you like them. I'm sorry that Zander was being a jerk. He's just jealous."

"I guess friends can get a little over protective sometimes."

ⵟ

Marco showed David to the guest suite. Everything was all laid out on the bed. Pajamas, a toiletry kit, a silk robe, and leather slippers. "Wow, I feel like royalty."

"Only the best for you. We want you to feel at home."

"Thanks." David yawned. Marco kissed him on the forehead. "Let's get you to bed before you fall asleep standing up." He gave Marco a sleepy smile. "I had a nice time tonight."

"Me too. If you need anything or get scared or something, text me and I'll sneak in and keep you company."

"Thanks, I just might do that." They kissed one more time and then Marco reluctantly made his way down the hall to his bedroom.

David got up after four and a half hours of restless sleep. He had fallen asleep as soon as his head hit the pillow, but woke up a couple of hour later thinking about Marco's friends. He wondered why some of them didn't like him. He tried to understand Zander's hostility. The only thing he could think of was that Zander probably had a secret crush on Marco. If that was the case he knew it would be a battle. He stopped feeling sorry for himself and decided not to let Zander get under his skin.

David spent the morning reading and working on a Fourier Transform. He was happy to be in his mathematical mindset. Rosa knocked on his door at eight-thirty. "I brought you some juice, coffee, and danish. You must be starving papi."

"Thank you. I am a little hungry."

"Did you have a nice time last night?"

"Yes I did. I enjoyed meeting Marco's friends."

"He was excited to have you meet them."

"What time does he usually wake up?"

"Around noon, but I'm going to wake him at ten."

"You don't have to do that. Let him sleep."

All of a sudden Marco peered around the door. "Are you two talking about me?"

"Of course we are," David said, with an infectious smile.

Rosa said good morning and kissed him on the cheek and then quietly left.

"Are you ready for a day of shopping Upper East Side style?"

"Sure, I didn't bring very much money, so I'll pretty much just be window shopping."

"No you won't. I'm treating you to the full experience. My father put an extra ten thousand on my card last night. He wants us to have a great time today."

"Marco, I know you and your father are trying to be nice, but I can't let you spend that kind of money on me."

"Yes you can. Remember, I'm showing you how I live just like you showed me how you live. Please let me do this, ok?"

David couldn't refuse his puppy dog look and finally relented.

They spent the entire afternoon going to Marco's favorite stores. They shopped at Salvatore Ferragano, Gucci, Luigi Borrelli, and Calvin Klein. Marco was in his element. He purchased a new leather jacket, five pairs of skinnys, and a half dozen new shirts. He made David try on some skinnys. This was a first for him. When he came out of the dressing room, Marco couldn't believe how thin he actually was. "God, you look extremely hot in those." Marco made him turn around so he could check him out at every angle. David felt self-conscious. "I don't think I'm cut out for these," he said, hoping Marco would understand.

"David, you look like a runway model." He leaned close and whispered, "You have a very cute ass."

"Thanks. S-so do you," David whispered back. Marco smiled. "Come on, let's get them so you can wear them to-night, ok?"

David knew he was going to lose this battle. "Ok." He was just about to go back to the dressing room when Marco asked him to wait. He grabbed two very stylish cardigan sweaters and two shirts he had found earlier.

"I think these will go nicely with your skinnys."

David was shocked that his new clothes cost over nine hundred dollars. He thanked Marco for being so generous.

They stopped at Gucci next and spent close to three thousand dollars in less than thirty minutes. Marco bought two new pairs of shoes for himself, and tried to do the same for David, but he wouldn't let him. He was finally able to talk David into some cool looking high tops. They were hand made with imported leather and even had arches built into them. David almost had a heart attack when he saw the seven hundred dollar price tag. He felt guilty about spending so much money, but he wanted to make Marco happy. They ended their afternoon of shopping and went to Marco's favorite Italian restaurant on 73rd Street. After a nice dinner they cabbed back to Marco's and relaxed.

⌘

It was just before midnight when Zander and Claire picked Marco and David up and headed to the East Village. Zander started using his charm as soon as they got into the limo.

"You guys look hot, especially you David."

"Stop hitting on my boyfriend," Marco playfully said.

Claire noticed too. "Both of you look very handsome."

David gave them a nervous smile. "You guys look nice too."

"Are you ready to party the night away?" Zander asked, as the limo pulled into traffic.

Marco was glowing. "Yeah, it's been a while since we've done this." He put his hand in David's and asked, "Are you ready for a night of dancing?"

"Yeah. It should be a lot of fun. But I have to warn you, I'm not a very good dancer."

"Don't worry. That's not the point. You'll see why when we get there."

A few minutes later things began to unravel. Claire put some Electro House Music on to get everyone in the mood. Marco and Zander started talking about some of the past raves they had been to and how much fun they were. David tried to listen but Claire wanted his complete attention. She was asking question after question trying to get to know him better. He smiled to himself because Melissa had done the same thing to Marco.

He was answering a question about growing up in the country when he noticed Zander pull a slim silver case out of his pocket. Zander opened it, smiling like he was opening up heaven.

"We have to do some Molly."

David saw a dozen little white pills scattered against the reflection. He turned to Marco wondering what was going on. Marco had the same look Zander had as he stared at the pills.

"David, have you ever taken Molly?"

"No. I've never even smoked weed. Sorry."

"Oh. no problem," Marco said, trying to reassure him. But Zander wouldn't give up.

"This is a low dose and only lasts a few hours. You don't have to be afraid. It's perfect for dancing because it makes you feel invincible. It's the perfect high. We've done it a thousand times. Marco, tell him." He gave Zander a look that could kill. "We don't need to take it tonight. David and I are going to party straight."

David was close to tears. He never thought for a second that Marco did drugs. He didn't want to ruin the evening, so he acquiesced. "You can take it if you want, but I'm not. I hope you understand."

"So you don't mind?"

"No."

Zander took a pill and swallowed it. Claire took one and swallowed it. Marco took one and looked at it. He put it back. "I have everything I need to feel invincible." He turned and kissed David.

The Escalade pulled up in front of the club a few minutes later. People dressed like runway models filled the sidewalk and blocked the entrance and smoked their cigarettes and posed with bored enticing smiles. David stayed close to Marco because the entire atmosphere felt bleak. It felt tragic.

Zander sent a text to see if any of their friends were inside yet. A couple of minutes later Adam and Tracy appeared at the entrance and motioned for them. They walked past the posers to the front of the line. Marco slipped the doorman a one hundred dollar bill as they walked in. They headed up a once opulent staircase to the second floor. David held on to Marco like his life depended on it. Music was blaring, the smell of weed covered the walls, the hypnotic droning bass vibrated through his body. Marco leaned in. "This is going to get a little crazy, so stay close, ok?"

"Don't worry, I will."

The flashing lights and the sea of hypnotized bodies made Marco, Zander, and Claire come alive as they entered the rave. David followed Marco as they walked the perimeter trying to find their friends. They found them at the bar drinking. Marco lied. He told David that his friends didn't drink. And before he knew it Marco handed him one.

"What is it?"

"Vodka and cranberry juice."

"Thanks, but I don't drink."

"Oh. Ok, no problem." David gave it back.

"Do you mind if I have a couple?"

"No, I guess not."

"Cool." Marco kissed him and finished off his drink. David felt out of place, but at the same time knew that Marco was trying to show him a good time. The boyfriend thing was new and he didn't know how it worked yet, so he decided to let Marco be Marco. He felt he would know him much better by the end of the night.

David stood next to Marco as he continued drinking and talking with his friends. He would smile and nod whenever they looked his way, but couldn't hear what they were saying with the music blaring at a billion decibels. Eventually he began watching other people with a detached curiosity. Chaos Theory came to mind while David tried to figure out the rave's allure. He pictured himself being caught inside the Butterfly Effect or the Double Pendulum and figured it must be some kind of adrenalin rush. No future or past. Only the present moment. That had to be it.

Marco finished his second drink and was ready to party. "Will you dance with me?"

"I'd love to. Remember, I'm not very good."

"You will be in five minutes." They kissed and started toward the dance floor. And that's when Zander, Adam, and some other guy walked up and blocked their way. All of Marco's friends looked like they had just seen a ghost. Marco froze when the guy walked right up and gave him a hug.

"It's been awhile," he said.

"Yeah, it has," Marco said, backing away.

Zander was all smiles as he put his arm around David and made the introduction.

"I'd like you to meet Patrick. He's one of my best friends."

"It's nice to meet you," David said as they shook hands.

"It's nice to meet you too. I heard about you and Marco. Congratulations."

"Thanks."

Patrick smiled as he looked David over. He gave Marco

an approving nod and then grabbed Zander and headed to the dance floor. Marco kissed David on the cheek and followed.

The night had now begun.

The music and lights began working their seductive magic as they danced their first dance. Marco showed David a few moves in a playful way. David began to forget about the madness around him and started having a good time. Marco was trying to be a caring boyfriend, but the thought of fucking David started creeping into his mind. He started dancing extra sexy and decided to see how far he could go. He slid his hands up and down the side of David's slender body as they moved to the music. David didn't seem to mind so Marco moved his hands around to his cute little ass and caressed it. David gave him a disapproving grin and moved his hands away.

Forty minutes later, exhausted and thirsty, they headed to the bar to get something to drink. Marco did the honorable thing and ordered cokes for both of them, and then apologized. "I'm sorry I got carried away out there."

"You don't have to apologize. It's just that I want to take things slow. I hope you understand."

"I understand completely and respect you for it."

"Thanks. I appreciate it."

"You are just too cute. May I have the honor of kissing you?" Marco asked.

"Yes you may."

Zander, Adam, and Patrick walked up just as they finished their kiss and ordered drinks.

"You guys looked great on the dance floor," Adam told

them. Zander and Patrick, who were holding hands, agreed. Then Zander leaned close to Marco and said something that made him nod in the affirmative. A minute later they got their drinks and said they were going to cruise around. "Your friends are really nice," David said, finally feeling like they were accepting him.

"They like you a lot. Are you having fun?"

"Yeah I am."

"Cool. Hey, I have to hit the bathroom. I'll be back in a few, ok."

"Sure, no problem." Marco walked away and disappeared into the crowd. Fifteen minutes went by and he still hadn't come back. David started to get worried. Claire noticed him standing at the bar by himself so she went over to say hi. "Someone as cute as you shouldn't be standing by themselves. Where is Marco?" she asked, slurring her words. David knew she was flying high with those words, and her glazed look. "He went to the bathroom, but that was fifteen minutes ago. I'm starting to get worried."

"Don't worry, the bathrooms get really crowded and it takes a while." She gave him an amorous smile and took him by the hand to where Tracy, Becca, and Debra were partying.

Another twenty minutes went by and Marco still hadn't come back. Total panic mode set in as David continued scanning the crowd. At the same time he was looking for his lost boyfriend, he was also trying to contain Claire. She kept hitting on him. "You're just the cutest thing. I wish you were straight so we could fuck. We should fuck anyway. Will you fuck me Davy? We'll keep it a secret." She leaned against his body and tried to kiss him. David knew the Molly had taken over so he tried to calm her down. He decided to keep an eye on her because he was afraid that someone would take advantage of the situation. The night was turning into one gigantic nightmare.

Claire decided that she wanted to dance. She kissed David on the cheek and led him to the dance floor. He kept looking for a Marco as they danced, but the lights made it difficult to see anything. Then another layer of craziness started happening when Tracy, Becca, and Debra joined them. He had four crazy girls trying to feel him up at the same time.

Marco finally showed up along with Zander, Adam, and Patrick and everyone started dancing together. David was happy to see Marco but could tell something was wrong. He had that same euphoric smile and glassy-eyed look Claire had. Marco was high. David turned and started walking away, but Marco grabbed him by the arm and flung him against his chest. His hands began caressing David's ass. He felt violated and tried to move away. Marco wouldn't let go. "Stop it Marco. Please let me go."

He wasn't listening. The words slurred off his tongue. "You're so fucking hot. You drive me fucking crazy." That glazed look frightened David. He didn't have any experience dealing with someone who was high. He decided to play along, hoping whatever Marco was on would wear off soon. But Marco just got crazier and more amorous as they danced.

While trying desperately to contain Marco, he was

suddenly being fondled by someone else. It was Zander. "Don't touch me," David yelled as he backed away.

"I wanna dance with you," Zander said, his words slurring out of his sick smile. He started dancing with David at the same time Adam, Sean, and Patrick grabbed Marco to dance with them.

David wanted to get Marco off the dance floor but Zander wouldn't let him go. He started touching David inappropriately again, trying to keep him distracted. He grabbed Zander's hands and yelled, "Keep your hands off of me." Zander backed off. "I'm sorry man. It's just that you're fucking hot and I'm feeling pretty good." David turned away not knowing what do, and that's when saw how erotically Marco was dancing with Patrick and Adam. He finally walked off the dance floor hoping Marco would eventually come down. Zander smiled as he watched what was happening. Marco was oblivious. David stood off to the side by himself, watching and realizing that he had jumped into the boyfriend thing way too soon. If lying, getting high, and disappearing was part of having a boyfriend, then he wanted nothing to do with it.

And that's when he decided to leave. He didn't know where he was going to go, but he was going. He found Claire hanging all over some half-dressed guy. He told her, "I'm leaving."

"Why? Aren't you having fun? Where's Marco?"

"He's on the dance floor." David turned around to show her, and that's when he saw Marco and Patrick dancing like they were having sex. He felt sick to his stomach as he watched their hands slide up and down each other's sweaty bodies with their eyes locked on each other and lips only inches apart. Tears welled up in David's eyes as he continued to watch in horror. Marco had spun Patrick around and was grinding his crotch against Patrick's ass like he was fucking him.

With that image forever burned into his retinas, David turned and walked away. He made it out to the hall before Claire caught up and grabbed him by the arm. "Please let me go. I have to get out of here now."

"David, please don't leave. I know this looks bad, but…"

"Looks bad. Are you fucking kidding me? Look at him. He doesn't care about us. It's all about him." Claire tried to calm David down. "Let's go outside and talk. Please? Then if you still want to leave I'll get you a cab, ok?" David nodded as tears streamed down his face.

When they got outside the cool air hit him like a tidal wave of reality. He wiped his eyes with his sleeve and looked aimlessly into the night. "David, I'm sorry you had to see that."

"Claire, what exactly did I see in there? Please explain it to me."

She hesitated for a moment, but then decided to tell the truth. "Marco and Patrick used to be boyfriends. They broke up last year. I don't even know why Patrick showed up tonight because he's not part of our crowd."

David looked at her with so much hurt. "Does Marco still like him? Please be honest with me."

"I don't think so. We talk all the time and Patrick never

came up once. All he talks about is you. He told me that he loves you. I know he does. Please believe me."

"So why is he pretending to have sex with Patrick right now if he loves me?"

"Honestly, I don't have an answer. The only thing I can think of is that he took some Molly. He gets that way whenever he takes it. So do I."

They stood there for another minute or so before David decided what he was going to do. First, he sent Melissa a text. "You were right. I'm in way over my head with Marco." Then he went back inside to tell Marco that he was leaving. When he got to the dance floor he found Marco sex dancing with Patrick and his other friend Sean. They had their hands all over each other lost in their own little world. David was through crying at that point. He started walking towards Marco when Zander stepped in his way with a contented smile on his face. "Don't they look fucking hot together?" David didn't say a word. It became obvious to him that Zander had set the whole thing up. And when he thought it couldn't get any worse, it did. "I think you're so fucking hot." Zander told David, and then tried to kiss him. David pushed him away and glared. Then he grabbed him by the arm and let him have it.

"Why don't you like me? Am I that much of a threat to you that you would try to get Marco and his old boyfriend back together just so you could get me out of the picture?"

Zander smiled his sick little smile again, realizing David was as perceptive as he was smart. "You need to back off. Please do that for Marco. Or is this the kind of shit friends do to each other in New York?" David looked at his boyfriend, shook his head, and walked out instead of confronting him. He knew it wouldn't matter because Marco had forgotten all about him.

With his eyes stinging again, David walked outside and tried to get his bearings. This time a bunch of drunk and stoned people were out front smoking cigarettes and partying. He walked a few feet to the side so he could think. He was seven hundred miles from home and needed to stay strong so he could get back safely. His parents told him to call if anything went wrong, so that's what he did. While waiting for his parents to answer the phone, David saw Marco run out of the club and into the street where he almost got hit by a car. He was yelling "David, David, David, fuck, fuck, I'm such a fucking asshole," at the top of his lungs. Everyone stared at him like he was a lunatic. Defeated, Marco turned around and started heading back to the club, and that's when he saw David looking at him with his phone to his ear. Marco stopped for a second, and then started walking towards him not knowing what was going to happen. His eyes filled with tears when he heard what David was saying. "Dad, I need to come home now." A few seconds went by as David listened. "Dad, I'm fine. I just need to come home now."

Marco felt his heart being ripped out of his chest with those words. He knew he had fucked everything up. "David, can we talk? Please? Please tell your dad you'll call him back, ok?"

David looked at Marco like he was a complete stranger. He hesitated for a few seconds. "Dad, let me call you back in a couple of minutes. I need to talk to Marco." David listened again. "Yes, I'm ok, really. I promise I'll call you back." His father asked where he was. "I'm just out with Marco and his friends. Please let me call you back. I'll explain everything then." David hung up and wiped his face with his sleeve.

"David, I'm so sorry for fucking everything up. Please let me explain."

"Marco, there is nothing to explain. I get it. You still like Patrick. It's that simple. You just need to admit it." David looked him hard in the eyes as he said those piercing words. It scared Marco to see such intensity coming from someone so gentle.

"I decided to take some Molly and it made me kind of crazy. It makes me so fucking horny whenever I take it. I'm still fucked up, so I hope I'm making sense. What you saw has nothing to do with Patrick, please believe me," Marco pleaded, trying like hell to come down.

"That's where you're wrong. It has everything to do with Patrick, can't you see that? Getting high on that shit when you said that I was enough to make you feel good, tells me you're afraid to love anyone but yourself. You revealed that truth real fast tonight. You left me alone to get stoned and fondle your old boyfriend. I really thought you were intelligent and sensitive, but you're not. You're not even close. You couldn't even see that you were set up by your best friend."

Marco stood there dumfounded at that revelation. "I'm sorry. You're right about everything. I am fucked up. Please give me another chance. Please."

"Look, I think you need to decide what you really want. I honestly don't think you're ready to get serious with one guy yet. You proved that tonight."

Marco leaned against the building and wiped his eyes. "I've been fucked up for so long. It's the only thing I know how to do well. Having meaningless relationships and getting high has been the only way I've felt connected to this shitty world. And then I met you and realized there was another way. I love you. I really love you. You need to know that. But you're right, I'm damaged goods. I don't want to get back with Patrick or anyone else. None of those guys mean anything to me because I want to be with you."

"I love you too, but I don't know if we should be together right now. You lied to me. I would never do that to you."

They stood there a few feet from each other. Silent. Afraid. A couple of minutes had gone by when David asked him, "So what do we do now?"

"Will you come back to my house so we can talk?"

David looked away for a few seconds trying to decide. "Let me call my dad back first." Marco breathed a sigh of relief. David made the call and told him everything was fine, and that he would explain what happened when he got home.

↯ ↘

Transitions reveal in tacit ways a longing to connect beyond spoken words that often muddy the truth. Transitions reveal loss of innocence, casual deception, aching desires to be loved. Desperate moments grab hold of that elusive mist and the city lights distorted in windows of the mind. That is where love so often plays its cruel game. In silence, two people hoping to find love walk the jagged edges of impossible summits. It was a long silent cab ride back to the Upper East Side.

They sat next to each other inside the rooftop terrace drinking coffee as a warm glow from streetlights filled a sleepy silent Park Avenue. Marco had wounds that were deep, and he was afraid to let David see them, but knew he had to. He finally spoke. "It scares the hell out of me loving you as much as I do. You are so beautiful, so perfect. I can't believe someone like you actually exists. And then I did what I did. I'm lucky to have you in my life, but it's like I want to destroy any happiness that comes my way so I can stay numb. So I can stay afraid or lonely or whatever it is that is going on inside my brain. I'm just fucked up on so many levels."

"I don't understand how someone like you can be afraid or lonely or want to destroy what makes you happy, but I want to try." It got quiet again for a while. They eventually curled up on the sofa with the hope that forgiveness and love might heal their wounds. They spent the rest of the night talking things out and eventually fell asleep in each other's arms just as the morning sun was welcoming a brand new day.

# Part Two

Time moves forward into unknown dimensions, emotionless to the will of the dreamer, artist, seeker of knowledge, and those who have found perfect love. As much as the human spirit tries to manipulate this cruel entity, time will not play the game. It never stands still.

It is a curving forward trajectory, a requirement of one's existence, a life capsule buried in the backyard of the mind, a scalpel that cuts mortally deep. It spares no one from the myriad of emotions that play out within each person who dares to love and be loved.

Deep is the heart that lives gracefully and is true to its core beliefs.

Deep is the heart that understands the human spirit must be nurtured and shared.

Deep is the heart when two people who love each other perfectly become blind to what is right in front of them.

# CHAPTER 19

The late summer winds were gently nudging David, Tyler, and Melissa into their brand new worlds. It had been a spring and summer filled with happy celebrations and sad goodbyes.

Tyler and Melissa had received their acceptance letters from the University of Michigan that spring. David was happy for them because they had gotten into their dream school just as he had. But the future still scared each of them more than they ever dared to lead on.

There were those quiet mystical moments whenever they were together that revealed connections that would never be broken. And even though they never expressed it in words, what they had went way beyond the other friendships that had come and gone through the years.

David loved Tyler and Melissa with all his heart and knew they felt the same way about him. He also knew that his love for Tyler had long ago entered that other realm. If only things could have worked out before meeting Marco.

Tyler felt the same way, but could never tell David the truth. He had fallen in love with David in middle school, but couldn't put it into a proper context back then. But he figured it out when they kissed. Things would have been different if only he had followed his heart. Knowing he had missed his chance, Tyler vowed to keep his love a secret because David had fallen in love with someone else. He finally understood that old saying, "Silence carries the heaviest burden of all." It was a burden he would have to endure so his best friend could be happy.

David and Marco visited each other in the spring and summer of that pivotal year, a year that would require David to become emotionally stronger as he journeyed into wide-eyed new territory. Just before Marco had come to visit, David decided that he had to let go of Tyler. He figured they were never meant to be. It was the hardest thing he had ever done because he loved Tyler with all his heart. He cried himself to sleep night after night holding one of Tyler's t-shirts against his chest. It was the t-shirt he had worn the last time he slept over. It still had his scent on it. Letting go was the only way David could move on.

Π

Having Marco visit that spring was just what David needed. It had been a snowy gray winter with very little sun. It made him depressed because he couldn't stargaze as much as he would have liked. The upside was being able to spend more time skyping with Marco. They had gotten to know each other better by being more open and honest about things. This new intimacy helped David get over what Marco had done that night at the rave. Melissa also helped put things into a proper context after he came home and told her what had happened.

DEEP IS THE HEART

"David, look at me and Brad. He pisses me off almost every day. He's always doing or saying something stupid. You have to understand that relationships are never perfect."

"Yeah, but it was like he was cheating on me when he was grinding away with his old boyfriend. He forgot all about me."

"Yeah he was being a selfish asshole. Brad gets that way at times. I see him looking at other girls every now an then, but I know he loves me."

"But Brad doesn't simulate having sex with them, right?"

"No. But Marco was stoned. That's what rich boys do when they party. Some of my friends in Chicago take Molly when they party. It's a stupid thing to do. I can't understand why they take it. Maybe it's a way to release the tension of their boring privileged lives. You have to understand that Marco's world is very different from yours. You either accept it or break up with him and move on."

"But I love him."

"He apologized, didn't he?"

"Yeah. He promised it would never happen again."

"Well, then I think you have to give him another chance. Just remember, let him know when things aren't going well, or when something is bothering you about the relationship. Talking to each other honestly is the only way real relationships survive."

David decided to take her advice. He forgave Marco and told him what his expectations were. Marco knew he had been given another chance and wasn't going to blow it again.

# CHAPTER 20

Tyler tried to make himself scarce during Marco's visit so David could have the space he needed with his boyfriend. But David innocently had other plans. He begged Tyler to have lunch with them one afternoon. He reluctantly agreed. They sat at the restaurant talking about school, music, and video games to kind of break the ice. Tyler felt like an intruder because he could see how happy David was. Marco sensed that Tyler really didn't want to be there by the inflection in his voice, and his body language. It was obvious to Marco, just like it was in December, that Tyler was in love with David. Their eyes met more than once while David talked enthusiastically about college life, New York City, and the first semester classes he had signed up for. The truth revealed itself whenever Tyler and Marco made eye contact. They were both emotionally wounded. Marco knew why Tyler was, but Tyler could not figure out the hurt emanating from Marco. It didn't make sense. After all, he was David's boyfriend and they were in love. So why did he look like he had just lost his best friend?

Tyler drove home that afternoon trying to figure out what was going on. He was afraid for David and didn't know why. Something just wasn't right about Marco. He could feel it in his bones. He pulled over to the side of the road and sat there for a couple of minutes thinking about the situation. He pounded his fist on the steering wheel and cursed at what a coward he had been. He turned his truck around and headed to the sand dunes to walk the trails and clear his head. He vowed to figure things out once and for all.

Tyler walked the mile of well-worn trail he had walked so many times in his young life. Twenty minutes later he was at his favorite beach with that deep blue body of water lapping serenely at his feet. It was a beautiful spring day with no one else in sight. He had been going there for years with David and Melissa, and it always felt perfect whenever they were together there. The sun was out and the temperature was a mild seventy degrees. He took his shirt off so he could feel the warmth that was missing in his life. With eyes looking toward the horizon, he wondered why Marco looked so sad and wounded. Something was terribly wrong. He needed to let David know somehow because the feeling he was feeling was making the hair on his arms stand straight up. Tyler didn't know if he was just overreacting because of jealously, or because he thought David was in danger. He decided to talk to Melissa first to see what she thought.

Tyler closed his eyes and started thinking about the one issue that had haunted him for years. He knew it was time to face the truth once and for all. He stretched his body out on the warm sand and started making a sand angel like he used to when he was a little kid. It felt perfect. He moved his arms and legs back and forth, running his hands on the surface of the sun drenched sand that surrounded his lean defined body. Those grains of sand sparkled all around him like millions of tiny diamonds. He took a handful of those precious grains and tried to hold them without letting them slip away. But he knew he couldn't. The tears welled up as they slipped through his fingers, back onto the beach where they were always meant to be.

With tears running down his cheeks, he sat back up and looked out at the lake. The sound of the waves caressed his mind while he thought about life. About his life. How he needed to honest with himself and the people he loved. It became an afternoon of self-reflection. Tyler decided to tell his mother and father that he was gay. It was the only way he could ever be happy. He hoped they would understand and accept him just as David's parents had.

Even though the tears kept coming, he smiled a real smile for the first time in months. The last time he felt that happy was when he kissed David. With each step he took on the trail back to his truck, he could feel a huge weight slowly being lifted off his shoulders. He felt like he was being reborn. The wind whipped around his body in a way that let him know how lucky he was to be who he was; a strong confident gay teenager.

Tyler came out to his parents that evening during dinner. It was the hardest thing he had ever done. He was extremely nervous but remained physically calm. "Mom, dad, I need to tell you something, but I need you to promise me that you won't say anything until I get everything out, ok?" They looked at him wondering if he was in some kind of trouble. "Is everything ok? What happened?" His father asked, with panic in his voice. Tyler sat there for a few seconds trying to find just the right words. "I need to tell you something about myself and I hope you'll understand. I'm gay." He waited to see what their reaction was going to be before he continued. They stayed surprisingly composed. "How long have you known?" his father asked.

"Since ninth grade. I've been trying to deal with it on my own, but I can't anymore. I need to be honest with myself and with you. I hope you'll still love me." Tyler sat there as tears came. Even though his parents were stunned by that revelation, they kept their response measured and empathetic. Tyler looked down at the table in shame as his father scooted his chair over and gave him a nice long hug. "We love you no matter what. Nothing is ever going to change that. Please don't feel guilty or ashamed of who you are. We love you just the same."

"Thank you for understanding," Tyler said, holding his father with all his might. His mother stood up and went over and kissed him on the cheek. She rubbed his back hoping to calm him down. "My baby boy. We love you so much and just want you to be happy." A weight the size of the earth had been finally lifted off Tyler's shoulders. All three were crying by this time, knowing a brand new chapter in their lives was beginning.

Those dark thoughts that had run through Tyler's mind so many times instantly disappeared. They ended up talking well into the evening about a lot of things. His parents were wise enough to let Tyler do most of the talking. He explained how he had struggled with his sexual identity since the age of fourteen, and how he tried to live up to their expectations of what a good son should be. "There were so many times when I felt like I was letting you down, like there was something wrong with me and I didn't want you to find out." he said, his body shaking from that truth.

"Tyler, we never meant to put that kind of pressure on you," his father said. "I feel like we let you down."

"Believe me dad, you didn't do anything wrong. You and mom have always treated me with respect and never pressured me in any way. I didn't come out because I put pressure on myself.

I wasn't being honest. That's the stupid thing I feel so bad about."

Tyler's parents tried to reassure him that what he had been going through was normal for teenagers questioning their sexuality. They even brought up David, which made Tyler open up even more. His mom asked, "You've talked to David about this, right?"

"Actually, no, but I wanted to many times."

"I'm surprised. He could have helped you like you helped him when he came out," his dad said. Tyler hesitated for a moment and then explained. "You see, things between me and David are a little complicated."

"In what way?"

"Well, for starters, I like him more than just as a friend. And when I finally got the nerve to tell him, it was too late.

He started seeing Marco. You know, that guy from New York. So I decided not to say anything."

"You have to tell him how you feel. You owe it to yourself and to him regardless of who he is seeing. He is your best friend."

"I know. You're right, but I want him to be happy for once in his life. He deserves it more than anyone I know. Look at the shit he's been through. They almost killed him because he's gay. If I tell him how I feel, it might jeopardize what he is building with Marco."

"How do you know for sure that will happen?"

"Because after I got the nerve to kiss him last fall, he told me that he'd had a crush on me since 7th grade. I kissed him because I wanted him to know how much I loved him as a friend. Plus I was trying to figure out if I was gay or straight. As soon as we kissed I knew, but I was still afraid to accept the truth, and afraid to tell him. I was panic-stricken. Then he met Marco a few days later when he was at Columbia. I knew I had blown my chance."

"Well, you need to tell him how you feel. You've been honest with us, and now you have to honest with him. You owe yourself and him that," his mother reiterated again.

"I know, but I just want him to be happy without any interference from me. I hope that makes sense?" His dad tried to find the right words of encouragement. "You know David is going to feel terrible if you don't tell him you're gay, and that you like him. You were there for him every step of the way after he came out, and you know he would want to be there for you."

"I know, but I can't tell him right now. Please understand. I plan on telling him when we're all home for Christmas break. Enough time will have passed by then."

His parents understood as best they could, and finally let the subject drop. They spent the rest of the evening getting to know each other through a brand new lens as they talked about the future, and reminisced about the past.

There are so many times when the pressures of everyday life get in the way of what a family is supposed to be. This had been the case for Tyler and his parents. He saw them in a brand new light, and they finally felt like they were part of his life as more than just the typical parent/child relationship. Rekindled love, respect, and a brand new friendship emerged between the three of them on that warm spring evening.

ƒ

Tyler invited Melissa over for lunch the next day on the premise that they were going to drive to Charlevoix and do some shopping. He needed to finally tell her the truth. It was the next step in coming out to the world. He was more nervous to tell her than he was his parents.

Melissa came over at noon. Tyler's parents went to visit his grandparents for the afternoon so he could have the house to himself. The look on his face when he let Melissa in made her wonder what was going on. "What's wrong?"

"Nothing. Everything is good. I made us a nice lunch before we head out. Are you hungry?"

"Yeah. That is so sweet of you." Melissa gave him a hug and

could feel his whole body shaking. She pulled away. "Tyler, please tell me what's going on. Did something bad happen?" He tried to calm down before speaking. "Look, I do have something to tell you, but you have to promise that you won't say anything to anyone about it right now. Promise?"

"Yes, of course."

"Good." They headed to the kitchen so he could finish preparing lunch. He tried to make small talk while he took the garlic bread out of the oven and the antipasto salad out of the refrigerator. Melissa got two glasses from the cupboard and poured lemonade. She couldn't take it anymore. "Please don't tell me you've decided not to go to Michigan. I'll kill you if you tell me that."

"Of course I'm still going to Michigan. That's been the plan all along."

He brought the salad to the table along with the garlic bread, and sat down. He was so nervous that he couldn't look her in the eyes. Melissa started giving him an exasperated look, the same one she had given Brad a million times. He finally looked at her as tears filled his eyes. He almost got up and walked out, but took a deep breath and held onto the table. "I…I don't know how to tell you this other than to just say it. I'm gay."

Melissa could see how hard this was for Tyler to actually say. She got up and hugged him.

"Thank you for telling me. I'm happy that you finally figured it out. I love you so much."

"I love you too."

Melissa held him. "Do you want to talk about it?" Tyler shook his head yes. "As you and David have known, I've been dealing with this for a long time. I started questioning a few months after David came out. I would always hug him whenever he got depressed or cried. It always made him feel better. He told me that he felt connected to me, which I figured out meant he liked me. It made me feel so good when he told me that. I felt the same way but didn't tell him. The thought of being gay frightened me to death. And for years I've felt so guilty for not accepting it, and keeping the truth from David. I've put both of us through hell because I'm a coward. I did everything I could to fight my feelings for him. But at least he's found someone who makes him happy." Tyler looked down at the table ashamed of his years hiding and denying. Melissa put her hand on top of his. "Why did you deny yourself the chance to be happy?"

His tears welled up again. "I wish I could go back and change things. I wish I could have been as brave as David."

"I'm sorry I asked that." Melissa said, now feeling terrible.

"Please don't be sorry. I need to talk about this honestly, and you're helping me do that. I started putting pressure on myself to get a girlfriend when I was in ninth grade. My parents overheard their friends bragging about their sons having girlfriends, so my mom and dad started asking if I liked any girls at school. I lied and said yes. Then I really felt like I had to get a girlfriend. That's when I started going out with Vanessa. And I really did like her. I know this is going to sound terrible, but a lot of times when we were making out I was pretending that I was making out with a guy. I knew I was at least bi at that point, but I still refused to accept it. I wanted to be the perfect hetero son. Someone my parents could be proud of."

"You should have said something to me or David. We could have helped."

"I know, but I didn't know how to deal with it. I still don't. You and my parents are the only people who know at the moment."

"Thank you for telling me. I love you and I'm here for you."

"I love you too."

"You do understand that David figured it out after you guys kissed, right?"

"I know he's had his suspicions."

Melissa tried to cheer Tyler up. "Can I ask you a question?"

"Yeah."

"Who was the guy you were pretending to kiss when you and Vanessa would make out?"

He smiled. "It was always David."

"I figured it was him," she said, giggling a little. That made him smile.

"What was it like when you finally got the nerve to kiss him?"

"It felt perfect. It was like we were made for each other. That's when I knew I was gay. That's when I knew I really loved him." He started feeling sad again.

"Coming out is never easy, so you shouldn't feel bad. And you know David's philosophy; a person has to come out when they're ready. He wanted you to figure it out before he said anything. I'm sure he has given you plenty of opportunities to talk about it, right?"

"Yeah, he has. I've just been a fucking coward about it."

"I can't believe my two best friends are gay. This is so cool. When are you going to tell David? Call him right now and have him come over. He has to know. He's been waiting a long time." Tyler looked at her knowing she was going to go ballistic at what he was about to say.

"I hope you'll understand, but I don't want to tell David right now.

"Why?"

"Because I don't want to complicate things for him. I mean, Marco is here and they're getting to know each other better, so coming out to him right now could cause problems."

"Tyler, that's bullshit and you know it. You know he's had a crush on you for years, right?"

"Yeah, he told me last fall. That's why I don't want to tell him. You can see where I'm coming from, can't you?"

"Yeah. FUCK! FUCK! is all I have to say." They sat there in silence trying to figure things out, but Melissa became frustrated thinking about what could have been.

"Can I ask you something?"

"Sure."

"You love David, right?"

"Yes. I love him more than anything."

"Well then, you have to fight for him. You have to tell him that you're in love with him and then let him choose."

"As much as I want to do that, I'm not going to. David is happy with Marco. I know he loves him, so I'm not going to make him choose."

Melissa disagreed, and was just about to say so when Tyler started to cry. She scooted over and put her arms around him. "It's going to be ok. Just let it all out." A few minutes later Tyler was able to pull himself together. "I love David so much and just want him to be happy. And now he is. You can see that, can't you?"

"Yes."

"You have to promise me that you won't say anything about me being in love with him or being gay. Please promise me."

"I promise," Melissa reluctantly said. "When are you going to tell him? You can't hide it from him forever."

"I've decided to tell him when we're home for Christmas break. Please promise that you won't say anything to anyone else until then, ok?"

"I promise."

"Thanks, I don't want him to hear it from some random person." Tyler gave Melissa a nice long hug.

# Chapter 21

David flew to New York a couple of weeks after graduation to celebrate that milestone together, and also have some private time before Marco left on a family vacation to Europe. This visit was completely different from his last one. For one thing, Zander and Claire weren't around. David found out that Marco and Zander weren't hanging out anymore. They talked about it one afternoon while walking across the Brooklyn Bridge on their way to have lunch at Grimaldi's Pizzeria.

"When are we going to get together with Zander and Claire?"

Marco stopped walking and looked out at the East River with a melancholy gaze. "Claire left for Paris right after graduation. Her father arranged an internship at the Louvre for the summer. She's also taking painting classes at the University of Paris in preparation for the fall. She was accepted at Brown University as an art major, so the internship and painting classes will be a nice little feather in her cap. Her parents own an apartment in Paris and she loves to spend her summers there. She was excited to get out of here and begin her new life."

"It sounds like it's going to be an incredible experience. Tell her I said hi next time you guys talk."

"She told me to tell you how sorry she was that she couldn't see you this time. She really likes you."

"I like her too. She made me feel welcome the last time I was here. And what about Zander?"

Marco turned and looked David square in the eyes. "Zander and I haven't really spoken since Christmas. I told him that we needed to take a break."

"I'm sorry if I screwed your friendship up."

"It doesn't have anything to do with you. Well, maybe a little because you were the catalyst for Zander's and my imma-ture behavior. He was so jealous of you that he wanted to scare you away. He knows how vulnerable I am in certain areas of my life, so he played me and he tried to play you. Getting away from him has been a good thing. It became obvious that he re-ally wasn't my friend."

"That's because he likes you more than just as a friend, right?" David asked, already knowing the answer.

"Yeah. I've known it for years. I guess I'm just as bad as he is in a lot of ways. I've used that against him a million times." Marco turned and looked out at the river trying to come to terms with certain flaws that ate at him night and day. "David, you need to know that I'm not perfect. I can be a real asshole at times."

"Why?"

"Honestly, I don't have a fucking clue. At least that's what I tell myself."

"Well, I hope you guys works things out at some point."

Marco turned back to him and asked, "How can you be so

perfect? I know I've told you this before, but I don't deserve you."

"I'm nowhere near the perfect person you think I am. Perfection doesn't exist and you know it. And it's not about deserving each other either. All I want is for us to be able to trust one another and let things develop as naturally as possible."

"Thank you for giving me another chance. I love you."

"I love you too."

⁘ ⸛

It turned out to be a very special week together. David and Marco got closer to what was important in their relationship. On the second day of David's visit they decided to check out their dorm buildings at Columbia. They had a blast walking around campus getting to know it better. They each displayed quiet confidence while walking around hand in hand, knowing their new journey was only weeks away. After completing their self-guided tour, they grabbed a cab and started doing all of the classic touristy things around the city, something Marco had never really experienced. Like most New Yorkers, he was always too busy with everyday life.

David loved seeing the city this way because they didn't have to spend a lot of money. It took the pressure off both of them as they explored the nooks and crannies with other wide-eyed tourists. David could see Marco starting to relax for the first time since they had met. He hoped sharing the simple things around the city would help them to get closer.

David enjoyed walking around it the most, because its

intimacy and rhythm slowly started to reveal itself. He began to understand why thousands of people just like him wanted to attend its great universities. Why young writers from small towns came to Manhattan in search of their creative souls. Why actors from those same small towns moved there so they could perform in hundreds of intimate old theaters. The ghosts of the past could be felt everywhere they went. David realized New York City was the modern day Athens and Rome all rolled into one. It was the place where the heartbeat of the entire human race pumped with a vengeance. He was slowly becoming part of this Victor Frankenstein-like creation and loved it. During their four day odyssey, David realized what could be achieved as individuals, and as boyfriends. The layers of apprehension and insecurity were finally being stripped away. The typical templates of their teenage existence were being replaced with a brand new layer of life, a layer that would end up teaching each of them valuable lessons. This was essence of the 'adolescence to adulthood' process that was about to hit David and Marco full force.

Near the end of David's visit they spent their last remaining days together at Marco's lake house in Connecticut. This was the first time they had been together without parents, friends, and pressures from the outside world. The insecurities each one brought with them seemed to vanish as they spent their time sailing, water-skiing, and enjoying the nightly campfires that kept them warm at night. It was just like being home for David. He looked up at that wondrous night sky and thanked the stars for finally granting his wish.

Their last night together became one of those life defining moments for David. He hadn't plan on it happening at all, but it did. They were both enjoying the campfire and the soft breeze coming off the lake when David nervously turned to Marco and said, "I really love you."

Marco smiled. "I really love you too."

David leaned in and kissed him with an intensity Marco had never felt before. Everything was just as David hoped this special moment would be: crickets chirping, the smell of the campfire, the stars looking down, and being with the boy he loved. He knew it needed to happen right then. "Marco, will you make love to me?" Marco had his arms around David and could feel his body shaking, not knowing if it was from the slight chill in the air, or from the realization of what he had just asked. "Are you sure you're ready? I don't want to put any pressure on you."

"Yes I'm sure. Please make love to me. I love you with all my heart," David said, and then kissed Marco lightly on the lips.

They put the campfire out and walked hand in hand back to the house without saying a word. David's body trembled with fear and excitement. Marco's emotions were going into brand new territory. He had never made love to another guy. For the first time in his life this was more than just calculated sex. This was the real thing.

They spent the entire night making love in the lakefront porch as the waves serenely lapped at the shore, and the rhythmic chirping of crickets sang to those two beautiful naked bodies that were intertwined with love. Marco was gentle and patient as he explored every crevice of David's slender body. David wanted Marco to make love to him any way he desired. He hoped Marco would find as much pleasure making love to him as he surely must have had with other guys from his past. David hated feeling insecure, but he was. He just hoped that giving up his virginity would be as special to Marco as it was to him.

# Chapter 22

It was a beautiful late August afternoon as David, Tyler, and Melissa picnicked on their favorite beach one last time before heading off to college. The time had finally arrived when they were all going their separate ways. David sat there wishing he could break the hands off the face of time and stop it at that very moment. He knew a demented time keeper loved to play games with those disappearing adolescent seconds. Sadly, there was no way to alter the inevitable.

It was the end of his childhood, his innocence, his life in the wilderness where he had come to know himself with no questions asked. Harbor Springs had given everything it could give, and now he, Tyler, and Melissa had to go chase their dreams in far-off lands.

They were leaving for college on the same day, just as they had planned. Melissa was standing in her driveway looking out at the lake when David and Tyler's SUVs pulled into the circular driveway in front of her house. It was a perfect sunny morning with a slight chill in the air. David and Tyler walked over to Melissa so they could all say goodbye to each other one last time. Their parents were kind enough to wait in their vehicles so they could have this special moment.

They walked to the back edge of the driveway to talk in private. No one wanted to be the first to speak, but Melissa finally relented and decided to be the brave one. "Well, this is it, what we've waited our entire lives for. How does it feel?"

"Not good. Not good at all," David said as the tears came.

"I know what you mean. This sucks big time," Tyler said, looking away as he wiped his eyes. Melissa was trying so hard not to cry. She tried to be optimistic about their new beginnings.

"Come on guys, this isn't the end of the world. This whole thing is an adventure of a lifetime. We're only going to be apart for a few months, then we'll be back together."

"Yeah, I know. You're right. But everything seems so complicated. I feel like I'm being torn apart." David said. He looked at Tyler with a sadness that made his heart break. Tyler wanted to say it. He wanted to scream it. He wanted to tell David that he was in love with him, but willed himself with all his might to stay silent. He looked away so David couldn't see the truth.

David looked at Melissa totally lost. She hugged him tight. "I'm going to miss you so much. I love you David Emerson."

"I love you too. I'm really going to miss you." They slowly let go of each other. She walked away so David and Tyler could be alone.

David was openly crying now as he looked at Tyler's beautiful face. He was trying hard to find the right words to say. He tried to say them but nothing came out. So he grabbed hold of Tyler and hugged him with every ounce of energy he had. "I love you Tyler Reed."

"I love you too David Emerson. Please don't forget me. Please," he pleaded, holding on to David, not wanting to let go. Melissa and their parents watched with sadness knowing how much they meant to each other. It broke their hearts watching them say goodbye.

"You better skype with me every night," David said, wiping his tears.

Tyler got it together a little. "You know I will. I'll always be here for you."

"I know. And I'll always be here for you too. Don't you ever forget that." David tried to smile. "I can't wait to hear all about your dorm room, the campus, and how you're classes are going. I wish I was going to Michigan with you guys."

"Yeah, it would've been awesome rooming together." Things got silent for a few seconds as they looked into each other's eyes. They both wanted to say it, but couldn't. Tyler felt like he was betraying his best friend with his silence. He finally spoke up. "I want you to do something for me." David looked at Tyler, trying to remain calm. "Sure, anything for you."

"If he ever hurts you, if anyone ever hurts you, please call me right away. I'll get to New York as fast as I can. Will you promise me that?"

"I promise." And with that, they slowly walked to where Melissa was standing and gave each other one last hug and then got into their SUVs and began brand new lives.

# CHAPTER 23

ON CAMPUS

Move-in day on the Columbia campus was a madhouse, but David loved every minute of it. His mom, dad, and sister helped him shuttle the Columbia blue moving bin from their SUV to his room at Hartley Residence Hall. They were lucky to get a parking space on 114th Street about half way down the block from his dorm. David brought only the essentials and had them packed as efficiently as possible so he could move in quickly. His dad couldn't believe the bins were free for only two hours. The University charged students after that. "I can't believe they would charge money for these things," he said, sounding disgusted.

"It's ok dad. I knew it ahead of time. It's only going to take us five or six trips. We'll be done in less than an hour."

"I just think it isn't very wise to start charging parents for an essential service as soon as we get here."

"Come on dad, I want to enjoy this with you," David said. They rolled the first full bin down the sidewalk to the entrance steps. He looked at his dad with pride as they lifted it up the steps and onto the campus sidewalk. David couldn't help but smile knowing it was really happening.

He pushed the bin down the red brick walkway towards

Hartley Hall. He turned and pushed it towards the entrance. He glanced at John Jay Residence Hall two buildings away knowing the guy he loved would be there soon. The pristine lawns and gardens in front of both buildings made David's heart pound. He had entered his perfect world.

A student coordinator stood in the garden area waiting to greet them. He had to sign in and was then handed a packet of information and two entrance cards. One for the lobby door, and one with the entrance code to his room on the seventh floor. They got everything moved in five trips. His mom and sister came with them on the last trip so they could see his room and help organize. David loved the reaction on their faces when they walked up the steps and saw the campus for the first time. He could actually see the magic enter both of them.

His parents watched with pride knowing their son was in his element. They saw the look on his face, his body language, and confident demeanor. It let them know that he was meant to be there. And that's when it finally hit them. Their son had grown up and was starting a brand new life. David and his parents put on their bravest faces because they knew. They knew life had changed the game. It all moves forward.

David loved the energy that filled the entire residence hall. Other sons and daughters and parents were doing the same things, feeling the same emotions as his family. His mind went into scientific overdrive at that point. He thought of each family as an independent universe, each with it's own unique characteristics and physical properties, yet all bound by spacetime and love and learning to let go. He could feel the gravitational pull of each parent still trying to protect their prized galaxies from rogue galaxies, but realizing it was futile. They would have to be content with watching from afar knowing they did the best they could. That was the heartbreak of time.

He came out of this thought and smiled knowing he was about to begin living in a human multiverse.

"What are you smiling about?" His mom asked, with a smile of her own.

"Oh, nothing in particular. It is just a perfect day and I get to share it with you guys. Thank you for letting me go to college here."

"Your dad and I are proud of you. It makes us happy to see you so happy." They both gave him a hug, keeping their promise not to cry until after they left.

David went to open another box and noticed Audrey standing in the doorway looking down the hall with dreamy eyes. He grabbed a box by the door and peaked outside.

He smiled when he saw a cute guy about Audrey's age helping his brother move in. "Here's five dollars. You look thirsty. There's a vending machine right past those two guys at the end of the hall and around the corner." She gave him a look. "Thanks. I am thirsty." Audrey started walking toward the cute boy.

The hardest part of the day for David was having to say goodbye. It was a rite of passage for each new freshman to experience this emotional, sad, exciting Shakespearian scene.

He stood on the sidewalk, and the tears came as he watched his mom, dad, and sister drive away.

♍

David decided to finish unpacking and get organized before Ryan, his roommate, arrived from California. He had received a text from him a few days earlier saying he wouldn't be on campus until later that afternoon. This gave David some time to put things away and get his space fixed up to his liking. As he did this, his thoughts drifted to Marco. He wanted to see him so bad but knew he would have to wait a little longer. Marco had sent him a text the night before saying that he wasn't going to be on campus until Sunday evening.

"I'm sorry I can't help you move in. My parents made me go with them to visit my uncle in Boston. I'm flying in at six and then heading straight to campus. I miss you and can't wait to see you."

"Please hurry."

"I will. I love you." Marco attached a selfie with a goofy grin.

David never felt more alive as he sat on his bed, looked around his room, still not quite believing where he was and how he got there. He was officially a college student, at Columbia, and his boyfriend was only one day away. He had finally made it.

David continued organizing his area while imagining what Marco's room looked like. They had talked about it earlier in the week and he knew how excited Marco was to see it. "My father arranged to have the moving company move some of my personal things and the new furniture my mother ordered."

"Columbia lets you remove their furniture?" David asked.

"Yeah. They just put it in storage."

"That's cool. I can't wait to see what your room looks like."

"Me too. She wouldn't tell me anything about it. It's a big surprise."

"I think it's nice that she wants to surprise you."

"Yeah…it's not like her at all. I hope there are no strings attached."

"Be nice. I think she has accepted the whole Columbia thing now, right?"

"You're right, she has. And it's nice to see her doing this for me. My mother does have extraordinary taste, so I know I'm going to like it."

David smiled knowing they were going to have many nights together in a beautiful setting.

♎ ♑

The hallways were filled with people talking, laughing, and just plain having a great time as they went from room to room introducing themselves. David was just about to join in this ritual when a group of students knocked on his slightly opened door.

"Ryyyan and Daaavid, it's time to come out and play," he heard a sing-songy voice say as his door opened wide. He turned around and saw a bunch of happy faces staring at him.

"Hi. I'm David Emerson. Ryan hasn't arrived yet." The guy who was singing David's name gave him a look that said he was instantly in love. "Oh my god, you are just…well, you just are! My name is Jay Holloway." He shook David's hand, gave him the biggest smile, and stared. David looked away feeling slightly embarrassment. It was obvious Jay was crushing on him.

"David Emerson. Your name has a nice ring to it. Where are you from?"

"Harbor Springs Michigan."

"That's bangin. I'm from London as you can probably tell from my impressive Harry Potter accent." Jay strategically moved next to David while everyone else squeezed into the room and introduced themselves. Cory Stratton was from Houston. Nikki Herrera was from Brooklyn. Clark Lancaster was from Boston. Justin Lee was from Japan. Amelia Lafleur was last to introduce herself. "Bonjour David, I'm from Paris."

"It's really nice to meet all of you." David knew this magical day was getting better by the minute. The seeds of friendship were already forming. They spent a few minutes talking about New York City, their dorm rooms, and how great the campus was. David always wanted to have friends from all over the world, and it was finally happening. He decided to join them as they continued going from room to room.

Everyone had a blast getting to know other people. Jay and Cory were naturals with the friendly banter. They were total extroverts, which helped David and the other quiet ones feel comfortable enough to say hi.

As they walked up to the eighth floor, David and Jay innocently lagged a dozen steps behind talking away. It was just the two of them for a moment and Jay got right to the point. "Gay, right?"

"Yes, extremely gay," David said, with a shy grin.

"Me too, as you probably guessed."

"Gaydar is a funny thing, isn't it?"

"Definitely. I hope I'm not being too forward, but are you seeing anyone? You know, do you have a boyfriend?" Before David could answer, Jay added, "I just think you are about the cutest guy I have ever seen." David totally blushed. "Thank you for saying that," he said, not knowing if he should return the compliment. He decided to answer the question instead. "Yes, I have a boyfriend. He's a freshman here too."

David could see the disappointment on Jay's face, even though he tried to hide it. "Hey, I'm happy for you, I really am," was all he could get out of his pouting mouth.

"I'd love to be friends with you," David said, trying to repair the damage.

Jay's smile returned slightly. "Me too."

Just as they got to the first room on the eighth floor, David said, "By the way, I think you're cute too."

"Really?"

"Yes, really. We have to find you a boyfriend. After we get settled, that can be our first quest. Deal?"

"Deal. I think you and I are going to become good friends."

Other students joined them on their pilgrimage going room to room and floor to floor.

They finally reached the tenth floor and entered an open lounge area where a bunch of students were hanging out. David couldn't believe how nice it was. It had leather couches, ornate Persian rugs, computer stations, and a small library with one of those rolling ladders to get to the books high up. He told Jay, "This is going to be the perfect place to hang out and study."

"You're right. I can't believe this is here."

The introductions continued and the mingling became more animated. It was like everyone knew how perfect the day was going and couldn't believe they were part of it. David was already taking a keen interest in his surroundings. He talked to a few people while listening to several other conversations at the same time. He didn't want to miss a thing.

A few minutes later he decided to check out the different areas of the lounge. He walked over to the library and pulled a few books off the shelf to see if anything interested him. He even got on the ladder and rolled himself from shelf to shelf checking more books out. While searching the upper shelves, David's entire body was hit by the sun's rays coming through an arched window to his right. He jumped off the ladder and walked over to the window. The view was incredible from that vantage point. He saw people walking in all directions, deep green manicured lawns, quiet gardens, and stately buildings that surrounded the main campus. It was as if he were looking at his dream from the top of his beloved hill.

But within a few seconds, that euphoria disappeared. David started feeling lonely and homesick. He put his forehead against the window and closed his eyes as his mind wandered back home, and then to Tyler and Melissa. He wondered how they were doing. It had only been thirty six hours, but he already missed them more than he could bear.

He was lost in his thoughts when a voice startled him back to reality. "I miss my friends too." David's whole body jumped. "Wow, you scared me," he said, to this kid with an infectious smile. "I'm sorry I startled you."

"It's ok," David told him, figuring it was someone's younger brother. He looked to be about fourteen or fifteen. Then he noticed a few similarities. They were both really thin, about the same height, and both had the shaggy emo hair happening. The only difference was the color. This guy's hair was pitch pitch black.

"My name is Miguel Montag. I'm a new freshman. I live just down the hall."

David stared in disbelief. "Nice to meet you Miguel. I'm David Emerson."

As soon as they shook hands, David started feeling dizzy. Miguel saw his eyes starting to role up and quickly grabbed his arm so he wouldn't fall. "Hey, are you ok? Miguel asked. "You don't look well." David leaned against the windowsill. "Yeah, I think so. I get dizzy spells every once in a while. I'll be fine in a minute or two." Feeling embarrassed, David turned around and looked out of the window again. "This is an awesome vantage point."

Miguel moved next to David to have a look. "It's unbelievable. I can't believe I'm a student here," he said.

"I know what you mean."

"Where are you from?"

"Michigan. I live in a small town called Harbor Springs. It's right on a Lake Michigan"

"That's wavy."

"Yeah, I love it there. Where are you from?"

"The Bronx. Just a few miles from here."

"Cool. My boyfriend is from the Upper East Side. He's a freshman here too."

"How did you guys meet?"

"We were both being interviewed for the Early Decision program when we met."

"Sounds like fate."

"I think you're right. So, what was it like growing up in the Bronx?"

"It's a lot different from where your boyfriend lives..lol It's a rough place. I'm gay, and that isn't a good thing to be in the Bronx. On top of that, my family is really messed up. I survived by staying away from all of the bullshit. You know, gangs, drugs, and violence. I stayed focused on my academics. That's how I got here."

"I'm sorry to hear about your family situation."

"Thanks. Shit happens."

David agreed. "Yeah, it definitely does."

The were silent for a minute or so as they watched people going every which way. Miguel finally spoke. "Some bad things happened to me, but bad things happen to everyone at some point, right?"

"Yeah. I know a little about that."

"I thought so. But here's the cool thing, we both survived and kept going after our dreams."

They locked eyes. David gave him a knowing smile. "You are extremely perceptive."

"Why thank you."

Curiosity was getting the best of David at this point. "I want to ask you something, and I hope it doesn't sound judgmental. How old are you? I mean, you don't look old enough to be in college."

Miguel laughed. "I've been asked that at least a dozen times today. I just turned sixteen a week ago. I could have graduated when I was twelve, but I decided not to. Some nasty things were going on at home and I needed to stay and protect my sister. I've been taking online college classes since seventh grade. Columbia wouldn't accept those credits, but it doesn't matter to me. I'm just glad to be here. My timing is perfect because I got to meet you."

"Awe, that is so nice of you to say."

Then it was Miguel's turn. "How old are you? Fifteen? Sixteen?"

David blushed. "I'm eighteen."

"There is no way you look eighteen. Sorry papi."

"I guess it's our curse. I just hope they take us seriously around here and not think we're still in middle school." They both laughed.

They were exchanging phone and room numbers when Jay, Cory, and a few others decided to join in on their conversation. David introduced Miguel to everyone, hoping the looks they were giving him weren't as condescending as they seemed. Miguel excused himself a few minutes later, saying he needed to finish unpacking. David walked with him out to the hall. "Would you like to hang out sometime this week?" He asked.

"Yeah, that would be great. Text me when you have some free time, or if you just feel like talking. Sometimes a person needs that."

Then Miguel did something that startled David. He placed his hand on David's chest and said, "You have a heart of gold," and then walked away.

David stood there for a few seconds pondering what Miguel had just said, and then went back to the lounge and joined in on Jay, Cory, and Clark's conversation. Jay gave him a look.

"That guy was rather strange looking. That goth or emo thing he has going is scary." Cory jumped in with additional criticism. "He looks sick to me. You know, like maybe he's anorexic or on drugs."

David got angry. "I don't think he looks strange, or sick, or on drugs. He's just being himself and I think it's cool. You shouldn't judge people until you get to know them first. He's really nice. Just give him a chance." They quickly apologized. Jay thought for sure he had fucked up their new friendship. "You're right. I'm sorry. My bitchy side is coming out already, and I promised myself that I would control it."

"Me too. I'm sorry," Cory said, feeling ashamed.

David was still angry. "I was relentlessly made fun of in

school for being a geek, for being too skinny, for being gay, for breathing. Miguel has a lot of courage. He just turned sixteen a week ago? Do you realize how brave he is coming here at that age?"

They were stunned. Another student who happened to be listening joined in on the conversation. "I overheard two guys talking about him earlier. They said he's a genius. His IQ is in the stratosphere, his test scores are off the charts, and he has a photographic memory." David smiled.

He excused himself at that point and went back to his room to finish unpacking. Within an hour everything was pretty much in its place, so he decided to text Tyler.

Tyler texted back a few seconds later. "Hey Ivy League boy. How is move-in day going?"

David smiled and then texted back. "Remember, you're attending one of the eight public Ivy League universities, so from one Ivy Leaguer to another, it's been unbelievable so far."

"Do you have time to skype?" Tyler asked.

"Yeah, right now as a matter of fact."

"Cool. I'm heading to my dorm. Should be there in a few."

Skyping with Tyler made David feel like he was back home. The first thing they did was take each other on a tour of their rooms. Then they talked about some of the people they had met, and what their campus atmospheres were like. Tyler said he had already walked all around Michigan's main campus trying to figure out where his classes were, and just getting the lay of the land. "My favorite part is the Diag."

"Yeah, me too." David said, thinking back to the six weeks

he spent there in Michigan's Summer Institute for the Gifted at the end of seventh grade.

"Most of my classes are in Angell Hall and the Chemistry building. I checked out the Law Quad a little while ago and felt like I was in the middle of Hogwarts."

David smiled because he had felt the same way. "Check their library out if you want to see something incredible."

"Yeah, I'll have to do that."

Things got quiet as they stared at one another. David finally looked away, knowing he was going to lose it any second.

"So, what is your campus like?" Tyler asked, breaking the silence.

"I haven't been out of my building since I got here. There is a lot of stuff going on out there though. I'm going to check it out in a little while. It's been a little crazy around here. But I did meet some cool people earlier and I went floor to floor with them saying hi and introducing ourselves. I met this guy named Miguel. He's so different from everyone else around here. Get this, he is only sixteen years old."

"Mmm...I take it he's a lot like you in the smarts department. Did you notice I didn't say that dreaded word?"

"Yeah. You're a goofball. He's really nice, and he's gay too."

"Cool. I hope to meet some people I can connect with."

"Don't worry, you will. Have you seen Melissa?"

"No, but we've texted. We are meeting up at Angell Hall in a couple of hours and then going out for dinner. Ann Arbor is the coolest place."

David started feeling sad. "I wish I could be there with you guys."

"Me too. It would have been perfect," Tyler lamented. "But hey, we can skype all we want. And we are going to visit each other at some point."

"You and Melissa are formally invited to come visit. Please come as soon as you can. I want to show you guys around New York. We'll have a blast."

They reluctantly said their goodbyes a few minutes later.

Ω ૩

David decided to take a walk around campus. He wanted to get the feel of his new surroundings. A gentle summer breeze greeted his body as soon as he walked outside. It gave him goosebumps. The infinite kind. The kind that happen when you hear a perfect song for the very first time. The heart-rending kind when you're with your best friends and everything feels perfect.

David rubbed his arms with a knowing grin as he walked through the garden to get a better view. He looked toward the center walkway and decided to head that way so he could check out all of the information booths. Hundreds of students mingled around. Some in groups, some with just a new friend or two, and some like him, by themselves checking things out with the hope of gathering enough courage to say hi to other lone students. It had always been difficult for him to make friends because of his shyness.

David walked straight into this frenzy hoping for the best.

He went from booth to booth checking everything out. They were selling posters, original paintings, books, school related supplies, and tons of Columbia University related items. There were also banks, credit card, phone, cable, and computer companies trying to sign up students for their services. David had everything he needed in those departments, so he decided to check out the fraternity booths. He wasn't quite sure if he wanted to join one, but thought he would introduce himself just in case. He talked with members of three fraternities and learned about the benefits of the greek system. The idea of becoming a fraternity brother excited him, especially after listening to what each house had to offer. It was the first time in his life meeting people who had many of the same interests as he did. That made him feel even more connected to his new surroundings. Each house gave him information about pledging, as well as private invitations to their first social events of the new semester.

After thanking each fraternity for the invitations, David decided to check out the Mathematics Building. He wanted to find the lecture halls where his math classes were going to be held. He also wanted to find out where his research team met. He had received an email in July from the math department telling him that he had been assigned to do research in Mathematical Physics.

Before heading there, he walked up the steps in front of Low Library to take some pictures. He snapped a few and sent them to his mom and dad, along with a short message. "Thank you for everything. I love it here. And I love you so much." Then he took a selfie with the lower campus as a backdrop. He grinned while texting it to Tyler and Melissa, knowing how dorky he looked. His message was short. "I really miss you guys."

There was singular awareness, a nuanced calm within David as the math building came into view. He stood at the edge of a wishbone walkway admiring its time-worn facade. It looked humble and wise surrounded by an expansive man-icured lawn, a wall of rectangular hedgerow, and branches swaying in the breeze. The scent of pine took his mind back home in a nanosecond. It felt right.

He looked toward the north hedgerow and it was just as he remembered. The lion. Standing alone just like him. They both stood there resolute and unwavering within their impa-tient convictions. The goosebumps came once again, and it all made sense. David walked to that weathered statue and put his hand on one of its paws. He felt honor and determina-tion, and understood how those attributes were requirements for his own success. He took a picture before leaving and up-loaded it to his Facebook cover. It would serve as a reminder to stay strong and focused in the coming years.

David entered the building with his heart beating fast. He now knew how Alice must have felt when she decided to go down the rabbit hole. It was a world he had only visualized in his mind's eye, and he couldn't believe that he was final-ly standing in the middle of it. An infinite dream. One that connected him to centuries of mathematical knowledge and empirical reasoning. His synapses were in love.

He was standing in the entryway trying to decide which

way to go when someone came around the corner and almost knocked him down. She apologized immediately. "I'm so sorry. Are you ok?"

"Yes, I'm fine. I was in your way. Sorry about that," David said, feeling like an idiot.

"You look a little lost. Are you looking for someone?"

"No, not really. I have a couple of classes here and I thought I would try to locate them before they start." What he was really hoping to do was run into Professor Eldridge.

She gave David a curious look, then smiled. "You must be a new student."

"Yes, I am. I just arrived on campus today."

"I hope this doesn't sound rude, but you look rather young to be a freshman."

David grinned. "I hear that a lot. I'm eighteen."

"Welcome to Columbia. I'm Professor Kapoor."

"It is nice to meet you Professor. My name is David Emerson."

"Yes, David. It is an honor to meet you. Your name has come up a number of times at our faculty meetings in the last few months. Professor Logan and his colleagues are impressed with your academic achievements." He was shocked to hear that. He managed a hesitant smile.

"I have a lot to learn. I hope I won't let them down."

She gave him a reassuring look. "Here's some advice. Don't ever feel pressured. Just have fun and let your mind fly. If you do that, you will learn and contribute in ways you never imagined."

"Thank you for the advice Professor."

"What classes are you taking?"

"Honors Math A and Introduction to Higher Mathematics."

"I'm impressed. Honor's will be held in Lecture Hall 4B on the fourth floor. And Higher Mathematics will be held in lecture hall 437."

"Thank you for your help."

"David, I'm so glad we were able to get acquainted. Good luck with your studies, and enjoy the rest of your tour around this fine old building."

"It was very nice meeting you Professor Kapoor. And thanks for the advice. I appreciate it."

He felt confident for the first time that day. He was in a state of excited calm as he began checking out the first floor. He loved the juxtaposition of early twentieth century architecture and twenty-first century technology and furnishings. Like one generation was handing off their knowledge and wisdom to the next.

He slowly made his way to the back of the building and found a cool winding marble staircase. He took his time walking to the fourth floor as his hand glided along the worn oak banister. The echo of each footstep guided the way. When he reached the fourth floor he could hear muffled voices talking in the offices that lined the main hall. He liked the fact that other people were around.

He got lost in the web of hallways, but finally found lecture hall 437. He tried to go inside but the door was locked. He wandered around until he found lecture hall 4B in the north quadrant. He checked to see if the doors were un-locked. Surprisingly one was. He carefully opened it, like he was afraid he might disturb the ghosts, and walked in. A few lights were on, casting long shadows, odd, angular, like textured brush strokes on canvas. It made the room look cryptic. He looked around trying to get a sense of its size and atmosphere. The numerous chalkboards on gliding pulleys made his mind come alive. He had always wanted one for his bedroom.

The goosebumps returned stronger than ever as he envisioned his first day of class. He closed the door behind him and continued on his self-guided tour.

David walked up to the fifth floor and entered the mathematics lounge. The arched entrance and foyer were decorated in decades-old hand carved oak. The marble floor created a slight echo effect as he walked into the main lounge area. He looked around with a huge grin knowing it was a going to be a place where he could study and relax. He could hear some talking, so he quietly peeked around a wall and saw a group of people at the far end of the lounge having an intense discussion. He turned to leave because it felt like he was intruding. He was almost to the door when he heard someone call his name. "David…David, please wait." He turned around and saw Professor Logan hurriedly walking towards him.

"David, it's good to see you. Welcome to Columbia."

"Thank you Professor Logan."

"Please come and join us."

He knew all eyes were on him as he followed the professor

back to the group. "Gene, I would like to introduce you to David Emerson."

"David, it is nice to make your acquaintance. I'm honored. You already have a fine reputation around here. Your abilities are astounding for someone so young."

David's mind raced and his heart was humbled. One of the most renowned mathematical geniuses in the world had just complimented him. "P-Professor Godard, I-it is an honor to meet you sir."

"Please call me Gene. I hate formalities."

David was then introduced to the others, all of whom were working on doctoral degrees. He tried to ignore their curious stares.

"Did you received an email from the Math Department about your research assignment?" Professor Logan asked.

"I did. It said that I was assigned to research Mathematical Physics."

"That's right. You are going to be working with Gene and I for the foreseeable future. You have a special gift, and I know you are going to help us forge new ground."

"Thank you sir. I'm looking forward to working with everyone on the team. Hopefully I'll be able to learn and contribute in a meaningful way."

David spent the next half hour listening and absorbing everything they discussed. It made him feel like he was already part of the team. Professor Logan took David on a tour of the research department when the meeting concluded, explaining new areas of math and physics and their future role in the quantum universe. They ended their tour in his office where two packets awaited. One contained information about research procedures and a schedule for the coming semester. The other contained an overview of the mathematical methods currently being researched.

David walked back into the campus frenzy with a new sense of purpose. Within seconds a group of female students surrounded him and introduced themselves. He spent the next half hour getting to know them as they went from booth to booth.

# Chapter 24

David's roommate was in the middle of four giant suitcases unpacking when he got back to his room. He looked slightly startled when David opened the door. "Hi Ryan. It's nice to finally meet you in person." They shook hands. "Likewise. This room is a little snug, but the view of campus is sick."

"Yeah, it is cramped, but being a student here makes it worth it. Do you need help unpacking?"

"Nah, I'm good. I need to relax, and unpacking is a way to relax. My mind is wound so tight from sitting in a plane for five hours. I hate flying. It scares the shit out of me. I always ask the person sitting next to me if they would be kind enough to talk to me. It helps keep my mind preoccupied during the takeoff and landing. Once the plane is flying smooth and steady I'm able to relax a little."

"I know what you mean. Flying makes me nervous too."

David was trying to figure out why Ryan looked so different from his picture.

"You used to have longer hair, right?" He asked.

"Yeah, I did, but I got sick of it."

"Shorter hair looks good on you. I almost didn't recognize you for a second."

"I also lost twenty pounds over the summer."

"Wow, that's amazing."

"Thanks. The dieting thing was hard at first, but I got the hang of it. You were the one who kind of inspired me."

"I did? How?"

"When I found out that you were going to be my roommate I checked you out on Facebook. I was curious to see what you looked like and what your interests were. I wasn't stalking you or anything..lol"

"Either was I," David, said, feeling as embarrassed as Ryan.

Ryan grinned. "First of all, you looked pretty young. You look younger in person." David laughed. "I guess."

"Then I saw how thin you were, so that inspired me to get my shit together and lose some weight."

David felt even more embarrassed. "I'm happy that I could motivate you that way."

"I feel a hundred percent better."

"Cool. Are you sure I can't help you unpack?"

"No, really, I'm good."

"When you're done, let the hall monitor know and he'll get one the maintenance guys to take your suitcases. He'll put them in the storage room."

"Cool. Thanks."

David sat at his desk and started going through the research packets Professor Logan had given him.

An hour had gone by, and David had forgotten to eat lunch in all the excitement of moving in, so he invited Ryan to have dinner with him at Lerner Hall. It was an opportunity for them to get to know each other. Ryan was quiet at first, like he had something on his mind, but was afraid to say it. David guessed that it probably had something to do with him being gay. "The food is really good. I can't believe the selections available," David said, while eating a chicken breast, baked potato, and green beans.

"Yeah, the food is excellent." Ryan was eating steamed vegetables and white rice. "I'm gunna have to stay away from this place so I don't gain that twenty pounds back."

"Me too," David said, empathizing with him.

"I'm sure you've never had to worry about getting fat. I mean, you can't weigh more than one hundred and twenty pounds, if that. I've always struggled with it."

"Just keep doing what you're doing diet wise and you'll be fine. I don't eat junk food, so there won't be any of that in our room, ok?"

"Thanks, but I don't want to change your lifestyle to suit me. Please don't feel like you have to be a certain way around me ok?" Ryan said, hoping he was making himself clear. David knew it was the perfect time to bring up the 'Tyrannosaurus Rex in the room' subject.

"Ryan, as you are probably aware by what it says on my Facebook page, I'm gay. I hope you're ok with that. If not, we can make other arrangements. I'll understand."

A few seconds of silence passed before Ryan looked up from his dinner. "Well, to tell you the truth, it did freak me out a little when I found out. I've never met anyone who is openly gay. I went to a boarding school in California, so I've been pretty sheltered. If anyone was gay, they were definitely in the closet. My school was all about making boys into men, just like it was back in the twentieth century. So, you're the first openly gay guy I've met. I know that sounds lame, but it's the truth."

"I'm not really that different from most people. Being gay is just one aspect of who I am. A lot of straight guys think the LGBTQ community is nothing more than people who are psychologically damaged and perverted. They think it's all about sex. You know, that we want to have sex with every guy we meet. It is such a sad perception, and totally untrue."

"I don't have a problem with it. You seem like a nice guy and I'm glad we're rooming together."

"Thanks. You seem like a nice guy too. I think we are going to have a lot of fun this year."

They ended up talking for a while and then finally made it back to their room a little after 7pm.

David put his headphones on and started reading more about his research assignment while Ryan continued unpacking and putting things away. David was in his own world reading away when someone knocked on their door. Ryan was putting some books on his shelf near the door, so he opened it and was greeted by a guy who looked like he had just stepped out of GQ magazine. "Hi. By any chance does David Emerson live here?" Marco asked.

"Yeah, he's right over there." Ryan opened the door a bit more so he could see. David had his back to them, oblivious to what was going on. "I want to surprise him."

"Sure, no problem. Ryan shut the door and then went over

and tapped David on the shoulder." David jumped slightly. He pulled his headphones off. "What's up?"

"Someone is here to see you."

"Thanks." David went to the door and opened it. Marco stood there grinning. David jumped into his arms and kissed him. A minute later they came up for air. "I can't believe you're here. How did…what happened?"

"There was no way I was staying in Boston with you here. My father loaned me his private jet so I could surprise you. That was his present to us."

"Tell him thank you so much from me."

"I will." David kissed him again, and it was gentle and loving and it made Marco's heart feel alive. A couple of girls walked by and giggled at the sight of two hot guys making out in the hall. They stopped and watched with curiosity. Finally one of them said. "Awe, that is so romantic." They walked around them and continued on their way.

"I've missed you." David whispered. He put his hand to Marco's face and traced his jaw line with his fingertips. "I love you so much."

"I love you too. I missed holding your body against mine. Being stuck in Europe sucked. I hated every minute. And then this stupid ass Boston trip. But it was worth it to see the look on your face."

David kissed him again, but this time it was intense, urgent, like he was slipping into some dark void and needed that kiss to save him.

"I need to make love to you," Marco whispered. David's

body trembled in his arms. "I want you so bad it hurts," David moaned.

"Let's head over to my place."

"Right now?"

"Yeah." Marco looked into David's blue eyes and could see pure love reflecting back at him. It was the kind of love he knew he didn't deserve. "I know you should be spending the first night with your roommate, but would you spend the night with me instead? I want to wake up next to you."

"I really want to, but it might seem rude." David looked into those dark brown eyes and smiled. "Let me ask Ryan if he wouldn't mind."

"Cool. I'll wait out here."

David went back in the room as saw Ryan at his computer with his back against the door. He had his headphones on which let David know that he was giving Marco and him some privacy. He thought it was a nice gesture. He tapped Ryan on the shoulder. "Can I ask a favor?"

"Sure."

"Would you mind if I stayed with my boyfriend tonight. I know it's a selfish thing to ask, but..." David felt ashamed.

"Hey, I understand completely. No problem."

"I promise to make it up to you. Thank you so much."

"Anytime."

David went to the door and let Marco in. "Ryan, I would like you to meet my boyfriend, Marco Valerio."

Ryan extended his hand. "It's nice to meet you."

"Nice to meet you too. Where are you from?"

"Carmel California."

David started packing some essentials while the two of them talked.

"Sweet. I've been there with my parents a few times. The scenery is unbelievable." Marco said.

"It is pretty cool from a geographical standpoint, but it's boring."

"How so?"

"Well, it's basically a playground for rich old prunes who love to pretend they're young. There is zero night life for teenagers. That's why I wanted to go to school here."

"That makes sense. David and I will have to show you around."

"Thanks, I'd like that."

They hung around the room for a few more minutes out of courtesy for Ryan, but kept looking at each other, anticipating their night together. Marco finally gave David a look that said he wanted to go. He made sure his area of the room was neat and tidy, like he was working out some guilt for leaving his roommate alone. He finally relented. "I'll see you sometime tomorrow. Thanks again for understanding."

"Anytime."

A brand new world greeted David and Marco as soon as they stepped outside. The sun had already set, creating a soft multi-colored evening sky. The buildings were lit up all across campus in a warm inviting glow. David stopped to take in the view. "This is amazing. Look at this place."

Marco was even awestruck. He held David's hand as they

both stood at the far edge of the garden. "This is like a perfect fairytale, and we get to live within it."

"I still can't believe that I go to school here." David rubbed the goosebumps on his arms. He could see his new reality. With all of the goodbyes from parents now part of the past, the campus had settled back into an academic haven once again. They watched people walking from building to building, people playing Frisbee on the south lawn in front of Butler, and lots of people sitting on the steps in front of Low library talking and laughing.

"Let's head over there for a few minutes to take this all in, ok?" Marco suggested.

"Sure."

As they walked, David could feel a real connection with Marco and their new home. It wasn't magic or Disney World giddiness; it was integrity and hard work that was a common bond between them. It was finding someone who wasn't afraid to be themselves. That was the foundation he knew would stand the test of time in any loving relationship.

They walked into the crowd of partying students, and kept on walking. They walked up the steps of Low Library and turned around to take it all in. They stood there hand in hand admiring the soft glow of the campus buildings against the darkening sky. It was an impressive sight.

"Olympus," David said, with a warm grin.

Marco squeezed his hand. "Zeus."

"Apollo."

"Definitely. It's good to be home." Zeus turned and kissed

Apollo, and all seemed right with the universe. "Are you ready to meet the mortals?"

"Definitely." Apollo answered. They descended those mighty steps and walked right back into the thick of the crowd. Within seconds people were introducing themselves. David stood there in awe as he watched Marco talk to complete strangers with ease, like he had known them for years. They spent the next half hour talking and laughing and exchanging social media info with a brand new group of friends. The thing David liked the most was that no one cared that they were gay. Not one flinch or condescending look happened whenever Marco put his arm around him, or held his hand, or kissed him. David finally found out what it felt like to be treated like a normal person. Sadly, he had to leave home to experience it.

At one point a couple of the girls asked if they wanted to hang out at their dorms. Marco politely declined and explained. "David and I are going on a date tonight. Let's get together sometime this week and party a little." A few minutes later they headed to Marco's building.

"I'm excited to see what my room looks like."

"Me too."

On their way over, Marco stopped walking, turned to David and hugged him. "I want my room to be our special place, ok?"

"I'd really like that," David said, feeling completely protected in his arms.

Marco checked in at the front desk so he could get his

packet of information, his entrance card, and the passcode to his room. The girl at the desk let him know that his suitcases had arrived from the airport. "They're in the storage room on the third floor. You can get them anytime you like." she said, giving Marco an "I'm available" smile.

David realized that he better get used to all the attention Marco was sure to attract. It was already happening. Marco continued his charm offensive. "What is your name?"

"Susan."

"Thank you for helping me out Susan."

"You're welcome. If there is anything else you need, please don't hesitate to ask."

"Thank you." Marco turned and kissed David. "Well, are you ready to see it?"

"Yeah."

Much to Marco's surprise, the elevator only went to the fourteenth floor, and it was extremely slow. "Man, this sucks," he said, as they climbed the stairs to the fifteenth floor. "I'm going to talk to my father about donating some money for a new elevator so we can ride all the way up. This is ridiculous."

"Hey, don't worry about it." David started kidding him. "Just think, you can tell your friends how hard you have it at college."

"Are you making fun of me, David Emerson?"

"Why yes I am." David playfully put his arms around Marco and started tickling him.

Marco grabbed hold of David's arms and pulled him close.

"I like the anticipation I'm feeling right now, knowing what awaits us."

"So do I."

They walked as quiet as they could up the steps so they wouldn't attract any attention. David followed Marco, admiring his cute little butt. He couldn't resist any longer and grabbed a cheek. "Is that all for me?" Marco turned and gave him an amorous grin. "Are you by any chance asking me to bottom for you?"

"No, but I wouldn't mind doing something else that you might enjoy."

"What do you have in mind?"

"Let me show you." David walked two steps up, leaned in and licked Marco's lips for a few seconds before inserting his tongue in deep. He loved the dreamy smile on Marco's face.

"Oh yeah, I'm definitely up for that." He spun David around and pinned his body against the stairwell wall. "I want to make love to you right here, right now." He gave David soft little kisses as his hands moved down to his slender hips, and then to his ass. David tensed up a little and whispered, "We should probably wait until we get to your room before we…. you know."

"Mmm. Yeah, we probably should." Marco grinned. They both composed themselves enough to finally enter the hallway.

It was fairly quiet as they walked past some of the dorm rooms. Different styles of music and muted conversations spilled out in muffled tones, indicating things had settled into the evening mode. They noticed a few doors were partially opened, so they tried being stealthy, but their luck had run out as they tried to sneak past the third open door. As soon as they walked by a tall lanky guy opened the door all the way and caught them. "Are you guys looking for someone in particular?" Marco turned around. "No, I live on this floor. I just arrived on campus." He extended his hand. "I'm Marco."

"Nice to meet you. I'm Grant. Welcome to John Jay." A second later Grant's roommate came out to see what was going on. He saw David and Marco holding hands. "I'm Rafi," he said, looking directly at Marco. Then he sighed. "Another cute one taken."

"I'm Marco. Nice to meet you. This is David, my boyfriend."

David shook both of their hands, "It's nice to meet you guys. Wasn't the campus crazy today with everyone moving in?" Rafi gave David an insincere smile. "Yes it was. The best part of the craziness was finally getting rid of my parents." No one laughed.

David noticed Rafi checking Marco out the whole time they talked. He felt insecure and out of place for some reason. He knew he had nothing to worry about, but that feeling was there. And then Rafi made it worse by getting in a little dig. "David, I take it you go to high school around here." David gave him a faint smile. "No. I'm a new freshman here."

"Sorry about that."

"It's ok. I've heard that a couple of times today. I take it as a compliment."

Marco glared at Rafi. "It was nice meeting you guys. We'll

have to hang out soon." And with that quick blow off, they headed down the hall.

"What a fucking asshole. I wanted to punch that fucker in the face," Marco said, seething. David grinned as he squeezed Marco's hand. "Rafi sure does have the hots for you."

"People like him never know when to back off."

"Don't worry, I didn't take it personally. I'm sure you get that kind of thing all the time, right?"

"Yeah, pretty much." Marco turned to David and apologized. "I'm really sorry about that."

"Don't be sorry for what other people do. I know you're irresistible. And I know you love me."

"Thanks for understanding."

They finally made it to Marco's door and stood there for a few seconds staring at it in wild anticipation. "Well, are you ready to see what it looks like?" Marco asked.

"Definitely. This is like Christmas in August."

Marco punched the code in and turned the handle until it clicked. He looked at David and smiled as he opened the door. It was dark except for a little moonlight coming through two arched windows. Marco found the wall switches and flipped them up. Several strategically placed lamps illuminated the room in a warm glow. "Aah, my mother knows how much I like mood lighting."

"Marco, this is unbelievable."

"Yeah, it is. My mother really outdid herself this time."

Staring them in the face was the most perfect dorm room imaginable. The first thing David noticed was how big it was.

It was at least three times the size of his room. He kissed Marco on the cheek. "Your mom has great taste."

"It's everything I envisioned." Floor to ceiling white bookshelves lined the far wall of the room. Marco's mother filled them with his favorite novels. A Bang & Olufsen sixty-five inch wireless flat screen and sound system were neatly centered. A docking station, Xbox One and PS4 lay on a pullout shelf. Two Avegant Glyphs were hung up on hooks, and mood lighting lit the entire area.

A black Cloten leather couch, a black Sydney premium leather chair, and two modern end tables with chrome lamps faced that entertainment area. Two burgundy and gray Persian rugs gave the room warmth within the sleek modern motif. There were two arched windows with perfect views of main campus. Under the left window was a white and gray desk with a MacBook Pro and iPad sitting there waiting to be put to use. Under the other window was a contemporary king bed. It had a chrome and gray bed frame, a burgundy comforter, and six overstuffed pillows. David couldn't get over it. "Just think of the view you are going to have every time you wake up."

"No, think of the view we are going to have when we wake up in each other's arms."

David smiled. Marco gently caressed his back as he contemplated asking him the question. A question that had been on his mind since that night at the lake. Marco had planned the lake visit so he could have emotionless sex with David. He fantasized about it for months. He knew David was a virgin and couldn't wait to fuck that virginity out of him. But something else happened instead. He felt love for the second time in his life as he held David's naked body in his arms. That night, David had taken him to emotional depths he never knew existed. Marco truly loved him and wanted to take the next step in their young relationship. And he did.

"David, I love you so much it hurts. I hate when we aren't together, so will you live with me? Here?" Marco was literally shaking as he asked. David was stunned. "What? I mean….. you…and…" his voice trailed off. Marco cupped David's face with his hands and gave him tiny gentle kisses. "I love you more than anything. Will you do me the honor and live with me?" David wanted to say yes in the worst way, but fought off the urge to give him an answer. He contemplated the significance of Marco's invitation, and then tried to explain his apprehension as best he could. "I'd love to live with you, but don't you think we might be moving a little fast?"

"No. I don't. Not at all. I love you and you love me, so what is there to think about?"

David looked into those pleading eyes and then down at the floor. He didn't want to say the wrong thing. "Will you give me a couple of days to think about it?"

Marco was disappointed, but understood. "Sure. I don't want you to feel pressured."

David knew he had hurt Marco's feelings and wanted to make it up to him. "I love you so much. Please make love to me now." Marco smiled as he put his hand in David's and led him over to the bed. His heart raced with wild anticipation as he held David in his arms and kissed him. A couple of minutes later he whispered, "I love you more than anything in this whole world." Marco gazed into David's piercing blue eyes and could see the truth. It was real love, something he thought he would never find again.

Marco began to slowly, gently, remove David's clothes until his slender ghost-like body was completely naked. David stood there vulnerable, exposed, wanting nothing more than to please the guy he loved. He watched as Marco took his clothes off, revealing a perfectly defined body that wanted only him. They made love all night long. Marco was gentle and loving. David was in heaven. In the early morning hours they finally fell asleep in each other's arms. A crescent moon streamed its celestial light through the arched window, making their perfect naked bodies glow in harmony with the rest of the universe.

# Chapter 25

It turned out to be a perfect morning on the first day of class. The residence halls had come alive at the same time the sun was waking up. The energy level, the anticipation, the day of reckoning began to ramp up in each young mind. David had already showered and dressed an hour earlier due to a restless night of sleep. It was a combination of nervous excitement, self-doubt, and being able to finally open the door that had always been just out of reach. It was hoping that he could slay the academic dragon that lay before him. His restless night's sleep was also caused by a terrible nightmare.

David had gone to bed early that night so he could make the morning come faster, but that didn't work at all. He tossed and turned for twenty minutes before deciding to read a book, hoping it would eventually make him sleepy. He finally fell asleep just after 1am, but was jarred awake a couple of hours later by a nightmare that played with his mind. He dreamt that he woke up late for class, had a major exam and forgot to study, went to his locker naked, and couldn't remember the combination. Then he started crying in front of all the people who were laughing at him as his naked body slid down the locker in shame. Then they started chanting, "You're a stupid faggot loser," over and over. He sat up in bed, his heart racing, his body shaking, as he tried to focus his eyes in the dark. He breathed a sigh of relief when he realized that he was still in his dorm room. There was no way his was going back to sleep after that dream. He put on his headphones and listened to *Snakes and Arrows* and *Clockwork Angels* as the early morning hours slowly ticked away.

Σ Ω

David and Marco met for breakfast at Lerner Hall. He was excited about the day ahead, but noticed that Marco seemed subdued and preoccupied, like something was on his mind.

"Is anything wrong?" David asked.

"No, everything's fine. I just didn't get very much sleep last night."

"Either did I. It must be catchy. I was going to text you but I figured you were fast asleep."

Marco smiled. "I was going to text you too." He changed the subject to get his mind off of his insecurities. "I can't believe the schedule you have. Are you sure you're going to be able to handle it?"

"I know it looks difficult, but I'm definitely up for it. I prioritize things a certain way and then everything falls into place. I've been doing it my whole life," David said.

"Just like a math proof, right?"

"Yep. Don't worry, I'll be fine. What classes do you have today?"

Marco didn't seem quite as thrilled or challenged.

"Philosophy and two boring English Lit classes. The English department is making me take them. It's a fucking waste of time."

"Come on, don't be negative. They're supposed to give you the foundation you need."

"Yeah, yeah, I know. But I just want to write. They're making me wait until next semester. It sucks."

"Just enjoy the whole experience and it will all work out. You write every night anyway, right?"

"My beautiful David, always the optimist. I can't believe you're already taking Honors Math, and what's that other one they put you in?" David gave Marco an embarrassed look.

"Intro to Higher Mathematics," he sheepishly said.

"Well, I guess everyone notices when you're a genius."

"Please don't say that. I'm not one of those. I just love math."

"Well, you're one of the smartest people I've ever met."

"Awe, thank you for saying that. You do know how smart you are, right?"

"I thought I did. But have you noticed that we're surrounded by smart people. I'm realizing how average I am."

"Believe me, you are not average. You are one of the smartest people I know. And you're right about the intelligence level around here. But here's the thing, it's not about comparing ourselves, it's about pursuing what we love at another level." David put his hand on Marco's to reassure him.

"What are you smiling about?" Marco asked.

"Everything. Me. You. Living here. Going to my first class. I've been waiting a long time for this moment."

Marco looked at David with a slightly lost look, like he was trying to find the perfect words to describe what he was feeling.

"Hey, are you ok?" David asked.

"I'm just admiring you."

David leaned close, close enough to where their lips were almost touching. He whispered, "I love you so much it scares me."

"I feel the same way." Marco knew it was the perfect moment to ask again. "Have you thought anymore about what I asked you last week?"

David's gaze dimmed ever so slight. "Yes, I have. A lot, actually..." Marco cut him off. "I'm glad. I-I want...David...I never thought I could love someone as much as I love you. I really mean that. Would you please do me the honor and live with me?"

"Marco, I...." He cut David off again. "Think how perfect it would be waking up next to each other every morning. I need to see your face and feel your body next to mine."

David had thought long and hard about Marco's invitation. It was easy to say yes from an emotional and physical standpoint. But he took in logical considerations while making his decision. "Marco, I love you and want to live with you some day, but I think we need to take things a little slower. I mean..."

Marco interrupted him. "Don't you love me?" He could feel David slipping away. He wasn't used to not getting his way. He was beside himself to the point where he couldn't fully comprehend what David was trying to say.

"Of course I love you. I just told you a second ago. That's not the issue."

"Then what is the issue? I don't get it. I don't get it at all," Marco said, in a condescending tone.

David knew he was going to be upset, so he kissed him on the cheek and tried to explain with more clarity. "I do want to live with you. You don't know how many times I've thought about it. About us being together for the rest of our lives. That's how much I love you. But we just got here, and we're finally getting to know each other in real terms. In day to day terms instead of the long distance thing. But, at the same time, I don't want to put any pressure on you, thinking that you always have to be with me every second of the day."

"I don't feel pressured about that at all. I love being with you."

"And I love being with you, but I also want us to have the normal college experience. You know, where we make new friends and hang out with them when we aren't together. I know it probably sounds dumb, but I have this romantic notion about college life. Making friends from all over the world. Finding out who I am as an individual. And seeing what I can achieve in the mathematical and physics community. It's what I've dreamt about since I was little."

Marco felt lost. Alone. "I want to be…" David put his finger to his lips to shush him. "And the most important thing of all, having a beautiful caring boyfriend take me out on dates, and me taking him on dates."

"Am I that boyfriend?" Marco asked, feeling rejected.

"Yes, of course you are. I like the idea of calling you up after a long day and asking you out for dinner and you saying 'I'd love to.' Then I go to my room and make myself look nice just for you. I walk over to your building, take the elevator, and climb the stairs to your floor with flowers in my hand. You open the door and I give them to you. I kiss you and tell you how much I love you. We walk hand in hand through the center of campus, out to Broadway, ending up at our favorite little restaurant. Then after dinner we go to the movies or just take a nice walk or go back to your room and make love. We lay in each other's arms knowing we were meant for each other. And I'll stay the whole night because I won't be able to leave. Other nights I'll go back to my room because the anticipation of being in your arms again gives me a high I can't explain."

Marco was broken hearted, but completely turned on. He wanted to forget about classes and take David back to his room and make love to him. And then fuck him. He wanted to fuck him until he moaned, "Yes I'll live with you," over and over.

"That is so romantic, but why….." Marco said, his voice trailing off.

"Why can't we have all of that and live together? That's what you were going to say, right?"

"Yeah." Marco pushed his tray away and slumped in his chair.

"Just know that I love you more than anything. We have lots of time."

They sat their in silence, looking out the window at

everyone crisscrossing the campus on their way to class. Marco finally turned to David. "I understand what you're saying. I really do. I want you to know that I'll wait until you're ready."

"Thank you for understanding." David gave him an amorous grin. "Will you go out with me on Friday?"

"I'd like that. Where are you taking me?"

"I thought we could take the subway to 72nd Street and go to Central Park for a romantic walk. Then I'll take you to this little Mexican restaurant on Columbus Avenue that I checked out online. We'll have dinner outside and enjoy the neighborhood atmosphere." He kissed Marco's pouting lips and gave him the look. "Then we could, you know…"

Marco grinned, "Do you wanna sleep over Friday night?"

"Why, yes I do," David said, with a seductive smile. "Should I bring my sleeping bag and pajamas with me?"

"Nah, I don't think you'll need those things."

Rafi and two girls walked up to their table just as they were getting ready to leave.

"Hey Marco, are we still on for tonight,"

David watched as Rafi put his hand on Marco's shoulder, giving it a slight caress. Then he turned to David, "Hi. It's good to see you again. I hope you had fun at our hall party."

"I did. It was nice meeting everyone."

Rafi's hand stayed firmly planted on Marco's shoulder. David was trying with all his might not to get jealous. After all, he had just given Marco his rationale about making friends.

"Hey Marco, it's good to see you again," Avani said, with

a smile that easily revealed her crush. Marco seemed oblivious to the fact that both of them were hitting on him. David was jealous. It was as simple as that. He tried to stay calm while they chatted away. He was in Marco's world and understood it was going to happen a lot. This is where trust would come into play. David trusted Marco implicitly, so he decided to enjoy Marco's friends.

While Marco, Rafi, and Avani talked, the other girl was giving David the once over. She interrupted Rafi. "Aren't you going to introduce me to these cute boys?"

"Forgive my rudeness. Olivia, I would like you to meet Marco, my hall mate. And this is his boyfriend David." Her smile faded, but remained gracious as she looked longingly at David.

Rafi noticed and gave a lamenting sigh. "Yes Olivia, the cute ones are always taken, or they're gay." Marco gave David a look that said, "Get used to this."

After the flirtatious episode ended, Marco asked what the plan was for later that evening.

"A bunch of us are going out for dinner, and then we're going to the Top of the Rock at Rockefeller Center to take in the views of the city."

"That sounds like a good plan." Marco asked David, "Would you like to go with me?"

"I'd love to, but I'm meeting with my research team at seven."

"Do you mind if I go?"

"Not at all. It sounds like a lot of fun."

"Cool."

They headed out to the main campus together. Rafi quickly positioned himself so he was walking next to Marco. They talked about a hall meeting that was coming up on Wednesday. Avani made small talk with David while Olivia continued to check him out. David was oblivious to it because he was concentrating on the flirting Rafi was engaged in with Marco.

Just as they were all about to go their separate ways, Rafi put his hand on Marco's back and said, "I'm really looking forward to hanging out with you tonight."

"Yeah, I think everyone is going to have a great time."

Once Rafi and the girls were safely out of sight, Marco turned to David. "I'm sorry about all that. Just know that I know what he's doing."

David grinned. "Yeah. It seems like someone is still crushing on you."

"I've tried to subtly get him to back off, but he just doesn't get it. I am really sorry."

"Don't be. You can't help it that you're so charming and handsome."

"Come on, don't make my ego any bigger than it already is." Marco grabbed David and started tickling him. "Cut it out you goofball or I'll wrestle you to the ground." David put his arms around him. "It's ok that other people find you so attractive."

"Does it bother you?"

"Not really. I trust you."

"I'm glad. You have nothing to worry about."

"I know. But Rafi really has it bad for you."

"Yeah, but he'll figure out that it is never going to happen between us."

"I hope he figures it out soon."

Marco kissed David on the forehead and then started grinning.

"What are you grinning at?"

"I'm jealous. Olivia was undressing you with her eyes. She wanted to get you naked in the worst way."

David's face turned five shades of red. "Yeah, that was uncomfortable."

"For your information Mr. Emerson, you are one of the cutest guys on campus. You are going to get hit on a lot, so you better get used to it too."

"That's not true and you know it," David said, feeling self-conscious.

"Sometimes it is hard to see certain things about oneself, so I'll fill you in. You are so cute that you give me goosebumps every time I look at you. You have a magic quality that is hard to explain. We've only been here a week and so many people have already checked you out. It makes me jealous, but it also makes me smile because you don't realize what you are doing to people around you.

So just know that girls and guys are going to continue to hit on you."

David seemed stunned. "You're just saying that to make me feel good, right?"

"I'm dead serious. So please be careful."

When they got to the upper campus, Marco asked David if he wanted to go out for lunch.

"Yeah, I'd love to."

"Cool. I'll meet you in front of the math building. Text me when you're done."

They kissed, wished each other good luck, and then headed in opposite directions.

# CHAPTER 26

The Mathematics Building was humming with students hurrying to make it to class on time. David savored every moment as he walked up the winding staircase to the fourth floor. The echoes of nervous voices and hurried footsteps gave him chills. He swore he could hear ghosts from the past giving him words of encouragement with each upward step.

He walked into the lecture hall fifteen minutes early hoping to find a few good seating choices. It was about a third full, with most of the students either sitting way up front, or way in the back. He decided to sit in the middle, about halfway up so he could visually take in the atmosphere. He scooted semi-sideways down an empty aisle, slipped his backpack off and sat down. His intense deep eyes scanned the entire room, etching everything into his brain. Emotions of a lifetime, the vast unknown, rushed through his veins like ripples through the universe. And it felt perfect.

Students started coming through the doors in droves a few minutes later. The first thing David noticed was how old everyone looked compared to him. Being the only freshman in the class was intimidating. Going into slight panic mode, he made himself as inconspicuous as possible. With his bangs covering his eyes, he scrunched down and kept his head low while powering up his laptop. He thought about Professor Godard teaching the class, hoping it would calm him down enough to get through the class in one piece.

People were staring at him when he finally got the nerve to look around again. He quickly averted his eyes, trying not to panic. He decided to text Marco to calm his nerves. "I know this sounds weird, but people are staring at me. I feel so out of place." Marco texted back. "You'll be fine. All those seniors aren't used to having a middle schooler in their class." It made David smile. "Cut that out. This is scary stuff. How is your class?"

"Hasn't started yet, but everyone seems cool. It's a small class, which I like. Don't be afraid. You belong there and you know it. Have fun with it. Love you."

"Thanks for the encouragement. Love you too."

With his heartbeat finally slowing and his confidence re-turning, he started thinking about Miguel and what he must be going through. He sent him a text. "Good luck today. We need to hang out soon." Within seconds Miguel responded. "You too. Do you wanna meet up for lunch today?"

"Sorry I can't. How about tomorrow?"

"Sure. I get out of class at 1:30"

"Me too. Let's meet at Lerner at 1:45."

Miguel texted two thumbs up and a smiley face. As David was slipping his phone into his pocket, he keyed in on a con-versation a group of students were having two rows behind him.

"Is he the one Professor Logan has been talking about?"

"He must be. Look how young he is."

"Awe, he's so cute."

"Can't be more than fifteen or sixteen."

"He's adorable. Love his hair."

"It's going to be nice having a cute genius running around here for a change."

The girls started giggling, knowing David had heard every word. He wished the professor hadn't said anything, but hated feeling sorry for himself, so he decided to deal with it like Marco suggested. He sat back up, moved his bangs out of his eyes and smiled, knowing at least a dozen sets of eyes were still focused on him. He even turned around and said hi to the girls. It was a simple way to let them know it was all good.

# Chapter 27

He stared, slunk down, silent, like a lion ready to devour its prey. This sleek sharp carnivore couldn't keep his eyes off of that pale blond snack. He crouched strategically at the far edge of the lecture hall, five rows back. The perfect angle. Infatuated by his adorable profile, his shaggy blond hair, and a skinny twink body, his hormones were being propelled beyond reason.

He needed to make his move. He got up, adjusted himself, and then quietly walked over to his row. "Is anyone sitting here?"

He looked up from his laptop and gave the carnivore a preoccupied smile. "No. Sorry." He moved his backpack and placed it between his feet. He couldn't believe how cute he was up close. How that slight glance set him on fire. He wanted this guy to be gay in the worst way. He wanted to do him right there. "My name is Jordan."

He looked up from his laptop again. "Hi, I'm David. Nice to meet you."

"Same here."

David's infectious smile was real, confident, and it made Jordan want him even more.

"Please don't take this the wrong way, but you look a little young to be in this class."

David stopped typing and grinned. "I guess. I turned eighteen over a month ago. Honest."

Jordan breathed a sigh of relief. "Cool. You must be one of those off the chart guys."

"What do you mean?"

"Only seniors are allowed to take this class. Plus you have to test in."

"Professor Godard gave me an override. I'm on his research team. He said this class would be nice starting point for me."

"I'm impressed."

David looked down at his laptop, indicating that he didn't want to talk anymore. Jordan wasn't going to let him get away that easy. "So, how do you like Columbia so far?"

"It's everything I envisioned. I'm happy classes are finally starting."

"It's a great place. The perfect college experience. Have you made any friends yet?"

"Yeah, I've made a few. I hope to make more once everything settles down."

"Cool. I'd love to hang out and show you around."

"Thanks. But are you sure you want to hang around with a freshman?"

Jordan laughed. "That's irrelevant. Friendships shouldn't have an age limit."

"I agree."

David had intoxicated Jordan by this point. He wanted to hold that slender body against his. He wanted that shy smile pressed against his lips. "Would you like to hang out later today?"

"I'd liked to, but I have three other classes today. Then I'm getting together with my research team."

"No problem. Let's exchange numbers. You can text me whenever you're free."

"That sounds good."

Everything got quiet when Professor Godard walked in. Jordan loved the excited look on David's face. It sent his mind back to when he was a young impressionable freshman. Sadly that was long ago and far away. His innocent smile faded, and then vanished. His sex-starved smile replaced it. He couldn't tell if David was gay or not, but it was a mathematical equation that needed to be solved soon.

The first class of the semester had now begun.

♫

Jordan and David were packing up their things and talking about the homework assignment when some of Jordan's friends spotted him. One look at David and they knew what Jordan was up to. They headed over to say hi. "We thought you skipped lecture today," this incredibly cute girl said. She gave Jordan a hug, but was eyeing David like he was a piece of delectable chocolate.

"Yeah, it wouldn't be the first time I skipped class."

"So, are you going to introduce us to your friend?" She asked, scooting closer to David.

"Guys, this is David. He's a new freshman." David tried to

stay calm so he could say something halfway intelligent. All that came out was a weak sounding "Hi."

Jordan introduced them one-by-one. "This is Marna, Joshua, and Chandler."

"It's nice to meet all of you."

Marna could tell that David was getting ready to leave, so she started asking him questions.

"So, how do you like it here so far?"

"I love it. The campus is great, and I love being in the city even though I haven't had a chance to see much of it yet." It was the perfect opportunity for Jordan to make his move.

"Well guys, we have to show our new friend what New York City life is all about. We're planning one of our regular Manhattan excursions this weekend. You know, hitting a few bars and dancing the night away. Would you be interested in joining us? It's a lot of fun."

David wanted to avoid the bar scene, so he tried to be tactful. "I'm not old enough to get into the bars, and I haven't received my research schedule for the weekend yet."

"No problem. There are quite a few bars that have something called college night. They let anyone in who is at least eighteen years old. It's alcohol free. All you have to do is show them your college ID."

"Oh, I didn't know that." Marna added, "We always go to the more upscale clubs where people aren't so overwhelming, if you know what I mean."

David's thoughts went to the night at the rave and knew exactly what she was talking about. "That's good to know."

Jordan jumped in. "Text me whenever you get your weekend schedule to let us know if you can make it or not."

David looked at his watch. "I have to head to my next class. It was nice meeting everyone."

Jordan didn't want him to leave. "What class do you have next?"

"Intro to Higher Mathematics."

"Are you kidding me? Holy fuck." He looked at David like he was an alien from another planet. Jordan and his friends had tried testing into that class multiple times and failed. He touched David's arm hoping that some of his intelligence or magic or whatever he possessed would rub off on him. "Do you know who is teaching that class?"

"No, but my other research professor told me that I would be pleasantly surprised."

"Professor Eldridge is teaching it."

A shy grin appeared on David's face. "Are you sure?"

"Yes I'm sure." Jordan was jealous and really turned on. He couldn't believe this hot twink was a genius too. "I don't know if you know this, but he's the most popular professor on campus."

"I figured. He's brilliant. He's been my hero since 8th grade. I can't believe I'm in his class. It feels unreal."

"Well, I'm sure you want to get going now that you know. Have fun."

"Thanks, I will." David walked to the aisle and started up the steps. He stopped and turned towards Jordan and his friends and waved, then he was out the door in a nanosecond.

Jordan looked at Chandler. "What?"

"It was so fucking obvious that you were coming onto to him. Take your time and plan it out, or you'll scare him away."

"Was I that obvious?"

"Duh. It looked like you were going to jump him any second."

Joshua went into protection mode. "Listen, you need to walk away from him. He's way too young for you."

Jordan grinned. "Yeah, he is young, but he's so fucking hot.

"How old is he anyway? Fifteen? Sixteen?"

"He is eighteen."

"You better cover up your woody. You're such a slut," Marna said, shaking her head and admiring the view. Jordan held his backpack in front of his crotch. "I want to have sex with him, but I think I like him too. He's definitely boyfriend material."

"Are you fucking kidding? You have feelings for someone other than yourself?" Chandler asked, totally stunned.

"Yeah, I can't believe it myself. I need to find out if he's gay. I don't want to waste my time on a straight guy. I hope he is. There is something magical about him, I fucking swear."

Marna gave Jordan the usual look. "You've said that about a few other guys in the past."

"Yeah, I know, but this feels completely different."

"I can't believe you just said that. Maybe our Jordan is finally growing up."

He stood there looking at the door David had just walked

out of. "Maybe I am."

"Well, if he is straight, I want my chance with him," Marna said. They looked at each other and sighed. Joshua tried to talk some sense into both of them. "You guys need to leave him alone. I mean, he's really young and doesn't seem to be jaded at all. So don't fuck him up."

Marna reluctantly agreed. "Did you see the look on his face when you told him about Eldridge? It was like he had just opened up the best Christmas present ever. I wanted to hug him."

"So did I." Jordan envisioned David in his arms.

They finally made their way out of the lecture hall and headed their separate ways.

# CHAPTER 28

David was still in shock when he walked out of Professor Eldridge's class. He couldn't believe how cool it was to see him in the flesh. To know that he was now one of his students. To realize that he was the only freshman in a graduate level class. The stares from the other students no longer mattered. He walked down the spiral staircase replaying the entire experience over in his mind.

Professor Eldridge looked at David several times during the lecture. He didn't see it coming the first time it happened. He was taking notes while trying to watch his every move and consume every word. The inflection, the cadence, the enthusiasm between the professor's words and voice sounded like movements of a theoretical symphony to his ears. They arched and weaved in energico as the rondo drove the meaning home. Those words spoke to him, like they were trying to reveal theories hidden between the heart and mind. Theories that would become realities of his journey forward.

As this symphony played, Eldridge looked directly at David while explaining the importance of reasoning like a mathematician. Their eyes locked for a couple of seconds, and he could swear that Eldridge gave him a slight smile. He

DEEP IS THE HEART

wasn't sure because he looked away, like he got caught doing something wrong. Like he didn't belong there.

A million thoughts flooded his mind. Was he a participant in some kind of cosmic Shakespearian tragedy? Was his hero human, or was he a god? Intimidation turned into fear, and then into doubt. Why was he born so different from everyone else? Why was he a recipient of the intelligence gift? And the overrides? He knew that every student around him had to work their asses off to get into that class, and there he sat with the one and only override. Sitting their like a golden child, he finally realized how intuitive his bullies had been over the years. He really was a freak of nature.

With his confidence shaken and synapses racing, he told himself to get it together. That he belonged there regardless of how it happened. That it was his destiny. He sat up again and continued to listen to the professor's words. They were measured and hopeful. His insecurities faded away as his confidence returned.

David vowed not to look away if the professor looked at him again. And sure enough, it happened a couple of minutes later. Eldridge was casually walking around the stage explaining mathematical foundations and ended up standing near David. Their eyes locked onto each other while Eldridge stressed that the mathematics of M-Theory, and M-Theory's existence, could be potential keys to help reconcile General Relativity and Quantum Mechanics.

David didn't look away. Instead he tried to let Eldridge know that he was up for the challenge with a nod of his head.

The professor acknowledged him with a brief pause and a determined look before continuing on. It was a moment David would never forget as long as he lived.

When he got to the first floor he texted Marco to come meet him. Marco responded a few seconds later. "I'm on my way. My classes are good. See you in a few. Love you."

"Hurry, I need to kiss you. I love you too! ;-)"

Just as David was ready to walk outside, he heard someone call his name. He turned around to see who it was. Jordan came running up. "Fancy meeting you here," he said. "Do you mind if I walk with you?"

"No, not at all."

"So, how was your hero's lecture?"

David's smile lit the entire hallway up. "It was the most unbelievable experience of my life."

"I figured it would be."

The first day of college had shown David that pursuing ones dreams, working diligently, and staying true to core beliefs were more than just theoretical aspirations. His life had finally aligned in gravitational perfection: He was in love, and was being loved. He was being challenged on an entirely new academic level. He was making new friends from all over the world. And he had the honor of being taught by three professors who were opening cosmological doors and letting him play.

With Jordan by his side, David looked around to see if Marco was there. He wasn't, so he looked towards the hedgerow hoping to spot him. His face lit up when he spotted Marco walking past the lion with two girls. He was wearing his sexy sunglasses and talking away.

David and Jordan were half way up the sidewalk when Marco came around the hedgerow and stopped dead in his tracks. His smile faded and was replaced by shear panic when he saw Jordan walking next to David. He tried to get it together as he walked up to them.

Even though they hadn't seen each other in almost a year, sparks flew in every direction as Marco and Jordan looked at each other. They could never forget their night of perfect sex.

David was oblivious to the sexual energy that had surrounded him. Marco felt like he was going to throw up, but tried his best to smile when David ran up and kissed him.

"I missed you so much."

Marco held David tight. "I missed you too."

"How were your classes?"

"Better than I thought. How were yours?"

"Surreal. You won't believe it. Professor Eldridge is teaching Intro to Higher Math this semester.

"Nice. I'm really happy for you." He gave David tiny little kisses, trying to hold back the tears. Jordan felt defeated as he watched this scene play out. David was taken by a guy he couldn't compete with. Marco looked over David's shoulder, locking eyes with Jordan again, hoping like hell that he wouldn't say anything about their night of sex.

David gave Marco one more kiss before introducing Jordan. "I'd like you to meet a new friend of mine. His name is…"

"Marco, it's good to see you again," Jordan said, with a measured grin.

Dead silence erupted. A chilly gust of wind suddenly whipped through the trees to let them know their chance meeting was more than some stupid fucking metaphor. In an instant Marco and Jordan had become a binary star system orbiting around a common point. One was trying to hold on, while the other was trying to take away. It was a dance without movement. A shadowed tragedy beginning to play out at the edges. Eventual singularity. David looked confused. "Do you guys know each other?"

"Kind of. We met last year," Jordan said, suddenly realizing all was not lost.

"That is so cool. Where did you meet?"

Jordan smiled at the thought of Marco's tight little bubble ass propped in the air with his back perfectly arched, moaning in ecstasy with each ravaging thrust. "We met at a gathering for college students in Chelsea about a year ago."

Marco thought for sure that Jordan was going to tell the truth. He breathed a sigh of relief knowing he had been given a temporary reprieve.

"Yeah, it was one of those conferences where future college students get to talk with current students," Marco added, hoping Jordan would keep playing along.

"Wow! It really is a small world. We definitely have to hang out." David's innocence began to cut Marco deep.

"So I take you two are boyfriends."

"Yeah," they both said in unison. Marco went into total

protection mode at that point, knowing David was going to be Jordan's next sexual conquest. "We've been going out for almost a year." He took his sunglasses off and gave Jordan a look that said don't even try. Marco made a vow right then and there. Even If David found out about them and then broke up with him, he would still do whatever was necessary to protect him.

Jordan ignored Marco's threatening look and congratulated them on their relationship. "David, you need to know that Marco is a very special guy. He's smart and has passion for many things in life. He is extremely talented. I know this first hand."

"I agree. I'm lucky to have met him," David said, as he squeezed Marco's hand.

Marco did his best to remain calm. "David, are you ready to get some lunch?"

"Yeah, I'm starving." He turned to Jordan and asked, "Do you want to have lunch with us?"

"Maybe next time. I'm meeting up with Marna and Chandler in a few. Thanks for the invite though." Jordan gave David a hug. "I'm glad you got into Eldridge's class. Show him what you're made of."

"Thanks. See you in a couple of days."

"Marco, it was nice seeing you again."

"Same here. I hope you have a good senior year."

"Thanks, I think I'm going to make it one to remember." Jordan gave Marco a coded smile. His arm brushed against Marco's as he walked past him, out to the main walkway.

Marco stood there, desperation distorting his handsome face. David noticed. "Are you ok? You have this weird look."

"It's nothing, I'm fine. It's just...." Marco's voice trailed off as his eyes veered from David to Jordan and then back to David. "It's been a long morning and I'm hungry."

"Me too."

David felt like a little kid. He held Marco's hand and semi-skipped as they headed toward the main gate. "It's still hard to believe that I'm in his class. I have to call my parents tonight and tell them. I can't wait to tell Tyler and Melissa too."

"I know they're going to be happy for you."

"Yeah. They know how influential he has been in my life. Marco, you won't believe this, but he looked at me several times during his lecture."

"Of course he did. He knows greatness when he sees it." Marco adjusted his sunglasses and his thoughts. He pulled David close and hugged him deep. Almost to the point where he was hurting him. "I love you so much it hurts."

"I love you too."

With fierce kisses and his deep infinite embrace, Marco tried to create a barrier between his past and the present. Between love and random sex. Between David and rest of the world.

That cool summer breeze swirled around their perfect bodies and their fragile vulnerabilities, trying to let them know that forever was a real place.

# CHAPTER 29

Spending the evening apart proved more difficult than David realized. He walked across campus that chilly morning to meet Marco for breakfast. They filled each other in on their night of research and fun. They had been together every evening since arriving on campus, so doing things separately with new friends was the beginning of the next phase in their relationship.

Their conversation further validated David's concerns about living together.

He understood that having alone time and hanging out with other people were normal components of a healthy relationship. It was also an important aspect of college life he wanted to experience. He trusted Marco, and hoped their time apart would make them realize how lucky they were to have each other.

Looking and sounding dead to the world, Marco asked, "So how did your research go last night?" David gave him an empathetic smile. "What time did you get in last night?"

"You mean this morning. Around four I think."

"You must have had a great time," David said, trying not to sound jealous.

"Yeah we did." Marco decided to change the subject. "So

tell me about your research. I mean, what is Mathematical Physics anyway?" Marco put his cup of coffee to his lips, drinking it like it was the elixir of life.

"Mathematical Physics covers a wide spectrum within both fields of study. For the most part though, it is coming up with new mathematical ways to further advance physical theories. You know, everything around us, including ourselves is mathematical. It's cool to think that we are probably living within one gigantic mathematical equation." David knew he was getting carried away, so he pulled back on the enthusiasm. "The math we are concentrating on deals with Relativity and Quantum Relativistic Theories. It's pretty cool stuff."

Marco gave David a weak smile. "That sounds amazing. I wish I knew more about it. The farthest I went in math was Calc I. And I took the easier science classes to keep my GPA up." Marco hated to admit his academic weaknesses.

"I know I'm a geek when it comes to this stuff, but…" David stopped and gave Marco a quizzical look. "Do you have a hangover?"

"Yeah, I'm sorry. Actually, I think I'm still a little drunk." Marco felt embarrassed.

David rubbed his hand. "Keep drinking your coffee and I'll be quiet."

"Thanks, but please keep talking. I need to hear your voice."

David scooted closer and gave him a kiss on the cheek. "Ok. So tell me all about your night of fun."

"We started off by having dinner at Keens Steakhouse. I have to take you there."

"I'd like that."

"I wanted to show them some old world New York ambiance and class. That place definitely has it. Then we went to the Top of the Rock at Rockefeller Center to check out the skyline. Of course everyone loved the view. Manhattan is magical at night."

"I wish I could have gone with you."

"Me too. You were all I thought about last night. I want to take you this weekend. Are you free Saturday night?"

"I'll make sure I am." Then David's insecurities slipped into the conversation. "So then what did you guys do after that?"

"Rafi, Avani, and Olivia wanted to go to a club. Somehow they got fake IDs and wanted to see if they worked. I had mine, so we cabbed to the village and hit this cool little piano bar. The whole place was in party mode. We were singing show tunes with everyone else and I got carried away with my drinking. I'm sorry. You probably think I'm an alcoholic now."

"No, I don't. I think you were just showing your friends a good time and things just kind of happened."

"Thanks for understanding. I promise, this isn't how I am."

"I know."

"Can I come over tonight?" Marco asked, with eyes closed and head throbbing.

"Yeah, I'd like that."

They finished breakfast and headed in different directions across campus.

# CHAPTER 30

David was quieter than usual that evening while sifting through research data with a couple of other students. Professor Logan noticed and tried to help when they had a few minutes alone. "You seem a little preoccupied tonight. If something is bothering you, I'm a good listener."

David hesitated for a moment, thinking about all those eyes on him the day before. "To be honest, I'm a little nervous about taking Particle Physics and Cosmology."

"Why is that?"

David felt embarrassed to tell him the truth. "Everyone was staring at me in both of my math classes yesterday. It was the weirdest experience. And I know it is going to happen in this class. Honestly, I felt so out of place, like I didn't belong, and somehow they knew it too. I know that probably sounds stupid."

"Not at all. I can empathize. Being in higher level and graduate classes can be intimidating, especially for someone as young as you. But you belong there, and every student in those classes will know that soon enough. I believe you are destined for an extraordinary career, and I am afraid that you are going to have to get used to people admiring your abilities. That is why they are staring."

"That's nice of you to say, but I'm not any different than they are."

"I hate to say this, but you are. And there is nothing wrong with that. You simply have abilities that make you stand out from the rest."

David sat there processing what he had just heard. He finally gave Professor Logan a half smile.

"I appreciate your kind words. I'll do my best not to let it bother me anymore."

"I'm glad. And just to let you know, you won't be alone in physics. I gave an override to one other freshman. His name is Miguel Montag. My hope is that the two of you will get to know each other." David couldn't believe what he had just heard. "Miguel and I are already friends. We met during move-in day. We live in the same residence hall."

"That is good to hear. You two have similar gifts, which should help you overcome any trepidation about being surrounded by doctoral students."

David was ecstatic about Miguel being in the same class. It was just what he needed to hear to calm his nerves. He felt bad about only seeing Miguel a couple of times since arriving on campus. As he walked back to the dorm that night, he vowed to be a better friend and even help Miguel deal with the age issue if he needed it. He walked through the entrance and headed straight to Miguel's room so he could tell him the good news. They talked for a few minutes and then David had to leave because Marco texted, saying he was on his way over.

♥ Ω ♥

It was close to noon the next day when David headed to Pupin Hall. As the sun peaked through cumulus cloud formations, he walked next to the hedgerow in front of the Mathematics Building with the palm of his hand skimming the freshly trimmed tips. The ticklish sensation instantly became a wormhole to the past. He was transported back to the days as a little kid when he would go backpacking in the woods. He remembered running down random trails with his arms spread out like he was flying. The tips of the virgin undergrowth would tickle his palms, making him giggle. That sensation always made him feel connected to the world. That long ago memory gave him a sliver of comfort as he continued on.

He looked ahead and saw the lion waiting, so he ran the last twenty meters. His hand flew off the hedgerow and landing on the lion's left paw. David looked up and greeted him with a smile before continuing on his way.

The anticipation of attending his first physics class with Miguel felt perfect. The best thing about it was being able to spend more time with his new friend. He entered Pupin, walked down one flight of stairs and entered a narrow hall where he could see the back of the lecture hall through the open doors. Taking a deep breath, he walked in and looked around hoping to find Miguel sitting somewhere. But no such luck. Just as he was ready to go find a seat, he felt a tap on his shoulder. It made him jump. He turned and there was Miguel smiling away. "Hey, what's up?"

"Man, you scared me. Where did you come from?"

"Sorry about that. I tend to do that to people for some

reason. My friends call me Ghost because I seem to appear out of nowhere. I'm just stealthy I guess."

"I'll say you are. That is quite a talent."

"Thanks. Do you mind if we sit in the middle? That way everyone can stare at us without having to strain their necks." David laughed. "That sounds like a plan. Might as well get it over with." Within seconds David almost tumbled down the steps because he wasn't watching where he was going. Fortunately Miguel grabbed him by his backpack and saved the day. "Hey, don't kill yourself on the first day."

"I'll try not to. I'm such a klutz. Thanks for saving me."

Miguel was concerned. "You didn't get dizzy again, did you?"

"No. Honest. I just wasn't looking where I was going."

They continued down and slipped into the middle row. Miguel grinned. "This should give everyone the perfect view."

"I love the way you're handling the age thing."

"After all the staring the last couple of days, I decided to give them what they want."

"I know what you mean. It felt really weird. I even overheard people taking about me. It was uncomfortable. But I guess since we can't control any of it, let them stare and talk and get it out of their system."

"Exactly."

David overheard a group of students a few rows down talking about Supersymmetry while he and Miguel were powering up their laptops. One by one they started looking their way. Two guys even did double takes. Once David had his file set up, he looked at them with a hesitant smile. Miguel was far more confident and engaging. He waved and said hi and things got back to normal. That is until the floodgates opened up. Students piled in and the inquisitive stares began once again. A couple of minutes later, just as Miguel had predicted, they got it out of their system.

There were still five minutes before class started, so it gave David and Miguel a chance to talk. "You never mentioned that you were a physics major when we first met. It is so cool that we are pursuing the same major," David said.

"Yeah, I agree. I've come to realize that us meeting is definitely some sort of destiny. We must have been drawn together by a common quantum energy field or something."

"What do you mean?"

"Um…even though I'm wired to think logically, I still believe in destiny. Sounds weird, doesn't it?"

"No, not at all. I've done my share of wishing for things to go a certain way, and when I'm about to give up, somehow it works out. So I think this life isn't as random as it seems."

"You and I are connected in some weird way. I just know it."

David felt it too but didn't understand how or why. "Why do you think that?"

"While I was unpacking my stuff the first day here, something, or some kind of feeling told me to go check out the lounge. So I did. When I walked in I saw you looking out the window and knew we had to meet. Sounds crazy, right?"

"Yeah, a little. But I'm glad you came over and talked to

me because I was already getting homesick. And I was afraid for some reason."

"Maybe you needing someone to talk to drew me to the lounge. I don't know how destiny works, but it does. And then you helped me," Miguel said, with an edge of seriousness.

"I did?"

"Yeah. You stood up for me when your friends came over to meet me. I knew they didn't like me, and I know you stuck up for me."

"How do you know that?"

"Jay saw me in the lobby the next day and apologized for being an asshole. Then he told me how angry you were and how you defended me. You were the first guy here who made me feel like I belonged. I really appreciate that. It helped me get through a strenuous first week of feeling like an outsider."

"I'm glad I could help. Believe me, I know how it feels to be an outsider. It's the story of my life. Being the only openly gay teenager in a small town. My nerdy predisposition for the academic world. And my lack of desire to try and fit in with the high school royalty made me the perfect outcast. If it wasn't for my two best friends I would never have survived."

"It's nice to have friends that you can count on. I consider you a good friend."

"Thanks. I feel the same way."

"I'm glad. I've actually been trying to hook up with you, but I haven't seen you around Hartley. I even stopped by your room the other day to see if you were there, but no one answered."

"Sorry about that. It's just that I've been busy getting up to speed with my research team, and I've been spending a lot of time with my boyfriend."

"I totally understand. What is his name?" Miguel asked.

"His name is Marco. And please don't get the wrong idea about me. He's a new student here too, but we didn't just meet. We met last year when we were being interviewed. We've been going out for nine months."

"That's cool. I understand completely. So I guess I won't be seeing you other than in this class."

"No, it's not going to be like that at all. Marco and I have a great relationship, and we've talked about how we both need to have our own space, and to make new friends, together and separately. I really like you and I'm looking forward to hanging out together."

"Same here."

"Do you want to meet up later and have dinner together?" David asked.

"Sure. I have a Literature class at six-thirty, so we'd have to meet before then."

"No problem. I have to meet with my research team at seven. How does five sound?"

"Perfect. I'll pick you up at your room and we can walk over to Lerner together," Miguel said. A couple of minutes later the professor walked in and class began.

# CHAPTER 31

Marco wondered if he should do it. It drove him crazy thinking about it all through class. He finally decided to send the text. "Can you meet me for lunch?"

He waited for a response while standing outside Philosophy Hall with a huge knot in his stomach. A couple of minutes later he received a reply. "Yeah, that sounds good. Where do you want to meet? And what time?"

"Let's meet at Le Monde at two. It's on the corner of 113th and B'way."

"Cool. See you soon ;-)"

Marco's hand was visibly shaking as he slipped the phone into his front pocket. Inner turmoil and mixed emotions were starting to get the best of him. He needed to calm down and chill, so he headed over to the steps in front of the library to relax. Once there, he took his sunglasses off and rubbed his eyes. A million thoughts raced through his mind as he watched his hands continue to shake. *Get your shit together. Remember, you can handle anything*, he told himself, knowing it was true.

With a little time to kill he started reading *Lust, Caution* by Eileen Chang. It was the first required reading for his Modern Lit class. Ten minutes into the book a cute girl walked up the steps and sat near him. He didn't notice, so she decided to get noticed.

"It's an unbelievable day, isn't it?"

Marco barely looked up. "Definitely. The sun feels great."

"I haven't seen you around campus. Are you a new student?"

He stopped reading and finally acknowledged her. "Yes I am. And you?"

"I'm a junior."

"Cool. I'm Marco."

"Nice to meet you Marco. I'm Nora."

"It's a pleasure to meet you." He could tell where the conversation was headed by the look in her eyes.

She scooted closer. "So, how do you like Columbia so far?"

"I like it a lot. The campus atmosphere suits me perfectly."

"Same here. This is my third year here and I want the whole thing to slow down. It's going by way too fast."

"Yeah, good things always seem to do that. If only we could control time, or even change the past somehow," Marco said, his mind drifting to one situation in particular.

"That would be awesome."

He looked towards Hartley Hall lost in his thoughts at the exact moment Nora decided to make her move. "Marco, I'd love to get to know you better. Maybe we could go out for dinner sometime."

That offer snapped him back to reality. Marco tried to let her down gently. "I'd love to, but I'm seeing someone right now. I hope you understand."

"Yeah, totally," she said, trying not to sound disappointed.

"Don't get me wrong. I think you're nice, and very beautiful, but here's the thing. I'm gay."

Nora's smile returned. "That is so cool. Maybe we could hang out as friends then."

"I'd like that." They exchanged phone numbers and talked a while longer.

❥ ≠

Marco sat at a table in the outdoor patio of Le Monde checking his messages and soaking in the sun. For some reason he had a slight chill that he couldn't shake. A few minutes later his confident persona re-emerged when he saw who was walking towards him.

"Marco, it's good to see you again. Thanks for inviting me to lunch. It definitely has been a while, hasn't it?" Jordan said, smiling seductively as he sat down. "You know, I tried texting you a few times last year hoping we could become fuck buddies, but you never responded. How come?"

Marco glared at him. Jordan looked away for a few seconds, then tried to seduce him again. "You know, I've thought about you a lot. I was hoping I would see you around campus so we could continue where we left off."

"Jordan, we need to talk about a few things," Marco said, in a sterile tone.

"Come on, please don't be this way. I take it this little lunch is going to be about David instead of us hooking up again."

Marco wasn't about to lower himself to Jordan's level by responding to his sexual overtures. He had played that game too many times himself. "Yes, this little meeting is about David. I want you to back off. I know what you're trying to set up. It was written all over your face yesterday. I can still see it."

Jordan grinned and then leaned in so no one could hear. "I just want to be friends with him. I mean, he's really nice, and he's a fucking genius. He would be a nice addition to my study group. And just for your information, that look on my face yesterday was me thinking back to our night together when I fucked your tight little ass all night long. It was heaven, wasn't it?"

Against his better judgment, that night of perfect sex came alive in Marco's mind. He loved how Jordan took control and humiliated him sexually and emotionally. Being Jordan's slutty bitch had sent him over the edge multiple times. No one had ever made him feel that good.

"Jordan, I'm not naive. I want you to back off."

"You can't be jealous of me. Or can you?"

"That's not the point at all and you know it."

"Then what is the point? I mean, you don't own him. And what if I do want to ask him out? Are you afraid he might say yes?"

Marco wanted to beat the shit of him, but needed to keep his cool. "Let's take a walk so we can talk in private." He pulled out a fifty and placed it under the empty dish. They walked to Riverside Park and found a row of empty benches and sat down.

Marco looked at Jordan with conflicted emotions. "Look, I'm serious about you staying away from David."

Jordan sat there enjoying his power over the situation. He enjoyed playing mind games with younger guys because it was so easy.

"Come on Marco, please don't be like this. I really like you. I won't hit on David, I promise. There is no way I would want to ruin anything you have with him. That's why I didn't say anything yesterday. I'm not heartless you know."

"Thanks for keeping us between us." Marco said, finally relaxing a little.

"So, how did you and David meet?"

"We met last year when we were at Columbia for our interviews."

"That's cool." Jordan started getting crude again. "I can just imagine how fine David is in bed. Is he as good as I think he is?"

"Please stop. It's not like that at all. I'm in love with him."

"You're serious, aren't you?" Marco didn't say a word. "So let me get this straight. You're in love with David and you've changed."

"Yeah, I've changed. I'm not like you anymore."

"So, you're telling me that you haven't cheated on him at all? I don't fucking believe that for a second."

"I would never cheat on someone I love," he reiterated again, trying not to think about the three way he had just before they started dating. Even though they weren't officially boyfriends, he had in fact cheated on David.

"I think you're bullshitting me, but good for you if it's true." Jordan changed tactics again. "Marco, you might think you love him, but you probably don't. And the reason why I say that is because you and I are exactly the same. We love sex, not people. We aren't capable of loving anyone but ourselves."

"Fuck you."

"It's true and you know it. I'm just trying to be honest about who we are. I mean, come on, we picked each other up last year so we could have the best sex of our lives. You loved it. I loved it. We were so into it that you begged me to fuck you raw, and I did because it connected us on an entirely different level."

"Fucking bareback was so fucking stupid. I had to get tested for the next six months to make sure you didn't give me HIV."

"I told you that night I was HIV negative. I would never lie about a thing like that."

"Well, it was a stupid thing to do anyway."

"I guess, but we both loved fucking each other's brains out. For guys like us, it's all about having sex with as many guys as we can. We didn't pretend to love each other, we just gave our bodies what we constantly crave."

Marco knew it was true but was doing his best to change because he really did love David. "Yeah, I used to be that way, but I'm not anymore."

"You're serious, aren't you?"

"Yes. I fell in love with David the moment I met him. And it had nothing to do with sex."

"I don't believe you."

"It's true. You mean to tell me that you've never been in love with anyone?"

"No," Jordan said, even though he was crushing on David.

"I feel sorry for you."

"Please don't. I'm happy the way I am. At least I've accepted it, unlike you."

Marco didn't respond to his taunt. Instead, he took a deep breath and said, "Please stay away from David, ok?"

"I already told you I won't hit on him. Can I at least be friends with him in class?"

Marco thought about it for a few seconds before deciding. He didn't want David to get upset or suspect anything if Jordan all of a sudden started ignoring him. "Yeah, but that's as far as I want your friendship to go."

"Ok, no problem. And I promise never to say anything about us. You know, maybe we could be friends at some point."

"I don't think that is going to work out."

They talked for a few more minutes and then headed back to campus. As soon as they walked through the front gates they went their separate ways.

# Chapter 32

It was 5pm when Miguel knocked on the slightly opened door. David didn't hear him knock because he was so immersed in homework. Miguel peaked in and saw him working away, so he knocked louder and called his name. David's body flinched. He turned around and saw Miguel with a slight grin. "Hey, come on in."

"I hope I didn't scare you again."

"Nah...Um, yeah you did. Don't worry though, it's good for the heart." David got up and gave him a hug. "Welcome to my home. So, what do you think of my Amsterdam Avenue penthouse?"

"Regal, yet understated," Miguel said, in an English accent. They both giggled.

David watched as Miguel scanned the room and then focused on the wall next to his bed.

"Impressive. I love your posters." His eyes went from one galaxy to the next. "I think Sombrero and M51 are my favorites."

"Yeah, they are unbelievable. Messie is pretty cool too. But the Milky Way will always be my favorite."

Miguel's eyes veered to a poster next to David's pillow. It was a picture of the Milky Way peeking through silhouetted treetops. The intensity, the clarity, the subtle colors behind those darkened branches seemed other worldly. Magical. "I love this poster," he said, pointing to it.

"I took that picture on the hill behind my house a few weeks ago."

"That's mad crazy. You see this from your backyard?"

"Yeah. All the time."

"I'm so jealous."

"Please don't be. I am officially inviting you to fly home with me on one of our breaks. You have to see this in person to really appreciate it. That hill is my favorite place on earth."

"Thanks. I accept your invitation."

"Cool."

Miguel checked out the music posters next. "Who is Rush?"

"They're my favorite rock group. I always listen to them whenever I stargaze. Their songs trigger my mathematical imagination for some reason, allowing my mind to fly through the universe even though my body is still on earth. I know that sounds a little weird, but it's the truth."

"I definitely have to listen to them."

"It's an acquired taste, but once you get hooked, that's it. The other thing I like about Rush is their decades old friendship." David pointed to Geddy and Alex. "These two have been friends since middle school. They are the embodiment of true friends. I hope to have that same longevity with my best friend Tyler."

"From what you've told me about him, I'm sure it will happen."

"That's him," David said, pointing to a picture of Tyler and him from eighth grade taped to the wall.

"He's hot."

"Yeah he is," David lamented, and then changed the subject. "I have an idea. Let's go to the observatory one night next week. I'll bring my docking station so we can listen to Rush while we stargaze."

"Cool. It's a date."

"What kind of music do you listen to?" David asked, knowing he had dominated the conversation. "I like lots of different styles. I'm really into Sam Smith right now. His voice is so emotional and soulful. And his songs hit my heart in a special way. They tell stories about him being used by the guys he falls in love with. That he is never enough to satisfy them."

"They sound really sad."

"Yeah, they are. But their sadness is beautiful in a way because at least he knows where he stands. I just hope he finds that special guy someday."

David got quiet as he thought about all of his lonely years. How it became so unbearable at times. "I know the feeling," he said, almost in a whisper.

"Me too, unfortunately."

"Are you ready to get some dinner?" David asked, as he glanced at the picture of him and Tyler smiling away.

"Yeah, I'm starving."

They headed to Lerner and were lucky enough to get a

table near the windows so they could people watch. During dinner their conversation began to reveal analogous life parallels, even though they had grown up in radically different environments. Both of them were passionate about math, physics, cosmology, music, and philosophy. Both had the courage to come out in spite of the consistent hatred shown by their communities against gay people. David couldn't believe how good it felt to be openly gay, to have gay friends, and to live in a city and attend a college that genuinely supported the gay community. Miguel agreed, telling David how Manhattan was light years ahead of the Bronx when it came to LGBTQ people.

Their conversation turned a bit darker when they decided to share their coming out stories. Each story revealed deep psychological wounds that lay hidden under the surface. Insidious monsters from the past, like a dormant virus striking at will, sent untold fear coursing through their veins every now and then. They could see it in each other's eyes as they shared their stories. Miguel went first. "I came out at school about a year ago, and that's when everything got mad intense. Then, a couple of days later I came out to my mom. She fuckin went crazy and hurt me real bad." The sadness in Miguel's voice made David shiver. "I'm so sorry that happened to you."

"It is what it is I guess."

"I don't mean to bring up bad memories, but what did she do to you?"

Miguel stopped eating and looked straight ahead, his eyes filling with tears. David felt terrible.

"I'm sorry. I shouldn't have asked."

"It's ok. Talking about it helps me deal with it. She beat the shit out of me so bad that I ended up in the hospital. I had a broken nose, a fractured cheekbone, three cracked ribs, and bruises all over my body. My right eye was swollen shut for over a week, and my left eye was seventy percent swollen shut. Fortunately my retinas weren't damaged."

David was horrified. He couldn't believe a mom could ever inflict that kind of brutality on their own child just because they were gay. "I'm so sorry." David gently rubbed Miguel's back, trying to comfort him as tears ran down his cheeks. Miguel gave a half smile. "Hey, everything is good now," he said, wiping his eyes. "There was a silver lining in the whole thing. She was arrested, and my sister and I were finally taken out of that nightmare. My mom is really messed up. She's a drug addict and an alcoholic. The perfect combination for terror. After I got out of the hospital I went to live with my boyfriend Gabriel and his mom."

"I'm glad you're safe now."

"So am I. Gabriel's mom is my legal guardian, so I never have to worry about my mom hurting me ever again. My sister lives with our aunt in Brooklyn, so she's safe too."

"That's good to hear. So, tell me about your boyfriend."

Miguel's face lit up.. "I love Gabriel more than anything. He's the nicest guy you could ever meet."

David understood completely. "Being in love is the best feeling in the world, isn't it?"

"Yeah. I'm lucky to have him in my life."

"Is Gabriel in college too?"

"No, he's a sophomore at my old high school. You have to meet him the next time he comes to visit me."

"I'd like that. I keep forgetting you're only sixteen."

"It's good to hear because this age thing really sucks." David smiled. "I wouldn't worry about it. You scare them and they need to deal with it, not you."

David looked at Miguel timidly, hoping he wouldn't ask about his story. Miguel gave him a sympathetic look. "You don't have to share if you don't feel like it. I'll understand."

He tried to gather his courage. "No, I don't mind." He hesitated for a few seconds.

"I came out to my parents a month before I started eighth grade. Then I came out to my friends three weeks after school started. Tyler and Melissa were my only friends from that moment on. All of the others hated me for being gay. I was constantly being bullied. Tyler and Melissa protected me as best they could. Then one day four of my former friends jumped me at school. They ducked taped my wrists and ankles and then took turns punching and kicking me. They knocked me out pretty quick and left me laying in a darkened classroom with my blood splattered all over the place. The doctors didn't think I was going to live and tried to prepare my parents for the inevitable..." David stopped again and gave Miguel a pleading look. "Please don't think I'm crazy for what I'm about to say, ok?"

"I would never think that. I'm sorry I made you talk about it."

"It's ok, really." He took a deep breath. "I left my body and saw myself hooked up to all these machines beeping away, trying to keep my body alive. I wasn't afraid at all because it made sense somehow. I stood there looking at my swollen face and all those stitches wondering why their hatred was so deep. So satisfying. Why they felt it was their duty to kill me just because I'm gay. That's when I decided to give them their victory. Just as I started to let go of this life, Tyler walked in and sat next to me. I felt so bad for him. He put his hand in mine and kissed me on the forehead. That's when I knew I couldn't leave him. I tried to get back inside my body, but couldn't. I screamed as I began to fade away. The monitor flat lined at that point and set off a Code Blue. Tyler pleaded and begged, 'David, please don't leave me. I need you. I love you. Please come back to me. Don't leave me here all alone.' As soon as he said that, I slipped back into my body and squeezed his hand. The monitor started beeping again. He squeezed my hand back and got right next to my face and whispered, 'I love you David Emerson.' I responded by moving my fingers in his hand just enough to let him know that I could hear him. I don't remember anything after that. I woke up two days later, and like you, I could only see a tiny bit out of one eye. I couldn't talk, so I moved my arm to let them know I was conscious. My mom, my sister, and Melissa were crying. My dad kissed me on the cheek and told me how much he loved me, and that I was a fighter. A few seconds later Tyler sat next to my bed and put his hand on mine to let me know that he was there. He didn't say anything, but he didn't need to. Anyway, you probably think I'm crazy, but I really did leave my body."

"I totally believe you. You guys must really love each other to have a connection like that."

"Yeah, we do. He is the one person I can talk to about anything."

"I can't wait to meet him so I can thank him for bringing you back."

David felt embarrassed. "I never told him what happened. I never told anyone what happened.

You're the first to know."

"I'm honored that you shared something so private. Personally though, I think you need to tell him. For some reason, I think he needs to know.

"You're right. I've wanted to tell him so many times, but things became complicated between us and I could never find the right moment. I promise I'll tell him during Christmas Break.

"Cool." Miguel then asked a favor. "Please promise me that you will never lose the special bond you guys have, ok?"

"I promise."

They sat there in quiet reflection trying to lock those brutal ghosts away for the final time.

A few minutes later they walked up the steps to upper campus, gave each other a hug, and then headed their separate ways.

Even though David was in a somber mood, he was looking forward to this particular evening with his research team.

Professor Godard and Professor Logan were adding another area of research; Black Hole Thermodynamics and Gravity. David had studied the laws of black hole mechanics and the Hawking Effect on his own in tenth grade, so he understood the math and the physics involved. Watching the equations come to life on the whiteboards made him smile because it validated several of his own theories he was quietly working on.

It was just after 8pm when David received a text from Marco. He was working on Fermionic Variables with Professor Logan and Lee at the time. He excused himself and walked over to the window to read it. "I'm not going to be able to see you tonight. I'm not feeling well. I think I have the flu or something. I have the chills. I'm going to get some sleep now. I'll text you in the morning. I love you :)" David was disappointed, but understood. He texted back. "My poor boy. Get under your comforter and keep warm. I love you too :)

"Is everything ok?" Professor Logan asked when David returned.

"My boyfriend isn't feeling well. He thinks he might have the flu."

"Lee and I can finish this up if you want to go check on him."

"Thanks for offering, but he was going straight to bed, so I don't want to disturb him. I'll check on him in the morning."

Marco sat alone at Starbucks drinking a Caramel Macchiato, feeling like shit. Lying to David about having the flu was the coward's way out. An easy task. A new reality for him. It was guilt and lust permeating through his veins that he didn't want David to see. It was meeting with Jordan and how it drained him on every emotional level possible. It was not knowing if he would keep his word. That situation was stabbing his heart harder and harder.

He sipped his coffee and watched people around him having fun without a care in the world. He wanted that feeling in the worst way. He even tried to summon the warm feeling he got whenever David was with him, but just couldn't do it. That night of pure sex with Jordan a year prior kept flooding his mind instead. His amorous grin said it all.

And then came the guilt. He made it to the restroom just in time to puke his guts out. When there was nothing more to puke up, he opened the stall door and walked to the sink and put some water on his face. When he finally had the courage to look in the mirror, the truth was staring back in full force.

# CHAPTER 33

*Ghost of a Chance*, one of David's favorites songs by Rush, filled his dorm room as he got ready for another day of classes. His mind was now in constant overdrive, just the way he liked it. He was only a few days into his Honor's Math class and was already a third of the way through the syllabus. He sent Professor Godard an email that morning explaining the situation. He requested additional homework.

Once the email was sent, he texted Marco to see how he was feeling. Marco responded five minutes later. "I still feel terrible. I'm going to stay in bed and try to sleep it off."

"I feel so bad for you. I'll stop by after my last class and take care of you."

"That is so sweet of you. Thanks."

Ten minutes later someone knocked on David's door. He opened it and there stood Marco with a devilish smirk. "Someone told me an extremely cute guy lives here, and they were right. You're hot." David giggled. "I thought you were deathly ill."

"I lied." Marco pulled David out of the room and into his arms. He kissed David like he hadn't seen him in years. A minute later other students began leaving for class and became spectators. They waited patiently for the lovebirds to come up for air so they could get by.

David heard some whispering, so he opened his eyes and saw a bunch of his hall mates smiling. He pulled Marco out of the way. "Sorry," he said, with a dreamy grin.

Debra, a pre-med student who lived three rooms down, told them they were adorable. As soon as the hallway emptied out Marco pinned David against the wall and kissed him with a lot more force. David's head actually banged against the wall, making him flinch in pain. Then Marco pressed his body hard against David's, not realizing that he was hurt. A panicky feeling came over David at that point. He tried to push Marco away because he couldn't breathe. He pleaded, "Marco, please stop. You're hurting me."

He came to his senses and eased up. "I'm sorry, but you get me so worked up, and I missed you last night." David rubbed his head and studied Marco's face. It looked different. It looked possessed. "I missed you too. I'm glad you're feeling better."

"Me too. I'm sorry I lied about still being sick this morning. I just wanted to surprise you."

"You totally surprised me. Let me get my laptop and backpack, and then we can go."

Marco followed David into the room, his eyes riveted on his perfect little ass. He wanted to fuck that ass. He wanted to have sex with that ass instead of making love to David. He had been jacking off to that fantasy for the last month, wanting it to become reality. Marco's fantasy consisted of treating David like a one night stand, like a slut who craved sex as much as he did. The idea of using David turned Marco on like nothing else ever had. It was driving him crazy. He decided to seduce him into having sex.

He walked over and started caressing David's back, and then his ass as he kissed the back of his neck. "I was just thinking, why don't we blow off our classes this morning and head back to my room? We can, you know, make love instead."

"I'd love to, but you know we can't do that." David turned and kissed Marco's pouting lips. "Can you wait until tonight?"

Marco wasn't listening. "I want you now." He moaned and nibbled on David's lower lip. "Please? I'm begging."

"I think someone is extremely turned on this morning." David leaned in and kissed Marco.

A few seconds later Marco grabbed his hand and placed it on his raging hard-on and moaned,

"I want you so bad."

"I love you," David whispered back as he moved his hand up and down. A few seconds later David pulled away. "I wish we could make love right now, but we need to get to class."

Marco gave him a seductive look and then started to unzip his jeans. "I love you."

"I love you too."

"Then let me fuck you right now. I want to fuck you so bad." The way Marco said those words, and the look in his eyes, frightened David. He tried to stay calm. "We need to go before we're late."

"Please David, it won't take long," Marco said, still trying to convince him.

"Believe me, I want to make love to you too, but I can't miss any of my classes, and neither can you." Marco looked totally dejected. He didn't say anything as he zipped his jeans back up.

David still couldn't believe that Marco said he wanted to fuck him. He didn't like hearing those words because they felt cold. He felt bad about turning Marco down, and wanted to make it up to him. "I'll be done with research by eight tonight, so I'll come right over so we can make love, ok?" He kissed Marco on the cheek.

"No...Yes...Fuck...I need..." Marco's voice disappeared into silence. "I'm sorry for getting carried away. It was stupid."

"It's ok. Don't worry about it. I'm glad I'm able to turn you on like that. It makes me feel special." It was the first time he had lied to Marco. Then he told him the truth. "I love you."

"I love you too."

"Can I sleep over tonight?" David asked, as he hugged Marco.

"I'd like that very much."

Marco hated having to wait all day, but knew it would be worth it.

Neither one said much as they walked across campus. David had a weird feeling. Marco was on fire. His mind raced and his body tingled at the thought of using David for sex. Making him feel dirty. Making him feel like an object. Like he was nothing. Making him feel exactly the way he did whenever he had random sex. That fantasy was nirvana, and he couldn't wait to get there.

⥲ ⩰

David was five minutes late for class. Fortunately Professor Godard was running late as well. He disliked being late for anything because it was impolite, and it made him feel rushed for the rest of the day.

The lecture hall was completely filled when he walked in. He looked around hoping to find an empty seat, and that's when he saw Jordan waving his arms, trying to get his attention. David smiled when he saw him and headed down the aisle to his row. Jordan stood up and waited as David slid past seven or eight pairs of legs. "I was getting worried that you weren't going to show up. Is everything ok?" Jordan asked.

"Yeah, everything's fine. Thanks for saving me a seat. I was running late because Marco and I were doing some last minute homework." David hated to lie, but his private life was private.

"You must have been having fun," Jordan said, with a mischievous grin.

"We always have fun doing homework together. Hey Marna, how are you?" David said, changing the subject.

"Hi David, I'm fine. Jordan, can you guys switch seats so David can sit between us?"

"Yeah, no problem." Jordan slid his body past David's making sure their crotches touched slightly while the maneuver took place. Jordan also put his hand on David's waist,

330

pretending to keep himself from falling off balance. That touch sent shockwaves through his body.

David sat down and was finally able to relax and focus.

Jordan continued to pry. "So, how is Marco doing these days?"

"Good. He loves his classes. He wasn't feeling well last night though."

"That's too bad. I hope he feels better soon. I hate being sick."

"He felt much better this morning. I think it was just nerves. Adjusting to college life is difficult, and I think everyone deals with it differently."

"You're probably right. Tell him I said hi."

"I will. It is so cool that you two know each other. We definitely have to hang out sometime."

"Yeah, for sure. Marco is a great guy. We had a blast at that college conference last year. I am formally inviting you and him to the next party I have."

"Thanks. I'll let Marco know. I'm sure he'd love to go."

"Do you guys live on campus?" Jordan asked, pumping David for more information.

"Yeah. I live at Hartley and Marco lives at John Jay. Do you live on campus?"

"I used to, but I have an apartment now. It's on 112th Street, between Broadway and Amsterdam. We are practically neighbors."

"It must be nice living in an apartment. Do you have roommates?"

"At one time I did, but it became a hassle. I enjoy my privacy."

"It must be expensive to live alone."

"It's free, actually. My parents bought it for me at the beginning of my sophomore year. I want to live in the city after I graduate, so it's an early graduation present."

"Wow. Having your own apartment in New York must be a dream come true."

"It really is. I'm one lucky guy."

"Marco's parents wanted to buy him an apartment too, but he turned them down so he could experience dorm life. But he did let his mother and her interior decorator remodel his dorm room."

"I'm sure it is awesome. Do you guys have roommates?"

"I do, but Marco doesn't. I'm a little jealous because his room is massive compared to mine. He has all the space a guy would ever want."

"Nice. I'm sure you spend a lot of time there."

"Not as much as I'd like. We've both been pretty busy adjusting to our crazy schedules."

"That will change once things settle down."

David was about to tell him he hoped so, but Professor Godard walked in, apologized for being late, and immediately began the day's lecture.

# CHAPTER 34

Marco was sitting on his bed in nothing but blue bikini briefs vehemently typing away. Throughout the evening ideas for new stories popped into his head like raindrops falling from the sky. He had entered a creative zone where words textured in dissonance and melody magically appeared from some other realm, coming alive on his computer screen. Those words were searching, crying, realizing. They were cutting him deep. And although he disliked the bloody mess, he continued to write because it was his destiny.

Conflicted emotions started taking their toll. An epic battle raged between what Marco desired and what he loved. He wanted both. He needed both. Those words became glimpses into love, pain, integrity, deceit, lust, sex, humiliation. His recognizable truths.

In-between creative outbursts Marco watched some of his favorite gay porn: Orgies, boyfriend swapping, three on ones, and domination. Everything he fantasized about, and needed. He couldn't wait for David to get there so he could introduce him to his sexual world. A place where he could dominate David by making him his bitch instead of his sweet innocent boyfriend. He was in love with the idea of David being the recipient of his sex fantasies, just like he had been for so many hot guys.

It was just after 8:15 when Marco heard a hesitant knock on the door. He knew it was David just by the gentleness of it. His heart began to race as he placed his laptop on the bed. He knew sex with David was only moments away. He adjusted himself for maximum effect and then walked to the door. In an amorous voice he asked, "Who is it?"

"My name is David. I'm looking for Marco Valerio, a gifted writer."

"He's not here right now. Would you like to come in and wait for him?"

"Sure, if it's not too much of a bother," David said with a slight giggle.

Marco opened the door, smiled, and then posed. "What do you think of my outfit?"

David's eyes grew wide at the sight of his boyfriend's perfect body and massive woody that was threatening to rip through his sexy Calvin Klein's. "I-I am very impressed," he stammered, feeling a little self-conscious. "Y-you are so beautiful. I really missed you today." David still couldn't believe someone so smart and good looking actually loved him.

"Thanks for the compliment. That Marco guy should be here in a little while. He's almost as hot as I am," he said, continuing to pretend.

David giggled. Marco grinned as he pulled him into the room and then into his arms.

"I missed you," David whispered, feeling a sense of contentment.

"I missed you too. You're all I've thought about all day." Marco loved the way David's warm breath felt on his chest. "I want you so bad," Marco whispered. He kissed David's lips soft and slow, just the way he liked. His hands found their way to the arch of David's back before continuing down to his perfect little ass.

David let out gentle moans while Marco's hands explored his body. He was about to make his move when David pulled away slightly so he could admire Marco's face. "You are so beautiful." He traced Marco's jawline with his fingers as he stared into those deep brown eyes. A moment later he whispered, "Make love to me like you did at the lake. I need to know how much you love me."

Marco pretended to want the same thing. He kissed David gently, just the way he liked, then started to lose control. He pulled away for a second, giving David a desperate look, and then went for it. "I want to have sex with you instead of making love to you. I want to strip you naked and lick every part of your hot twink body, and then I wanna fuck you all night long."

"Marco, I don't under…."

"Shhh, don't say anything. Just let it happen," Marco whispered, putting his finger to David's lips. He kissed David on the forehead and then grabbed his arms and pushed him onto the bed. "David didn't say a word or even resist as he tried to process Marco's words.

"You're so fucking hot," Marco murmured over and over as he ripped David's clothes off, exposing his slender pale body, and his innocence. Marco needed to take his innocence so they would be equal. He stood in front of David playing with himself as he slowly slipped off his bikini briefs. "Do you like what you see? It's just for you. Tell me you want it deep inside you. I want you to fucking beg for it."

"I love you," David told him.

Marco straddled David's body and began his sexual ascent by licking his bellybutton. He slowly worked his way up to David's nipples, and then to his neck. "Does it feel good?"

"Yes. I love you. Do you love me?" David asked.

Marco didn't answer. Instead, he raised his body and pinned David's arms with his legs. Then he looked down at him with a possessed stare as his raging hard-on hovered just above David's face. "Suck me. Suck me good," he commanded in a cool detached voice. With David's voice quivering and panic setting in, he pleaded, "Marco, you're hurting me. Please let me up. What's wrong with you?"

"Nothing is wrong. I'm just trying to, you know...." Marco moved his legs off of David's arms and quickly changed strategies. He leaned down and kissed David's chest just the way he liked. He hoped by giving David a little of what he wanted, it would lead to what he wanted. Sure enough, David began to relax and enjoy Marco's tender foreplay. Within minutes he had worked David into a frenzy just the way he always did. Then he went for it again. "I want to fuck you. I want to fuck you hard. I want to give you the best sex you've ever had."

"Make love to me," David whispered back.

"Not tonight. I want to try something different. I want to

make our bodies come alive through sex, not love. Trust me, please. I know you'll love it if you give it a chance."

"I don't think I'm ready for…."

"Please let me have sex with you. Do you love me?"

"Yes."

"I love you too. Having sex together through fantasy play is another way to express our love. Let yourself go and you'll see how hot sex can be."

"I'll try, if it'll make you happy."

"Marco smiled, then started licking David's soft full lips. He moaned as his naked body slithered all over David's. He began to nibble those lips, gently at first, and then harder. David tensed up and pulled back slightly because it hurt. Marco stopped and went back to licking them before thrusting his tongue deep inside his mouth while forcefully pressing his body against David's.

Within minutes Marco was giving David commands, telling him to moan, telling him to let go of his inhibitions. Each time David moaned Marco became more aggressive, his body moving in an almost violent sexual rhythm. Marco licked his way down to David's chest and then took turns biting each nipple. They were tender bites at first, almost playful, but the biting got progressively harder and painful. Every guy Marco had ever been with loved it and always begged for more. David winced in pain but didn't stop Marco because he wanted to please him. So he pretended to like it by moaning for more. Marco had gone over the edge knowing David enjoyed pain. It made his body come alive on an entirely new level.

It was time to initiate another of his kinky turn-ons. Marco cooed seductively in David's ear.

"I want to talk dirty to you while we have sex. And I want you to talk dirty to me. It'll be so fucking hot, believe me. Ok?"

David felt like crying. He knew he should have said no, but decided to experience everything Marco wanted to do, hoping he would understand why it turned him on.

"Ok."

"Are you sure?"

"Yes, I'm sure. Talk dirty to me," he whispered, and then braced himself.

Marco started exploring David's body aggressively while humiliating him with dirty talk. "I want to fuck your little bitch ass hard. Are you my little bitch? Tell me you're my little slutty bitch."

The tears came as David did as he was told. "Yes, I'm your little slutty bitch."

Marco looked at him with a sick smile. "Beg me to fuck your ass. Beg like I know you can bitch."

"I want you to fuck me. Fuck me hard. Please fuck me hard."

That was all Marco needed to hear. He flipped David over, almost violently, onto his stomach and gave the next command. "Get on your fucking knees and arch your back. You are so fucking hot." David did as he was told, and for the next two hours Marco had his way with him in every conceivable position possible while calling him every filthy name he could think of.

Marco couldn't believe how much he loved using David. His multiple orgasms were so intense, almost God-like as he made the guy he loved feel dirty and worthless.

David hated it. He hated the way Marco found pleasure in emotionless sex. Most of all, he hated himself. He was caught in a nightmare of his own making and didn't know what to do about it.

When it was all over, they lay next to each other in the dim light and the smell of empty sex. Marco's thin muscular body glistened with sweat and satisfaction. David's slender body was covered in sweat and humiliation. He kept his eyes closed, hoping that it was finally over. Neither one said anything for a long while. The silence felt wounded, satisfied, powerful, sad.

And then, just as David remembered, Marco's voice became gentle once again. "I love you more than anything. You made me feel so good." David kept his eyes closed because he couldn't bear to see his satisfaction. "It makes me happy to make you happy," he whispered, hating himself for lying.

Marco gave David little kisses all over his face while gently stroking his hair. Within minutes he had fallen fast asleep. David lay there, tears falling, body shivering, as he tried to figure out what to do. Should he endure Marco's sex fetish, hoping he would eventually outgrow it? Or should he break up with him and move on? He would make a decision soon.

Twenty minutes later David needed to leave. A long shower and the comfort of his own bed were needed to help him forget. He quietly slipped out of bed and put his clothes on. Then he took the comforter that had been thrown on the floor and covered Marco. He stood there looking at the guy he loved wondering why he enjoyed humiliating him so much. He realized a couple of things as he walked back to his building in the chilly evening air. He was alone once again, and love was just a cruel extreme.

# CHAPTER 35

David barely listened to the physics lecture as he stared blankly at his laptop. His mind was still trying to process what had happened a few hours earlier. All those things Marco did to his body. Hearing immense pleasure in Marco's voice whenever he called him his bitch, his little slut, his skinny ass twink. He felt so dirty. He felt so ashamed. But what he hated most was allowing it to happen in the first place. Playing along with Marco's domination fetish should never have happened.

And then the tears came when he realized how much Marco loved treating him like a one night stand. Knowing how much he enjoyed physically hurting him with sex. Inflicting additional pain by pulling his hair and straining his neck while Marco sexually ravaged him from behind. Tears began to fall on his hands and keyboard.

"David, what's wrong?" Miguel asked.

He didn't answer right away. He kept his head down and wiped his eyes with his sleeve.

"Nothing, I'm ok. It's just…"

Miguel gently rubbed David's arm trying to comfort him. He looked at Miguel, and then the humiliation came. He put his laptop into his backpack, got up and walked out of the lecture hall. Miguel grabbed his things and followed.

"David, please wait," Miguel yelled, as soon as he was in the hallway. David was just about to head upstairs when he finally stopped. Miguel ran to him. "What's going on? Are you ok?" He gave Miguel a wounded look and then hugged him with all his might. "Everything is just so wrong right now," he said, no longer fighting back the tears.

"It's ok. Everything is going to be ok. I'm here for you. Let's go outside and get some air." They walked outside and found a bench away from the main walkway so they could have some privacy. David sat there with his eyes closed, trying to hide from the world. Trying to hide his shame. Wondering what was happening between him and Marco.

"I thought I had an idea of what love was supposed to be, but now I'm not so sure."

"That makes two of us. It is the most complex emotion we will ever experience. Just when you think you understand it, it changes in an instant."

David sighed. "I know what you mean. Especially after last night."

Miguel tried to give him some sound advice. "Sometimes what we think is love is a total miscalculation on our part. We miscalculate because we fail to look close enough, or we are held spellbound by beauty and charm. Or just wanting to be loved by anyone because we're lonely. David, I have a feeling that you know what real love is. You have experienced it, right?" David didn't say anything for a few seconds as he thought back to the night Tyler and him kissed. "Yes. And it felt perfect. But it wasn't meant to be."

"Remember, circumstances change. People change over the course of time, especially when they are searching for the truth."

"Sometimes they can, sometimes not."

"Did you and Marco have a fight?"

"No, but something else happened. I can't talk about it right now."

"I understand." They sat there in silence for a while, which allowed David to rationally gather his thoughts. Miguel finally spoke. "It might not be any of my business, and you don't have to answer the question, but, do you still love Marco?"

"Yes."

"Does he still love you?" David hesitated. "I think he does. It's just…" David's voice trailed off into silence once again.

"Did he hurt you in any way? David, please tell me the truth. Because you can't allow anyone to hurt you physically or mentally. That kind of situation becomes extremely dangerous if you aren't careful. I know this first hand."

David turned and looked at Miguel, knowing those intense brown eyes could see the truth. Embarrassed, he looked away for a few seconds before speaking. "Our relationship became a bit more complicated last night, and I realize that I need to sort some things out. I'm not in any danger or anything, so please don't worry about that. Marco loves me and would never do anything to hurt me."

"Well, I'm happy to hear that."

"Yeah," David said, hoping it was true.

"You and I are good friends, right?" Miguel asked.

"Of course we are. Actually, you remind me so much of Tyler it's scary."

"Well, I take that as the ultimate compliment. Thanks."

"You're welcome."

They sat there for a few more minutes until David suggested they go back and catch the last part of class. He gave Miguel a nice long hug. "Thanks for being here for me."

"Anytime. I want to give you some advice that I think Tyler would give if he were here. Don't ever let anyone talk you into doing something that you aren't comfortable doing, ok?"

"I won't, I promise." They headed back to class.

# CHAPTER 36

Everything had settled in somewhat nicely over the course of the next six weeks. David had taken Miguel's advice and was honest with Marco, telling him how uncomfortable he was participating in his sex fantasies. How it made him feel used and unloved. Marco apologized and promised it would never happen again. It never did.

They also made time from their busy schedules so they could be together more. Going on dates became an important part of their relationship. Marco surprised David with front row seats for Rush in early October. He spared no expense, making sure his blond haired angel had the time of his life. His father's limo picked them up at the front gates of campus and took them to King's Carriage House, one of the finest restaurants on the Upper East Side. Marco had reserved one of the more intimate dining areas just for them. A table was placed near the fireplace with Rush music playing in the background. Marco felt terrible when they were taken to their table and David started to cry. "David, what's wrong?" he asked, all panicky.

"Nothing is wrong. I'm just a little overwhelmed. This is beautiful and you are so romantic and I feel like I'm in a fairytale. I love you so much." David wiped his tears and kissed Marco.

"I love you too. I hope the music is ok," Marco said, with a sly grin.

"It's perfect. How did you know I liked Rush?" David said, as his smile retuned.

An hour later they were on their way to the Barkley Center in Brooklyn. The anticipation of seeing Rush for the first time overwhelmed David. He sat next to Marco holding his hand in quiet reflection. His hill, the billions of stars that always welcomed him, and songs like *Tom Sawyer, Roll the Bones, New World Man,* and countless others had kept him sane through the years by making him feel like he belonged in the world. David finally snapped out of his trepidation, squeezed Marco's hand and kissed his cheek. "Thank you for making this happen."

All during the concert Marco enjoyed watching the look on David's face with each song Rush played. It was three and a half hours of heaven for both of them.

After the concert was over they took the scenic route through Manhattan before returning to campus, ending their date by making love and falling asleep in each other's arms.

Two weeks later David surprised Marco with tickets to see Young The Giant. Both of them loved their music, so he called his father to see if he would lend him the money for tickets, promising to pay him back when he received his next paycheck from the university. His dad was more than happy to help out, and even put an extra $150 dollars on David's debit card, explaining it was a gift to be used any way he wanted.

Unfortunately there was one little problem after David surprised Marco with the tickets. The Algarotti Ballroom, the venue where the concert was being held, was for a twenty-one and over crowd. Marco easily solved the problem a day later by surprising David with a fake ID.

This was the first date David had ever planned and hoped Marco would enjoy himself. They had dinner at an inexpensive Thai restaurant a few blocks from campus. Then they took the subway to midtown. He wanted to take a cab because Marco hated the subway, but couldn't afford it. Plus, he wanted to make sure he had some money to spend at the concert.

David was apprehensive about using the fake ID. Marco kept trying to get him to relax while they stood in line waiting to get in. "You are so cute when you're nervous. Don't worry, we'll get in."

"I hope so."

"We are getting in. Just act like you belong here. Honestly, they don't care as long as the ID looks real. I would say at least twenty five percent of the people here are under twenty-one. Look around and see for yourself." David did and knew he was right. A few minutes later they received their wristbands and were through the front doors.

They walked into the ballroom and were met by hundreds of people partying away. Marco loved the grittiness of the place. David looked around in awe. A few minutes later he shocked Marco when he asked, "Can I buy you a drink?"

Marco grinned. "Are you trying to get me drunk so you can take advantage of me later?"

"You are so perceptive." David said, grinning back.

"I'll let you buy me one if I can buy you one."

"Ok."

"Are you sure about this?"

"Yes. After all we are twenty one. At least that's what our IDs say." They both laughed.

It turned out to be one of the best concerts they had ever been to. They spent the whole night jumping up and down to songs like *My Body, Cough Syrup, Apartment,* and *Crystallized.*

When the last encore was over they decided to cab back to campus because they were feeling pretty good. Marco insisted on paying for the cab, but David told him that he had enough money to cover it, which he did by saving every extra penny of his living expense money for two weeks. David's roommate was gone for the weekend so they spent the night there. It was the first time he had the room to himself. And it was also the first time he had made love to Marco as a top.

# CHAPTER 37

Relationships are like vibrating strings. No two are alike, yet the attraction, the quantum gravitational pull cannot be denied when it comes to love. David and Marco were caught in each other's gravitational fields trying to maneuver through pulling forces from all directions in their search to find equilibrium. Spending time apart, and hanging out with new friends had become part of this new equation. They talked about it several times. Marco didn't like it one bit, but finally agreed with David that it would strengthen their relationship, not tear it apart.

Making new friends was an important component of David's college experience. The academic setting, and trying hard not to be so shy, made it a lot easier for him to meet people. As a result of these new friendships, David began seeing the world through a different lens.

His closest friend on campus was Miguel. They had so many things in common. It was almost as if they had known each other for years. They studied together almost every day, helping each other out with homework. In-between homework they theorized about all sorts of weird concepts as a way of exercising their brains. New mathematical equations, rotating universes, theories about what Dark Energy was, how the

Big Bang and all the other probable ones happened, humans as infinite energy being able to exist without bodies or brains, and so on. It became a new game to see who could come up with the weirdest theory.

David was also teaching Miguel how to play the guitar after Miguel found out that playing a musical instrument makes the brain communicate at superior levels. David found it hard to believe how much they were alike even though they had come from different worlds.

For Marco, making friends was a nonissue, a boring endeavor, an easy commodity. He understood all about so-called friendships, degrees of friendships, calculated acquaintances. It was a game that needed to be played. A social requirement. And he always won.

Marco's decided to let Avani and Rafi partially into his world since they lived on the same floor and were always inviting him to hang out. He had to admit that he liked both of them. They were funny and seemed sincere. Marco thought Rafi was really cute and enjoyed being his not so secret crush.

Marco also decided to become friends with Thomas and Reid, two guys that were in one of his literature classes. He actually liked them because they were crazy aspiring writers just like him. They even decided to form a writing group and got together several times a week to write and share ideas.

And as usual, Marco became one of the popular guys around campus. He was the guy everyone wanted to know and be seen with. He never consciously drew attention to himself, but he understood how his physical attributes and cordial charm made people gravitate to him. Word had also gotten around that he was extremely wealthy. That he lived in a penthouse on the Upper East Side, and had one of the private luxury dorm rooms.

People started dropping by to hang out. Marco didn't mind at first, but finally had to put a stop to it because it was getting way out of hand.

Marco wasn't the only one getting his share of attention. David was too, but in a different way. He was constantly impressing professors and peers with his academic prowess. While some students enjoyed letting others know how intelligent they were, David just went about his studies in his usual quiet manner. He never drew attention to himself because that kind of thing got in the way of what he was trying to achieve.

It became apparent to everyone around him just how intelligent he was, especially when they listened to him in the discussion sections. Graduate students taught these small classes where students discussed the lectures in more detail, and received help with the homework whenever it was needed. David had to attend them because it was a requirement to pass the class. But whenever he did ask a question, other students listened closely because his questions were never about the homework. His questions were always some sort of theoretical concept that either added to a given lecture, or challenged it like any good physicist would. His ideas went way beyond what was being taught.

David was also getting his share of attention from the gay community. At least a half dozen guys had asked him out since the beginning of the semester. He always politely declined, telling them he already had a boyfriend. A few girls had even asked him out, but he told them the same thing. Getting all that attention was nice, but it felt alien. He had been pretty much an outcast all through middle school and most of high school. He couldn't believe how things had changed so quickly.

With David's crazy schedule still consuming most of his days and early evenings, he started sleeping at Marco's more often because it became the only time they could be together. David started to rethink Marco's offer about living together. He decided to talk to Melissa about it to see what she thought, and would then let Marco know either way when they returned to campus from the Thanksgiving holiday.

# CHAPTER 38

David and Miguel sat in physics class listening to a lecture on gravitational waves and how their existence could possibly lead to mathematical harmony between General Relativity and Quantum Mechanics. David's phone buzzed just as the professor began to delve deeply into this theory. He discreetly pulled it out to see who it was. It was Marco. "I'm sorry, but I can't meet up for lunch today. Something came up. I'll make it up to you tonight ;-)"

David was disappointed, but smiled at the thought of Marco making it up to him. He texted back. "No problem. See you tonight."

Miguel leaned in and whispered, "Is everything ok?"

"Yeah, it was Marco. He can't meet me for lunch. Something came up."

"Oh. Do you wanna have lunch with me?"

"Sure. We can compare notes while we eat."

They both refocused their attention back to the professor.

♍

A few seconds later Marco sent another text. "Hey, it's all set. See you in an hour." He sat in class trying to stay focused while waiting for a response. Thirty seconds later it came. "Cool, can't wait." Marco smiled knowing it was going to be another magical afternoon. He walked out of Philosophy Hall with Thomas and Reid when class was over, thinking it would never end.

"I'm starving. Do you guys want to grab some lunch?" Thomas asked.

"Sounds good to me," Reid said.

"I can't today. I'm meeting up with David in a few minutes," Marco told them.

"Next time then." They walked together until they got to lower campus, then Marco headed toward the 114th Street campus exit.

# CHAPTER 39

The sun was just beginning to peak through the buildings as David lay next to Marco admiring his handsome face. He still couldn't believe that sleeping angel actually loved him, that fate had brought them together. For David, the last couple of weeks had been way too busy with research, meetings with professors, and homework. The guilt he felt about hardly seeing Marco was taking its toll, so he decided to talk to Professor Logan about cutting back on attending so many department meetings with him.

David snuggled next to Marco just as he was waking up. "You look like a little boy when you sleep," David whispered, before kissing him on the cheek.

Marco stretched and then turned on his side. "How long were you watching me? Was I drooling enough for you?"

David smiled. "No drool this time. Just fluttering eye lids. You must have been having a good dream."

"I had several, and you were in all of them."

"Awe, I love you. I'm sorry I haven't been around lately. Everything's been so hectic with my research and those department meetings. I've decided to make a change in my schedule so we can spend more time together. I'm going to see if I can make it happen today."

"Don't worry about it. I understand. I've been busy too. Just do what you need to do."

"Thanks for understanding."

"Will you spend the night again?"

"Yeah, of course." David put his head on Marco's chest and started tracing his sexy v-lines with his fingers. Marco giggled, "That tickles."

"Your body is so beautiful."

"Thanks. It was made just for you." Marco said as he caressed David's back. A few seconds later he whispered, "I'll make you feel good anyway you'd like tonight."

"Mmm…Well, I'll take you up on that offer. I might just surprise you with my request."

"Oh really?" Marco said, and then started tickling David. An all-out tickle fight ensued for the next minute or so before finally collapsing in each other's arms.

Within their exhausted embrace Marco began to maneuver. "Do we really have to go to Jordan's party tonight? Let me take you out for dinner instead. Then we'll come back here and make love. I want to be alone with you tonight."

David kissed Marco's pouting lips. "Believe me, that sounds so good, but I promised Jordan we would show up this time. I don't want to back out again."

"Come on, please?"

"I'll tell you what, we will only stay for an hour or so, ok?"

"Ok. I'm going to set the timer on my phone for exactly an hour, and then I will sweep you up in my arms and carry you back here."

"Promise?"

"Promise."

"I appreciate you going with me. To be honest, I'm kind of curious to see what Jordan's apartment looks like. Marna says it's really nice."

Marco looked up at the ceiling. "I'm sure it is," he said, and then changed the subject. "We better shower and get some breakfast, or we're going to be late for class."

≠ ≠

David was eating his omelet and explaining Density Matrix Theory to Marco, who was pretending to listen while he moved his food around with his fork. David noticed his far away stare. "I am now going to quiz you on atomic and molecular physics."

"What? I-I'm sorry. My mind keeps wandering to this story I've been writing." Marco said, knowing he was caught.

"It's ok. I know math isn't the most exciting thing people like to hear about." David changed the subject. "So how is your study group going?"

"It's been great actually. I've learned a lot from Thomas and Reid. They're really good writers."

"That sounds awesome. I'm sure it is nice having other people to bounce ideas off of. That's why I like doing my homework with Miguel. We talk about the future of math, and we discuss our own theories. It's a lot of fun."

Marco smiled. "I can just imagine what you two geniuses come up with. Just don't blow up the universe, ok?"

"I promise. I like the idea of belonging to a study group."

"Me too. It has helped my writing. Maybe you and Miguel could find one and join."

"Jordan asked me to join his. He has invited me several times, but I've been too busy to go." Marco put his fork down and looked at David, trying hard not to lose it. "Oh, I didn't know that. Why didn't you say anything about it before?"

"I guess I forgot. I'd like to attend one to see what it's like. Marna told me they hold them at Jordan's apartment, and he always has lunch catered, and he even has Apple TV so everyone can sync their laptops together." Marco didn't want David anywhere near Jordan's apartment, but didn't know how to stop it from happening. In a defeated tone he managed to sound enthused.

While walking across campus David reminded Marco that he was spending Saturday in the Bronx with Miguel. "What time are you leaving?"

"Around ten or so. We should be back by nine."

Marco didn't like it one bit. "David, you have to be careful. The Bronx can be very dangerous. Do you really have to go?"

"Yes. I wouldn't want to insult Miguel. He wants me to meet his boyfriend, and show me around his neighborhood. I promise I'll be careful. Anyway, Miguel said that he would be my guardian angel and protect me." Marco visualized a sixteen-year-old kid protecting David and almost had a panic attack. "Do you want me to come with you? I can change my plans."

"I'd love it if you could, but you need to go see your parents."

"Yeah, I know. My father has been bugging me about getting together."

All of a sudden Marco's phone buzzed. He pulled it out to see who it was. "Are you coming over this afternoon?" He messaged back. "Yeah," and then slipped it back into his pocket.

"Who was that?"

"Thomas. He wants to meet up after class this afternoon to discuss a story he's been writing."

"Cool." David kissed Marco. "I'll see you later. Have fun today. I love you."

"I love you too."

As soon as David disappeared around the corner Marco sent another text. "Hey, I just want to let you know that I'm free all day tomorrow too if you wanna get together again?" His body was alive with anticipation as he waited for a response. It came as he approached Philosophy Hall.

"Oh yeah ;-) Very cool. Um, I have a couple of friends who want to join us. Are you interested in a four-way?" Marco smiled. "Hmm…sounds fucking hot. Can't wait."

"Cool, I'll let them know ;-) Now go learn something."

"I'll try, but it's gunna be hard."

"Yeah. I like it hard, and so do you ;-)

# CHAPTER 40

Marco lay on David's bed waiting for him to finish showering. He dreaded going to Jordan's with him. Everything was getting way too complicated and he didn't know what to do. Instead of trying to get his life under control, Marco let his mind replay his secret afternoon of sex. It was so perfect because there was no emotion involved. Just two bodies giving each other sexual pleasure.

Then guilt and jealousy brought him back to reality. He knew Jordan wanted to take David away from him. He wanted to use David to get off, just like they were doing with each other. He knew Jordan was using the study group as a ploy to achieve his goal. The only thing that kept Marco from going insane was knowing that David would never cheat on him.

A couple of minutes later David came out of the bathroom with a towel wrapped around his waist and walked over to the bed. "You look very enticing in that position."

"So do you sexy boy." Marco pulled the towel off, exposing David's semi-hard dick. He sat up and began kissing David's bellybutton and gently stroking him. "Let's stay here and make love just the way you like."

"You know I'd love to. I promise we'll leave after an hour,

360

and then we can finish this, ok?" David bent down and kissed Marco.

They walked out of Hartley hand and hand, filling each other in about their day. When they got to the end of the sidewalk, David started walking toward the Broadway exit.

"Hey, where are you going?"

David stopped. "Jordan said his apartment is on 112th Street and Broadway."

"What's the address?"

"234"

"Let's take a shortcut," Marco suggested. They headed to the campus exit on 114th Street instead. A minute later they were on Amsterdam Avenue walking towards 112th Street. As soon as they turned onto 112th they saw the address on a green canopy one building away. "Wow, how did you know it was so close to Amsterdam?"

"I've lived here my whole life silly, so I know how the numbers work."

The doorman acknowledged Marco with a nod and then let them in. Marco was unusually quiet on the ride up to the twelfth floor. "Thanks for coming with me. It means a lot," David said, as he squeezed Marco's hand.

"You're welcome. Anything for you."

Marco stood nervously behind David as he knocked on Jordan's door. No one answered, so he knocked harder because the party seemed to already be in high gear. A few seconds later it opened and there stood Marna with a flirty smile and a drink in her hand. "David," she said, in a giddy voice, and then proceeded to give him a hug while looking over his shoulder at the most gorgeous guy she had ever seen. She kissed David on the cheek and asked, "Is this the guy that makes your heart go pitter patter?"

"Yes. Marna, I'd like you to meet my boyfriend Marco."

"I'm happy to finally meet you. You're all David talks about when he's not talking about math." Marco tried his best to smile before receiving her awkward hug. "It's nice to meet you Marna."

They locked eyes for a split second. Marco knew she knew. "Come with me boys." She put her arm around David's waist and guided him into the living room as Marco followed close behind.

The living room was packed with people in full party mode as *Radioactive* by Imagine Dragons blasted away. Marco scanned the room trying to find Jordan, and that's when some guy tapped him on the shoulder and passed him a blunt. He turned around so David couldn't see and took a couple of hits off it, then he passed it back. "Thanks. I needed that."

"Anytime. My name is Cole."

"I'm Marco."

"I've seen you around campus."

"Cool. Excuse me, but I have to catch up to my boyfriend."

"Let me know if you need a couple of hits later. I'll save a blunt just for you."

"Thanks." Marco's slid his fingers down Cole's forearm and smiled, then he worked his way through the crowd and caught up with David. At that point, Marna introduced them to everyone. A few seconds later Joshua walked up and gave David a hug. "I'm glad you decided to show up."

"Me too. I've wanted to hang out, but I've been kind of busy. Joshua, this is my boyfriend Marco."

"Nice to meet you."

"Joshua, nice to meet you too."

"Can I get you guys something to drink?" he asked.

"No thanks," David said. Marco wanted something strong, but held off. "I'll have something in a little while. Thanks."

"No problem. Excuse me while I go and make myself one."

Two seconds later someone announced that the appetizers were being served. Marco turned around and saw Jordan and another guy placing two large trays of food on the dining room table. His heart beat frantically thinking about how good Jordan had made him feel just a few hours earlier.

Walking this tightrope without a safety net excited Marco like nothing else, even though he knew he could lose his balance and fall.

A moment later Jordan looked up and locked Marco into his sights. He smiled and started walking towards him. Marco turned around and pretended to be listening to David and Marna's conversation. Jordan's hand caressed Marco's ass as he squeezed past. "David, I'm happy that you finally decided to come to one of my parties," he said, while giving him a hug. Then he turned around and hugged Marco, and discreetly caressed his ass again. "It's good to see you. Thanks for coming again." Marco felt sick to his stomach. David was all smiles. "I really like your apartment."

"Thanks. I'll take you on a personal tour in a few minutes."

A few seconds later Joshua and Chandler squeezed through the crowd and joined them.

"It's about time you showed up to one of our parties," Chandler told David.

"I'm glad I could finally make it. This is my boyfriend Marco."

Chandler extended his hand. "I've heard a lot about you."

All eyes were on Marco as he exchanged pleasantries. A subtle game of chess was being played between everyone except David. This particular game had two winners, and all the players knew who they were.

Jordan excused himself a few minutes later. "I'll be back. I need to get the rest of the appetizers prepared. Help yourselves to food and drinks."

Marco finally relax a little knowing his secret was staying secret. He enjoyed watching David have a good time. The party really started poppin when someone put on *The End*, by Linkin Park. Drinks were being consumed and blunts were being toked by open windows. At one point Marco was able to slip away to toke with Cole. With a perfect buzz going, he asked Cole if he wanted to hook up sometime. Cole said yes instantly, so they made a play date for Tuesday.

Marco made his way back to David and asked if he wanted something to drink. "Yeah, thanks. I'd love some juice or vitamin water."

"Don't you want something stronger?"

"No, not tonight. You can though."

DEEP IS THE HEART

He walked over to the bar and made himself a Black Russian, and then got a vitamin water out of one of the coolers. Just as he was about to head back, Jordan walked up with two gorgeous guys. Marco's eyes darted to David for a quick second and then he relaxed when he saw him deep in conversation. Jordan leaned close. "This afternoon was fucking unbelievable. I hope you enjoyed it as much as I did."

Marco grinned. "I didn't want it to end."

"Don't worry, tomorrow is only a few hours away."

"Hmm…"

"I'd like you to meet Adam and Dominic." Marco liked what he saw. "Very nice."

"You are definitely everything Jordan said you were," Adam said, as he focused on Marco's package.

Marco grinned. "Cool. Do you want to fuck me?"

"Oh yeah."

"Dominic, do you want to fuck me too?"

"I'd love to fuck you right now."

Marco smiled as he scanned their perfect bodies.

What time can you come over?" Jordan asked.

"Ten thirty. I'll text you when I'm on my way."

"I promise that you are going to have the best sex you've ever had."

"I'm counting on it."

Jordan grinned. "You better get back to your boyfriend before he starts to miss you."

Those words brought Marco back to reality. "Hey, don't forget, you have to take us on a tour of your apartment."

365

"Oh yeah, Give me a couple of minutes to let my woody die down a little."

David and Marco ended up staying a lot longer than planned. Marco didn't want to spoil his evening by making him leave, so he sat next to him and engaged in whatever topics David and his friends were discussing. He enjoyed seeing his boyfriend in his element. How everyone listened to every word he said, knowing he was light years ahead of them. Himself included.

They ended up leaving the party around 2 am. Marco had his arm around David as they walked home. As soon as they were in his room, David collapsed on the bed and closed his eyes. "This feels so comfy." Marco hung his jacket in the closet and then walked to the bed and kissed David on the forehead.

"I'll be back in a minute. I have to pee." He spent a few minutes freshening up, and then stripped down to his Calvin Klein's. He came out of the bathroom walking seductively towards the bed only to find David fast asleep. Marco looked at his angel and smiled. He took the comforter and covered him, and then slid under it himself. He kissed the back of David's head and whispered, "I love you more than you will ever know. I'm sorry for everything."

Marco lay there as the tears fell, wondering how he could make it all work.

# CHAPTER 41

Spending Saturday in the Bronx was one of the biggest reality checks David had ever experienced. There were hard edges of poverty encasing everything that he encountered.

The looks of despair in so many older eyes. The aggression of teenage girls towards other teenage girls, thinking it was a sign of power instead of ignorance.

Guys smoking blunts and yelling sex come-ons to every girl who walked by. It was a side of the city that left David feeling like he was an alien from another world. Hanging in the hood, as Miguel called it, was an eye-opening journey that made him realize just how fortunate he was.

It also made him aware of how brave Miguel and Gabriel had to be. Especially Miguel.

The constant violence that surrounded him. The emptiness he surely felt being hated by his father, and physically abused by his mother. And then there was the other side of this irrational equation. Miguel and Gabriel finding each other on those mean streets, and falling in love.

Being taken in by Gabriel's mother and protecting him by becoming his legal guardian. That was the most powerful display of love David could think of. As the day continued to unfold, he knew his friendship with Miguel would be a lifelong one.

When the 2 train pulled into the 3rd Avenue subway station and stopped, Gabriel was standing on the platform directly in front of the train doors where David and Miguel were.

Miguel smiled. "This is perfect timing."

David couldn't believe his eyes when he saw Gabriel. "We could be brothers."

"Weird, isn't it?"

The doors opened and Miguel flew into Gabriel's arms. David got off and stood to the side trying not to watch. After they finished kissing, Miguel turned to him, "This is Gabriel."

"Hi. It is nice to meet you."

Gabriel looked as startled as David. "Wow, it's almost like looking in the mirror. Miguel said we looked a little alike, but this is unreal. I've been looking forward to meeting you." He gave David a hug. "Miguel talks about you all the time. He says you're in the academic stratosphere."

David smiled. "He has it all wrong. He's the one in the stratosphere." Gabriel shook his head. "I can see why you guys are friends."

"I really like your accent," David told Gabriel.

"Thanks. I was born in Manhattan, but lived in London for many years."

"Wow. That sounds fascinating."

As they headed up the steps, Miguel warned David, "This area is mad different from Manhattan, so be prepared." The subway steps led them into the middle of a crazy intersection where five roads converged into utter chaos. People were walking into on-coming traffic, horns were honking, and curse word after curse word bombarded them from every direction. David was surprised by the aggressiveness of everything as they stood there deciding which way to go. "I'll bet this is a little different than Harbor Springs," Miguel said, after seeing the shock on David's face.

"Yeah, it is. I'd be lying if I didn't say it scares me a little."

"This area is always like this. You have to careful when crossing the streets around here," Miguel warned. "This corner is a lot like Chaos Theory. Totally crazy, but it works."

Miguel took Gabriel's hand in his and began showing David around. Within minutes they were being verbally harassed by a group of older Hispanic men. They were yelling the word jotos at them while making dick sucking gestures. Miguel said joto was the Spanish word for faggot. Then, as soon as they got to the next block, four guys, probably fifteen or sixteen years old, started following them. Within seconds they started calling David, Miguel, and Gabriel their bitches and demanding that they suck their dicks.

David tried not to show any fear, but felt himself going into panic mode. All of a sudden Gabriel turned around and calmly asked, "Which one of you mother fuckers wants to die first?" He got into a martial arts stance and waited. One guy yelled, "fuck off faggot, and then they quickly walked away.

"I'm sorry about all of this. This kind of shit happens all the time around here," Gabriel said.

"I thought being gay in New York was acceptable."

Miguel shook his head. "Not really. There are still plenty of places in the city where we are hated. Especially around here. It's sad, but Gabriel and I refuse to be intimidated by ignorant assholes."

"I always thought people were more tolerant in the city."

"The affluent areas are tolerant, and so are a few people here. But for the most part, poverty and ignorance breeds intolerance. They hate what they can't understand," Miguel said, hoping to calm David down. Fortunately, no one else harassed them for the rest of their walk. They eventually ended up at Miguel and Gabriel's apartment a couple of hours later.

As David got to know Gabriel, he realized just how intelligent he was. At one point he even asked, "Why aren't you going to Columbia with Miguel?"

"Here are the simple facts. I'm not a genius like Miguel and you."

Miguel gave him that same exasperated look David gave whenever anyone said that to him.

Gabriel shook his head. "That fact is obviously true whether you guys want to admit it or not. I have to work really hard to get good grades. I do have some good news though. My counselor told me last week that I am on track to graduate in June. I've been receiving additional credits by testing out of classes I would normally have to take in my junior and senior years."

"Congratulations! You have to apply to Columbia so we can all go to school together," David said. Miguel grinned. "Gabriel is just like us, but won't admit it."

David smiled. "I figured as much."

They spent the rest of the afternoon listening to music, playing video games, and talking about anything and everything that came to mind. Most of the conversations centered around math, physics, and philosophy. At one point Gabriel shared his thoughts about the math required in order to attain the coveted Unified Theory. He didn't know where to start, but he had some interesting theories. Their conversation went into mathematical overdrive at that point.

An hour later Gabriel's mom knocked on his bedroom door to let them know dinner was ready. They spent the rest of the evening around the dinner table eating a real home cooked meal, something David really missed, and talking on a variety of topics. By the time they were ready to leave, David realized how kind and loving Gabriel and his mother really were. It made him homesick.

꙰

While David was bonding with his friends in the Bronx, Marco was having sex with three guys. He was in heaven as they dominated his perfect naked body with the best sex he had ever had. His body came more alive with each intense orgasm. Marco loved to be used. He loved being a sexual object. He moaned and begged for more and more as they fucked him every way imaginable. The Molly he had taken, and the poppers he was sniffing, made it even more intense and satisfying. Having three hot guys do him at the same time made Marco feel special. Almost loved. Random sex always made him feel that way. He wanted it to last forever.

Eventually they were all spent, but Marco's three on one ended the way he always fantasized; laying on the bed covered in sweat and baby oil, watching three hot guys on their knees shooting all over his body with total satisfaction on their faces. When the last drips had fallen, Jordan complimented Marco. "You were such a good little slut for us today."

"I loved every second," Marco said, in a dreamy voice.

"You are so fucking hot. We need to do this again real soon," Adam said, with Dominic and Jordan agreeing. They eventually headed to the bathroom and took showers together.

9:30 Saturday Evening

Marco was busy doing homework when David knocked on his door. He tried his best to conceal the guilt that had now crept all over his skin, hoping like hell it wouldn't reveal the truth. Taking an added breath, he opened the door and hoped for the best. David jumped into his arms and kissed him. "I missed you so much."

"I missed you too." Marco shut the door and kissed David again, hoping it would bring him back to what was truly important in his life.

"Did you have a good time with your parents? How are they?"

"Yeah, I actually had great time," Marco said, telling the

truth and lying. He couldn't believe how good he was at the game. "They want us to come over for dinner when we have some time."

"That sounds nice. I really like your parents. Hopefully your mom will eventually like me at some point."

"She does like you. We've talked and she thinks you are very sweet."

"Awe, I'm glad."

"We even talked about you today." Then Marco changed the subject because he was tired of lying. He asked David about his day in the Bronx. As he listened, his mind drifted to some of the tragic plays he had read over the years, realizing he was living one of his own making.

# CHAPTER 42

Two black holes merge together within the gravitational pull of spacetime, trying desperately to achieve loving singularity. The ultimate quest. A unified theory. They dance that mystical dance to binary rhythms that can be felt all across a lonely violent universe. Two beating hearts can love each other with a gravitational pull so powerful that their lifecycle only lasts a finite time.

Real love has always traveled faster than the speed of light.

Real love is more than just gravitational attraction, or the touch of skin on skin, or gentle words spoken between two beating hearts.

Real love is an emotional equation that requires patience, passion, and truth.

Real love resides on that omnipresent event horizon where truth and lies play out within entropy, eventually breaking down into degradation. It doesn't have to be this way, but sadly, more often than not, one heart miscalculates what is truly important, and then breaks the other heart into infinite invisible strings where mathematical calculations no longer exist.

$$\Delta \ \oint \ \forall$$

David was excited about his upcoming trip to Princeton University. His research team had been invited to attend a scientific conference on Supergravity, Strings, and Quantum Field Theory. It had always been a dream of his to attend conferences like this one, and now it was becoming a reality.

This particular conference was potentially groundbreaking because of the recent advances in M-Theory and Supergravity Mathematics. David realized how fortunate he was in terms of timing. Matriculating at Columbia, being part of a research team, and new forms of mathematics being discovered had become his perfect storm. In the back of his mind he thought destiny was playing a hand, even though he vacillated about its existence.

David felt a sense of pride in his own mathematical abilities, but looked forward to meeting other students and scientists who had far greater abilities. The United States, Switzerland, Germany, Great Britain, France, and Japan were the countries being represented by their math and physics communities. And on top of all that, Professor Eldridge decided to be the chairperson of David's research team for this particular conference. Professor's Godard and Logan had informed everyone the first week of November.

The reality of the situation finally hit David with just a week left to go before the conference. He worked vehemently all week helping to put the final touches on their presentation. And then Thursday evening, it happened. All those years David studied by himself, his passion for empirical knowledge that revealed real truths, being constantly belittled and taunted just for being intelligent, for being gay, had finally been recognized.

David was in his zone working away as the two white-boards in front of him slowly came to life. He wanted to see where the integration of M-Theory and Loop Quantum Gravity mathematics would take him. Little did he know that a certain theoretical physicist was standing a few meters away, watching him with interest. David stood back after he was finished and scanned his calculations to see if they made sense.

"I'm impressed," a voice behind him said. David turned around and almost fainted. He was standing face to face with Benjamin Eldridge. "P-Professor Eldridge, I-I..," was all David could get out of his mouth as they shook hands.

"David, how are you?"

"I-I'm... It's an honor to meet you sir," David said, trying to stay calm.

"The honor is all mine. Are you enjoying my math class?"

"Yes, very much. Having you as a professor is a dream come true."

"Thank you. It is a privilege to teach students of your cali-ber. Just think, we get to go on this journey together."

"It's been unbelievable so far."

Eldridge turned back to the whiteboards to have another look. "This is very interesting." He held out his hand, "Do you mind?"

"No, not at all." David gave him the marker and watched greatness unfold before his eyes. For the next ten minutes they both stood at the whiteboards theorizing and calculating by letting logic and creativity guide the way. They finally stood back and looked at what they had just accomplished. David was so nervous his hands were trembling. Eldridge put his hand on David's shoulder and said, "Only eighteen years old. I'm impressed."

"Thank you, sir."

Professor Godard and Professor Logan finally came over to see how David was holding up.

A couple of minutes later the conversation began to focus on the conference. David listened intently as the professors shared some of their experiences from past conferences. He had to keep pinching himself to make sure he wasn't dreaming.

# CHAPTER 43

Marco was entertaining Rafi, Avani, and a few other people from his floor. His room had become an enticing destination for the chosen few. With the latest toys and an atmosphere that screamed Upper East Side modern, it made all the other dorm rooms feel like jail cells. Marco had been protective of his privacy, but recently started letting a few people hang out because David was rarely around.

Being alone did not suit Marco one bit, so he began to take advantage of other options. Rafi was one of those options. Marco invited him to his room whenever David or Jordan weren't available. Rafi understood the situation and gave Marco all the sex he wanted without pressuring him, hoping it would eventually lead to becoming boyfriends.

Marco sat at his computer doing homework while *The A Team*, by Ed Sheerin played in the background. Tim and Olivia were playing video games. Avani and Gia were on their computers socializing. Rafi was sprawled out on the bed reading his bio chem book and taking notes. Marco was in a typing frenzy when his phone buzzed. It was a message from Jordan. He grinned knowing what was in store for the weekend. "Hey, are we gunna meet up for some fun this weekend?" Marco

378

texted back. "Can you come over on Sunday?"

"Yeah. Can I fuck you on Saturday too? I don't think I can wait until Sunday. I'm ready to bust now."

"I wish you could, but I have to attend a wedding in Connecticut with my parents."

Jordan sent a sad face back. Another text followed a few seconds later. "What about David?"

"No worries there. He's going to Princeton for a conference and won't be back until Monday afternoon."

"Can I spend the night?"

Marco's body came alive at the thought of Jordan fucking him all night long.

"Yeah, of course."

"Cool. What time should I come over?"

"I'll be back on campus around four. I'll text you when I'm here. Can't wait."

"Me either."

Marco put the phone back on the desk and looked out the window trying to calm down. His life was caught in a massive vortex. He loved having sex with Jordan, Rafi, and Cole, but he was in love with David. Marco sat there deep in thought. In the end he realized that he needed to have it all. He tried the other way one more time just to make sure. He closed his eyes and tried to think only of David and the love they shared, but couldn't do it. Marco opened his eyes and glanced over at Rafi, who was laying on his bed with that cute little ass of his positioned perfectly for his viewing pleasure. They had been fucking nonstop for the past two weeks. With a sexy body only six feet away, a new sexual fantasy popped into his brain; fucking Rafi while everyone in the room watched. His dick was hard in an instant thinking about it. But then, whatever guilt was left surfaced, leaving him slightly depressed. His mind raced in all directions, like a schizophrenic tide, trying to hang onto the love he had for David.

Everyone left Marco's room by seven that evening. He barely noticed because he was still in the zone. He was writing another story that paralleled his own life once again. The alarm on his phone went off in the middle of a pivotal chapter, bringing him back to earth. He sat there reading what he had just written and grinned. The main theme was living life to its fullest, and he pledged to continue doing just that regardless of the consequences. A few minutes later he went to meet David so they could have dinner together.

Marco leaned against the math building enjoying the cool night air waiting for David to come out. He was also texting with Claire trying to catch up with her life. She told him that she was seeing a guy who was in one of her art classes. "His name is Jamie. He's so sweet. Very cute too. He reminds me so much of David it isn't funny. He has blond hair and grew up in the mid-west."

"Cool, then he must be a great guy. They make them sexy cute in the mid-west...lol"

"Yeah, you're right about that. I'm just so sick of pretentious guys."

All of a sudden David walked out with a group of students. Marco sent one last text. "I have to go, David's here. Love you."

"Tell him I said hi."

Marco waited patiently in the shadows while David finished up the conversation he was involved in. After everyone said their goodbyes, Marco stepped into the light. "Hey handsome scientist," he said, startling David. He gave Marco a nice long kiss. "I missed you so much today. I hate that we haven't been able to spend any time together."

"It's ok. I understand, so please don't worry about it."

David held Marco. "I do worry about it, but I have some good news."

"Oh yeah? What is it?"

"My research team is taking a three week break as soon as we come back from the conference."

"That's fantastic. I know this is going to sound selfish, but I feel so lost when we aren't together."

"Me too." David looked at Marco in a way that frightened him.

"What's wrong?"

"Nothing's wrong, but I do have something I want to discuss with you as soon as I get back from Princeton, ok?"

Marco gave him a panicked look. "Why can't you just tell me now?"

"I want it to be a surprise."

"You know how much I hate surprises, so just tell me now." Marco started tickling David to get him to tell. David tried to get away, but they ended up rolling around on the ground laughing and kissing.

They had dinner at Max Soha's, their favorite Italian

restaurant a couple of blocks from campus. Marco loved how playful and giddy David was being by suggesting that they use their fake IDs to get some wine to go with their meal. He grinned a little at the suggestion.

"What are you grinning about?" David asked.

"Nothing. I'd love to get some wine too, but, honestly, you really do look like you're only about fifteen. Those IDs are only good for places that don't care how old you are."

"Well, it was a good idea anyway." Then David laughed. "If I only look like I'm fifteen, then I guess I'm jail bate. Shame on you."

"Thank goodness you're legal." They both laughed.

"Thank you for taking me out to dinner. I just wish you were going with me this weekend," David said, caressing Marco's hand with his.

"Me too. But I know you're going to have a great time being around all of those science guys. Anyway, I have to go to that wedding with my parents, so everything kind of worked out for the best."

"I forgot about that. When are you leaving?"

"Friday, right after my last class. Max is picking me up because my parents are having an early pre-wedding dinner party. Then we're driving to Connecticut right after that. The wedding is an all day affair, which I hate."

"When are you going to get back to campus?"

"I'm planning on being back by three on Sunday. I have a lot of homework this weekend."

That made David relax because he was planning on

surprising Marco by coming back Sunday evening instead of Monday afternoon. "That's good. Getting back by then should give you enough time to get it finished."

"I hope so," Marco said. "What time are you leaving tomorrow?" he casually asked, trying to make sure David's conference schedule hadn't changed.

"Early. We are meeting at the Math Building at seven thirty. Professor Godard is having breakfast catered. He wants to make sure everyone has eaten and is prepared. I just hope I can get some sleep tonight."

"What time are you getting back on Monday?"

"We should be back by one or two in the afternoon."

That made Marco relax knowing his plans didn't have to change. "I know you're going to have a great time. I can't wait to hear all about it. Are you sure you can't sleep over tonight?"

"I'd love to, but I have some reading I have to do, plus I need to get some sleep, which I know I won't get if I stay with you." Marco gave him a pouty look. David smiled. "I promise that I'll make it up to you."

"Are you sure?"

"Yes I'm sure." Then David put his finger tips against Marco's and leaned close. "I love you beautiful boy."

# CHAPTER 44

The conference was an experience far beyond anything David had ever imagined. Every emotion he had come to know were reminders that his journey had been worth every breathing second of his young life. That conference validated everything he had worked so hard to attain. That his desire to solve the mysteries of the universe weren't just crazy notions, it had become his destiny. David had now joined an honored group of individuals who were also seeking the same empirical truths.

The confidence Professor's Eldridge, Logan, and Godard had shown towards his abilities meant the most to him. They never treated him or anyone else on the team as lesser entities. They included him in every meeting, every discussion group, and even introduced him to other world renown physicists. David had to pinch himself more than once because it had actually happened. And it happened at Princeton University, the home of Albert Einstein.

Over the course of three incredible days David engaged in conversations with dozens of other students and professors about Quantum Variants, Conformal Field Theory and Strings, Sigma Models, and new mathematical developments within M-Theory.

Little did David know, but Saturday evening had become a turning point in his life, and the physicist he admired most made it happen. Professor Eldridge was the guest speaker on the topics of M-Theory and the Unified Theory. Ten minutes into his talk, he surprised everyone by inviting David and one other student named Elaine up to the stage to partake in the discussion. Everyone applauded as they made their way across the stage and sat down. David wasn't nervous at all because he could hear his father's voice telling him to just be himself. And he was. And everyone listened as he, Eldridge, and Elaine shared their ideas about theories that might one day lead to a Unified Theory. What surprised David the most was being applauded after explaining his belief that solving the mysteries of M-Theory and Dark Energy would lead the scientific world to a unified theory.

After the talk was over, Professor Eldridge shook David and Elaine's hands and thanked them for participating. Then he asked David to stay for a minute so they could talk. "David, you have a real knack for explaining your ideas. I am very impressed."

"Thank you sir. And thank you for inviting me on stage. It was an honor."

The next words David heard almost made him faint. "I was wondering if you would be interested in joining my research team. I've talked with Gene and Tim and they think it is an excellent idea." At that point some of their colleagues made their way to the stage to congratulate them just as David was accepting his invitation. "Professor, it would be an honor to work with you." Eldridge shook his hand again. "Welcome to the team." For the next half hour David received congratulatory handshakes and talked with as many people as he could. He was humbled by the entire experience.

SUNDAY EVENING

It was a few minutes past 7pm when David's cab arrived at Princeton to take him to the train station. He was excited about surprising Marco. He couldn't wait to make love to him and then cuddle afterwards. He wanted to hear all about the wedding, and then tell him about the conference. He also decided to let Marco know that he was ready to live together and couldn't wait to see the look on his face.

David was on the train a half hour later heading back to Manhattan. He closed his eyes and tried to get some sleep, but some memories began to escape from the neatly stored drawers of his mind. Parts of his life began playing out before him:

His first memory occurring at the age of two years, three months, seven days, six hours and thirty-two minutes, walking into the kitchen and asking his father if he could have a cup of coffee with him. His father picking him up, giving him a hug, and putting him in the chair next to him at the kitchen table. His father making him a very sweet and milky cup of coffee. How that part of the morning became their special time together through the years.

The next memory was of his father taking him to the hill for the first time at the age of three, sitting in his lap and looking up at the Milky Way, knowing it was trying to show him its secrets. That it was calling for him to come out and play whenever he was ready.

Memory after memory unfolded before his smiling eyes.

Figuring out Calculus and Differential Geometry by the age of eleven, and then scaring his 6th grade teacher to the point where she summoned the principal to watch him fill the entire whiteboard with advanced equations while explaining Einstein's General Relativity to his classmates.

His parents being in shock by his abilities after being called to the school to see what he had done.

Countless trips to Ann Arbor where he went through series after series of intelligence tests that tried to determine the level of his unique capabilities.

Getting his first guitar at the age of nine and learning how play it well within six weeks. Learning how to read music at an advanced level in the same time frame because it was just like a mathematical concept.

The first time he heard side one of *2112* by Rush.

Spending two summers taking math and physics classes at the University of Michigan and the Massachusetts Institute of Technology.

Realizing he was gay.

Meeting Tyler, crushing on him, and then falling in love with him.

Coming out to his parents.

Being beaten into a coma by his friends just because he was gay. Almost dying and then learning how to forgive so he could move on with his life.

Tyler and Melissa's friendship.

His first kiss. And then his second later that same night.

His life in New York City as a college student at Columbia University.

Meeting Marco and falling in love.

David smiled as memory after memory reminded him of just how fortunate he was. How all of those life experiences, and the people he loved, were instrumental in shaping his life in some significant way.

When those memories were finally back into their proper place, David looked out the window into the pitch dark night and began going over a new proof that he had been working on in his spare time. He let his thoughts wander through mathematical calculations, inserting and eliminating as if his mind were a whiteboard, trying to capture multiple dimensions of loop spaces and somehow make them slow dance with General Relativity.

Every mathematical concept he had learned so far floated in space while he calculated and thought abstractly, hoping to see what the missing pieces within Quantum Field Theory might be. This went on for the next hour or so until several potential paths made their appearance. David got his laptop out and added them to his math journal. Time flew by, and before he knew it the train had pulled into Grand Central Station.

David grabbed his suitcase and walked through the main Concourse and then outside to 42nd Street. Luckily he got a cab right away and was back on campus within twenty minutes. He decided to stop at his room before heading to Marco's so he could drop his suitcase off and freshen up. Ryan was startled when David walked in. "Hey, this is a surprise. Is everything all right?" Ryan asked. "I thought you weren't coming back until tomorrow?"

"Everything is good. I came back early because the conference ended at five today and I wanted to surprise Marco. That has been my plan all along."

"Oh, nice. So how was the conference?"

"It was unbelievable. I had a blast. I met so many interesting people from all over the world. It was everything I thought it would be, and more."

"Cool." They continued talking while David changed into a purple t-shirt and skinny jeans. A couple of minutes later he was out the door.

While walking over to Marco's building, David began to panic slightly at a couple of possible scenarios. What if Marco was out with his friends? Or decided to spend the night at home with his parents? He hesitated for a moment before deciding there was only one way to find out. Two girls were coming out of John Jay and held the door for him. The guy at the front desk said hi and let him through. David noticed it was a bit quieter than usual as he walked to the elevators. He hoped Marco's floor wasn't in party mode because he didn't want anyone ruining his surprise, plus he wanted some privacy.

David stood there waiting for an elevator with the giddiness of a little boy. A minute later one finally came down. A half dozen girls dressed for an evening out gave him the once over as they walked by him. He shyly looked away as he entered the elevator. His heart started pounding in anticipation as he pushed the button. He got out on the fourteenth floor and walked up one flight of stairs as quiet as possible. When he got to the landing, he peaked down the hall to see if anyone was coming. The entire floor was quiet except for some jazz music coming from a room down the other hall. He walked slowly trying his hardest not to make the floor squeak. His heart raced and his smile grew wider with each step he took, knowing what awaited him less than ten meters away. He was glad no one had come out of their rooms while inching closer to the guy of his dreams.

But then it happened. He could hear it. With only four meters left to go, David froze and just stood there. His smile disappeared as he listened to the bed's rhythmic squeaks and someone moaning and someone else talking dirty. Within seconds the moaning got louder. He was moaning and giving sex commands between the moans. It was Marco's voice. Tears started streaming down David's cheeks as he stood there paralyzed, wanting to die as he listened to Marco having sex with someone else. "Fuck me good. Fuck me hard papi. Fuck me as hard as you can," Marco commanded.

David put his hand on the wall to steady himself. He felt like he had just been kicked in the stomach and couldn't breathe. He wiped his face with his sleeve as he stood there.

A few seconds later he heard the other voice. "You are such a good little slut. Your tight ass feels so fucking good." It instantly clicked. That voice. He heard that voice three times a week in math class. It was Jordan.

The moaning and fucking and dirty talk sliced David at every possible angle, leaving him blood drenched in humiliation. He wiped the tears from his face again and started walking away. He stopped when he got to the stairs and stood there for a few seconds before turning around and walking back. Everything went dead silent as soon as he knocked. David waited about fifteen seconds and then knocked again. The silence remained. "Marco, please open the door," David said, trying to stay calm. Marco didn't respond, but he could hear them scrambling around, probably trying to fix the bed or trying to get their clothes on. "Marco, please open the door. I know Jordan is in there with you." Again, David was met by silence as he stood in front of the door trying his hardest not to cry. David finally heard footsteps coming towards him. Marco was on the other side of the locked door, just inches away, crying. "I'm so sorry David. I'm so sorry," he said through breathless sobs.

David leaned his head against the door, caught between anger and a broken heart. "If you wanted to fuck around, why didn't you just break up with me? Why couldn't you have been honest with me?" Marco was silent. A few seconds later David heard Jordan trying to console Marco, and lost it. "Marco, I take it you get off by using and humiliating people. It must be part of the kinky sex you love so much. You know something,

I really loved you, and I thought you loved me too, but I was so wrong. I just hope tha….." Jordan interrupted him.

"David, this is all my fault, please don't blame Marco."

"Jordan, this isn't any of your business, so shut the fuck up."

"David, please it wa…."

"Please stop talking Jordan. Just stop, ok? Marco, it's over."

David wiped his eyes and walked away. He could hear Marco crying and pleading to give him another chance, but he didn't care. He ran down all fifteen flights of stairs so he could get out of there as fast as he could. By the time David got to the first floor, he was crying uncontrollably. The guy at the desk got up and ran to him. "Hey, are you ok? What happened" Through his sobs, David said, "No I'm not ok."

"Did somebody hurt you?"

"Yes, but I don't want to talk about it. I just need to go."

"I'm going to call security. What is your name?"

"I'm ok. You don't have to do that." David hurried out the door and headed toward his building. The cool night air grabbed hold of his entire body, trying to make him realize that he was still alive even though he was badly wounded. With his eyes stinging and everything a blur, he found his way to the garden area and sat down on a bench. He buried his head in his hands and rocked his body back and forth, trying ease the pain.

Out of nowhere he heard a familiar voice. "David, are you all right? What happened?" Miguel was standing right in front of him. David looked up and wiped his eyes. He could barely get the words out. "I caught Marco having sex with my friend Jordan, the guy I told you about from math class." Miguel looked towards Marco's building and then back at David. "I'm so sorry." He sat down and put his arm around David to console him. "I know it must hurt like hell, but you will get through this. You'll see."

David buried his head in Miguel's shoulder and sobbed. Miguel held him tight and let him cry. A few minutes later David had finally calmed down. Miguel gently stroked his hair and kissed him on the cheek to let him know that he was loved. "Thank you," David whispered.

"I'll always be here for you," Miguel whispered back, as his own tears began to fall. "You are the most beautiful person I have ever met. There is so much love inside of you." They held on each other in that lonely darkness, Miguel doing his best to protect his friend with warmth and love. A few minutes went by before David sat up and kissed Miguel on the cheek. He gave him a faint smile. "Thank you for everything. You are the best friend anyone could ever have. I love you."

"I love you too." Then Miguel made a suggestion. "Why don't we head up to the lounge and relax?"

"Ok. I need to rest my eyes because I can feel a bad headache coming on."

As soon as they stood up they could hear someone running frantically down the sidewalk towards them. Miguel stood in front of David knowing who it was. Two seconds later Marco appeared at the garden entrance looking like someone who had lost everything that was important to him.

"Marco, you need to leave right now," Miguel told him. David stood behind Miguel looking down at the ground.

"David, I'm so sorry for what I've done to you. I love you more than anything in this world. I want you to know that. I'm so fucked up I can't....."

"Just stop Marco. Don't say another word," David said, as he moved next to Miguel and stared him down. "I've heard this speech before, but this time I'm not falling for it. How long have you been cheating on me? I'll bet a million dollars you've been having sex with Jordan the whole time we've been here, right? RIGHT? Tell me the fucking truth for once in your pathetic life," he yelled.

"Yes. You're right. I've been cheating on you the whole time." Marco said through his sobs. David turn away, feeling like he had been stabbed in the heart once again. Miguel put his arm around David and told him, "He won't hurt you anymore."

Marco started to walk towards them, but Miguel put his hand up. "Marco, you need to leave, NOW! You've caused enough pain to last a lifetime."

David couldn't bear to look at Marco as he spoke, "Please go. Leave me alone. I don't ever want to see you again. I mean it."

David and Miguel turned and walked away, leaving Marco standing all alone in the garden of dreams.

David didn't say a word while the elevator made its way to

the tenth floor. He just stared straight ahead in a daze. When they got to the tenth floor, Miguel put his arm around him. "Let's go to my room first so I can get some pillows and blankets for you."

"Thanks. I feel cold, and my head is killing me."

While Miguel was getting pillows and blankets from his closest, David stood in the doorway looking at his posters. "The universe is so beautiful. It is the only thing that always tells the truth," he said, in a barely audible whisper. "Sometimes it feels like I don't belong here."

"The universe is a beautiful place, but so is the earth. And so are you. David, you have to believe me when I say that you belong here."

"Thank you. I don't know what I would have done if you hadn't found me." He walked over to Miguel and hugged him. Miguel rubbed David's back and whispered, "Remember, a lot of people love you, myself included. Everything will turn out just the way you want it to. It might be hard to fathom right now, but believe me, good things happen to good people."

Miguel was happy to see that they had the lounge all to themselves. The lights were dimmed perfectly, giving off the same warm glow that he was giving to David.

"Hey, our favorite couch is empty," Miguel said, trying to cheer him up. "I'll get it set up nice and comfy for you." As Miguel arranged the blankets and pillows, David walked over to the window and looked down at the campus. A moment later Miguel walked over and stood next to him. "It is so beautiful. It all feels like a dream sometimes," David whispered.

"It is beautiful. And it is a dream. It is your dream, and it is my dream. No one ever said it would be easy, and that's what makes this dream so special."

"You're right." David wiped his eyes.

"Come lay down for a while."

"Ok. I need to close my eyes. This headache is making me dizzy."

"Grab hold of me." Miguel told him, with a worried look. He put his arm around David's waist and took him to the couch. David gave him a slight smile as he lay down. Miguel covered him with a blanket and then knelt beside him. "Let me rub your temples a little. It will help you relax."

"Ok." Miguel gently massaged David's temples as he lay quietly with his eyes closed. "That feels so good. Your fingers are really warm," David whispered.

A moment later Miguel asked, "How do you feel now?" David opened his eyes. "I don't feel dizzy anymore. And my headache is gone."

"I'm glad." Miguel kissed David on the forehead. "Get some sleep now. Everything will be much better in the morning. I promise."

"Ok. Please don't leave me."

"I won't. I'll be right here when you wake up. Remember what I told you before? I'm your guardian angel."

"I remember." A moment later David was fast asleep.

A few minutes later Miguel quietly got up and made his way through the doorway and down the hall to one of the alcoves. He took out his phone and made a call.

"Hi. Is this Tyler Reed?"

"Yeah. Who is this?"

"My name is Miguel. I'm a friend of David's. We go to college together."

"Oh." Tyler said. Then he remembered. "Yeah. David said you guys are good friends." Then a panicky feeling overcame him. "What's wrong? Is David there? Please let me talk to him."

"He's sleeping right now. Something happened to him tonight."

Tyler's voice was shaking. "What happened? Is David all right?"

"Do you remember what you told him just before you guys left for college?"

Tyler didn't say anything for a couple of seconds, seemingly in shock. "I told David that if anyone ever hurts him I would fly to New York as fast as I could. Please tell me what's going on. Please," Tyler pleaded.

"Marco hurt David pretty bad tonight. He needs you here."

# Part Three

Soon

## A note to my readers

This book is dedicated to all of the gay and straight people who have ever been in love. If you have any questions or comments, please email me at <u>avzeppa@gmail.com</u>

## Other books by A.V. Zeppa

*Miguel's Secret Journal*

(Outskirts Press 2011)

*Miguel's Secret Journal – The Four Corners of Earth*

(Outskirts Press 2013)

Deep is the Heart

Long ago we looked into the darkness
eyes steady, looking for love.
calculating infinite shadows
into a dream, deep is the heart.
Once upon a time love was all I ever wanted
but it was just a cruel extreme,
broken hearted theories explode into forever,
forever, an impossible dream.

I close my eyes and listen to echoes
innocent dreams drifting down stream.
Years of fear were gone in an instant
teardrops knowing, deep is the heart.
Interstellar motion was bringing us together
fingertips just inches apart,
you just need to say it, don't leave me here forever
waiting for your beautiful heart.


Written, performed, and produced by A.V. Zeppa
Available for viewing on YouTube

.

CPSIA information can be obtained
at www.ICGtesting.com
Printed in the USA
FFOW03n1602020615
13884FF